TWO BY FRANCIS

TWO _BY_ FRANCIS

FORFEIT
& SLAYRIDE

DICK FRANCIS

HARPER & ROW, PUBLISHERS, New York
Cambridge, Philadelphia, San Francisco,
London, Mexico City, São Paulo, Sydney _1817_

Library of Congress Cataloging in Publication Data

Francis, Dick.
    Two by Francis.
      Contents: Forfeit—Slayride.
      1. Detective and mystery stories, English.
I. Francis, Dick. Slay-ride. 1983. II. Title.
PR6056.R27A6 1983   823′.914   82-48488
ISBN 0-06-015126-9

83 84 85 86 87 10 9 8 7 6 5 4 3 2 1

Contents

FORFEIT

One

The letter from *Tally* came on the day Bert Checkov died. It didn't look like trouble; just an invitation from a glossy to write an article on the Lamplighter Gold Cup. I flicked it across the desk to the sports editor and went on opening the mail which always accumulated for me by Friday. Luke-John Morton grunted and stretched out a languid hand, blinking vacantly while he listened to someone with a lot to say on the telephone.

"Yeah . . . yeah. Blow the roof off," he said.

Blowing the roof off was the number-one policy of the *Sunday Blaze,* bless its cold heart. Why didn't I write for the *Sunday Times,* my wife's mother said, instead of a rag like the *Sunday Blaze?* They hadn't needed me, that was why. She considered this irrelevant, and when she couldn't actively keep it quiet, continued to apologize to every acquaintance for my employment. That the *Blaze* paid twenty-eight per cent more than the *Times,* and that her daughter was expensive, she ignored.

I slit open a cheap brown envelope and found some nut had written to say that only a vicious, unscrupulous bum like myself would see any good in the man I had defended last Sunday. The letter was written on lavatory paper and spite oozed from it like marsh gas. Derry Clark read it over my shoulder and laughed.

"Told you you'd stir them up."

"Anything for an unquiet life," I agreed.

Derry wrote calm uncontroversial articles each week assessing form and firmly left the rebel stuff to me. My back, as he constantly pointed out, was broader than his.

Eight more of my correspondents proved to be thinking along the same general lines. All anonymous, naturally. Their problems, I reflected, dumping their work in the wastebasket, were even worse than mine.

"How's your wife?" Derry said.

"Fine, thanks."

He nodded, not looking at me. He'd never got over being embarrassed about Elizabeth. It took some people that way.

Luke-John's conversation guttered to a close. "Sure . . . sure. Phone it through by six at the latest." He put down the receiver and focused on my letter from *Tally*, his eyes skidding over it with professional speed.

"A study in depth . . . how these tarty magazines love that phrase. Do you want to do it?"

"If the fee's good."

"I thought you were busy ghosting Buster Figg's autobiography."

"I'm hung up on Chapter Six. He's sloped off to the Bahamas and left me no material."

"How far through his horrid little life have you got?" His interest was genuine.

"The end of his apprenticeship and his first win in a classic."

"Will it sell?"

"I don't know." I sighed. "All he's interested in is money, and all he remembers about some races is the starting price. He bled in thousands. And he insists I put his biggest bets in. He says they can't take away his license now he's retired."

Luke-John sniffed, rubbing a heavily freckled hand across the prominent tendons of his scrawny neck, massaging his walnut-

sized larynx, dropping the heavy eyelid hoods while he considered the letter from *Tally*. My contract with the *Blaze* was
restrictive: books were all right, but I couldn't write articles for
any other paper or magazine without Luke-John's permission,
which I mostly didn't get.

Derry pushed me out of his chair and sat in it himself. As I
spent only Fridays in the office, I didn't rate a desk and usurped
my younger colleague's whenever he wasn't looking. Derry's
desk held a comprehensive reference library of form books in
the top three drawers and a half bottle of vodka, two hundred
purple hearts, and a pornographic film catalogue in the bottom
one. These were window dressing only. They represented the
wicked fellow Derry would like to be, not the lawful, temperate
semidetached man he was.

I perched on the side of his desk and looked out over the
Friday morning clatter, a quarter acre of typewriters and tele-
phones going at half speed as the week went on toward Sunday.
Tuesdays, the office was dead; Saturdays, it buzzed like flies
squirted with D.D.T. Fridays, I felt part of it. Saturdays, I went
to the races. Sundays and Mondays—officially off. Tuesdays to
Thursdays, think up some galvanizing subject to write about,
and write it. Fridays, take it in for Luke-John, and then for the
editor to read and veto.

Result—a thousand words a week, an abusive mailbag, and
a hefty check which didn't cover my expenses.

Luke-John said, "Are you or Derry doing the Lamplighter?"

Without giving me a second Derry jumped in: "I am."

"That all right with you, Ty?" Luke-John asked dubiously.

"Oh, sure," I said. "It's a complicated handicap. Right up his
street."

Luke-John pursed his thin lips and said with unusual generosity, *"Tally* says they want background stuff, not tips. . . . I don't see why you shouldn't do it, if you want to."

He scribbled a large "O.K." at the bottom of the page and signed his name. "But of course," he added, "if you dig up any dirt, keep it for *us."*

Generous be damned, I thought wryly. Luke-John's soul belonged to the *Blaze* and his simple touchstone in all decisions was "Could it possibly, directly or indirectly, benefit the paper?" Every member of the sports section had at some time or other been ruthlessly sacrificed on his altar. For canceled holidays, smashed appointments, lost opportunities, he cared not one jot.

"Sure," I said mildly. "And thanks."

"How's your wife?" he asked.

"Fine, thanks."

He asked every week without fail. He had his politenesses, when it didn't cost the *Blaze.* Maybe he really cared. Maybe he only cared because when she wasn't "fine" it affected my work.

I pinched Derry's telephone and dialed the number.

"Tally magazine, can I help you?" A girl's voice very smooth, West Ken, and bored.

"I'd like to talk to Arnold Shankerton."

"Who's calling?"

"James Tyrone."

"One moment, please." Some clicks and a pause. "You're through."

An equally smooth, highly sophisticated tenor voice proclaimed itself to be Arnold Shankerton. Features. I thanked him for his letter and said I would like to accept his commission. He said that would be very nice, in moderately pleased tones, and I gently added, "If the price is right, naturally."

"Naturally," he conceded. "How much do you want?"

Think of a number and double it. "Two hundred guineas, plus expenses."

Luke-John's eyebrows rose and Derry said, "You'll be lucky."

"Our profit margin is small," Shankerton pointed out a little plaintively. "One hundred is our absolute limit."

"I pay too much tax."

His sigh came heavily down the wire. "A hundred and fifty, then. And for that it'll have to be good."

"I'll do my best."

"Your best," he said, "would scorch the paper. We want the style and the insight but not the scandal. Right?"

"Right," I agreed without offense. "How many words?"

"It's the main feature. Say three thousand five hundred, roughly speaking."

"How about pictures?"

"You can have one of our photographers when you're ready. And within reason, of course."

"Of course," I said politely. "When do you want it by?"

"We go to press on that edition—let's see—on November twenty-first. So we'd like your stuff on the morning of the seventeenth, at the very latest. But the earlier the better."

I looked at Derry's calendar. Ten days to the seventeenth.

"All right."

"And when you've thought out how you'd like to present it, send us an outline."

"Will do," I said; but I wouldn't. Outlines were asking for trouble in the shape of editorial alterations. Shankerton could, and would, chop at the finished article to his heart's content, but I was against him getting his scissors into the embryo.

Luke-John skimmed the letter back and Derry picked it up and read it.

"In depth," he said sardonically. "You're used to the deep end. You'll feel quite at home."

"Yeah," I agreed absent-mindedly. Just what *was* depth, a hundred and fifty guineas' worth of it?

I made a snap decision that depth in this case would be the background people, not the stars.

The stars hogged the headlines week by week. The background people had no news value. For once, I would switch them over.

Snap decisions had got me into trouble once or twice in the past. All the same, I made this one. It proved to be the most trouble-filled of the lot.

Derry, Luke-John, and I knocked off soon after one and walked down the street in fine drizzle to elbow our way into the bar of the Devereux, in Devereux Court opposite the Law Courts.

Bert Checkov was there, trying to light his stinking old pipe and burning his fingers on the matches. The shapeless tweed which swathed his bulk was as usual scattered with ash and as usual his toecaps were scuffed and gray. There was more glaze in the washy blue eyes than one-thirty normally found there: an hour too much, at a rough guess. He'd started early.

Luke-John spoke to him and he stared vaguely back. Derry bought us a half pint each and politely asked Bert to have one, though he'd never liked him.

"Double Scotch," Bert mumbled, and Derry thought of his mortgages and scowled.

"How's things?" I asked, knowing that this, too, was a mistake. The Checkov grumbles were inexhaustible.

For once, however, the stream was dammed. The watery eyes focused on me with an effort and another match sizzled on his skin. He appeared not to notice.

"Gi' you a piesh o' advishe," he said, but the words stopped there. The advice stayed in his head.

"What is it?"

"Piesh o' advishe." He nodded solemnly.

Luke-John raised his eyes to the ceiling in an exasperation that wasn't genuine. For old-time journalists like Bert he had an unlimited regard which no amount of drink could quench.

"Give him the advice, then," Luke-John suggested. "He can always do with it."

The Checkov gaze lurched from me to my boss. The Checkov mouth belched uninhibitedly. Derry's pale face twisted squeamishly, and Checkov saw him. As a gay lunch, hardly a gas. Just any Friday, I thought: but I was wrong. Bert Checkov was less than an hour from death.

Luke-John, Derry, and I sat on stools around the bar counter and ate cold meat and pickled onions, and Bert Checkov stood swaying behind us, breathing pipe smoke and whiskey fumes down our necks. Instead of the usual steady rambling flow of grousing to which we were accustomed, we received only a series of grunts, the audible punctuation of the inner Checkov thoughts.

Something on his mind. I wasn't interested enough to find out what. I had enough on my own.

Luke-John gave him a look of compassion and another whiskey, and the alcohol washed into the pale blue eyes like a tide, resulting in pinpoint pupils and a look of blank stupidity.

"I'll walk him back to his office," I said abruptly. "He'll fall under a bus if he goes on his own."

"Serve him right," Derry said under his breath, but carefully so that Luke-John shouldn't hear.

We finished lunch with cheese and another half pint. Checkov lurched sideways and spilt my glass over Derry's knee and the pub carpet. The carpet soaked it up good-temperedly, which was more than could be said for Derry. Luke-John shrugged resignedly, half laughing, and I finished what was left of my beer with one swallow, and steered Bert Checkov through the crowd and into the street.

"Not closing time yet," he said distinctly.

"For you it is, old chum."

He rolled against the wall, waving the pipe vaguely in his chubby fist. "Never leave a pub before closing. Never leave a story while it's hot. Never leave a woman on her doorstep. Paragraphs and skirts should be short and pheasants and breasts should be high."

"Sure," I said, sighing. Some advice.

I took his arm and he came easily enough out onto the Fleet Street pavement. His tottering progress up toward the City end produced several stares but no actual collisions. Linked together, we crossed during a lull in the traffic and continued eastward under the knowing frontages of the *Telegraph* and the black glass *Express*. Fleet Street had seen the lot: no news value in an elderly racing correspondent being helped back from lunch with a skinful.

"A bit of advice," he said suddenly, stopping in his tracks, "a bit of advice."

"Yes?" I said patiently.

He squinted in my general direction.

"We've come past the *Blaze*."

"Yeah."

He tried to turn me around to retrace our steps.

"I've business down at Ludgate Circus. I'm going your way today," I said.

"Zat so?" He nodded vaguely and we shambled on. Ten more paces. He stopped again.

"Piece of advice."

He was looking straight ahead. I'm certain that he saw nothing at all. No bustling street. Nothing but what was going on inside his head.

I was tired of waiting for the advice which showed no signs of materializing. It had begun to drizzle again. I took his arm to try and get him moving along the last fifty yards to his paper's florid front door. He wouldn't move.

"Famous last words," he said.

"Whose?"

"Mine. Naturally. Famous last words. Bit of advice."

"Oh, sure." I sighed. "We're getting wet."

"I'm not drunk."

"No."

"I could write my column anytime. This minute."

"Sure."

He lurched off suddenly, and we made it to his door. Three steps and he'd be home and dry.

He stood in the entrance and rocked unsteadily. The pale blue eyes made a great effort toward sobering up, but the odds were against it.

"If anyone asks you," he said finally, "don't do it."

"Don't do what?"

An anxious expression flitted across his pallid fleshy face. There were big pores all over his nose, and his beard was growing out of stiff black millimetres. He pushed one hand into his jacket pocket, and the anxiety turned to relief as he drew it out again with a half bottle of Scotch attached.

" 'Fraid I'd forgotten it," he mumbled.

"See you, then, Bert."

"Don't forget," he said. "That advice."

"Right." I began to turn away.

"Ty?"

I was tired of him. "What?"

"You wouldn't let it happen to you, I know that . . . but sometimes it's the strong ones get the worst clobbering . . . in the ring, I mean. . . . They never know when they've taken enough. . . ."

He suddenly leaned forward and grasped my coat. Whiskey fumes seeped up my nose and I could feel his hot breath across the damp air.

"You're always broke, with that wife of yours. Luke-John told me. Always bloody stony. So don't do it. . . . Don't sell your sodding soul. . . ."

"Try not to," I said wearily, but he wasn't listening.

He said, with the desperate intensity of the very drunk, "They buy you first and blackmail after."

"Who?"

"Don't know . . . don't sell . . . don't sell your column."

"No." I sighed.

"I *mean* it." He put his face even closer. "Never sell your column."

"Bert . . . Have you?"

He closed up. He pried himself off me and went back to rocking. He winked, a vast caricature of a wink.

"Bit of advice," he said, nodding. He swiveled on rubbery ankles and weaved an unsteady path across the lobby to the lifts. Inside he turned around and I saw him standing there under the light clutching the half bottle and still saying over and over, "Bit of advice, bit of advice."

The doors slid heavily across in front of him. Shrugging, puzzled a little, I started on my way back to the *Blaze*. Fifty yards along, I stopped off to see if the people who were servicing my typewriter had finished it. They hadn't. Call back Monday, they said.

When I stepped out into the street again, a woman was screaming.

Heads turned. The high-pitched agonized noise pierced the

roar of wheels and rose clean above the car horns. With everyone else, I looked to see the cause.

Fifty yards up the pavement a knot of people was rapidly
forming, and I reflected that in this particular place droves of
regular staff reporters would be on the spot in seconds.
Nevertheless I went back. Back to the front door of Bert's
paper, and a few steps farther on.

Bert was lying on the pavement. Clearly dead. The shining
fragments of his half bottle of whiskey scattered the paving
slabs around him, and the sharp smell of the spilt spirit mixed
uneasily with that of the pervading diesel oil.

"He fell! He fell!" The screaming woman was on the edge
of hysterics and couldn't stop shouting. "He fell. I saw him.
From up there. He fell!"

Luke-John said "Christ" several times and looked badly
shocked. Derry shook out a whole pot of paper clips onto his
desk and absent-mindedly put them back one by one.

"You're sure he was dead?" he said.

"His office was seven floors up."

"Yeah." He shook his head disbelievingly. "Poor old boy."
Nil nisi bonum. A sharp change of attitude.

Luke-John looked out of the *Blaze* window and down along
the street. The smashed remains of Bert Checkov had been
decently removed. The pavement had been washed. People
tramped unknowingly across the patch where he had died.

"He was drunk," Luke-John said. "Worse than usual."

He and Derry made a desultory start on the afternoon work. I
had no need to stay as the editor had O.K.'d my copy, but I
hung around anyway for an hour or two, not ready to go.

They had said in Bert's office that he came back stoned from
lunch and simply fell out of the window. Two girl secretaries

saw him. He was taking a drink out of the bottle of whiskey, and he suddenly staggered against the window, which swung open, and he toppled out. The bottom of the window was at hip height. No trouble at all for someone as drunk as Bert.

I remembered the desperation behind the bit of advice he had given me.

And I wondered.

Two

Three things immediately struck you about the girl who opened
the stockbroker-Tudor door at Virginia Water. First, her poise.
Second, her fashion sense. Third, her color. She had honey-toast
skin, large dark eyes, and a glossy shoulder-length bounce of
black hair. A slightly broad nose and a mouth to match en-
hanced a landscape in which Negro and Caucasian genes had
conspired together to do a grand job.

"Good afternoon," I said. "I'm James Tyrone. I telephoned. . . ."

"Come in." She nodded. "Harry and Sarah should be back at
any minute."

"They are still playing golf?"

"Mmm." She turned, smiling slightly, and gestured me into
the house. "Still finishing lunch, I expect."

It was three-thirty-five. Why not?

She led me through the hall (well-polished parquet, careful
flowers, studded leather umbrella stand) into a chintz and
chrysanthemum sitting room. Every window in the house was a
clutter of diamond-shaped leaded lights which might have had
some point when glass could only be made in six-inch squares
and had to be joined together to get anywhere. The modern
imitation obscured the light, and the view and was bound to
infuriate window cleaners. Harry and Sarah had opted also for
uncovered dark oak beams with machine-made chisel marks.
The single picture on the plain cream walls made a wild

contrast: a modern impressionistic abstract of some cosmic explosion, with the oils stuck on in lumps.

"Sit down." She waved a graceful hand at a thickly cushioned sofa. "Like a drink?"

"No, thank you."

"Don't journalists drink all day?"

"If you drink and write, the writing isn't so hot."

"Ah, yes," she said. "Dylan Thomas said he had to be stone cold for any good to come of it."

"Different class." I smiled.

"Same principle."

"Absolutely."

She gave me a long inspection, her head tilted an inch to one side and her green dress lying in motionless folds down her slender body. Terrific legs in the latest in stockings ended in shiny green shoes with gold buckles, and the only other accessory on display was a broad-strapped gold watch on her left wrist.

"You'll know me again," she said.

I nodded. Her body moved subtly inside the green dress.

She said slowly, with more than simple meaning, "And I'll know you."

Her voice, face, and manner were quite calm. The brief flash of intense sexual awareness could have been my imagination. Certainly her next remark held no undertone and no invitation.

"Do you *like* horses?"

"Yes, I do," I said.

"Six months ago I would have said the one place I would never go would be to a race meeting."

"But you go now?"

"Since Harry won Egocentric in that raffle, life has changed in this little neck of the woods."

"That," I said, "is exactly what I want to write about."

I was on *Tally* business. Background to the Lamplighter. My choice of untypical racehorse owners, Harry and Sarah Hunterson, came back at that point from their Sunday golf-course lunch, sweeping in with them a breeze compounded of healthy links air, expensive cigar smoke, and half-digested gin.

Harry was big, sixtyish, used to authority, heavily charming, and unshakably Tory. I guessed that he read the *Telegraph* and drove a three-litre Jaguar. With automatic transmission, of course. He gave me a hearty handshake and said he was glad to see his niece had been looking after me.

"Yes, thank you."

Sarah said, "Gail, dear, you didn't give Mr. Tyrone a drink."

"He didn't want one."

The two women were coolly nice to each other in civilized voices. Sarah must have been about thirty years older, but she had worked hard at keeping nature at bay. Everything about her looked careful, from the soft gold rinse via the russet-colored dress to the chunky brown golfing shoes. Her well-controlled shape owed much to the drinking-man's diet, and only a deep sag under the chin gave the game away. Neither golf nor gin had dug wrinkles anywhere except around her eyes. Her mouth still had fullness and shape. The wrappings were good enough to hold out hopes of a spark-striking mind, but these proved unrealistic. Sarah was all-of-a-piece, with attitudes and opinions as tidy and well-ordered and as imitative as her house.

Harry was easy to interview in the aftermath of the nineteenth hole.

"I bought this raffle ticket at the golf-club dance, you see. Some chap was there selling them, a friend of a friend, you know, and I gave him a quid. Well, you know how it is at a dance. For charity, he said. I thought a quid was a bit steep for a raffle ticket, even if it was for a horse. Though I didn't want a horse, mind you. Last thing I wanted. And then damn me if I didn't go and win it. Bit of a problem, eh? To suddenly find yourself saddled with a racehorse?" He laughed, expecting a reward for his little joke.

I duly obliged. Sarah and Gail were both wearing the expressions which meant they had heard him say "saddled with a racehorse" so often that they had to grit their teeth now at each repetition.

"Would you mind," I said, "telling me something of your background and history?"

"Life story, eh?" He laughed loudly, looking from Sarah to Gail to collect their approval. His head was heavily handsome, though a shade too fleshy around the neck. The bald sunburned crown and the well-disciplined mustache suited him. Thread veins made circular patches of color on his cheeks. "Life story," he repeated. "Where shall I start?"

"Start from birth," I said, "and go on from there."

Only the very famous who have done it too often, or the extremely introverted, or the sheer bloody-minded, can resist such an invitation. Harry's eyes lit up, and he launched forth with enthusiasm.

Harry had been born in a Surrey suburb in a detached house a size or two smaller than the one he now owned. He had been to a day school and then a minor public school, and was turned down by the Army because as soon as he left school he had pleurisy. He went to work in the City, in the head office of a finance company, and had risen from junior clerk to director, on the way using occasional snippets of information to make himself modest capital gains via the stock market. Nothing shady, nothing rash; but enough so that there should be no drop in his standard of living when he retired.

He married at twenty-four and five years later a lorry rammed his car and killed his wife, his three-year-old daughter, and his widowed mother. For fifteen years, much in demand at dinner parties, Harry "looked around." Then he met Sarah in some Conservative Party committee rooms where they were doing voluntary work addressing pamphlets for a by-election, and they had married three months later. Below the confident fruitiness of successful Harry's voice there was an echo of the motivation of this second marriage. Harry had begun to feel lonely.

As lives went, Harry's had been uneventful. No *Blaze* material in what he had told me, and precious little for *Tally*. Resignedly I asked him if he intended to keep Egocentric indefinitely.

"Yes, yes, I think so," he said. "He has made quite a remarkable difference to us."

"In what way?"

"It puts them several notches up in lifemanship," Gail said coolly. "Gives them something to boast about in pubs."

We all looked at her. Such was her poise that I found it impossible to tell whether she meant to be catty or teasing, and, from his uncertain expression, so did her uncle. There was no ducking it, however, that she had hit to the heart of things, and Sarah smoothly punished her for it.

"Gail, dear, would you go and make tea for all of us?"

Gail's every muscle said she would hate to. But she stood up ostentatiously slowly, and went.

"A dear girl," Sarah said. "Perhaps sometimes a little trying." Insincerity took all warmth out of her smile, and she found it necessary to go on, to make an explanation that I guessed she rushed into with every stranger at the first opportunity.

"Harry's sister married a barrister. . . . Such a clever man, you know . . . but, well . . . *African.*"

"Yes," I said.

"Of course we're *very* fond of Gail, and as her parents have gone back to his country since it became independent, and as she was born in England and wanted to stay here, well, we—well, she lives here with us."

"Yes," I said again. "That must be very nice for her."

Sad, I thought, that they felt any need to explain. Gail didn't need it.

"She teaches at an art school in Victoria," Harry added. "Fashion drawing."

"Fashion *design,*" Sarah corrected him. "She's really quite good at it. Her pupils win prizes, and things like that." There was relief in her voice now that I understood, and she was prepared to be generous. To do her justice, considering the far-back embedded prejudices she clearly suffered from, she had made a successful effort. But a pity the effort showed.

"And you," I said. "How about your life? And what do you think of Egocentric?"

She said apologetically that her story wasn't as interesting as Harry's. Her first husband, an optician, had died a year before she met Harry, and all she had done, apart from short excursions into voluntary work, was keep house for the two of them. She was glad Harry had won the horse, she liked going to the races as an owner, she thought it exciting to bet, but ten shillings was her usual, and she and Gail had found it quite fun inventing Harry's racing colors.

"What are they?"

"White with scarlet and turquoise question marks, turquoise sleeves, red cap."

"They sound fine." I smiled. "I'll look out for them."

Harry said his trainer was planning to fit in one more race for

Egocentric before the Lamplighter, and maybe I would see him then. Maybe I would, I said, and Gail brought in the tea.

Harry and Sarah rapidly downed three cups each, simultaneously consulted their watches, and said it was time to be getting along to the Murrows' for drinks.

"I don't think I'll come," Gail said. "Tell them thanks, but I have got some work to do. But I'll come and fetch you, if you like, if you think it might be better not to drive home. Give me a ring when you're ready."

The Murrow drinks on top of the golf-club gin were a breathalizer hazard in anyone's book. Harry and Sarah nodded and said they would appreciate it.

"Before you go," I said, "could you let me see any newspaper cuttings you have? And any photographs?"

"Certainly, certainly," Harry agreed. "Gail will show them to you, won't you, honey? Must dash now, old chap. The Murrows, you know. . . . President of the golf club. Nice to have met you. Hope you've got all the gen you need. . . . Don't hesitate to call if you want to know anything else."

"Thank you," I said, but he was gone before I finished. They went upstairs and down, and shut the front door, and drove away. The house settled into quiet behind them.

"They're not exactly alcoholic," Gail said. "They just go eagerly from drink to drink."

Gail's turn to explain. But in her voice, only objectivity: no faintest hint of apology, as there had been in Sarah's.

"They enjoy life," I said.

Gail's eyebrows rose. "Do you know," she said, "I suppose they do. I've never really thought about it."

Self-centered, I thought. Cool. Unaffectionate. Everything I disliked in a woman. Everything I needed one to be. Much too tempting.

"Do you want to see those photographs?" she asked.

"Yes, please."

She fetched an expensive leather folder and we went through them one by one. Nothing in the few clippings that I hadn't learnt already. None of the photographs were arresting enough for *Tally*. I said I'd come back one day soon, with a photographer. Gail put the folder away and I stood up to go.

"It'll be two hours yet before they ring up from the Murrows'. Stay and have that drink now?"

I looked at my watch. There was a train every thirty minutes. I supposed I could miss the next. There was Elizabeth. And there was Gail. And it was only an hour.

"Yes," I said. "I will."

She gave me beer and brought one for herself. I sat down again on the sofa and she folded herself gracefully into a large velvet cushion on the floor.

"You're married, of course?"

"Yes," I said.

"The interesting-looking ones always are."

"Then why aren't you?"

Her teeth flashed liquid white in an appreciative smile. "Ah . . . marriage can wait."

"How long?" I asked.

"I suppose . . . until I find a man I can't bear to part with."

"You've parted with quite a few?"

"Quite a few." She nodded and sipped her beer, and looked at me over the rim. "And you? Are you faithful to your wife?"

I felt myself blink. I said carefully, "Most of the time."

"But not always?"

"Not always."

After a long considering pause she said one short word.

"Good."

"And is that," I asked, "a philosophic comment, or a proposition?"

She laughed. "I just like to know where I stand."

"Clear-eyed and wide-awake?"

"I hate muddle," she said.

"And emotional muddle especially?"

"You're so right."

She had never loved, I thought. Sex, often. Love, never. Not what I liked, but what I wanted. I battened down the insidious whisper and asked her, like a good little journalist, about her job.

"It serves." She shrugged. "You get maybe one authentic talent in every hundred students. Mostly their ambition is five times more noticeable than their ideas."

"Do you design clothes yourself?"

"Not for the rag trade. Some for myself, and for Sarah, and for the school. I prefer to teach. I like being able to turn vaguely artistic ignorance into competent workmanship."

"And to see your influence all along Oxford Street?"

She nodded, her eyes gleaming with amusement. "Five of the biggest dress manufacturers now have old students of mine on their design staff. One of them is so individual that I can spot his work every time in the shop windows."

"You like power," I said.

"Who doesn't?"

"Heady stuff."

"All power corrupts?" She was sarcastic.

"Each to his own corruption," I said mildly. "What's yours, then?"

She laughed. "Money, I guess. There's a chronic shortage of the folding stuff in all forms of teaching."

"So you make do with power."

"If you can't have everything"—she nodded—"you make do with *something*."

I looked down into my beer, unable to stop the contraction I could feel in my face. Her words so completely summed up my perennial position. After eleven years I was less resigned to it than ever.

"What are you thinking about?" she asked.

"Taking you to bed."

She gasped. I looked up from the flat brown liquid ready for any degree of feminine outrage. I could have mistaken her.

It seemed I hadn't. She was laughing. Pleased.

"That's pretty blunt."

"Mmm."

I put down the beer and stood up, smiling. "Time to go," I said. "I've a train to catch."

"After that? You can't go after that."

"Especially after that."

For answer she stood up beside me, took hold of my hand, and put my fingers into the gold ring at the top of the zipper down the front of her dress.

"Now go home," she said.

"We've only known each other three hours," I protested.

"You were aware of me after three minutes."

I shook my head. "Three seconds."

Her teeth gleamed. "I like strangers."

I pulled the ring downward and it was clearly what she wanted.

Harry and Sarah had a large white fluffy rug in front of their fireplace. I imagined it was not the first time Gail had lain on it. She was brisk, graceful, unembarrassed. She stripped off her stockings and shoes, shook off her dress, and stepped out of the diminutive green bra and panties underneath it. Her tawny skin looked warm in the gathering dusk, and her shape took the breath away.

She gave me a marvelous time. A generous lover as well as

practiced. She knew when to touch lightly, and when to be vigorous. She had strong internal muscles, and she knew how to use them. I took her with passionate gratitude, a fair substitute for love.

When we had finished, I lay beside her on the rug and felt the released tension weighing down my limbs in a sort of heavy languorous weakness. The world was a million light-years away and I was in no hurry for it to come closer.

"Wow," she said, half breathless, half laughing. "Boy, you sure needed that."

"Mmm."

"Doesn't your wife let you. . . ?"

Elizabeth, I thought. Oh God, Elizabeth. I must sometimes. Just sometimes.

The old weary tide of guilt washed back. The world closed in.

I sat up and stared blindly across the darkening room. It apparently struck Gail that she had been less than tactful, because she got up with a sigh and put her clothes on again, and didn't say another word.

For better or worse, I thought bitterly. For richer, for poorer. In sickness and in health keep thee only unto her as long as you both shall live. I will, I said.

An easy vow, the day I made it. I hadn't kept it. Gail was the fourth girl in eleven years. The first for nearly three.

"You'll miss your train," she observed prosaically, "if you sit there much longer."

I looked at my watch, which was all I had on. Fifteen minutes.

She sighed, "I'll drive you along to the station."

We made it with time to spare. I stepped out of the car and politely thanked her for the lift.

"Will I see you again?" she said. Asking for information. Showing no anxiety. Looking out at me through the open window of the station wagon outside Virginia Water station, she was giving a close imitation of any suburban wife doing the train run. A long cool way from the rough and tumble on the rug. Switch on, switch off. The sort of woman I needed.

"I don't know," I said indecisively. The signal at the end of the platform went green.

"Goodbye," she said calmly.

"Do Harry and Sarah," I asked carefully, "always play golf on Sundays?"

She laughed, the yellow station lighting flashing on teeth and eyes.

"Without fail."

"Maybe. . . ."

"Maybe you'll ring, and maybe you won't." She nodded. "Fair enough. And maybe I'll be in, and maybe I won't." She gave me a lengthy look which was half smile and half amused detachment. She wouldn't weep if I didn't return. She would accommodate me if I did. "But don't leave it too long, if you're coming back."

She wound up the window and drove off without a wave, without a backward glance.

The green electric worm of a train slid quietly into the station to take me home. Forty minutes to Waterloo. Underground to King's Cross. Three-quarters of a mile to walk. Time to enjoy the new ease in my body. Time to condemn it. Too much of my life was a battlefield in which conscience and desire fought constantly for the upper hand; and whichever of them won, it left me the loser.

Elizabeth's mother said with predictable irritation, "You're late."

"I'm sorry."

I watched the jerks of her crossly pulling on her gloves. Coat and hat had already been in place when I walked in.

"You have so little consideration. It'll be nearly eleven when I get back."

I didn't answer.

"You're selfish. All men are selfish."

There was no point in agreeing with her, and no point in arguing. A disastrous and short-lived marriage had left hopeless wounds in her mind which she had done her best to pass on to her only child. Elizabeth, when I first met her, had been pathologically scared of men.

"We've had our supper," my mother-in-law said. "I've stacked the dishes for Mrs. Woodward."

Nothing could be more certainly relied upon to upset Mrs. Woodward than a pile of congealed plates first thing on Monday morning.

"Fine," I said, smiling falsely.

"Goodbye, Elizabeth," she called.

"Goodbye, Mother."

I opened the door for her and got no thanks.

"Next Sunday, then," she said.

"That'll be nice."

She smiled acidly, knowing I didn't mean it. But since she worked as a receptionist-hostess in a health farm all week, Sunday was her day for seeing Elizabeth. Most weeks I wished she would leave us alone, but that Sunday it had set me free to go to Virginia Water. From the following Sunday, and what I might do with it, I wrenched my thoughts away.

When she had gone, I walked across to Elizabeth and kissed her on the forehead.

"Hi."

"Hi yourself," she said. "Did you have a good afternoon?"

Straight jab.

"Mmm."

"Good. . . . Mother's left the dishes again."

I said, "Don't worry, I'll do them."

"What would I do without you!"

We both knew the answer to that. Without me, she would have to spend the rest of her life in a hospital ward, a prisoner with no possibility of escape. She couldn't breathe without the electrically driven pump which hummed at the foot of her high bed. She couldn't cut up her own food or take herself to the bathroom. Elizabeth, my wife, was ninety per cent paralyzed from poliomyelitis.

Three

We lived over a row of lockup garages in a mews behind Gray's Inn Road. A development company had recently knocked down the old buildings opposite, letting in temporary acres of evening sunshine, and was now at the girder stage of a block of flats. If these made our place too dark and shut in when they were done, I would have to find us somewhere else. Not a welcome prospect. We had moved twice before and it was always difficult.

Since race trains mostly ran from London, and to cut my traveling time down to a minimum, we lived ten minutes' walk from the *Blaze*. It had proved much better, in London, to live in a backwater than in a main street; in the small mews community the neighbors all knew about Elizabeth and looked up to her window and waved when they passed, and a lot of them came upstairs for a chat and to bring our shopping.

The district nurse came every morning to do Elizabeth's alcohol rubs to prevent bedsores, and I did them in the evenings. Mrs. Woodward, a semitrained but unqualified nurse, came Mondays through Saturdays from nine-thirty to six, and was helpful about staying longer if necessary. One of our main troubles was that Elizabeth could not be left alone in the flat even for five minutes in case there was an electricity failure. If the main current stopped, we could switch her breathing pump over to a battery, and we could also operate it by hand, but someone had to be there to do it quickly.

Mrs. Woodward was kind, middle-aged, reliable, and quiet,

35

and Elizabeth liked her. She was also very expensive, and since the Welfare State turns a blind eye on incapacitated wives, I could claim not even so much as a tax allowance for Mrs. Woodward's essential services. We had to have her, and she kept us poor; and that was that.

In one of the garages below the flat stood the old Bedford van which was the only sort of transport of any use to us. I had had it adapted years ago with a stretcher-type bed so that it would take Elizabeth, pump, batteries, and all, and although it meant, too, much upheaval to go out in it every week, it did sometimes give her a change of scenery and some country air. We had tried two holidays by the sea in a caravan, but she had felt uncomfortable and insecure, and both times it had rained, so we didn't bother any more. Day trips were enough, she said. And although she enjoyed them, they exhausted her.

Her respirator was the modern cuirass type: a Spiroshell, not the old totally enclosing iron lung. The Spiroshell itself slightly resembled the breastplate of a suit of armor. It fitted over the entire front of her chest, was edged with a thick roll of latex, and was fastened by straps around her body. Breathing was really a matter of suction. The pump, which was connected to the Spiroshell by a thick flexible hose, alternately made a partial vacuum inside the shell and then drove air back in again. The vacuum period pulled Elizabeth's chest wall outward, allowing air to flow downward into her lungs. The air-in period collapsed her chest and pushed the used breath out again.

Far more comfortable, and easier for everyone caring for her than a box respirator, the Spiroshell had only one drawback. Try as we might, and however many scarves and cardigans we might stuff in around the edges between the latex roll and her nightdress, it was eternally drafty. As long as the air in the flat was warm, it did not worry her. Summer was all right. But cold air continually blowing onto her chest—not surprisingly—distressed her. Cold also reduced to nil the small movements she had retained in her left hand and wrist, and on which she depended for everything. Our heating bills were astronomical.

In the nine and a half years since I had extricated her from hospital, we had acquired almost every gadget invented. Wires and pulleys trailed all around the flat. She could read books, draw the curtains, turn on and off the lights, the radio, and television, use the telephone, and type letters. An electric box of tricks called Possum did most of these tasks. Others worked on a system of levers set off by the feather-light pressure of her left forefinger. Our latest triumph was an electric pulley which raised and rotated her left elbow and forearm, enabling her to eat some things on her own, without always having to be fed. And with a clipped-on electric toothbrush she could now brush her own teeth.

I slept on a divan across the room from her with a bell beside my ear for when she needed me in the night. There were bells, too, in the kitchen and the bathroom, and the tiny room I used for writing in, which with the large sitting room made up the whole of the flat.

We had been married three years, and we were both twenty-four, when Elizabeth caught polio. We were living in Singapore, where I had a junior job in the Reuters office, and we flew home for what was intended to be a month's leave.

Elizabeth felt ill on the flight. The light hurt her eyes, and she had a headache like a rod up the back of her neck, and a stabbing pain in her chest. She walked off the aircraft at Heathrow and collapsed halfway across the tarmac, and that was the last time she ever stood on her feet.

Our affection for each other had survived everything that followed. Poverty, temper, tears, desperate frustrations. We had

emerged after several years into our present comparative calms
of a settled home, a good job, a reasonably well-ordered existence. We were firm close friends.

But not lovers.

We had tried, in the beginning. She could still feel of course,
since polio attacks only the motor nerves, and leaves the sensory
nerves intact. But she couldn't breathe for more than three or
four minutes if we took the Spiroshell right off, and she
couldn't bear any weight or pressure on any part of her wasted
body. When I said after two or three hopeless attempts that we
would leave it for a while, she had smiled at me with what I
saw to be enormous relief, and we had rarely even mentioned
the subject since. Her early upbringing seemed to have easily
reconciled her to a sexless existence. Her three years of thawing
into a satisfying marriage might never have happened.

On the day after my trip to Virginia Water I set off as soon as
Mrs. Woodward came and drove the van northeast out of
London and into deepest Essex. My quarry this time was a
farmer who had bred gold dust in his field in the shape of
Tiddely Pom, antepost favorite for the Lamplighter Gold Cup.

Weeds luxuriantly edged the potholed road which led from a
pair of rotting gateless gateposts into Victor Roncey's farmyard.
The house itself, an undistinguished arrangement of mud-
colored bricks, stood in a drift of sodden unswept leaves and
stared blankly from symmetrical grubby windows. Colorless
paint peeled quietly from the woodwork and no smoke rose
from the chimneys.

I knocked on the back door, which stood half open, and
called through a small lobby into the house, but there was no
reply. A clock ticked with a loud cheap mechanism. A smell of
Wellington boots richly acquainted with cow pat vigorously as-

saulted the nose. Someone had dumped a parcel of meat on the edge of the kitchen table from which a thread of watery blood, that had soaked through the newspaper wrapping, was making a small pink pool on the floor.

Turning away from the house, I wandered across the untidy yard and peered into a couple of outbuildings. One contained a tractor covered with about six years' mud. In another, a heap of dusty-looking coke rubbed shoulders with a jumbled stack of old broken crates and sawed-up branches of trees. A larger shed housed dirt and cobwebs and nothing else.

While I hovered in the center of the yard wondering how far it was polite to investigate, a large youth in a striped knitted cap with a scarlet pompon came around a corner at the far end. He also wore a vast sloppy pale blue sweater, and filthy jeans tucked into heavyweight gum boots. Fair-haired, with a round weather-beaten face, he looked cheerful and uncomplicated.

"Hullo," he said. "You want something?" His voice was light and pleasant, with a touch of local accent.

"I'm looking for Mr. Roncey."

"He's round the roads with the horses. Better call back later."

"How long will he be?"

"An hour, maybe." He shrugged.

"I'll wait, then, if you don't mind," I said, gesturing toward my van.

"Suit yourself."

He took six steps toward the house and then stopped, turned around, and came back.

"Hey, you wouldn't be that chap who phoned?"

"Which chap?"

"James Tyrone?"

"That's right."

"Well, for crying out loud why didn't you say so? I thought you were a traveler. . . . Come on into the house. Do you want some breakfast?"

"Breakfast?"

He grinned. "Yeah. I know it's nearly eleven. I get up before six. Feel peckish again by now."

He led the way into the house through the back door, did nothing about the dripping meat, and added to the Wellington smell by clumping across the floor to the furthest door, which he opened.

"Ma?" he shouted. "Ma."

"She's around somewhere," he said, shrugging and coming back. "Never mind. Want some eggs?"

I said no, but when he reached out a half-acre frying pan and filled it with bacon I changed my mind.

"Make the coffee," he said, pointing.

I found mugs, powdered coffee, sugar, milk, kettle, and spoons all standing together on a bench alongside the sink.

"My Ma," he explained, grinning, "is a great one for the time-and-motion bit."

He fried six eggs expertly and gave us three each, with a chunk of new white bread on the side.

We sat at the kitchen table, and I'd rarely tasted anything so good. He ate solidly and drank coffee, then pushed his plate away and lit a cigarette.

"I'm Peter," he said. "It isn't usually so quiet around here, but the kids are at school and Pat's out with Pa."

"Pat?"

"My brother. The jockey of the family. Point-to-points, mostly, though. I don't suppose you would know of him?"

"I'm afraid not."

"I read your column," he said. "Most weeks."

"That's nice."

He considered me, smoking, while I finished the eggs. "You don't talk much, for a journalist."

"I listen," I said.

He grinned. "That's a point."

"Tell me about Tiddely Pom, then."

"Hell, no. You'll have to get Pa or Pat for that. They're crazy on the horses. I just run the farm." He watched my face carefully, I guessed for surprise, since in spite of being almost my height he was still very young.

"You're sixteen?" I suggested.

"Yeah." He sniffed, disgusted. "Waste of effort, though, really."

"Why?"

"Why? Because of the bloody motorway, that's why. They've nearly finished that bloody three-lane monster and it passes just over there, the other side of our ten-acre field." He gestured toward the window with his cigarette. "Pa's going raving mad wondering if Tiddely Pom'll have a nervous breakdown when those heavy lorries start thundering past. He's been trying to sell this place for two years, but no one will have it, and you can't blame them, can you?" Gloom settled on him temporarily. "Then, see, you never know when they'll pinch more of our land, they've had fifty acres already, and it doesn't give you much heart to keep the place right, does it?"

"I guess not," I said.

"They've talked about knocking our house down," he went on. "Something about it being in the perfect position for a service station with restaurants and a vast car park and another slip road to Bishop's Stortford. The only person who's pleased about the road is my brother Tony, and he wants to be a rally driver. He's eleven. He's a nut."

There was a scrunch and clatter of hoofs outside, coming nearer. Peter and I got to our feet and went out into the yard, and watched three horses plod up the bumpy gravel drive and rein to a halt in front of us. The rider of the leading horse slid off, handed his reins to the second, and came toward us. A trim wiry man in his forties, with thick brown hair and a mustard-colored mustache.

"Mr. Tyrone?"

I nodded. He gave me a brisk hard handshake in harmony with his manner and voice, and then stood back to allow me a clear view of the horses.

"That's Tiddely Pom, that bay." He pointed to the third horse, ridden by young man very like Peter, though perhaps a size smaller. "And Pat, my son."

"A fine-looking horse," I said insincerely. Most owners expected praise, but Tiddely Pom showed as much high quality to the naked eye as an uncut diamond. A common head, slightly U-necked on a weak shoulder, and herring-gutted into the bargain. He looked just as uncouth at home as he did on a racecourse.

"Huh," snorted Roncey. "He's not. He's a doer, not a looker. Don't try and butter me up. I don't take to it."

"Fair enough," I said mildly. "Then he's got a common head and neck, a poor shoulder, and doesn't fill the eye behind the saddle, either."

"That's better. So you do know what you're talking about. Walk him round the yard, Pat."

Pat obliged. Tiddely Pom stumbled around with the floppy gait that once in a while denotes a champion. This horse, bred from a thoroughbred hunter mare by a premium stallion, was a spectacular jumper endowed with a speed to be found nowhere in his pedigree. When an ace of this sort turned up unexpectedly, it took the owner almost as long as the public to realize it. The whole racing industry was unconsciously geared against belief that twenty-two-carat stars could come from tiny owner-trained stables. It had taken Tiddely Pom three seasons to become known, while from a big fashionable public stable he would have been newsworthy in his first race.

"When I bred him, I was hoping for a point-to-point horse for the boys," Roncey said. "So we ran him all one season in point-to-points and, apart from one time Pat fell off, he didn't get beat. Then last year we thought we would have a go in hunter chases as well, and he went and won the Foxhunters at Cheltenham."

"I remember that," I said.

"Yes. So last year we tried him in open handicaps, smallish ones—"

"And he won four out of six," I concluded for him.

"It's your job to know, I suppose. Pat!" he shouted. "Put him back in his box." He turned to me again. "Like to see the others?"

I nodded, and we followed Pat and the other two horses across the yard and around the corner from which Peter had originally appeared.

Behind a ramshackle barn stood a neat row of six well-kept wooden horse boxes, with shingle roofs and newly painted black doors. However run-down the rest of the farm might be, the stable department was in tiptop shape. No difficulty in seeing where the farmer's heart lay: with his treasure.

"Well, now," Roncey said, "we've only the one other race-horse, really, and that's Klondyke, that I was riding just now. He ran in hunter chases in the spring. Didn't do much good, to be honest." He walked along to the second box from the far end, led the horse in, and tied it up. When he took the saddle off, I saw that Klondyke was a better shape than Tiddely Pom, which was saying little enough, but the health in his coat was conspicuous.

"He looks well," I commented.

"Eats his head off," said Roncey dispassionately, "and he can stand a lot of work, so we give it to him."

"One-paced," observed Pat regretfully over my shoulder. "Can't quicken. Pity. We won just the two point-to-points with him. No more."

There was the faintest glimmer of satisfaction in the laconic voice, and I glanced at him sideways. He saw me looking and wiped the expression off his face but not before I had seen for certain that he had mixed feelings about the horses' successes. While they progressed to National Hunt racing proper, he didn't. Older amateur riders had been engaged, and then professionals. The father-son relationship had needles in it.

"What do you have in the other boxes?" I asked Roncey as he shut Klondyke's door.

"My old gray hunter at the end, and two hunter mares here, both in foal. This one, Piglet, she's the dam of Tiddely Pom, of course; she's in foal to the same sire again."

Unlikely, I thought, that lightning would strike twice.

"You'll sell the foal," I suggested.

He sniffed. "She's in the farm accounts."

I grinned to myself. Farmers could train their horses and lose the cost on the general farm accounts, but if they sold one it then came under the heading of income and was taxed accordingly. If Roncey sold either Tiddely Pom or his full brother, nearly half would go to the Revenue.

"Turn the mares out, Joe," he said to the third rider, a patient-looking old man with skin like bark, and we watched while he set them loose in the nearest field. Peter was standing beside the gate with Pat: bigger, more assured, with far fewer knots in his personality.

"Fine sons," I said to Roncey.

His mouth tightened. He had no pride in them. He made no reply at all to my fishing comment, but instead said, "We'll go into the house and you can ask me anything you want to know. For a magazine, you said?"

I nodded.

"Pat!" he shouted. "You give these three mares a good strapping and feed them and let Joe get on with the hedging. Peter, you've got work to do. Go and do it."

Both his boys gave him the blank acquiescing look which covers seething rebellion. There was a perceptible pause before they moved off with their calm accepting faces. Lids on a lot of steam. Maybe one day Roncey would be scalded.

He led the way briskly back across the yard and into the kitchen. The meat still lay there dripping. Roncey by-passed it and gestured me to follow him through the far door into a small dark hall.

"Madge?" he shouted. "Madge?"

Father had as little success as son. He shrugged in the same way and led me into a living room as well worn and untidy as the rest of the place. Drifts of clutter, letters, newspapers, clothing, toys, and indiscriminate bits of junk lay on every flat surface, including the chairs and the floor. There was a vase of dead and desiccated chrysanthemums on a window sill, and some brazen cobwebs networked the ceiling. Cold ash from the day before filled the grate. A tossup, I thought, whether one called the room lived-in or squalid.

"Sit down if you can find somewhere," Roncey said. "Madge lets the boys run wild in the house. Not firm enough. I won't have it outside, of course."

"How many do you have?"

"Boys? Five."

"And a daughter?" I asked.

"No," he said abruptly. "Five boys."

The thought didn't please him. "Which magazine?"

"*Tally*," I said. "They want background stories to the Lamplighter, and I thought I would give the big stables a miss and shine a bit of the spotlight on someone else for a change."

"Yes, well," he said defensively, "I've been written up before, you know."

"Of course," I said soothingly.

"About the Lamplighter, too. I'll show you." He jumped up and went over to a kneehole desk, pulled out one of the side drawers bodily, and brought it across to where I sat at one end of the sofa. He put the drawer in the center, swept a crumpled jersey, two beaten-up dinky cars, and a gutted brown paper parcel onto the floor, and seated himself in the space.

The drawer contained a heap of clippings and photographs all thrust in together. No careful sticking into expensive leather folders, like the Huntersons.

My mind leapt to Gail. I saw Roncey talking to me but I was thinking about her body. Her roundnesses. Her fragrant pigmented skin. Roncey was waiting for an answer and I hadn't heard what he'd asked.

"I'm sorry," I said.

"I asked if you know Bert Checkov." He was holding a lengthy clipping with a picture alongside and a bold headline, "BACK TIDDELY POM NOW."

"Yes . . . and no," I said uncertainly.

"How do you mean?" he said brusquely. "I should have thought you would have known him, being in the same business."

"I did know him. But he died. Last Friday."

I took the clipping and read it while Roncey went through the motions of being shocked, with the indifference uppermost in his voice spoiling the effect.

Bert Checkov had gone to town with Tiddely Pom's chances in the Lamplighter. The way he saw it, the handicapper had been suffering from semiblindness and mental blocks to put Tiddely Pom into the weights at ten stone seven, and all punters who didn't jump on the band wagon instantly needed to be wet-nursed. He thought the antepost market would open with generous odds, but urged everyone to hurry up with their shirts, before the bookmakers woke up to the bonanza. Bert's pungent phraseology had given Roncey's horse more boost than a four-stage rocket.

"I didn't know he'd written this," I admitted. "I missed it."

"He rang me up only last Thursday and this was in the paper on Friday. That must have been the day you said he died. In point of fact I didn't expect it would appear. When he telephoned, he was, to my mind, quite drunk."

"It's possible," I conceded.

"I wasn't best pleased about it, either."

"The article?"

"I hadn't got my own money on, do you see? And there he went spoiling the price. When I rang up my bookmaker on Friday, he wouldn't give me more than a hundred to eight and today they've even made him favorite at eight to one, and there's still nearly three weeks to the race. Fair enough he's a good horse, but he's not Arkle. In point of fact I don't understand it."

"You don't understand why Checkov tipped him?"

He hesitated. "Not to that extent, then, let's say."

"But you do hope to win?"

"Hope," he said. "Naturally, I hope to win. But it's the biggest race we've ever tried. . . . I don't *expect* to win, do you see?"

"You've as good a chance as any," I said. "Checkov had his

column to fill. The public won't read halfhearted stuff; you have to go all out for the positive statement."

He gave me a small tight smile laced with a sneer for the soft option. A man with no patience or sympathy for anyone else's problems, not even his sons'?

The sitting-room door opened and a large woman in a sunflower yellow dress came in. She had thick hair down on her legs but no stockings, and a pair of puffed ankles bulged over the edges of some battered blue bedroom slippers. Nevertheless she was very light on her feet and she moved slowly, so that her progress seemed to be a weightless drift—no mean feat considering she must have topped twelve stone.

A mass of fine light brown hair hung in an amorphous cloud around her head, from which a pair of dreamy eyes surveyed the world as though she were half asleep. Her face was soft and rounded, not young, but still in a way immature. Her fantasy life, I guessed uncharitably, was more real to her than the present. She had been far away in the past hour, much farther than upstairs.

"I didn't know you were in," she said to Roncey.

He stood up several seconds after me. "Madge, this is James Tyrone. I told you he was coming."

"Did you?" She transferred her vague gaze to me. "Carry on, then."

"Where have you been?" Roncey said. "Didn't you hear me calling?"

"Calling?" She shook her head. "I was making the beds, of course." She stood in the center of the room, looking doubtfully around at the mess. "Why didn't you light the fire?"

I glanced involuntarily at the heap of ashes in the grate, but she saw them as no obstacle at all. From a scratched oak box beside the hearth, she produced three firelighters and a handful of sticks. These went on top of the ashes, which got only a desultory poke. She struck a match, lit the firelighters, and made a wigwam of coal. The new fire flared up good-temperedly on the body of the old while Madge took the hearth brush and swept a few cinders out of sight behind a pile of logs.

Fascinated, I watched her continue with her housework. She drifted across to the dead flowers, opened the window, and threw them out. She emptied the water from the vase after them, then put it back on the window sill and shut the window.

From behind the sofa where Roncey and I sat, she pulled out a large brown cardboard box. On the outside was stenciled "KELLOGG'S CORNFLAKES, 12 x 12 FAMILY SIZE," and on the inside it was half filled with the same sort of jumble which was lying around the room. She wafted methodically around in a large circle, taking everything up and throwing it just as it was into the box, a process which took approximately three minutes. She then pushed the box out of sight again behind the sofa and plumped up the seat cushions of two armchairs on her way back to the door. The room, tidy and with the brightly blazing fire, looked staggeringly different. The cobwebs were still there but one felt it might be their turn tomorrow. Peter was right. Ma had got the time-and-motion kick completely buttoned up, and what did it matter if the motive was laziness?

Roncey insisted that I should stay to lunch and filled in the time beforehand with a brisk but endless account of all the horses he had ever owned. Over lunch—cold beef and pickles and cheese and biscuits served at two-thirty on the kitchen table—it was still he who did all the talking. The boys ate steadily in silence and Madge contemplated the middle distance with eyes which saw only the scenes going on in her head.

When I left shortly afterward, Pat asked for a lift into

Bishop's Stortford and braved his father's frown to climb into
the front seat of the van. Roncey shook hands firmly, as before,
and said he hoped to receive a free copy of *Tally*. "Of course,"
I said. But *Tally* was notoriously mean; I would have to send it
myself.

He waved me out of the yard and told Pat brusquely to come
straight back on the four-o'clock bus, and we were barely out
through the sagging gateposts before Pat unburdened himself
of a chunk of bottled resentment.

"He treats us like children. . . . Ma's no help, she never
listens. . . ."

"You could leave here," I pointed out. "You're what—
nineteen?"

"Next month. But I can't leave and he knows it. Not if I
want to race. I can't turn professional yet; I'm not well enough
known and no one would put me up on their horses. I've got to
start as an amateur and make a name for myself, Pa says so.
Well, I couldn't be an amateur if I left home and got an ordinary job somewhere, I couldn't afford all the expenses and I
wouldn't have any time."

"A job in a stable. . . ." I suggested.

"Do me a favor. The rules say you can't earn a salary in any
capacity in a racing stable and ride as an amateur, not even if
you're a secretary or an assistant or anything. It's bloody unfair.
And don't say I could get a job as a lad and do my two and have
a professional license—of course I could. And how many lads
ever get far as jockeys doing that? None. Absolutely none. You
know that."

I nodded.

"I do a lad's work now, right enough. Six horses we've got,
and I do the bloody lot. Old Joe's the only labor we've got on
the whole farm, except us, believe it or not. Pa's always got a

dozen jobs lined up for him. And I wouldn't mind the work, and getting practically no pay, I really wouldn't, if Pa would let me ride in anything except point-to-points, but he won't; he says I haven't enough experience, and if you ask me he's making bloody sure I never get enough experience. . . . I'm absolutely fed up, I'll tell you straight."

He brooded over his situation all the way into Bishop's Stortford. A genuine grievance, I thought. Victor Roncey was not a father to help his sons get on.

Four

They held the inquest on Bert Checkov on that Monday afternoon. Verdict: Misadventure. Dead drunk he was, said the girl typists who saw him fall. Dead drunk.

And after he hit the pavement, just dead.

When I went into the office on Tuesday morning, Luke-John and Derry were discussing whether or not to go to the funeral on the Wednesday.

"Croxley," Derry said. "Where's that?"

"Near Watford," I said. "On the Metropolitan line. A straight run in to Farringdon Street."

"What Fleet Street needs," said Derry gloomily, "is a tube station a lot nearer than blooming Farringdon. It's three-quarters of a mile if it's an inch."

"If you're right, Ty, we can manage it easily," Luke-John said authoritatively. "We should all go, I think."

Derry squinted at the small underground map in his diary. "Croxley. Next to Watford. What do you know?"

I'd had a girl in Watford once. The second one. I'd spent a lot of time on the Metropolitan line while Elizabeth was under the impression I was extra busy at the *Blaze*. Guilt and deceit were old familiar traveling companions. From Watford, from Virginia Water, from wherever.

"Ty," Luke-John was saying sharply.

"Huh?"

"The funeral is at two-thirty. An hour, say, to get there?"

"Not me," I said. "There's this *Tally* article to be done. It'll take me at least another two days in interviews."

He shrugged. "I'd have thought . . ."

"What depths have you plumbed so far?" Derry asked. He was sitting with his feet up on the desk. No work in a Sunday paper on Tuesday.

"The Roncey family," I said. "Tiddely Pom."

Derry sniffed. "Antepost favorite."

"Will he be your tip?" I asked with interest.

"Shouldn't think so. He's won a few races but he hasn't beaten much of any class."

"Bert tipped him strongly. Wrote a most emphatic piece about catching the odds now before they shorten. He wrote it last Thursday; it must have been straight after the handicap was published in the racing calendar, and it was in his paper on Friday. Roncey showed me the clipping. He said Bert was drunk when he rang up."

Luke-John sighed. Derry said decisively, "That does it, then. If Bert tipped him, I'm not going to."

"Why not?"

"Bert's heavy long-distance tips were nearly always non-starters."

Luke-John stretched his neck until the tendons stood out like strings, and massaged his nobbly larynx. "Always the risk of that, of course. It happens to everyone."

"Do you mean that seriously?" I asked Derry.

"Oh, sure. Sorry about your *Tally* article and all that." He grinned. "But I'd say just about the time it's published you'll find Tiddely Pom has been taken out of the Lamplighter."

Derry twiddled unconcernedly with a rubber band and Luke-John shuffled absent-mindedly through some papers. Neither of them felt the shiver traveling down my spine.

"Derry," I said, "are you sure?"

"Of what?"

"That Bert always tipped nonstarters for big races."

Derry snapped the band twice in his fingers. "To be precise, if you want me to be precise, Bert tipped a higher percentage of big-race nonstarters than anyone else in the street, and he has been at his best in this direction, or worst—or, at any rate, his most consistent—during the past year. He'd blow some horse up big, tell everyone to back it at once, and then, wham, a day or two before the race it would be scratched."

"I've never noticed," said Luke-John forbiddingly, as if it couldn't have happened without.

Derry shrugged. "Well, it's a fact. Now, if you want to know something equally useless about that puffed-up Connersley of the *Sunday Hemisphere,* he has a weird habit of always tipping horses which start with his own initial, C. Delusions of grandeur, I imagine."

"You're having us on," Luke-John said.

Derry shook his head. "Uh-uh. I don't just sit here with my eyes shut, you know; I read the newspapers."

"I think," I said suddenly, "I will fetch my typewriter."

"Where is it?"

Over my shoulder on the way to the door I said, "Being cleaned."

This time the typewriter was ready. I collected it and went farther along the street, to Bert's paper. Up in the lift, to Bert's department. Across the busy floor to the sports desk. Full stop beside the assistant sports editor, a constant racegoer, a long-known bar pal.

"Ty! What's the opposition doing here?"

"Bert Checkov," I said.

We discussed him for a while. The assistant sports editor was hiding something. It showed in half looks, unfinished gestures, an unsuccessfully smothered embarrassment. He said he was shocked, shattered, terribly distressed by Bert's death. He said everyone on the paper would miss him, the paper would miss him, they all felt his death was a great loss. He was lying.

I didn't pursue it. Could I, I asked tentatively, have a look at Bert's clippings book? I would very much like to reread some of his articles.

The assistant sports editor said kindly that I had little to learn from Bert Checkov, or anyone else for that matter, but to go ahead. While he got back to work, I sorted out the records racks at the side of the room and eventually found three brown paper clippings books with Bert's work stuck into the pages.

I took my typewriter out of its carrying case and left it lying on an inconspicuous shelf. The three clippings books went into the carrying case, though I had to squeeze to get it shut, and I walked quietly and unchallenged out of the building with my smuggled goods.

Luke-John and Derry goggled at the books of cuttings.

"How on earth did you get them out? And why on earth do you want them?"

"Derry," I said, "can now set about proving that Bert always tipped nonstarters in big races."

"You're crazy," Luke-John said incredulously.

"No," I said regretfully. "If I'm right, the *Blaze* is on the edge of the sort of scandal it thrives on. A circulation explosion. And all by courtesy of the sports section."

Luke-John's interest sharpened instantly from nil to needles. "Don't waste time then, Derry. If Ty says there's a scandal, there's a scandal."

Derry gave me a sidelong look. "Our truffle hound on the scent, eh?" He took his feet off the desk and resignedly got to work checking what Bert had forecast against what had actually happened. More and more form books and racing calendars were brought out, and Derry's written lists slowly grew.

"All right," he said at last. "Here it is, just as I said. These books cover the last three years. Up till eighteen months ago he tipped runners and nonrunners in about the same proportion as the rest of us poor slobs. Then he went all out suddenly for horses which didn't run when it came to the point. All in big races, which had antepost betting." He looked puzzled. "It can't be just coincidence, I do see that. But I don't see the point."

"Ty?" said Luke-John.

I shrugged. "Someone has been working a fiddle."

"Bert wouldn't." His voice said it was unthinkable.

"I'd better take these books back before they miss them," I said, packing again into the typewriter case.

"Ty!" Luke-John sounded exasperated.

"I'll tell you when I come back," I said.

There was no denunciation at Bert's office. I returned the books to their shelf and retrieved my typewriter, and thanked the assistant sports editor for his kindness.

"You still here? I thought you'd gone." He waved a friendly hand. "Any time."

"All right," said Luke-John truculently when I got back to the *Blaze*. "I won't believe Bert Checkov was party to any fiddle."

"He sold his soul," I said plainly. "Like he told me not to."

"Rubbish."

"He sold his column. He wrote what he was told to write."

"Not Bert. He was a newspaperman, one of the old school."

I considered him. His thin face looked obstinate and pugnacious. Loyalty to an old friend was running very strong.

"Well, then," I said slowly, "Bert wrote what he was forced to write."

A good deal of the Morton tension subsided and changed course. He wouldn't help to uncover a scandal an old friend was responsible for, but he'd go the whole way to open up one he'd been the victim of.

"Clever beast," said Derry under his breath.

"Who forced him?" Luke-John said.

"I don't know. Not yet. It might be possible to find out."

"And *why?*"

"That's much easier. Someone has been making an antepost book on a certainty. What Bert was doing—being forced to do—was persuading the public to part with their money."

They both looked contemplative. I started again, explaining more fully. "Say a villain takes up bookmaking. It can happen, you know."

Derry grinned. "Say one villain hits on a jolly scheme for making illegal gains in a foolproof way with very little effort. He only works it on big races which have antepost betting, because he needs at least three weeks to rake in enough to make it worth the risk. He chooses a suitable horse, and he forces Bert to tip it for all his column's worth. Right? So the public put their money on, and our villain sticks to every penny that comes his way. No need to cover himself against losses. He knows there won't be any. He knows he isn't going to have to pay out on that horse. He knows it's going to be scratched at or after the four-day forfeits. Very nice fiddle."

After a short silence Derry said, "How does he know?"

"Ah, well," I said, shrugging, "that's another thing we'll have to find out."

"I don't believe it," Luke-John said skeptically. "All that just because Bert tipped a few nonstarters."

Derry looked dubiously at the lists he had made. "There were too many nonstarters. There really were."

"Yes," I said.

"But you *can't* have worked out all that just from what I said, from just that simple casual remark. . . ."

"No," I said. "There was something else, of course. It was something Bert himself said, last Friday, when I walked back with him from lunch. He wanted to give me a piece of advice."

"That's right," Derry said. "He never came out with it."

"Yes, he did. He did indeed. With great seriousness. He told me not to sell my soul. Not to sell my column."

"No," Luke-John said.

"He said, 'First they buy you and then they blackmail you.' "

Luke-John said "No" again, automatically.

"He was very very drunk," I said. "Much worse than usual. He called the advice he was giving me his famous last words. He went up in the lift with a half bottle of whiskey, he walked right across his office, he drank from the bottle, and without a pause he fell straight out of the window."

Luke-John put his freckled fingers on his thin mouth, and when he spoke his voice was low, protesting, and thick: "No. . . . My *God.*"

After leaving the *Blaze* I collected the van and drove down to a racing stable in Berkshire to interview the girl who looked after the best-known horse in the Lamplighter.

Zig Zag was a household name, a steeplechaser of immense reputation and popularity, automatic headline material; but any day the cracks would begin to show, since he would be turning eleven on January 1st. The Lamplighter, to my mind, would be his last bow as grand old man before the younger brigade shouldered him out. Until Bert Checkov had rammed home the telling difference in weights, Zig Zag, even allotted a punitive twelve stone ten pounds, had been the automatic choice for antepost favorite.

His girl groom was earnest and devoted to him. In her twenties, unsophisticated, of middling intelligence, Sandy Willis's every sentence was packed with pithy stable language which she used unself-consciously and which contrasted touchingly with her essential innocence. She showed me Zig Zag with proprietary pride and could recite, and did, his every race from the day he was foaled. She had looked after him always, she said, ever since he came into the yard as a leggy untried three-year-old. She didn't know what she'd do when he was retired; racing wouldn't be the same without him somehow.

I offered to drive her into Newbury to have tea in a café or a hotel, but she said no, thank you, she wouldn't have time because the evening work started at four. Leaning against the door of Zig Zag's box, she told about her life, hesitantly at first, and then in a rush. Her parents didn't get on, she said. There were always rows at home, so she'd cleared out pretty soon after leaving school, glad to get away; her old man was so mean with the housekeeping and her mum did nothing but screech, nag, nag, at him mostly but at her, too, and her two kid sisters, right draggy the whole thing was, and she hoped Zig Zag would be racing at Kempton on Boxing Day so she'd have a good excuse not to go home for Christmas. She loved her work, she loved Zig Zag, the racing world was the tops, and no, she wasn't in any hurry to get married; there were always boys around if she wanted them and honestly whoever would swap Zig Zag for a load of draggy housework, especially if it turned out like her mum and dad. . . .

She agreed with a giggle to have her photograph taken if Zig Zag could be in the picture, too, and said she hoped that *Tally* magazine would send her a free copy.

"Of course," I assured her, and decided to charge all free copies against expenses.

When I left her, I walked down through the yard and called on the trainer, Norton Fox, whom I saw almost every time I went racing. A businesslike man in his fifties, with no airs and few illusions.

"Come in, Ty," he said. "Did you find Sandy Willis?"

"Thank you, yes. She was very helpful."

"She's one of my best lads." He waved me to an armchair and poured some oak-colored tea out of a silver pot. "Sugar?" I shook my head. "Not much in the upstairs department, but her horses are always jumping out of their skins."

"A spot of transferred mother love," I said. I tasted the tea. My tongue winced at the strength of the tannin. Norton poured himself another cup and took three deep swallows.

"If I write her up for *Tally*," I said, "you won't do the dirty on me and take Zig Zag out of the Lamplighter at the last minute?"

"I don't plan to."

"Twelve stone ten is a prohibitive weight," I suggested.

"He's won with twelve thirteen." He shrugged. "He'll never come down the handicap."

"As a matter of interest," I said, "what happened to Brevity just before the Champion Hurdle?"

Norton clicked his tongue in annoyance. "You can rely on it, Zig Zag will *not* be taken out at the last minute. At least not for no reason, like Brevity."

"He was favorite, wasn't he?" I knew he was; I'd checked carefully from Derry's list. "What exactly happened?"

"I've never been so furious about anything." The eight-month-old grievance was still vivid in his voice. "I trained that horse to the minute. To the minute. We always had the Champion Hurdle as his main target. He couldn't have been more fit.

He was ready to run for his life. And then what? Do you know what? I declared him at the four-day stage, and the owner—the *owner,* mark you—went and telephoned Weatherbys two days later and canceled the declaration. Took the horse out of the race. I ask you! And on top of that he hadn't even the courtesy —or the nerve, probably—to tell me what he'd done, and the first I knew of it was when Brevity wasn't in the overnight list of runners. Of course I couldn't believe it and rang up Weatherbys in a fury and they told me old Dembley himself had struck his horse out. And I still don't know why. I had the most God-almighty row with him about it and all he would say was that he had decided not to run, and that was that. He never once gave me a reason. Not one, after all that planning and all that work. I told him to take his horses away, I was so angry. I mean, how can you train for a man who's going to do that to you? It's impossible."

"Who trains for him now?" I asked sympathetically.

"No one. He sold all three of his horses, including Brevity. He said he'd had enough of racing; he was finished with it."

"You wouldn't still have his address?" I asked.

"Look here, Ty, you're not putting all that in your wretched paper!"

"No," I assured him. "Just one day I might write an article on owners who've sold out."

"Well . . . yes, I still have it." He copied the address from a ledger and handed it to me. "Don't cause any trouble."

"Not for you," I said. Trouble was always Luke-John's aim, and often mine. The only difference was that I was careful my friends shouldn't be on the receiving end. Luke-John had no such difficulties. He counted no one, to that extent, a friend.

Mrs. Woodward and Elizabeth were watching the news on television when I got back. Mrs. Woodward took a quick look at

her watch and made an unsuccessful attempt at hiding her disappointment. I had beaten her to six o'clock by thirty seconds.
She charged overtime by the half hour, and was a shade over-
businesslike about it. I never got a free five minutes: five past
six and it would have cost me the full half hour. I understood
that it wasn't sheer miserliness. She was a widow whose teen-
age son had a yearning to be a doctor, and as far as I could see
it would be mainly Tyrone who put him through medical
school.

The timekeeping war was conducted with maximum politeness and without acknowledgment that it existed. I simply
synchronized our two clocks and my watch with the B.B.C. time
signal every morning, and paid up with a smile when I was late.
Mrs. Woodward gave me a warmer welcome at ten past six than
at ten to, but never arrived a minute after nine-thirty in the
mornings. Neither of us had let on to Elizabeth how acutely the
clock was watched.

Mrs. Woodward was spare and strong, with a little of her
native Lancashire in her voice and a lot in her character. She
had dark hair going gray, rich brown eyes, and a determined
jaw line which had seen her through a jilting fiancé and a work-
shy husband. Unfailingly gentle to Elizabeth, she had never yet
run out of patience, except with the vacuum cleaner, which
occasionally regurgitated where it should have sucked.

In our flat she wore white nylon uniforms which she knew
raised her status to nurse from home help in the eyes of visitors,
and I saw no reason to think any worse of her for it. She took
off the uniform and hung it up, and I helped her into the dark
blue coat she had been wearing every single day for at least
three years.

"Night, Mr. Tyrone. Night, luv," she said, as she always
said. And as always I thanked her for coming, and said I'd see
her in the morning.

"Did you have a good day?" Elizabeth asked when I kissed her forehead. Her voice sounded tired. The Spiroshell tugged her chest up and down in a steady rhythm, and she could only speak easily on the outgoing breaths.

"I went to see a girl about a horse," I said, smiling, and told her briefly about Sandy Willis and Zig Zag. She liked to know a little of what I'd been doing, but her interest always flagged pretty soon, and after so many years I could tell the exact instant by the microscopic relaxation in her eye muscles. She rarely said she was tired and had had enough of anything, because she was afraid I would think her complaining and querulous and find her too much of a burden altogether. I couldn't persuade her to say flatly, "Stop, I'm tired." She agreed each time I mentioned it that she would, and she never did.

"I've seen three of the people for the *Tally* article," I said. "Owners, owner-trainer, and stable girl. I'm afraid after supper I'd better make a start on the writing. Will you be all right watching television?"

"Of course." She gave me the sweet brilliant smile which made every chore for her possible. Occasionally I spotted her manufacturing it artificially, but no amount of reassurance seemed able to convince her that she needn't perform tricks for me, that I wouldn't shove her back into hospital if she lost her temper, that I didn't need her to be angelic, that she was safe with me, and loved, and, in fact, very much wanted.

"Like a drink?" I said.

"Love one."

I poured us both a J & B with Malvern water, and took hers over and fastened it into a holder I'd rigged up, with the bent drinking straw near to her mouth. Using that, she could drink in her own time, and a lot less got spilt on the sheets. I tasted appreciatively the pale fine Scotch, slumping into the big armchair beside her bed, sloughing off the day's traveling with a comfortable feeling of being at home. The pump's steady soft thumping had its usual soporific effect. It sent most of our visitors fast asleep.

We watched a brain-packed quiz game on television and companionably answered most of the questions wrong. After that I went into the kitchen and looked at what Mrs. Woodward had put out for supper. Plaice coated in bread crumbs, a bag of frozen chips, one lemon. Stewed apples, custard. Cheddar cheese, square crackers. The Woodward views on food didn't entirely coincide with my own. Stifling thoughts of underdone steak, I cooked the chips in oil and the plaice in butter, and left mine to keep hot while I helped Elizabeth. Even with the new pulley gadget, some foods were difficult; the plaice broke up too easily and her wrist got tired, and we ended up with me feeding her as usual.

While I washed the dishes, I made coffee in mugs, fixed Elizabeth's into the holder, and took mine with my typewriter into the little room which would have been a child's bedroom if we'd ever had a child.

The *Tally* article came along slowly, its price tag reproaching me for every sloppy phrase. The Huntersons, the Ronceys, Sandy Willis. Dissect without hurting, probe but leave whole. Far easier, I thought resignedly, to pick them to bits. Good for *Tally*'s sales, too. Bad for the conscience, lousy for the Huntersons, the Ronceys, Sandy Willis. To tell all so that the victim liked it. . . . This was what took the time.

After two hours I found myself staring at the wall, thinking only of Gail. With excruciating clearness I went through in my mind every minute of that uninhibited lovemaking, felt in all my limbs and veins an echo of passion. Useless to pretend that once was enough, that the tormenting hunger had been anesthetized for more than a few days. With despair at my weakness

I thought about how it would be on the next Sunday. Gail with no clothes on, graceful and firm. Gail smiling with my hands on her breasts, Gail fluttering her fingers on the base of my spine.

The bell rang sharply above my head. One ring: not urgent. I stood up slowly, feeling stupid and ashamed. Daydreaming like Madge Roncey. Just as bad. Probably much worse.

Elizabeth was apologetic. "Ty, I'm so sorry to interrupt you. . . ."

How can I do it, I thought. And knew I would.

"My feet are awfully cold."

I pulled out the hot-water bottle, which had no heat left. Her feet were warm enough to the touch, but that meant nothing. Her circulation was so poor that her ankles and feet ached with cold if they were not constantly warmed from outside.

"You should have said," I protested.

"Didn't want to disturb you."

"Any time," I said fiercely. "Any time." And preferably twenty minutes ago. For twenty minutes she'd suffered her cold feet and all I'd done was think of Gail.

I filled her bottle and we went through her evening routine. Rubs with surgical spirit. Washing. Bedpan.

Her muscles had nearly all wasted to nothing so that her bones showed angularly through the skin, and one had to be careful when lifting her limbs, as pressure in some places hurt her. That day Mrs. Woodward had painted her toenails for her instead of only her fingernails as usual.

"Do you like it?" she said. "It's a new color, Tawny Pink."

"Pretty," I nodded. "It suits you."

She smiled contentedly. "Sue Davis brought it for me. She's a pet, that girl."

Sue and Ronald Davis lived three doors away: married for six months and it still showed. They had let their euphoria spill over onto us. Sue brought things in to amuse Elizabeth and Ronald used his Rugger-bred strength to carry the pump downstairs when we went out in the van.

"It matches my lipstick better than the old color."

"Yes, it does," I said.

When we married, she had had creamy skin and hair as glossy as new peeled chestnuts. She had had sun-browned agile limbs and a pretty figure. The transition to her present and forever state had been as agonizing for her mentally as it had been physically, and at one point of that shattering progress I was aware she would have killed herself if even that freedom hadn't been denied her.

She still had a good complexion, fine eyebrows, and long-lashed eyes, but the russet lights had turned to gray in both her irises and her hair, as if the color had drained away with the vitality. Mrs. Woodward was luckily expert with shampoo and scissors and I, too, had long grown accurate with a lipstick, so that Elizabeth always turned a groomed and attractive head to the world and could retain at least some terrifically important feminine assurance.

I settled her for the night, slowing the rate of the breathing pump a little and tucking the covers in firmly around her chin to help with the draft. She slept in the same half-sitting propped-up position as she spent the days; the Spiroshell was too heavy and uncomfortable if she lay down flat, besides not dragging as much air into her lungs.

She smiled when I kissed her cheek. "Good night, Ty."

"Good night, honey."

"Thanks for everything."

"Be my guest."

Lazily I pottered round the flat, tidying up, brushing my teeth, rereading what I'd written for *Tally*, and putting the cover on the typewriter. When I finally made it to bed, Elizabeth was asleep, and I lay between the lonely sheets and thought about Bert Checkov and the nonstarters like Brevity in the Champion Hurdle, planning in detail the article I would write for the *Blaze* on Sunday.

Sunday.

Inevitably, inexorably, every thought led back to Gail.

Five

I telephoned to Charles Dembley, the ex-owner of Brevity, on Wednesday morning, and a girl answered, bright fresh voice, carefree and inexperienced.

"Golly, did you say Tyrone? *James* Tyrone? Yes, we do have your perfectly frightful paper. At least we used to. At least the gardener does, so I often read it. Well, of course come down and see Daddy, he'll be frightfully pleased."

Daddy wasn't.

He met me outside his house, on the front step, a smallish man nearing sixty with a gray mustache and heavy pouches under his eyes. His manner was courteous stone-wall. .

"I am sorry you have had a wasted journey, Mr. Tyrone. My daughter Amanda is only fifteen and is apt to rush into things. . . . I was out when you telephoned, as I expect she told you. I hope you will forgive her. I have absolutely nothing to say to you. Nothing at all. Good afternoon, Mr. Tyrone."

There was a tiny twitch in one eyelid and the finest of dews on his forehead. I let my gaze wander across the front of his house (genuine Georgian, not too large, unostentatiously well kept) and brought it gently back to his face.

"What threat did they use?" I asked. "Amanda?"

He winced strongly and opened his mouth.

"With a fifteen-year-old daughter," I commented, "one is dangerously vulnerable."

He tried to speak but achieved only a croak. After clearing

his throat with difficulty he said, "I don't know what you're talking about."

"How did they set about it?" I asked. "By telephone? By letter? Or did you actually see them face to face?"

His expression was a full giveaway, but he wouldn't answer.

I said, "Mr. Dembley, I can write my column about the last-minute unexplained withdrawal of favorites, mentioning you and Amanda by name, or I can leave you out of it."

"Leave me out," he said forcefully. "Leave me out."

"I will," I agreed, "if in return you will tell me what threat was made against you, and in what form."

His mouth shook with a mixture of fear and disgust. He knew blackmail when he heard it. Only too well.

"I can't trust you."

"Indeed you can," I said.

"If I keep silent, you will print my name and they will think I told you anyway—" He stopped dead.

"Exactly," I said mildly.

"You're despicable."

"No," I said. "I'd simply like to stop them doing it to anyone else."

There was a pause. Then he said, "It *was* Amanda. They said someone would rape her. They said I couldn't guard her twenty-four hours a day for years on end. They said to make her safe all I had to do was call Weatherbys and take Brevity out of the Champion Hurdle. Just one little telephone call, against my daughter's—my daughter's health. So I did it. Of course I did. I had to. What did running a horse in the Champion Hurdle matter compared with my daughter?"

What indeed.

"Did you tell the police?"

He shook his head. "They said . . ."

I nodded. They would.

"I sold all my horses, after," he said. "There wasn't any point going on. It could have happened again, anytime."

"Yes."

He swallowed. "Is that all?"

"No. . . . Did they telephone, or did you see them?"

"It was one man. He came here, driven by a chauffeur. In a Rolls. He was, he seemed to me, an educated man. He had an accent; I'm not sure what it was, perhaps Scandinavian, or Dutch, something like that. Maybe even Greek. He was civilized . . . except for what he said."

"Looks?"

"Tall. About your height. Much heavier, though. Altogether thicker, more flesh. Not a crook's face at all. I couldn't believe what I was hearing him say. It didn't fit the way he looked."

"But he convinced you," I commented.

"Yes." He shuddered. "He stood there watching me while I telephoned to Weatherbys. And when I'd finished he simply said, 'I'm sure you've made a wise decision, Mr. Dembley,' and he just walked out of the house and the chauffeur drove him away."

"And you've heard no more from him at all?"

"No more. You will keep your bargain, too, like him?"

My mouth twisted. "I will."

He gave me a long look. "If Amanda comes to any harm through you, I will see it costs you—costs you—" He stopped.

"If she does," I said, "I will pay."

An empty gesture. Harm couldn't be undone, and paying wouldn't help. I would simply have to be careful.

"That's all," he said. "That's all." He turned on his heel, went back into his house, and shut the front door decisively between us.

For light relief on the way home, I stopped in Hampstead to interview the man who had done the handicap for the Lamplighter. Not a well-timed call. His wife had just decamped with an American colonel.

"Damn her eyes," he said. "She's left me a bloody note." He waved it under my nose. "Stuck up against the clock, just like some ruddy movie."

"I'm sorry," I said.

"Come in, come in. What do you say to getting pissed?"

"There's the unfortunate matter of driving home."

"Take a taxi, Ty, be a pal. Come on."

I looked at my watch. Four-thirty. Half an hour to home, counting rush-hour traffic. I stepped over the threshold and saw from his relieved expression that company was much needed. He already had a bottle out with a half-full glass beside it, and he poured me one the same size.

Major Colly Gibbons, late forties, trim, intelligent, impatient, and positive. Never suffered fools gladly and interrupted rudely when his thoughts leaped ahead, but was much in demand as a handicapper, as he had a clear comprehensive view of racing as a whole, like a master chess player winning ten games at once. He engineered more multiple dead heats than anyone else in the game; the accolade of his profession and a headache to the interpreters of photo finishes.

"A bloody colonel," he said bitterly. "Outranked, too."

I laughed. He gave me a startled look and then an unwilling grin.

"I suppose it *is* funny," he said. "Silly thing is, he's very like me. Looks, age, character, everything. I even like the guy."

"She'll probably come back," I said.

"Why?"

"If she chose a carbon copy of you, she can't hate you all that much."

"Don't know as I'd have her," he said aggressively. "Going off with a bloody colonel, and a Yank at that."

His pride was bent worse than his heart: nonetheless painful. He sloshed another stiff whiskey into his glass and asked me why, as a matter of interest, I had come. I explained about the *Tally* article, and, seeming to be relieved to have something to talk about besides his wife, he loosened up with his answers more than I would normally have expected. For the first time I understood the wideness of his vision and the grasp and range of his memory. He knew the form book for the past ten years by heart.

After a while I said, "Can you remember about antepost favorites which didn't run?"

He gave me a quick glance which would have been better focused three drinks earlier. "Is this for *Tally*, still?"

"No," I admitted.

"Didn't think so. Question like that's got the *Blaze* written all over it."

"I won't quote you."

"Too right you won't." He drank deeply, but seemed no nearer oblivion. "Put yourself some blinkers on and point in another direction."

"Read what I say on Sunday," I said mildly.

"Ty," he said explosively. "Best to keep out."

"Why?"

"Leave it to the authorities."

"What are they doing about it? What do they know?"

"You know I can't tell you," he protested. "Talk to the *Blaze*? I'd lose my job."

"Mulholland went to jail rather than reveal his sources."

"All journalists are not Mulholland."

"Same secretive tendencies."

"Would you," he said seriously, "go to jail?"

"It's never cropped up. But if my sources want to stay unrevealed, they stay unrevealed. If they didn't, who would tell me anything?"

He thought it over. "Something's going on," he said at last.

"Quite," I said. "And what are the authorities doing about it?"

"There's no evidence. . . . Look, Ty, there's nothing you can put your finger on. Just a string of coincidences."

"Like Bert Checkov's articles?" I suggested.

He was startled. "All right, then. Yes. I heard it on good authority that he was going to be asked to explain them. But then he fell out of the window. . . ."

"Tell me about the nonrunners," I said.

He looked gloomily at the note from his wife, which he still clutched in his hand. He took a deep swallow and shrugged heavily. The caution barriers were right down.

"There was this French horse, Polyxenes, which they made favorite for the Derby. Remember? All last winter and spring there was a stream of information about it, coming out of France—how well he was developing, how nothing could stay with him on the gallops, how he made all the three-year-olds look like knock-kneed yearlings? Every week, something about Polyxenes."

"I remember," I said. "Derry Clark wrote him up for the *Blaze*."

Colly Gibbons nodded. "So there we are. By Easter, six-to-one favorite for the Derby. Right? They leave him in through all the forfeit stages. Right? They declare him at the four-day declarations. Right? Two days later he's taken out of the race.

Why? He knocked himself out at exercise and his leg's blown up like a football. Can't run a lame horse. Too bad, everybody who'd backed him. Too bad. All their money down the drain. All right. Now I'll tell you something, Ty. That Polyxenes, I'll never believe he was all that good. What had he ever done? Won two moderate races as a two-year-old at Saint-Cloud. He didn't run this year before the Derby. He didn't run the whole season in the end. They said his leg was still bad. I'll tell you what I think. He never was good enough to win the Derby, and from the start they never meant him to run."

"If he were as bad as that, they could have run him anyway. He wouldn't have won."

"Would you risk it if you were them? The most fantastic outsiders *have* won the Derby. Much more certain not to run at all."

"Someone must have made thousands," I said slowly.

"More like hundreds of thousands."

"If they know it's going on, why don't the racing authorities do something about it?"

"What *can* they do? I told you, no evidence. Polyxenes *was* lame, and he stayed lame. He was seen by dozens of vets. He had a slightly shady owner, but no shadier than some of ours. Nothing, absolutely nothing, could be proved."

After a pause I said, "Do you know of any others?"

"God, Ty, you're a glutton. Well . . . yes. . . ."

Once started, he left little out. In the next half hour I listened to the detailed case histories of four more antepost favorites who hadn't turned up on the day. All could have been bona-fide hard-luck stories. But all, I knew well, had been overpraised by Bert Checkov.

He ran down, in the end, with a faint look of dismay.

"I shouldn't have told you all this."

"No one will know."

"You'd get information out of a deaf-mute."

I nodded. "They can usually read and write."

"Go to hell," he said. "Or, rather, don't. You're four behind me; you aren't trying." He waved the bottle in my general direction and I went over and took it from him. It was empty.

"Got to go home," I said apologetically.

"What's the hurry?" He stared at the letter in his hand. "Will your wife give you gip if you're late? Or will she be running off with some bloody Yankee colonel?"

"No," I said unemotionally. "She won't."

He was suddenly very sober. "*Christ,* Ty . . . I forgot."

He stood up, as steady as a rock. Looked forlornly around his comfortable wifeless sitting room. Held out his hand.

"She'll come back," I said uselessly.

He shook his head. "I don't think so." He sighed deeply. "Anyway, I'm glad you came. Needed someone to talk to, you know. Even if I've talked too much . . . better than getting drunk alone. And I'll think of you, this evening. You . . . and your wife."

I got hung up in a jam at Swiss Cottage and arrived home at eight minutes past seven. An hour and a half overtime. Mrs. Woodward was delighted.

"Isn't she sweet?" Elizabeth said when she had gone. "She never minds when you are late. She never complains about having to stay. She's so nice and kind."

"Very," I said.

As usual I spent most of Thursday at home, writing Sunday's article. Mrs. Woodward went out to do the week's shopping and to take and collect the laundry. Sue Davis came in and made coffee for herself and Elizabeth. Elizabeth's mother telephoned to say she might not come on Sunday; she thought she could be getting a cold.

No one came near Elizabeth with a cold. With people on artificial respiration, colds too often meant pneumonia, and pneumonia too often meant death.

If Elizabeth's mother didn't come on Sunday, I couldn't go to Virginia Water. I spent much of the morning unproductively trying to persuade myself it would be better if the cold developed, and knowing I'd be wretched if it did.

Luke-John galloped through the article on nonstarting favorites, screwed his eyes up tight, and leaned back in his chair with his face to the ceiling. Symptoms of extreme emotion. Derry reached over, twitched up the typewritten sheets, and read them in his slower, intense, shortsighted-looking way. When he'd finished, he took a deep breath.

"Wowee," he said. "Someone's going to love this."

"Who?" said Luke-John, opening his eyes.

"The chap who's doing it."

Luke-John looked at him broodingly. "As long as he can't sue, that's all that matters. Take this down to the lawyers and make sure they don't let it out of their sight."

Derry departed with a folded carbon copy of the article and Luke-John permitted himself a smile.

"Up to standard, if I may say so."

"Thanks," I said.

"Who told you all this?"

"Couple of little birds."

"Come off it, Ty."

"Promised," I said. "They could get their faces pushed in, one way or another."

"I'll have to know. The editor will want to know."

I shook my head. "Promised."

"I could scrub the article altogether. . . ."

"Tut, tut," I said. "Threats, now?"

He rubbed his larynx in exasperation. I looked around the vast busy floor space, each section, like the sports desk, collecting and sorting out its final copy. Most of the feature stuff went down to the compositors on Fridays, some even on Thursdays, to be set up in type. But anything like a scoop stayed under wraps upstairs until after the last editions of the Saturday evening papers had all been set up and gone to press. The compositors were apt to make the odd ten quid by selling a red-hot story to reporters on rival newspapers. If the legal department and the editor both cleared my article, the printshop wouldn't see it until too late to do them any good. The *Blaze* held its scandalous disclosures very close to its chest.

Derry came back from the lawyers without the article.

"They said they'd have to work on it. They'll ring through later."

The *Blaze* lawyers were of Counsel standard on the libel laws. They needed to be. All the same they were true *Blaze* men with "publish and be damned" engraved on their hearts. The *Blaze* accountants allowed for damages in their budget as a matter of course. The *Blaze*'s owner looked upon one or two court cases a year as splendid free advertising, and watched the sales graphs rise. There had, however, been four actions in the past six months and two more were pending. A mild memo had gone around, saying to cool it just a fraction. Loyal forever, Luke-John obeyed even where he disapproved.

"I'll take this in to the editor," he remarked. "See what he says."

Derry watched his retreating back with reluctant admiration.

"Say what you like, the sports pages sell this paper to people who otherwise wouldn't touch it with gloves on. Our Luke-John, for all his stingy little ways, must be worth his weight in gumdrops."

Our Luke-John came back and went into a close huddle with a soccer correspondent. I asked Derry how the funeral had been, on the Wednesday.

"A funeral's a funeral." He shrugged. "It was cold. His wife wept a lot. She had a purple nose, blue from cold and red from crying."

"Charming."

He grinned. "Her sister told her to cheer up. Said how lucky it was Bert took out all that extra insurance."

"He did what?"

"Yeah. I thought you'd like that. I chased the sister up a bit. Two or three weeks ago Bert trebled his life insurance. Told his wife they'd be better off when he retired. Sort of self-help pension scheme."

"Well, well," I said.

"So it had to be an accident." Derry nodded. "In front of witnesses. The insurance company might not have paid up if he'd fallen out of the window with no one watching."

"I wonder if they'll contest it."

"Don't see how they can, when the inquest said misadventure."

The editor's secretary came back with my piece. The editor's secretary was an expensive package tied up with barbed wire. No one, reputedly, had got past the prickles to the goodies.

The editor had scrawled "O.K. on the lawyers' say-so" across the top of the page. Luke-John stretched out a hand for it, nodded in satisfaction, and slid it into the lockable top drawer of his desk, talking all the while to the soccer man. There was no need for me to stay longer. I told Derry I'd be at home most of the day if they wanted me and sketched a goodbye.

I was halfway to the door when Luke-John called after me.

"Ty . . . I forgot to tell you. A woman phoned, wanted you."

"Mrs. Woodward?"

"Uh-uh. Let's see, I made a note. . . . Oh, yes, here it is. A Miss Gail Pominga. Would you ring her back. Something about *Tally* magazine."

He gave me the slip of paper with the telephone number. I went across to the underpopulated news desk and picked up the receiver. My hands were steady. My pulse wasn't.

"The Western School of Art. Can I help you?"

"Miss Pominga."

Miss Pominga was fetched. Her voice came on the line, as cool and uninvolved as at the railway station.

"Are you coming on Sunday?" Crisp. Very much to the point.

"I want to." Understatement. "It may not be possible to get away."

"Well . . . I've been asked out to lunch."

"Go, then," I said, feeling disappointment lump in my chest like a boulder.

"Actually, if you are coming I will stay at home."

Damn Elizabeth's mother, I thought. Damn her and her cold.

"I want to come. I'll come if I possibly can," I said.

There was a short silence before she said, "When can you let me know for sure?"

"Not until Sunday, really. Not until I go out to catch the train."

"Hmm." She hesitated, then said decisively, "Ring me in any case, whether you can come or whether you can't. I'll fix it so that I can still go to lunch if you aren't coming."

"That's marvelous," I said with more feeling than caution.

She laughed. "Good. Hope to see you then. Anytime after ten. That's when Harry and Sarah go off to golf."

"It would be eleven-thirty or so."

She said "All right," and "Goodbye," and disconnected. I went home to write up Colly Gibbons for *Tally* and to have lunch with Elizabeth and Mrs. Woodward. It was fish again, unspecified variety and not much flavor. I listened to Elizabeth's sporadic conversation and returned her smiles and hoped fiercely not to be there with her forty-eight hours later. I ate automatically, sightlessly. By the end of that meal, treachery tasted of salt.

Six

Time was running short, *Tally*-wise. With their deadline only
two days ahead I went to Heathbury Park races on Saturday to
meet Dermot Finnegan, an undistinguished jockey with an
undistinguished mount in the Lamplighter.

For a while I couldn't understand a word he said, so impene-
trable was his Irish accent. After he had sipped unenthusiastically at a cup of lunch-counter coffee for ten minutes, he
relaxed enough to tell me he always spoke worse when he was
nervous, and after that we got by with him having to repeat
some things twice, but not four or five times, as at the beginning.

Once past the language barrier, Dermot unveiled a resigned
wit and an accepting contented way of life. Although by most
standards his riding success was small, Dermot thought it great.
His income, less than a dustman's, seemed to him princely
compared with the conditions of his childhood. His father had
fed fourteen children on the potatoes he had grown on two and
a half exhausted acres. Dermot, being neither the strong eldest
nor the spoilt youngest, had usually had to shove for his share
and hadn't always got it. At nineteen he tired of the diet and
took his underdeveloped physique across the sea to Newmarket,
where an Irish accent, irrespective of previous experience, guar-
anteed him an immediate job in the labor-hungry racing industry.

He had "done his two" for a while in a flat-racing stable, but couldn't get a ride in a flat race because he hadn't been apprenticed. Philosophically he moved down the road to a stable which trained jumpers as well, where the "Governor" gave him a chance in a couple of hurdle races. He still worked in the same stable on a part-time basis, and the Governor still put him up as his second-string jockey. How many rides? He grinned, showing spaces instead of teeth. Some seasons maybe thirty. Two years ago, of course, it was only four, thanks to breaking his leg off a brainless divil of a knock-kneed spalpeen.

Dermot Finnegan was twenty-five, looked thirty. Broken-nosed and weather-beaten, with bright sharp blue eyes. His ambition, he said, was to take a crack at Aintree. Otherwise he was all right with what he had: he wouldn't want to be a classy top jockey; it was far too much responsibility. "If you only ride the scrubbers round the gaffs at the back end of the season, see, no one expects much. Then they gets a glorious surprise if you come in."

He had ridden nineteen winners in all, and he could remember each of them in sharp detail. No, he didn't think he would do much good in the Lamplighter, not really, as he was only in it because his stable was running three. "I'll be on the pacemaker, sure. You'll see me right up there over the first, and maybe for a good while longer, but then my old boy will run out of steam and drop out of the back door as sudden as an interrupted burglar, and if I don't have to pull him up it'll be a bloody miracle."

Later in the afternoon I watched him start out on some prospective ten-year-old dogmeat in a novice chase. Horse and rider disappeared with a flurry of legs into the second open ditch, and when I went to check on his injuries some time after the second race, I met Dermot coming out of the ambulance room wearing a bandage and a grin.

"It's only a scratch," he assured me cheerfully. "I'll be there for the Lamplighter sure enough."

Further investigation led to the detail of a fingernail hanging on by a thread. "Some black divil" had leant an ill-placed hoof on the Finnegan hand.

To complete the *Tally* roundup, I spent the last half of the afternoon in the Clerk of the Course's office, watching him in action.

Heathbury Park, where the Lamplighter was to be held a fortnight later, had become under his direction one of the best-organized courses in the country. Like the handicapper, he was ex-forces, in this case R.A.F., which was unusual in that the racing authorities as a rule leant heavily toward the Army and the Navy for their executives.

Wing Commander Willy Ondroy was a quiet effective short-ish man of forty-two who had been invalided out after fractur-ing his skull in a slight mishap with a Vulcan bomber. He still, he said, suffered from blackouts, usually at the most incon-venient, embarrassing, and even obscene moments.

It wasn't until after racing had finished for the day that he was really ready to talk, and even then he dealt with a string of people calling into his office with statistics, problems, and keys.

The Lamplighter was his own invention, and he was mod-estly proud of it. He'd argued the Betting Levy Board into putting up most of the hefty stake money, and then drawn up entry conditions exciting enough to bring a gleam to the hardest-headed trainer's eye. Most of the best horses would conse-quently be coming. They should draw an excellent crowd. The gate receipts would rise again. They'd soon be able to afford to build a warm modern nursery room, their latest project, to at-tract young parents to the races by giving them somewhere to park their kids.

Willy Ondroy's enthusiasm was of the enduring, not the bubbling, kind. His voice was as gentle as the expression in his amber eyes, and only the small self-mockery in his smile gave any clue to the steel within. His obvious lack of need to assert his authority in any forceful way was finally explained after I'd dug, or tried to dig, into his history. A glossed-over throwaway phrase about a spot of formation flying turned out to be his version of three years as a Red Arrow, flying two feet away from the jet pipe of the aircraft in front. "We did two hundred displays one year," he said apologetically. "Entertaining at air shows. Like a concert party on Blackpool pier—no difference, really."

He had been lucky to transfer to bombers when he was twenty-six, he said. So many R.A.F. fighter and formation pilots were grounded altogether when their reaction times began to slow. He'd spent eight years on bombers, fifteen seconds knowing he was going to crash, three weeks in a coma, and twenty months finding himself a civilian job. Now he lived with his wife and twelve-year-old twins in a house on the edge of the racecourse, and none of them wanted to change.

I caught the last train when it was moving and made a start on Dermot and Willy Ondroy on the way back to London.

Mrs. Woodward departed contentedly at a quarter to seven, and I found she had for once left steaks ready in the kitchen. Elizabeth was in good spirits. I mixed us a drink each and relaxed in the armchair, and only after a strict ten minutes of self-denial asked her casually if her mother had telephoned.

"No, she hasn't." She wouldn't have.

"So you don't know if she's coming?"

"I expect she'll ring, if she doesn't."

"I suppose so," I said. Damn her eyes, couldn't she at least settle it, one way or another?

Trying to shut my mind to it, I worked on the *Tally* article; cooked the supper; went back to *Tally;* stopped to settle Elizabeth for the night; and returned to the typewriter until I'd finished. It was then half past two. A pity, I thought, stretching, that I wrote so slowly, crossed out so much. I put the final version away in a drawer with only the fair copy to be typed the next day. Plenty of time for that even if I spent the rest of it on the primrose path making tracks for Gail.

I despised myself. It was five before I slept.

Elizabeth's mother came. Not a sniffle in sight.

I had spent all morning trying to reconcile myself to her nonappearance at ten-fifteen, her usual time of arrival. As on past occasions, I had turned a calm and everyday face to Elizabeth and found I had consciously to stifle irritation at little tasks for her that normally I did without thought.

At ten-seventeen the doorbell rang, and there she was, a well-groomed good-looking woman in her mid-fifties with assisted tortoise-shell hair and a health-farm figure. When she showed surprise at my greeting, I knew I had been too welcoming. I damped it down a little to more normal levels and saw that she felt more at home with that.

I explained to her, as I already had to Elizabeth, that I still had people to interview for *Tally,* and by ten-thirty I was walking away down the mews feeling as though a safety valve were blowing fine. The sun was shining, too. After a sleepless night, my conscience slept.

Gail met me at Virginia Water, waiting outside in the station wagon. "The train's late," she said calmly as I sat in beside her. No warm, loving, kissing hello. Just as well, I supposed.

"They work on the lines on Sunday. There was a delay at Staines."

She nodded, let in the clutch, and cruised the three-quarters of a mile to her uncle's house. There she led the way into the sitting room and without asking poured two beers.

"You aren't writing today," she said, handing me the glass.

"No."

She gave me a smile that acknowledged the purpose of my visit. More businesslike about sex than most women. Certainly no tease. I kissed her mouth lightly, savoring the knowledge that the deadline of the Huntersons' return was three full hours ahead.

She nodded as if I'd spoken. "I approve of you," she said.

"Thanks."

She smiled, moving away. Her dress that day was of a pale cream color which looked wonderful against the gilded coffee skin. She was no darker, in fact, than many southern Europeans or heavily suntanned English; her mixed origin was distinct only in her face. A well-proportioned, attractive face, gathering distinction from the self-assurance within. Gail, I imagined, had had to come to terms with herself much earlier and more basically than most girls. She had done almost too good a job.

A copy of the *Sunday Blaze* lay on the low table, open at the sports page. Editors or subeditors write all the headlines, and Luke-John had come up with a beauty. Across the top of my page, big and bold, it said, "DON'T BACK TIDDELY POM—YET." Underneath, he'd left in word for word every paragraph I'd written. This didn't necessarily mean he thought each word was worth its space in print, but was quite likely because there weren't too many advertisements that week. Like all newspapers, the *Blaze* lived on advertising; if an advertiser wanted to pay for space, he got it, and out went the deathless prose of the columnists. I'd lost many a worked-on sentence to the late arrival of spiels on Whosit's cough syrup or Whammo's hair tonic. It was nice to see this intact.

I looked up at Gail. She was watching me.

"Do you always read the sports page?" I asked.

She shook her head. "Curiosity," she said. "I wanted to see what you'd written. That article—it's disturbing."

"It's meant to be."

"I mean, it leaves the impression that you know a great deal more than you've said, and it's all bad, if not positively criminal."

"Well," I said, "it's always nice to hear one has done exactly what one intended."

"What usually happens when you write in this way?"

"Repercussions? They vary from a blast from the racing authorities about minding my own business to abusive letters from nut cases."

"Do wrongs get righted?"

"Very occasionally."

"Sir Galahad," she mocked.

"No. We sell more papers. I apply for a raise."

She laughed with her head back, the line of her throat leading tautly down into her dress. I put out my hand and touched her shoulder, suddenly wanting no more talk.

She nodded at once, smiling, and said, "Not on the rug. More comfortable upstairs."

Her bedroom furnishings were pretty but clearly Sarah's work. Fitted cupboards, a cozy armchair, bookshelves, a lot of pale blue carpet, and a single bed.

At her insistence, I occupied it first. Then while I watched, like the time before, she took off her clothes. The simple, un-dramatized, unself-conscious undressing was more ruthlessly arousing than anything one could ever pay to see. When she had finished, she stood still for a moment near the window, a pale bronze naked girl in a shaft of winter sun.

"Shall I close the curtains?"

"Whichever you like."

She screwed my pulse rate up another notch by stretching up to close them, and then in the midday dusk she came to bed.

At three she drove me back to the station, but a train pulled out as we pulled in. We sat in the car for a while, talking, waiting for the next one.

"Do you come home here every night?" I asked.

"Quite often not. Two of the other teachers share a flat, and I sleep on their sofa a night or two every week, after parties, or working late, or a theatre, maybe."

"But you don't want to live in London all the time?"

"D'you think it's odd that I stay with Harry and Sarah? Quite frankly, it's because of money. Harry won't let me pay for living here. He says he wants me to stay. He's always been generous. If I had to pay for everything myself in London, my present standard of living would go down with a reverberating thump."

"Comfort before independence," I commented mildly.

She shook her head. "I have both." After a considering pause she said, "Do you live with your wife? I mean, have you separated, or anything?"

"No, we've not separated."

"Where does she think you are today?"

"Interviewing someone for my *Tally* article."

She laughed. "You're a bit of a bastard."

Nail on the head. I agreed with her.

"Does she know you have—er—outside interests? Has she ever found you out?"

I wished she would change the subject. However, I owed her quite a lot, at least some answers, which might be the truth and nothing but the truth, but would certainly not be the whole truth.

"She doesn't know," I said.

"Would she mind?"

"Probably."

"But if she won't—sleep with you—well, why don't you leave her?"

I didn't answer at once. She went on, "You haven't any children, have you?" I shook my head. "Then what's to stop you? Unless, of course, you're like me."

"How do you mean?"

"Staying where the living is good. Where the money is."

"Oh . . ." I half laughed, and she misunderstood me.

"How can I blame you"—she sighed—"when I do it myself? So your wife is rich. . . ."

I thought about what Elizabeth would have been condemned to without me: to hospital ward routine, hospital food, no privacy, no gadgets, no telephone, lights out at nine and lights on at six, no free will at all, forever and ever.

"I suppose you might say," I agreed slowly, "that my wife is rich."

Back in the flat I felt split in two, with everything familiar feeling suddenly unreal. Half my mind was still down in Surrey. I kissed Elizabeth and thought of Gail. Depression had clamped down in the train like drizzle and wouldn't be shaken off.

"Some man wants to talk to you," Elizabeth said. "He telephoned three times. He sounded awfully angry."

"Who?"

"I couldn't understand much of what he said. He was stuttering."

"How did he get our number?" I was irritated, bored; I didn't want to have to deal with angry men on the telephone. Moreover our number was ex-directory, precisely so that Elizabeth should not be bothered by this sort of thing.

"I don't know. But he did leave his number for you to ring back; it was the only coherent thing he said."

Elizabeth's mother handed me a note pad on which she had written down the number.

"Victor Roncey," I said.

"That's right," agreed Elizabeth with relief. "That sounds like it."

I sighed, wishing that all problems, especially those of my own making, would go away and leave me in peace.

"Maybe I'll call him later," I said. "Right now I need a drink."

"I was just going to make some tea," said Elizabeth's mother reprovingly, and in silent fury I doubled the quantity I would normally have taken. The bottle was nearly empty. Gloomy Sunday.

Restlessly I took myself off into my writing room and started the clean unscribbled-on retype for *Tally*, the mechanical task eventually smoothing out the rocky tensions of my guilt-ridden return home. I couldn't afford to like Gail too much, and I did like her. To come to love someone would be too much hell altogether. Better not to visit Gail again. I decided definitely not to. My body shuddered in protest, and I knew I would.

Roncey rang again just after Elizabeth's mother had left.

"What the devil do you mean about this—this trash in the paper? Of course my horse is going to run. How dare you—how dare you suggest there's anything shady going on?"

Elizabeth had been right; he was stuttering still, at seven in the evening. He took a lot of calming down to the point of admitting that nowhere in the article was it suggested that he personally had anything but good honest upright intentions.

"The only thing is, Mr. Roncey, as I said in the article, that some owners have in the past been pressured into not running their horses. This may even happen to you. All I was doing was giving punters several good reasons why they would be wiser to wait until half an hour before big races to put their money on. Better a short starting price than losing their money in a swindle."

"I've read it," he snapped. "Several times. And no one, believe me, is going to put any pressure on *me*."

"I very much hope not," I said. I wondered whether his antipathy to his elder sons extended to the smaller ones; whether he would risk their safety or happiness for the sake of running Tiddely Pom in the Lamplighter. Maybe he would. The stubborn streak ran through his character like iron in granite.

When he had calmed down to somewhere near reason, I asked him if he'd mind telling me how he'd got my telephone number.

"I had the devil's own job, if you want to know. All that ex-directory piffle. The inquiries people refused point-blank to tell me, even though I said it was urgent. Stupid, I call it, but I wasn't to be put off by that. If you want to know, your colleague on the paper told me. Derrick Clark."

"I see," I said resignedly, thinking it unlike Derry to part so easily with my defenses. "Well, thank you. Did the *Tally* photographer find you all right?"

"He came on Friday. I hope you haven't said anything in *Tally* about—" His anger was on its way up again.

"No," I said decisively. "Nothing like that at all."

"When can I be sure?" He sounded suspicious.

"That edition of *Tally* is published on the Tuesday before the Lamplighter."

"I'll ask for an advance copy from the editor. Tomorrow. I'll demand to see what you've written."

"Do that," I agreed. Divert the buck to Arnold Shankerton. Splendid.

He rang off still not wholly pacified. I dialed Derry's number and prepared to pass the ill temper along to him.

"*Roncey?*" He said indignantly. "Of course I didn't give your number to Roncey." His baby girl was exercising her lungs loudly in the background. "What did you say?"

"I said, who *did* you give it to?"

"Your wife's uncle."

"My wife hasn't got any uncles."

"Oh Christ. Well, he said he was your wife's uncle, and that your wife's aunt had had a stroke, and that he wanted to tell you but he'd lost your number."

"Lying crafty bastard," I said with feeling. "And he accused me of misrepresenting facts."

"I'm sorry, Ty."

"Never mind. Only check with me first, next time, huh? Like we arranged."

"Yeah. Sure. Sorry."

"How did he get hold of your number, anyway?"

"It's in the *Directory of the British Turf*, unlike yours. My mistake."

I put the receiver back in its special cradle near to Elizabeth's head and transferred to the armchair, and we spent the rest of the evening as we usually did, watching the shadows on the goggle box. Elizabeth never tired of it, which was a blessing, though she complained often about the shutdowns in the day-time between all the child-orientated programs. Why couldn't they fill them, she said, with interesting things for captive adults?

Later I made some coffee and did the alcohol rubs and other jobs for Elizabeth, all with a surface of tranquil domesticity, going through my part with my thoughts somewhere else, like an actor at the thousandth performance.

On the Monday morning I took my article to the *Tally* offices and left the package at the reception desk, virtuously on the deadline.

After that I caught the race train to Leicester, admitting to myself that although it was technically my day off I did not want to stay in the flat. Also the Huntersons' raffle horse Egocentric was to have its pre-Lamplighter warm-up, which gave me an excellent overt reason for the journey.

Raw near-mist was doing its best to cancel the proceedings and only the last two fences were visible. Egocentric finished fourth without enough steam left to blow a whistle, and the jockey told the trainer that the useless bugger had made a right bloody shambles of three fences on the far side and couldn't jump for peanuts. The trainer didn't believe him and engaged a different jockey for the Lamplighter. It was one of those days.

The thin Midland crowd of cloth caps and mufflers strewed the ground with betting slips and newspapers and ate a couple of hundredweight of jellied eels out of little paper cups. I adjourned to the bar with a colleague from the *Sporting Life,* and four people commented on my nonstarters with varying degrees of belief. Not much of a day. One, on the whole, to forget.

The journey home changed all that. When I forget it, I'll be dead.

Seven

Thanks to having left before the last race, I had a chance in the still empty and waiting train of a forward-facing window seat in a nonsmoker. I turned the heating to "hottest," and opened the newspaper to see what "Spyglass" had come up with in the late editions.

"Tiddely Pom will run, trainer says. But is your money really safe?"

Amused, I read to the end. He'd cribbed most of my points and rehashed them. Complimentary. Plagiarism is the sincerest form of flattery.

The closed door to the corridor slid open and four book-makers' clerks lumbered in, stamping their feet with cold and discussing some luckless punter who had lost an argument over a betting slip.

"I told him to come right off it, who did he think he was kidding? We may not be archangels, but we're not the ruddy mugs he takes us for."

They all wore navy-blue overcoats, which after a while they shed onto the luggage racks. Two of them shared a large packet of stodgy-looking sandwiches and the other two smoked. They were all in the intermediate thirty-forties, with London Jewish accents in which they next discussed their taxi drive to the station in strictly non-Sabbath-day terms.

"Evening," they said to me, acknowledging I existed, and one of them gestured with his cigarette to the nonsmoking notice on the window and said, "O.K. with you, chum?"

I nodded, hardly taking them in. The train rocked off southward, the misty day turned to foggy night, and five pairs of eyelids fell gently shut.

The door to the corridor opened with a crash. Reluctantly I opened one eye a fraction, expecting the ticket collector. Two men filled the opening, looking far from bureaucratic. Their effect on my four fellow travelers was a spine-straightening mouth-opening state of shock. The larger of the newcomers stretched out a hand and pulled the blinds down on the inside of the corridor-facing windows. Then he gave the four clerks a contemptuous comprehensive glance, jerked his head toward the corridor, and said with simplicity, "Out."

I still didn't connect any of this as being my business, not even when the four men meekly took down their navy-blue overcoats and filed out into the train. Only when the large man pulled out a copy of the *Blaze* and pointed to my article did I have the faintest prickle on the spine.

"This is unpopular in certain quarters," remarked the larger man. Thick sarcastic Birmingham accent. He pursed his lips, admiring his own heavy irony. "Unpopular."

He wore grubby overalls from shoes to throat, with above that a thick neck, puffy cheeks, a small wet mouth, and slicked-down hair. His companion, also in overalls, was hard and stocky with wide eyes and a flat-topped head.

"You shouldn't do it, you shouldn't really," the large man said. "Interfering and that."

He put his right hand into his pocket and it reappeared with a brass ridge across the knuckles. I glanced at the other man. Same thing.

I came up with a rush, grabbing for the communication cord. Penalty for improper use, twenty-five pounds. The large man moved his arm in a professional short jab and made havoc of my intention.

They had both learned their trade in the ring; that much was clear. Not much else was. They mostly left my head alone, but they knew where and how to hit to hurt on the body, and if I tried to fight off one of them, the other had a go. The most I achieved was a solid kick on the smaller man's ankle, which drew from him four letters and a frightening kidney punch. I collapsed onto the seat. They leant over me and broke the Queensberry rules.

It crossed my mind that they were going to kill me, that maybe they weren't meaning to, but they were killing me. I even tried to tell them so, but if any sound came out they took no notice. The larger one hauled me bodily to my feet and the small one broke my ribs.

When they let go, I crumpled slowly onto the floor and lay with my face against cigarette butts and the screwed-up wrappings of sandwiches. Stayed quite motionless, praying to a God I had no faith in not to let them start again.

The larger one stooped over me.

"Will he cough it?" the smaller one said.

"How can he? We ain't ruptured nothing, have we? Careful, aren't I? Look out the door, time we was off."

The door slid open and presently shut, but not for a long time was I reassured that they had completely gone. I lay on the floor breathing in coughs and jerky shallow breaths, feeling sick. For some short time it seemed in a weird transferred way that I had earned such a beating not for writing a newspaper article but because of Gail; and to have deserved it, to have sinned and deserved it, turned it into some sort of expurgation. Pain flowed through me in a hot red tide, and only my guilt made it bearable.

Sense returned, as sense does. I set about the slow task of picking myself up and assessing the damage. Maybe they had ruptured nothing; I had only the big man's word for it. At the receiving end it felt as though they had ruptured pretty well everything, including self-respect.

I made it up to the seat, and sat vaguely watching the lights flash past, fuzzy and yellow from fog. Eyes half shut, throat closing with nausea, hands nerveless and weak. No one focus of pain, just too much. Wait, I thought, and it will pass.

I waited a long time.

The lights outside thickened and the train slowed down. London. All change. I would have to move from where I sat. Dismal prospect. Moving would hurt.

The train crept into King's Cross and stopped with a jerk. I stayed where I was, trying to make the effort to stand up and not succeeding, telling myself that if I didn't get up and go I could be shunted into a siding for a cold uncomfortable night, and still not raking up the necessary propulsion.

Again the door slid open with a crash. I glanced up, stifling the beginnings of panic. No heavy man with overalls and knuckle-duster. The guard.

Only when I felt the relief wash through me did I realize the extent of my fear, and I was furious with myself for being so craven.

"The end of the line," the guard was saying.

"Yeah," I said.

He came into the compartment and peered at me. "Been celebrating, have you, sir?" He thought I was drunk.

"Sure," I agreed. "Celebrating."

I made the long-delayed effort and stood up. I'd been quite right about it. It hurt.

"Look, mate, do us a favor and don't throw up in here," said the guard urgently.

I shook my head. Reached the door. Rocked into the corridor.

The guard anxiously took my arm and helped me down onto the platform, and as I walked carefully away I heard him behind me say to a bunch of porters, half laughing, "Did you see that one? Greeny gray and sweating like a pig. Must have been knocking it back solid all afternoon."

I went home by taxi and took my time up the stairs to the flat. Mrs. Woodward for once was in a hurry for me to come, as she was wanting to get home in case the fog thickened. I apologized. "Quite all right, Mr. Tyrone. You know I'm usually glad to stay. . . ." The door closed behind her and I fought down a strong inclination to lie on my bed and to groan.

Elizabeth said, "Ty, you look terribly pale," when I kissed her. Impossible to hide it from her completely.

"I fell," I said. "Tripped. Knocked the breath out of myself, for a minute or two."

She was instantly concerned, with the special extra anxiety for herself apparent in her eyes.

"Don't worry," I comforted her. "No harm done."

I went into the kitchen and held on to the table. After a minute or two I remembered Elizabeth's pain-killing tablets and took the bottle out of the cupboard. Only two left. There would be. I swallowed one of them, tying a mental knot to remind me to ring the doctor for another prescription. One wasn't quite enough, but better than nothing. I went back into the big room and, with a fair try at normality, poured our evening drinks.

By the time I had done the supper and the jobs for Elizabeth and got myself undressed and into bed, the main damage had resolved itself into two or possibly three cracked ribs low down on my left side. The rest slowly subsided into a blanketing ache. Nothing had ruptured, like the man said.

I lay in the dark breathing shallowly and trying not to cough, and at last took time off from simply existing to consider the

who and why of such a drastic roughing up, along with the pros
and cons of telling Luke-John. He'd make copy of it, put it on
the front page, plug it for more than it was worth, write the
headlines himself. My feelings would naturally be utterly dis-
regarded as being of no importance compared with selling
papers. Luke-John had no pity. If I didn't tell him and he found
out later, there would be frost and fury and a permanent
atmosphere of distrust. I couldn't afford that. My predecessor
had been squeezed off the paper entirely as a direct result of
having concealed from Luke-John a red-hot scandal in which he
was involved. A rival paper got hold of it and scooped the
Blaze. Luke-John never forgave, never forgot.

I sighed deeply. A grave mistake. The cracked ribs stabbed
back with unnecessary vigor. I spent what could not be called a
restful, comfortable, sleep-filled night, and in the morning
could hardly move. Elizabeth watched me get up and the raw
anxiety twisted her face.

"Ty!"

"Only a bruise or two, honey, I told you, I fell over."

"You look . . . hurt."

I shook my head. "I'll get the coffee."

I got the coffee. I also looked with longing at Elizabeth's last
pill, which I had no right to take. She still suffered sometimes
from terrible cramp, and on these occasions had to have the
pills in a hurry. I didn't need any mental knots to remind me to
get some more. When Mrs. Woodward came, I went.

Dr. Antonio Perelli wrote the prescription without hesitation
and handed it across.

"How is she?"

"Fine. Same as usual."

"It's time I went to see her."

"She'd love it," I said truthfully. Perelli's visits acted on her

like champagne. I'd met him casually at a party three years
earlier, a young Italian doctor in private practice in Welbeck
Street. Too handsome, I'd thought at once. Too feminine, with
those dark, sparkling eyes. All bedside manner and huge fees,
with droves of neurotic women patients paying to have their
hands held.

Then, just before the party broke up, someone told me he
specialized in chest complaints and not to be put off by his youth
and beauty, he was brilliant; and by coincidence we found
ourselves outside on the pavement together, hailing the same
taxi, and going the same way.

At the time I had been worried about Elizabeth. She had to
return to hospital for intensive nursing every time she was ill,
and with the virtual stamping out of polio the hospitals geared
to care for patients on artificial respiration were becoming
fewer and fewer. We had just been told she could not expect to
go back any more to the hospital that had always looked after
her.

I shared the taxi with Perelli and asked him if he knew of
anywhere I could send her quickly if she ever needed it. Instead
of answering directly he invited me into his tiny bachelor flat
for another drink, and before I left he had acquired another
patient. Elizabeth's general health had improved instantly
under his care and I paid his moderate fees without a wince.

I thanked him for the prescription and put it in my pocket.

"Ty . . . are the pills for Elizabeth or for you?"

I looked at him, startled. "Why?"

"My dear fellow, I have eyes. What I see in your face is . . .
severe."

I smiled wryly. "All right. I was going to ask you. Could you
put a bit of strapping on a couple of ribs?"

He stuck me up firmly and handed me a small medicine glass

containing, he said, Disprins dissolved in nepenthe, which worked like a vanishing trick: now you feel it, now you don't.

"You haven't told Elizabeth?" he said anxiously.

"Only that I fell and winded myself."

He relaxed, moving his head in a gesture of approval. "Good."

It had been his idea to shield her from worries which ordinary women could cope with in their stride. I had thought him unduly fussy at first, but the strict screening he had urged had worked wonders. She had become far less nervous, much happier, and had even put on some badly needed weight.

"And the police? Have you told the police?"

I shook my head and explained about Luke-John.

"Difficult. Um. Suppose you tell this Luke-John simply that those men threatened you? You'll not be taking your shirt off in the office." He smiled in the way that made Elizabeth's eyes shine. "These two men, they will not go about saying they inflicted so much damage."

"They might." I frowned, considering. "It could be a good idea if I turned up in perfect health at the races today and gave them the lie."

With an assenting gesture he mixed me a small bottleful of the Disprin and nepenthe. "Don't eat much," he said, handing it over. "And only drink coffee."

"O.K."

"And do nothing that would get you another beating like this."

I was silent.

He looked at me with sad understanding. "That is too much to give up for Elizabeth?"

"I can't just . . . crawl away," I protested. "Even for Elizabeth."

He shook his head. "It would be best for her. But . . ." He shrugged, and held out his hand in goodbye. "Stay out of trains, then."

I stayed out of trains. For ninety-four minutes. Then I caught the race train to Plumpton and traveled down safely with two harmless strangers and a man I knew slightly from the B.B.C.

Thanks to Tonio's mixture, I walked about all day and talked and laughed much the same as usual. Once I coughed. Even that caused only an echo of a stab. For maximum effect, I spent a good deal of my time walking about the bookmakers' stalls, inspecting both their prices and their clerks. The fraternity knew something had happened. Their heads swiveled as I passed and they were talking behind my back, nudging each other. When I put ten shillings on a semi-outsider with one of them, he said, "You feeling all right, chum?"

"Why not?" I said in surprise. "It's a nice enough day."

He looked perplexed for a second, and then shrugged. I walked on, looking at faces, searching for a familiar one. The trouble was I'd paid the four clerks in the compartment so little attention that I wasn't sure I'd recognize any one of them again, and I wouldn't have done if he hadn't given himself away. When he saw me looking at him, he jerked, stepped down off his stand, and bolted.

Running was outside my repertoire. I walked quietly up behind him an hour later when he had judged it safe to go back to his job.

"A word in your ear," I said at his elbow.

He jumped six inches. "It was nothing to do with me."

"I know that. Just tell me who the two men were. Those two in overalls."

"Do me a favor. Do I want to end up in hospital?"

"Twenty quid?" I suggested.

"I dunno about that. . . . How come you're here today?"

"Why not?"

"When those two've seen to someone, they stay seen to."

"Is that so? They seemed pretty harmless."

"No, straight up," he said curiously, "didn't they touch you?"

"No."

He was puzzled.

"A pony. Twenty-five quid," I said. "For their names, or who they work for."

He hesitated. "Not here, mate. On the train."

"Not on the train." I was positive. "In the press box. And now."

He got five minutes off from his grumbling employer and went in front of me up the stairs to the aerie allotted to newspapers. I gave a shove-off sign to the only press man up there, and he obligingly disappeared.

"Right," I said. "Who were they?"

"They're Brummies," he said cautiously.

"I know that. You could cut their accents."

"Bruisers," he ventured.

I stopped myself just in time from telling him I knew that, too.

"They're Charlie Boston's boys." It came out in a nervous rush.

"That's better. Who's Charlie Boston?"

"So who hasn't heard of Charlie Boston? Got some betting shops, hasn't he, in Birmingham and Wolverhampton and such like."

"And some boys on race trains?"

He looked more puzzled than ever. "Don't you owe Charlie

no money? So what did they want, then? It's usually bad debts they're after."

"I've never heard of Charlie Boston before, let alone had a bet with him." I took out my wallet and gave him five fivers. He took them with a practiced flick and stowed them away in a pocket like Fort Knox under his left armpit. "Dirty thieves," he explained. "Taking precautions, aren't I?"

He scuttled off down the stairs, and I stayed up in the press box and took another swig at my useful little bottle, reflecting that when Charlie Boston unleashed his boys on me he had been very foolish indeed.

Luke-John reacted predictably with a bridling "They can't do that to the *Blaze*" attitude.

Wednesday morning. Not much doing in the office. Derry with his feet up on the blotter, Luke-John elbow deep in the dailies' sports pages, the telephone silent, and every desk in the place exhibiting the same feverish inactivity.

Into this calm I dropped the pebble of news that two men, adopting a threatening attitude, had told me not to interfere in the nonstarters racket. Luke-John sat up erect like a belligerent bullfrog, quivering with satisfaction that the article had produced tangible results. With a claw hand he pounced on the telephone.

"Manchester office? Give me the sports desk. . . . That you, Andy? Luke Morton. What can you tell me about a bookmaker called Charlie Boston? Has a string of betting shops around Birmingham."

He listened to a lengthy reply with growing intensity.

"That adds up. Yes. Yes. Fine. Ask around and let me know."

He put down the receiver and rubbed his larynx. "Charlie

Boston changed his spots about a year ago. Before that he was apparently an ordinary Birmingham bookmaker with about six shops and a reasonable reputation. Now, Andy says, he's expanded a lot and become a bully. He says he's been hearing too much about Charlie Boston lately. Seems he hires two ex-boxers to collect unpaid debts from his credit customers, and as a result of all this he's coining it."

I thought it over. Charlie Boston of Birmingham with his betting shops and bruisers didn't jell at all with the description Dembley had given me of a quiet gentleman in a Rolls with a chauffeur and a Greek, Dutch, or Scandinavian accent. They even seemed an unlikely pair as shoulder-to-shoulder partners. There might of course be two separate rackets going on, and if so, what happened if they clashed? And by which of them had Bert Checkov been seduced? But if they were all one outfit, I'd settle for the Rolls gent as the brains and Charlie Boston the muscles. Setting his dogs on me had been classic muscle-bound thinking.

Luke-John's telephone rang and he reached out a hand. As he listened, his eyes narrowed and he turned his head to look straight at me.

"What do you mean, he was pulped? He certainly was not. He's here in the office at this moment and he went to Plumpton races yesterday. What your paper needs is a little less imagination. . . . If you don't believe me, talk to him yourself." He handed me the receiver, saying with a grimace, "Connersley. Bloody man."

"I heard," said the precise malicious voice on the phone, "that some Birmingham heavies took you to pieces on the Leicester race train."

"A rumor," I said with boredom. "I heard it myself yesterday at Plumpton."

"According to my informant, you couldn't have gone to Plumpton."

"Your informant is unreliable. Scrap him."

A small pause. Then he said, "I can check if you were there."

"Check away." I put the receiver down with a brusque crash and thanked my stars I had reached Luke-John with my version first.

"Are you planning a follow-up on Sunday?" he was asking. Connersley had planted no suspicions: was already forgotten. "Hammer the point home. Urge the racing authorities to act. Agitate. You know the drill."

I nodded. I knew the drill. My bruises gave me a protesting nudge. No more, they said urgently. Write a nice mild piece on an entirely different, totally innocuous subject.

"Get some quotes," Luke-John said.

"O.K."

"Give with some ideas," he said impatiently. "I'm doing all your ruddy work."

I sighed. Shallowly and carefully. "How about us making sure Tiddely Pom starts in the Lamplighter? Maybe I'll go fix it with the Ronceys. . . ."

Luke-John interrupted, his eyes sharp. "The *Blaze* will see to it that Tiddely Pom runs. Ty, that's genius. Start your piece with that. The *Blaze* will see to it. . . . Splendid. Splendid."

Oh God, I thought. I'm the world's greatest bloody fool. Stay out of race trains, Tonio Perelli had said. Nothing about lying down on the tracks.

Eight

Nothing much had changed at the Ronceys'. Dead leaves, cob-webs still in place. No dripping meat on the kitchen table; two unplucked pheasants sagged with limp necks there instead. The sink overflowed with unwashed dishes and the Wellington smell had intensified.

I arrived unannounced at two-thirty and found Roncey him-self out in the yard watching Pat and the old man saw up a large hunk of dead tree. He received me with an unenthusiastic glare but eventually took me through into the sitting room with a parting backward instruction to his son to clean out the tack room when he'd finished the logs.

Madge was lying on the sofa, asleep. Still no stockings, still the blue slippers, still the yellow dress, very dirty now down the front. Roncey gave her a glance of complete indifference and gestured me to one of the armchairs.

"I don't need help from the *Blaze*," he said, as he'd said outside in the yard. "Why should I?"

"It depends on how much you want Tiddely Pom to run in the Lamplighter."

"Of course he's going to run." Roncey looked aggressive and determined. "I told you. Anyone who tries to tell me otherwise has another think coming."

"In that case," I said mildly, "one of two things will happen. Either the men operating the racket will abandon the idea of preventing Tiddely Pom from running, as a result of all the publicity they've been getting. Or they will go ahead and stop him. If they've any sense, they'll abandon the idea. But I don't see how one can count on them having any sense."

"They won't stop him." Pugnacious jaw, stubborn eyes.

"You can be sure they will, one way or another, if they want to."

"I don't believe you."

"But would you object to taking precautions, just in case? The *Blaze* will foot the bills."

He stared at me long and hard. "This is not just a publicity stunt to cover your sensation-hunting paper with glory?"

"Dual purpose," I said. "Half for you and the betting public. Half for us. But only one object: to get Tiddely Pom safely off in the Lamplighter."

He thought it over.

"What sort of precautions?" he said at last.

I sighed inwardly with mixed feelings, a broken-ribbed skier at the top of a steep and bumpy slope, with only myself to thank.

"There are three main ones," I said. "The simplest is a letter to Weatherbys, stating your positive intention to run in the Lamplighter, and asking them to check carefully with you if they should receive any instructions to strike out the horse either before or after the four-day declaration stage next Tuesday. You do realize, don't you, that I or anyone else could send a telegram or telex striking out the horse, and nothing you could do would get him put back again?"

His mouth dropped open. *"Anyone?"*

"Anyone signing your name. Of course. Weatherbys receive hundreds of cancellations a week. They don't check to make sure the trainer really means it. Why should they?"

"Good God," he said, stunned. "I'll write at once. In fact I'll ring them up." He began to stand up.

"There won't be that much urgency," I said. "Much more likely a cancellation would be sent in at the last moment, in order to allow as much time as possible for antepost bets to be made."

"Oh . . . quite." A thought struck him as he sat down again. "If the *Blaze* declares it is going to make Tiddely Pom safe and then he *doesn't* run for some reason, you are going to look very silly."

I nodded. "A risk. Still . . . We'll do our best. But we do need your wholehearted cooperation, not just your qualified permission."

He had made up his mind. "You have it. What next?"

"Tiddely Pom will have to go to another stable."

That rocked him. "Oh, no."

"He's much too vulnerable here."

He swallowed. "Where, then?"

"To one of the top trainers. He will still be expertly prepared for the race. He can have the diet he's used to. We'll give you a report on him every day."

He opened and shut his mouth several times, speechless.

"Thirdly," I said, "your wife and at least your three youngest sons must go away for a holiday."

"They can't," he protested automatically.

"They must. If one of the children were kidnaped, would you set his life against running Tiddely Pom?"

"It isn't possible," he said weakly.

"Just the threat might be enough."

Madge got up and opened her eyes. They were far from dreamy. "Where and when do we go?" she said.

"Tomorrow. You will know where after you get there."

She smiled with vivid delight. Fantasy had come to life. Roncey himself was not enchanted.

"I don't like it," he said, frowning.

"Ideally, you should all go. The whole lot of you," I said.

Roncey shook his head. "There are the other horses, and the farm. I can't leave them. And I need Pat here, and Peter."

I agreed to that, having gained the essentials. "Don't tell the children they are going," I said to Madge. "Just keep them home from school in the morning, and someone will call for you at about nine. You'll need only country clothes. And you'll be away until after the race on Saturday week. Also, please do not on any account write any letters straight to here, or let the children send any. If you want to write, send the letters to us at the *Blaze,* and we will see that Mr. Roncey gets them."

"But Vic can write to us?" Madge said.

"Of course . . . but also via the *Blaze.* Because he won't know where you are."

They both protested, but in the end saw the sense of it. What he didn't know, he couldn't give away, even by accident.

"It won't only be people working the racket who might be looking for them," I explained apologetically. "But one or two of our rival newspapers will be hunting for them, so as to be able to black the *Blaze's* eye. And they are quite skilled at finding people who want to stay hidden."

I left the Ronceys looking blankly at each other and drove the van back to London. It seemed a very long way, and too many aches redeveloped on the journey. I'd finished Tonio's mixture just before going into the office in the morning and was back on Elizabeth's pills, which were not as good. By the time I got home, I was tired, thirsty, hurting, and apprehensive.

Dealt with the first three: armchair and whiskey. Contemplated the apprehension, and didn't know which would be worse, another encounter with the Boston boys or a complete failure with Tiddely Pom. It would likely be one or the other. Could even be both.

"What's the matter, Ty?" Elizabeth looked and sounded worried.

"Nothing." I smiled at her. "Nothing at all, honey."

The anxious lines relaxed in her face as she smiled back. The pump hummed and thudded, pulling air into her lungs. My poor, poor Elizabeth. I stretched my hand over and touched her cheek in affection, and she turned her head and kissed my fingers.

"You're a fantastic man, Ty," she said. She said something like it at least twice a week. I twitched my nose and made the usual sort of answer, "You're not so bad yourself." The disaster that a virus had made of our lives never got any better. Never would. For her it was total and absolute; for me there were exits, like Gail. When I took them, the guilt I felt was not just the ordinary guilt of an unfaithful husband, but that of a deserter. Elizabeth couldn't leave the battlefield; but when it got too much for me, I just slid out and left her.

At nine o'clock the next morning Derry Clark collected Madge and the three Roncey boys in his own Austin and drove them down to Portsmouth and straight on to the Isle of Wight car ferry.

At noon I arrived at the farm with a car and Rice trailer borrowed from the city editor, whose daughters went in for show jumping. Roncey showed great reluctance at parting with Tiddely Pom, and loaded the second stall of the trailer with sacks of feed and bales of hay, adding to these the horse's saddle and bridle, and also three dozen eggs and a crate of beer. He had written out the diet and training regime in four-page detail scattered with emphatic underlinings. I assured him six times I would see that the new trainer followed the instructions to the last full stop.

Pat helped with the loading with a twisting smile, not unhappy that his father was losing control of the horse. He gave
me a quick look full of ironic meaning when he saw me watching him, and said under his breath as he humped past with some
hay, "Now he knows what it feels like."

I left Victor Roncey standing disconsolately in the center of
his untidy farmyard watching his one treasure depart, and drove
carefully away along the Essex lanes, heading west to Berkshire. About five miles down the road I stopped at a telephone
box and rang up the Western School of Art.

Gail said, "Surprise, surprise."

"Yes," I agreed. "How about Sunday?"

"Um." She hesitated. "How about tomorrow?"

"Won't you be teaching?"

"I meant," she explained, "tomorrow night."

"Tomorrow . . . *all* night?"

"Can you manage it?"

I took so deep a breath that my sore ribs jumped. It depended
on whether Mrs. Woodward could stay, as she sometimes did.

"Ty?" she said. "Are you still there?"

"Thinking."

"What about?"

"What to tell my wife."

"You slay me," she said. "Is it yes or no?"

"Yes," I said with a sigh. "Where?"

"A hotel, I should think."

"All right," I agreed. I asked her what time she finished
work, and arranged a meeting point at King's Cross railway
station.

When I called the flat, Elizabeth answered.

"Ty! Where are you?"

"On the road. There's nothing wrong. It's just that I forgot to ask Mrs. Woodward before I left if she could stay with you tomorrow night . . . so that I could go up to Newcastle ready for the races on Saturday." Louse, I thought. Mean, stinking louse. Lying, deceiving louse. I listened miserably to the sounds of Elizabeth asking Mrs. Woodward and found no relief at all in her answer.

"She says yes, Ty, she could manage that perfectly. You'll be home again on Saturday?"

"Yes, honey. Late, though."

"Of course."

"See you this evening."

"Bye, Ty," she said with a smile in her voice. "See you."

I drove all the way to Norton Fox's stable wishing I hadn't done it. Knowing that I wouldn't change it. Round and round the mulberry bush and a thumping headache by Berkshire.

Norton Fox looked curiously into the trailer parked in the private front drive of his house.

"So that's the great Tiddely Pom. Can't say I think much of him from this angle."

"Nor from any other," I added. "It's good of you to have him."

"Happy to oblige. I'm putting him in the box next to Zig Zag, and Sandy Willis can look after both of them."

"You won't tell her what he is?" I asked anxiously.

"Of course not." He looked resigned at my stupidity. "I've recently bought a chaser over in Kent. I've just postponed collecting it a while, but Sandy and all the other lads think Tiddely Pom is him."

"Great."

"I'll just get my head lad to drive the trailer into the yard and unload. You said on the phone that you wanted to stay out of sight. . . . Come inside for a cuppa?"

Too late, after I'd nodded, I remembered the near-black tea of my former visit. The same again. Norton remarked that his housekeeper had been economizing; he never could get her to make it strong enough.

"Did the *Tally* photographer get here all right?" I asked as he came in from the yard, filling his cup, and sat down opposite me.

He nodded. "Took dozens of pics of Sandy Willis and thrilled her to bits." He offered me a slice of dry-looking fruit-cake and, when I said no, ate a large chunk himself, undeterred. "That article of yours last Sunday," he said past the currants. "That must have been a bombshell in certain quarters."

I said, "Mmm, I hope so."

"Brevity—that Champion Hurdler of mine—that was definitely one of the nonstarters you were talking about, wasn't it? Even though you didn't mention it explicitly by name?"

"Yes, it was."

"Ty, did you find out *why* Dembley struck his horse out, and then sold out of racing altogether?"

"I can't tell you why, Norton," I said.

He considered this answer with his head on one side and then nodded as if satisfied. "Tell me one day, then."

I smiled briefly. "When and if the racket is extinct."

"You go on the way you are, and it will be. If you go on exposing it publicly, the antepost market will be so untrustworthy that we'll find ourselves doing as the Americans do, only betting on a race on the day of the race, and never before. They don't have any off-the-course betting at all over there, do they?"

"Not legally."

He drank in big gulps down to the tea leaves. "Might shoot our attendances up if punters had to go to the races to have a bet."

"Which would shoot up the prize money, too. . . . Did you see that their champion jockey earned well over three million dollars last year? Enough to make Gordon Richards weep."

I put down the half-finished tea and stood up. "Must be getting back, Norton. Thank you again for your help."

"Anything to prevent another Brevity."

"Send the accounts to the *Blaze*."

He nodded. "And ring the sports desk every day to give a report, and don't speak to anyone except you or Derry Clark or a man called Luke-John Morton. Right?"

"Absolutely right," I agreed. "Oh, and here are Victor Roncey's notes. Eggs and beer in Tiddely Pom's food every night."

"I've one owner," Norton said, "who sends his horse champagne."

I drove the trailer back to the city editor's house, swapped it for my van, and went home. Ten to seven on the clock. Mrs. Woodward was having a grand week for overtime and had cooked a chicken à la king for our supper, leaving it ready and hot. I thanked her. "Not at all, Mr. Tyrone, a pleasure I'm sure. Ta-ta, luv, see you tomorrow. I'll bring my things for stopping the night."

I kissed Elizabeth, poured the drinks, ate the chicken, watched a TV program, and let a little of the day's tension trickle away. After supper there was my Sunday article to write. Enthusiasm for the project: way below zero. I went into the writing room determined to put together a calm played-down sequel to the previous week, with a sober let's-not-rush-our-fences approach. Somewhere along the line most of these good intentions vanished. Neither Charlie Boston nor the foreign gent in the Rolls was going to like the result.

Before setting off to the office in the morning I packed an

overnight bag, with Elizabeth reminding me to take my alarm
clock and a clean shirt.

"I hate it when you go away," she said. "I know you don't go
often, probably not nearly as much as you ought to. I know you
try not to get the faraway meetings. Derry nearly always does
them, and I feel so guilty because his wife has those tiny children to look after all alone. . . ."

"Stop worrying," I said, smiling. "Derry likes to go." I had
almost convinced myself that I really was taking the afternoon
train to Newcastle. Gail was hours away, unreal. I kissed
Elizabeth's cheek three times and dearly regretted leaving her.
Yet I left.

Luke-John and Derry were both out of the office when I
arrived. Luke-John's secretary handed me a large envelope
which she said had come for me by hand just after I left on
Wednesday. I opened it. The galley proofs of my *Tally* article:
please would I read and O.K. immediately.

"*Tally* telephoned for you twice yesterday," Luke-John's
secretary said. "They go to press today. They wanted you
urgently."

I read the article. Arnold Shankerton had changed it about
here and there and had stamped his own slightly pedantic views
of grammar all over it. I sighed. I didn't like the changes, but a
hundred and fifty guineas plus expenses softened the impact.

Arnold Shankerton said in his perfectly modulated tenor,
with a mixture of annoyance and apology, "I'm afraid we've
had to go ahead and print, as we hadn't heard from you."

"My fault. I've only just picked up your letter."

"I see. Well, after I'd worked on it a little I think it reads
very well, don't you? We're quite pleased with it. We think it
will be a success with our readers. They like that sort of intimate human touch."

"I'm glad," I said politely. "Will you send me a copy?"

"I'll make a note of it," he said suavely. I thought I would probably have to buy one on a bookstall. "Let me have your expenses. Small, I hope?"

"Sure," I agreed. "Tiny."

Luke-John and Derry came back as I disconnected and Luke-John without bothering to say good morning stretched out a hand for my Sunday offering. I took it out of my pocket and he unfolded it and read it.

"Hmph," he said. "I expected a bit more bite."

Derry took one of the carbon copies from me and read it.

"Any more bite and he'd have chewed up the whole page," he said.

"Couldn't you emphasize a bit more that only the *Blaze* knows where Tiddely Pom is?" Luke-John said. "You've only implied it."

"If you think so."

"Yes, I do think so. As the *Blaze* is footing the bills, we want all the credit we can get."

"Suppose someone finds him—Tiddely Pom?" I asked mildly. "Then we'd look right nanas, hiding him, boasting about it, and then having him found."

"No one will find him. The only people who know where he is are us three and Norton Fox. To be more precise, only you and Fox know *exactly* where he is. Only you and Fox know which in that yardful of sixty horses is Tiddely Pom. Neither of you is going to tell anyone else. So how is anyone going to find him? No, no, Ty. You make that article absolutely definite. The *Blaze* is keeping the horse safe, and only the *Blaze* knows where he is."

"Charlie Boston may not like it," Derry observed to no one in particular.

"Charlie Boston can stuff it," Luke-John said impatiently.

"I meant," Derry explained, "that he might just send his thug-uglies to take Ty apart for so obviously ignoring their keep-off-the-grass."

My pal. Luke-John considered the possibility for two full seconds before shaking his head. "They wouldn't dare."

"And even if they did," I said, "it would make a good story if you could sell more papers."

"Exactly." Luke-John started nodding and then looked at me suspiciously. "That was a joke?"

"A feeble one." I sighed, past smiling.

"Change the intro, then, Ty. Make it one hundred per cent specific." He picked up a pencil and put a line through the first paragraph. Read the next, rubbed his larynx thoughtfully, let that one stand. Axed the next. Turned the page.

Derry watched sympathetically as the pencil marks grew. It happened to him, too, often enough. Luke-John scribbled his way through to the end and then returned to the beginning, pointing out each alteration that he wanted made. He was turning my moderately hard-hitting original into a bulldozing battering ram.

"You'll get me slaughtered," I said, and I meant it.

I worked on the rewrite most of the morning, fighting a rearguard action all the way. What Luke-John finally passed was a compromise between his view and mine, but still left me so far out on a limb as to be balancing on twigs. Luke-John took it in to the editor, stayed there while he read it, and brought it triumphantly back.

"He liked it. Thinks it's great stuff. He liked Derry's piece yesterday, too, summing up the handicap. He told me the sports desk is a big asset to the paper."

"Good," Derry said cheerfully. "When do we get our next raise?"

"Time for a jar at the Devereux," Luke-John suggested, looking at his watch. "Coming today, Ty?"

"Norton Fox hasn't rung through yet."

"Call him, then."

I telephoned to Fox. Tiddely Pom was fine, ate his feed the previous evening, had settled in well, had done a mile at a working canter that morning, and no one had looked at him twice. I thanked him and relayed the news to Roncey, who sounded both agitated and depressed.

"I don't like it," he said several times.

"Do you want to risk having him at home?"

He hesitated, then said, "I suppose not. No. But I don't like it. Don't forget to ring tomorrow evening. I'll be at Kempton races all afternoon."

"The sports editor will ring," I assured him. "And don't worry."

He put the receiver down saying an explosive "Huh." Luke-John and Derry were already on the way to the door and I joined them to go to lunch.

"Only a fortnight since Bert Checkov died," observed Derry, sitting on a bar stool. "Only ten days since we spotted the non-starters. Funny."

Hilarious. And eight more days to go to the Lamplighter. This Monday, I decided, I would stay safely tucked away at home.

"Don't forget," I said to Derry. "Don't tell anyone my phone number."

"What brought that on all of a sudden?"

"I was thinking about Charlie Boston. My address isn't in the phone book. . . ."

"Neither Derry nor I will give your address to anyone," Luke-John said impatiently. "Come off it, Ty, anyone would think you were frightened."

"Anyone would be so right," I agreed, and they both laughed heartily into their pints.

Derry was predictably pleased that I wanted to go to Newcastle instead of Kempton, leaving the London meeting for once for him.

"Is it all right," he said, embarrassed. "With your wife, I mean?"

I told him what Elizabeth had said, but as usual anything to do with her made him uncomfortable. Luke-John said dutifully "How is she?" and I said "Fine."

I kicked around the office all the afternoon, arranging a travel warrant to Newcastle, putting in a chit for expenses for Heathbury Park, Leicester, and Plumpton, and collecting the cash from Accounts. Luke-John was busy with a football columnist and the golfing correspondent, and Derry took time off from working out his tips for every meeting in the following week to tell me about taking the Roncey kids to the Isle of Wight.

"Noisy little devils," he said disapprovingly. "Their mother has no control over them at all. She seemed to be in a dream most of the time. Anyway, none of them actually fell off the ferry, which was a miracle considering Tony—that was the eldest one—was trying to lean over far enough to see the paddles go round. I told him they were under the water. Made no difference."

I made sympathetic noises, trying not to laugh out of pity for my ribs. "They were happy enough, then?"

"Are you kidding? No school and a holiday at the sea? Tony said he was going to bathe, November or no November. His mother showed no signs of stopping him. Anyway, they settled into the boarding house all right, though I should think we shall get a whacking bill for damage, and they thought it tremendous fun to change their names to Robinson—no trouble there. They thought Robinson was a smashing choice; they would all pretend they were cast away on a desert island. . . . Well, I tell you, Ty, by the time I left them I was utterly exhausted."

"Never mind. You can look forward to bringing them back."

"Not me," he said fervently. "Your turn for that."

At four I picked up my suitcase and departed for King's Cross. The Newcastle train left at five. I watched it go.

At five-forty-eight she came up from the underground, wearing a beautifully cut darkish-blue coat and carrying a creamy white suitcase. Several heads turned to look at her, and a nearby man who had been waiting almost as long as I had watched her stedfastly until she reached the corner where I stood.

"Hallo," she said. "Sorry I'm late."

"Think nothing of it."

"I gather," she said with satisfaction, "that you fixed your wife."

Nine

She moved against me in the warm dark and put her mouth on the thin skin somewhere just south of my neck. I tightened my arms around her, and buried my nose in her clean sweet-scented hair.

"There's always something new," she said sleepily. "Broken ribs are quite a gimmick."

"I didn't feel them."

"Oh, yes, you did."

I stroked my hands slowly over her smooth skin and didn't bother to answer. I felt relaxed and wholly content. She had been kind to my ribs, gentle to my bruises. They had even in an obscure way given her pleasure.

"How did it happen?"

"What?"

"The black-and-blue bit."

"I lost an argument."

She rubbed her nose on my chest. "Must have been quite a debate."

I smiled in the dark. The whole world was inside the sheets, inside the small private cocoon wrapping two bodies in intimate primeval understanding.

"Ty?"

"Mmm?"

"Can't we stay together all weekend?"

I said through her hair, "I have to phone in a report from Newcastle. Can't avoid it."

"Damn the *Blaze.*"

"There's Sunday, though."

"Hurrah for the golf club."

We lay quiet for a long while. I felt heavy with sleep and fought to stay awake. There were so few hours like this. None to waste.

For Gail time was not so precious. Her limbs slackened and her head slid down onto my arm, her easy breath fanning softly against my chest. I thought of Elizabeth lying closely curled against me like that when we were first married, and for once it was without guilt, only with regret.

Gail woke of her own accord a few hours later and pulled my wrist around to look at the luminous hands on my watch.

"Are you awake?" she said. "It's ten to six."

"Do you like it in the morning?"

"With you, Ty, anytime." Her voice smiled in the darkness. "Any old time you care to mention."

I wasn't that good. I said, "Why?"

"Because you're normal, maybe. Nice bread-and-butter love." She played the piano down my stomach. "Some men want the weirdest things. . . ."

"Let's not talk about them."

"O.K.," she said. "Let's not."

I caught the Newcastle express at eight o'clock with ten seconds in hand. It was a raw cold morning with steam hissing up from under the train. Hollow clanking noises and unintelligible station announcements filled the ears, and bleary-eyed shivering passengers hurried grayly through the British Standard dawn.

I took my shivering bleary-eyed self into the dining car and tried some strong black coffee, but nothing was going to shift the dragging depression which had settled in inexorably as soon as I left Gail. I imagined her as I had left her, lying warm and luxuriously lazy in the soft bed and saying Sunday was tomorrow, we could start again where we'd left off. Sunday was certainly tomorrow, but there was Saturday to get through first. From where I sat it looked like a very long day.

Four and a half hours to Newcastle. I slept most of the way, and spent the rest remembering the evening and night which were gone. We had found a room in a small private hotel near the station and I had signed the register "Mr. and Mrs. Tyrone." No one there had shown any special interest in us; they had presently shown us to a clean uninspiring room and given us the key, had asked if we wanted early tea, had said they were sorry they didn't do dinners, there were several good restaurants round about. I paid them in advance, explaining that I had an early train to catch. They smiled, thanked me, withdrew, asked no questions, made no comment. Impossible to know what they guessed.

We talked for a while and then went out to a pub for a drink and from there to an Indian restaurant where we took a long time eating little, and an even longer time drinking coffee. Gail wore her usual air of businesslike poise and remained striking-looking even when surrounded by people of her own skin color. I, with my pale face, was in a minority.

Gail commented on it. "London must be the best place in the world for people like me."

"For anyone."

She shook her head. "Especially for people of mixed race. In so many countries I'd be on the outside looking in. I'd never get the sort of job I have."

"It never seems to worry you, being of mixed race," I said.

"I accept it. In fact I wouldn't choose now to be wholly white or wholly black, if I could alter it. I am used to being me. And with people like you, of course, it is easy, because you are un-affected by me."

"I wouldn't say that, exactly," I said, grinning.

"Damn it, you know what I mean. You don't mind me being brown."

"You're brown and you're beautiful. A shattering combination."

"You're not being serious," she complained.

"And you're glossy to the bone."

Her lips curved in amusement. "If you mean I've a hard core instead of a soft center, then I expect you're right."

"And one day you'll part from me without a twinge."

"Will we part?" No anxiety, no involvement.

"What do you think?"

"I think you wouldn't leave your wife to live with me."

Direct, no muddle, no fluffy wrappings.

"Would you?" she asked when I didn't quickly answer.

"I'll never leave her."

"That's what I thought. I like to get things straight. Then I can enjoy what I have, and not expect more."

"Hedging your bets."

"What do you mean?" she asked.

"Insuring against disappointment."

"When people desperately want what they can never have, they *suffer*. Real grinding misery. That's not for me."

"You will be luckier than most," I said slowly, "if you can avoid it altogether."

"I'll have a damned good try."

One day uncontrollable emotion would smash up all that organized levelheadedness. Not while I was around, if I could help it. I prized it too much. Needed her to stay like that. Only while she demanded so little could I go on seeing her, and since she clearly knew it we had a good chance of staying safely on the tightrope for as long as we wanted.

With the coffee we talked, as before, about money. Gail complained that she never had enough.

"Who has?" I said sympathetically.

"Your wife, for one." There was a faint asperity in her voice, which made me stifle my immediate impulse to deny it.

"Sorry," she said almost at once. "Shouldn't have said that. What your wife has is quite irrelevant. It's what I haven't got that we're talking about. Such as a car of my own, a sports car, and not having to borrow Harry's all the time. And a flat of my own, a sunny one overlooking a park. Never having to budget every penny. Buying lavish presents for people if I feel like it. Flying to Paris often for a few days, and having a holiday in Japan. . . ."

"Marry a millionaire," I suggested.

"I intend to."

We both laughed, but I thought she probably meant it. The man she finally didn't part with would have to have troubles with his surtax. I wondered what she would do if she knew I could only afford that dinner and the hotel bill because *Tally's* fee would be plugging for a while the worst holes in the Tyrone economy. What would she do if she knew that I had a penniless paralyzed wife, not a rich one. On both counts, wave a rapid goodbye, probably. For as long as I could, I wasn't going to give her the opportunity.

I missed the first Newcastle race altogether and only reached the press stand halfway through the second. Delicate probes among colleagues revealed that nothing dramatic had happened in the hurdle race I had spent urging the taxi driver to go above twenty. Luke-John would never know.

After the fourth race I telephoned through a report, and another after the fifth, in which one of the top northern jockeys broke his leg. Derry came on the line and asked me to go and find out from the trainer who would be riding his horse in the Lamplighter instead, and I did his errand thanking my stars I had had the sense actually to go to Newcastle, and hadn't been tempted to watch the racing on television and phone through an "on-the-spot" account from an armchair three hundred miles away, as one correspondent of my acquaintance had been known to do.

Just before the last race someone touched my arm. I turned. Colly Gibbons, the handicapper, looking harassed and annoyed.

"Ty. Do me a favor."

"What?"

"You came by train? First class?"

I nodded. The *Blaze* wasn't mean about comfort.

"Then swap return tickets with me." He held out a slim booklet which proved to be an air ticket, Newcastle to Heathrow.

"There's some damn meeting been arranged here which I shall have to go to after this race," he explained. "And I won't be able to catch the plane. I've only just found out and—it's most annoying. There's a later train. . . . I particularly want to get to London tonight."

"Done," I said. "Suits me fine."

He smiled, still frowning simultaneously. "Thanks. And here are the keys to my car. It's in the multistory park opposite the Europa building." He told me its number and position. "Drive yourself home."

"I'll drive to your house and leave the car there," I said. "Easier than bringing it over tomorrow."

"If you're sure. . . ." I nodded, giving him my train ticket.

"A friend who lives up here was going to run me back to the airport," he said. "I'll get him to take you instead."

"Have you heard from your wife?" I asked.

"That's just it. She wrote to say we'd have a trial reconciliation and she'd be coming home today. If I stay away all night, she'll never believe I had a good reason. She'll be gone again."

"Miss the meeting," I suggested.

"It's too important, especially now I've got your help. I suppose you couldn't explain to her, if she's there, that I'm on my way?"

"Of course," I said.

So the friend whisked me off to the airport, and I flew to Heathrow, collected the car, drove to Hampstead, explained to Mrs. Gibbons, who promised to wait, and arrived home two and a half hours early. Elizabeth was pleased, even if Mrs. Woodward wasn't.

Sunday morning. Elizabeth's mother didn't come.

Ten-fifteen, ten-thirty. Nothing. At eleven someone telephoned from the health farm and said they were so sorry, my mother-in-law was in bed with a virus infection, nothing serious, don't worry, she would ring her daughter as soon as she was a little better.

I told Elizabeth. "Oh, well," she said philosophically, "we'll have a nice cozy day on our own."

I smiled at her and kept the shocking disappointment out of my face.

"Do you think Sue Davis would pop along for a moment while I get us some whiskey?" I asked.

"She'd get it for us."

"I'd like to stretch my legs. . . ."

She smiled understandingly and rang Sue, who came at

twelve with flour down the sides of her jeans. I hurried round corners to the nearest phone box and gave the Huntersons' number. The bell rang there again and again, but no one answered. Without much hope I got the number of Virginia Water station and rang there: no, they said, there was no young woman waiting outside in a station wagon. They hadn't seen one all morning. I asked for the Huntersons' number again. Again, no reply.

Feeling flat, I walked back to our local pub and bought the whiskey, and tried yet again on the telephone too publicly installed in the passage there.

No answer. No Gail.

I went home.

Sue Davis had read out to Elizabeth my piece in the *Blaze*.

"Straight between the eyeballs," she observed cheerfully. "I must say, Ty, no one would connect the punch you pack in that paper with the you we know."

"What's wrong with the him you know?" asked Elizabeth with real anxiety under the surface gaiety. She hated people to think me weak for staying at home with her. She never told anyone how much nursing she needed from me, always pretended Mrs. Woodward did everything. She seemed to think that what I did for her would appear unmanly to others; she wanted in public a masculine never-touch-the-dishes husband, and since it made her happy I played that role except when we were alone.

"Nothing's wrong with him," Sue protested. She looked me over carefully. "Nothing at all."

"What did you mean, then?" Elizabeth was smiling still, but she wanted an answer.

"Oh . . . only that this Ty is so quiet, and that one"—she

pointed to the paper—"bursts the eardrums." She put her head on one side, summing me up, then turned to Elizabeth with the best of motives and said, "This one is so gentle. That one is tough."

"Gentle nothing," I said, seeing the distress under Elizabeth's laugh. "When you aren't here, Sue, I throw her round the room and black her eyes regularly on Fridays." Elizabeth relaxed, liking that. "Stay for a drink," I suggested to Sue, "now that I've fetched it."

She went, however, back to her half-baked Yorkshire pudding, and I avoided discussing what she had said by going out to the kitchen and rustling up some omelets for lunch. Elizabeth particularly liked them, and could eat hers with the new feeding gadget, up to a point. I helped her when her wrist tired, and made some coffee and fixed her mug in its holder.

"Do you really know where the horse is?" she asked.

"Tiddely Pom? Yes, of course."

"Where is it?"

"Dark and deadly secret, honey," I said. "I can't tell anyone, even you."

"Oh, go on," she urged. "You know I won't tell either."

"I'll tell you next Sunday."

Her nose wrinkled. "Thanks for nothing." The pump heaved away, giving her breath. "You don't think anyone would try to . . . well . . . *make* you tell. Where he is, I mean." More worry, more anxiety. She couldn't help it. She was always on the edge of a precipice, always on the distant lookout for anything which would knock her over.

"Of course not, honey. How could they?"

"I don't know," she said; but her eyes were full of horrors.

"Stop fussing," I said with a smile. "If anyone threatened me with anything really nasty, I'd say quick enough where he is.

No horse is worth getting in too deep for." Echoes of Dembley. The matrix which nurtured the germ. No one would sacrifice himself or his family for the sake of running a horse.

Elizabeth detected the truth in my voice and was satisfied. She switched on the television and watched some fearful old movie which bored me to death. Three o'clock came and went. Even if I'd gone to Virginia Water, I would have been on the way back again. And I'd had Friday night. Rare unexpected Friday night. Trouble was, the appetite grew on what it fed on, as someone else once said. The next Sunday was at the wrong end of a telescope.

Drinks, supper, jobs for Elizabeth, bed. No one else called, no one telephoned. It crossed my mind once or twice, as I lazed in the armchair in our customary closed-in little world, that perhaps the challenge implicit in my column had stirred up, somewhere, a hive of bees.

Buzz buzz, busy little bees. Buzz around the *Blaze*. And don't sting me.

I spent all Monday in and around the flat. Washed the van, wrote letters, bought some socks, kept off race trains from Leicester.

Derry telephoned twice, to tell me (a) that Tiddely Pom was flourishing, and (b) the Roncey children had sent him a stick of peppermint rock.

"Big deal," I said.

"Not bad kids."

"You'll enjoy fetching them."

He blew a raspberry and hung up.

Tuesday morning I walked to the office. One of those brownish late-November days, with saturated air and a sour

scowl of fog to come. Lights shone out brightly at 11 A.M.
People hurried along Fleet Street with pinched mean eyes,
working out whose neck to scrunch on the next rung of the
ladder, and someone bought a blind man's matches with a poker
chip.

Luke-John and Derry wore moods to match.

"What's the matter?" I asked mildly.

"Nothing's happened," Derry said.

"So?"

"So where's our reaction?" Luke-John inquired angrily. "Not
a letter. No one's phoned, even. Unless"—he brightened—"unless Charlie Boston's boys have called on you with a few more
threats?"

"They have not."

Relapse into gloom for the sports desk. I alone wasn't sorry
the article had fallen with a dull thud. If it had. I thought it
was too soon to be sure. I said so.

"Hope you're right, Ty," Luke-John said skeptically. "Hope
it hasn't all been a coincidence—Bert Checkov and the nonstarters. Hope the *Blaze* hasn't wasted its time and money for
nothing on Tiddely Pom."

"Charlie Boston's boys were not a coincidence."

"I suppose not." Luke-John sounded as though he thought I
might have misunderstood what the Boston boys had said.

"Did your friend in Manchester find out any more about
Charlie B.?" I asked.

Luke-John shrugged. "Only that there was some talk about
his chain of betting shops being taken over by a bigger concern.
But it doesn't seem to have happened. He is still there, anyway,
running the show."

"Which bigger concern?"

"Don't know."

To pass the time, we dialed four of the biggest London bookmaking businesses which had chains of betting shops all over the country. None of them admitted any immediate interest in buying out Charlie Boston. But one man was hesitant, and when I pressed him he said, "We did put out a feeler, about a year ago. We understood there was a foreign buyer also interested. But Boston decided to remain independent and turned down both offers."

"Thanks," I said, and Luke-John commented that that took us a long way, didn't it. He turned his attention crossly to a pile of letters which had flooded in contradicting one of the football writers, and Derry began to assess the form for the big race on Boxing Day. All over the vast office space the Tuesday picking of teeth and scratching of scabs proceeded without haste, the slow week still slumbering. Tuesday was gossip day. Wednesday, planning. Thursday, writing. Friday, editing. Saturday, printing. Sunday, *Blaze* away. And on Mondays the worked-on columns lit real fires or wrapped up fish-and-chips. No immortality for a journalist.

Tuesday was also *Tally* day. Neither at home nor at the office had a copy come for me by post. I went downstairs to the next-door magazine stand, bought one, and went back inside the *Blaze*.

The pictures were offbeat and rather good, the whole article well presented. One had to admit that Shankerton knew his stuff. I forgave him his liberties with my syntax.

I picked up Derry's telephone and got through to the *Tally* dispatch department. As expected, they didn't send free copies to the subjects of any articles: not their policy. Would they send them? Oh, sure, give us the addresses, we'll let you have the bill. I gave them the six addresses, Huntersons, Ronceys, Sandy Willis, Colly Gibbons, Dermot Finnegan, Willy Ondroy.

Derry picked up the magazine and plodded through the article, reading at one-third Luke-John's wide-angled speed.

"Deep, deep," he said ironically, putting it down. "One hundred and fifty fathoms."

"Sixty will go in tax."

"A hard life." Derry sighed. "But if you hadn't picked on Roncey, we would never have cottoned on to this nonstarter racket."

Nor would I have had any cracked ribs. With them, though, the worst was over. Only coughing, sneezing, laughing, and taking running jumps were sharply undesirable. I had stopped eating Elizabeth's pills. In another week, the cracks would have knitted.

"Be seeing you," I said to Derry. Luke-John waved a freckled farewell hand. Carrying *Tally,* I went down in the lift and turned out of the front door up toward the Strand, bound for a delicatessen shop that sold Austrian apple cake which Elizabeth liked.

Bought the cake. Came out into the street. Heard a voice in my ear. Felt a sharp prick through my coat abeam the first lumbar vertebra.

"It's a knife, Mr. Tyrone."

I stood quite still. People could be stabbed to death in busy streets and no one noticed until the body cluttered up the fairway. Killers vanished into crowds with depressing regularity.

"What do you want?" I said.

"Just stay where you are."

Standing on the Fleet Street pavement, holding a magazine and a box of apple cake. Just stay where you are. For how long?

"For how long?" I said.

He didn't answer. But he was still there, because his knife

was. We stood where we were for all of two minutes. Then a black Rolls came to a silent halt at the curb directly opposite where I stood. The door to the back seat swung open.

"Get in," said the voice behind me.

I got in. There was a chauffeur driving, all black uniform and a stolid acne-scarred neck. The man with the knife climbed in after me and settled by my side. I glanced at him, knew I'd seen him somewhere before, didn't know where. I put *Tally* and the apple cake carefully on the floor. Sat back. Went for a ride.

Ten

We turned north into the Aldwych and up Drury Lane to St. Giles' Circus. I made no move toward escape, although we stopped several times at traffic lights. My companion watched me warily, and I worked on where I had seen him before and still came up with nothing. Up Tottenham Court Road. Left, right, left again. Straight into Regent's Park and around the semicircle. Stopped smoothly at the turnstile entrance to the Zoo.

"Inside," said my companion, nodding.

We stepped out of the car, and the chauffeur quietly drove off.

"You can pay," I remarked.

He gave me a quick glance, tried to juggle the money out of his pocket one-handed, and found he couldn't manage it if he was to be of any use with his knife.

"No," he said. "You pay. For us both."

I paid, almost smiling. He was nowhere near as dangerous as he wanted to be thought.

We checked through the turnstiles. "Where now?" I said.

"Straight ahead. I'll tell you."

The Zoo was nearly empty. On that oily November Tuesday lunchtime, not even the usual busloads from schools. Birds shrieked mournfully from the aviary and a notice board said the vultures would be fed at three.

A man in a dark overcoat and black homburg hat was sitting on a seat looking toward the lions' outdoor compounds. The cages were empty. The sun-loving lions were inside under the sun lamps.

"Over there," said my companion, nodding.

We walked across. The man in the black homburg watched us come. Every line of his clothes and posture spoke of money, authority, and high social status, and his manner of irritating superiority would have done credit to the Foreign Office. As Dembley had said, his subject matter was wildly at variance with his appearance.

"Did you have any trouble?" he asked.

"None at all," said the knife man smugly.

A bleak expression crept into pale gray eyes as cold as the stratosphere. "I am not pleased to hear it."

The accent in his voice was definite but difficult. A thickening of some consonants, a clipping of some vowels.

"Go away, now," he said to the knife man. "And wait."

My nondescript abductor in his nondescript raincoat nodded briefly and walked away, and I nearly remembered where I'd seen him. Recollection floated up, but not far enough.

"You chose to come," the man in the homburg said flatly.

"Yes and no."

He stood up. My height, but thicker. Yellowish skin, smooth except for a maze of wrinkles around his eyes. What I could see of his hair was nearly blond, and I put his age down roughly as five or six years older than myself.

"It is cold outside. We will go in."

I walked around with him inside the big cats' house, where the strong feral smell seemed an appropriate background to the proceedings. I could guess what he wanted. Not to kill: that could have been done in Fleet Street or anywhere on the way. To extort. The only question was how.

"You show too little surprise," he said.

"We were waiting for some—reaction. Expecting it."

"I see." He was silent, working it out. A bored-looking tiger blinked at us lazily, claws sheathed inside rounded pads, tail swinging a fraction from side to side. I sneered at him. He turned and walked three paces and three paces back, around and around, going nowhere.

"Was last week's reaction not enough for you?"

"Very useful," I commented. "Led us straight to Charlie Boston. So kind of you to ask. That makes you a sidekick of his."

He gave me a frosty glare. "I *employ* Boston."

I looked down, not answering. If his pride was as easily stung as that, he might give me more answers than I gave him.

"When I heard about it, I disapproved of what they did on the train. Now I am not so sure." His voice was quiet again, the voice of culture, diplomacy, tact.

"You didn't order it, then?"

"I did not."

I ran my hand along the thick metal bar which kept visitors four feet away from the animals' cages. The tiger looked tame, too gentle to kill. Too indifferent to maul, to maim, to scrape to the bone.

"You know what we want," said the polite tiger by my side. "We want to know where you have hidden the horse."

"Why?" I said.

He merely blinked at me.

I sighed. "What good will it do you? Do you still seriously intend to try to prevent it from running? You would be much wiser to forget the whole thing and quietly fold your tent and steal away."

"You will leave that decision entirely to me." Again the pride stuck out a mile. I didn't like it. Few enemies were as

ruthless as those who feared a loss of face. I began to consider
before how wide an acquaintanceship the face had to be pre-
served. The wider, the worse for me.

"Where is it?"

"Tiddely Pom?" I said.

"Tiddely Pom." He repeated the name with fastidious disgust. "Yes."

"Quite safe."

"Mr. Tyrone, stop playing games. You cannot hide forever
from Charlie Boston."

I was silent. The tiger yawned, showing a full set of fangs.
Nasty.

"They could do more damage next time," he said.

I looked at him curiously, wondering if he seriously thought I
would crumble under so vague a threat. He stared straight back
and was unmoved when I didn't answer. My heart sank slightly.
More to come.

"I suspected," he said conversationally, "when I heard that
you were seen at Plumpton races the day following Boston's ill-
judged attack, that physical pressure would run us into too
much difficulty in your case. I see that this suspicion was correct.
I directed that a different lever should be found. We have, of
course, found it. And you will tell us where the horse is
hidden."

He took out the black crocodile wallet and removed from it a
small sheet of paper, folded once. He gave it to me. I looked.
He saw the deep shock in my face and he smiled in satisfaction.

It was a photocopy of the bill of the hotel where I had stayed
with Gail. Mr. and Mrs. Tyrone, one double room.

"So you see, Mr. Tyrone, that if you wish to keep this interesting item of news from your wife, you must give us the
address we ask."

My mind tumbled over and over like a dry-cleaning machine, and not a useful thought came out.

"So quiet, Mr. Tyrone? You really don't like that, do you? So you will tell us. You would not want your wife to divorce you, I am sure. And you have taken such pains to deceive her that we are certain you know she would throw you out if she discovered this. . . ." He pointed to the bill. "How would she like to know that your mistress is colored? We have other dates, too. Last Sunday week, and the Sunday before that. Your wife will be told it all. Wealthy women will not stand for this sort of thing, you know."

I wondered numbly how much Gail had sold me for.

"Come along, Mr. Tyrone. The address."

"I need time," I said dully.

"That's right," he said calmly. "It takes time to sink in properly, doesn't it? Of course you can have time. Six hours. You will telephone to us at precisely seven o'clock this evening." He gave me a plain white card with numbers on it. "Six hours is all, Mr. Tyrone. After that, the information will be on its way to your wife, and you will not be able to stop it. Do you clearly understand?"

"Yes." I said. The tiger sat down and shut its eyes. Sympathetic.

"I thought you would." He moved away from me toward the door. "Seven o'clock precisely. Good day, Mr. Tyrone."

With erect easy assurance he walked straight out of the cat house, turned a corner, and was gone. My feet seemed to have become disconnected from my body. I was going through the disjointed floating feeling of irretrievable disaster. A disbelieving part of my mind said that if I stayed quite still the nutcracker situation would go away.

It didn't, of course. But after a while I began to think normally instead of in emotional shock waves; began to look for a hole in the net. I walked slowly away from the tiger, out into the unwholesome air, and down toward the gate, all my attention turned inward. Out of the corner of my eye I half caught sight of my abductor in his raincoat standing up a side path looking into an apparently empty wire-netted compound, and when I'd gone out of the turnstile onto the road it hit me with a thump where I'd seen him before. So significant a thump that I came to a rocking halt. Much had urgently to be understood.

I had seen him at King's Cross station while I waited for Gail. He had been standing near me; had watched her all the way from the underground until she had reached me. Looking for a lever. Finding it.

To be watching me at King's Cross, he must have followed me from the *Blaze*.

Today he had picked me up outside the *Blaze*.

I walked on slowly, thinking about it. From King's Cross in the morning I had gone on the train to Newcastle, but I hadn't come back on my return ticket. Colly Gibbons had. I'd taken that unexpected roundabout route home, and somewhere, maybe back at Newcastle races, I'd shaken off my tail.

Someone also must either have followed Gail or have gone straight into the hotel to see her after I left. I balked at thinking she would sell me out with my imprint still on our shared sheets. But maybe she would. It depended on how much they had offered her, I supposed. Five hundred would have tempted her mercenary heart too far.

No one but Gail could have got a receipt from the hotel. No one but Gail knew of the two Sunday afternoons. No one but Gail thought my wife was rich. I coldly faced the conclusion that I had meant little to her. Very little indeed. My true deserts. I had sought her out because she could dispense sex without involvement. She had been consistent. She owed me nothing at all.

I reached the corner and instinctively turned my plodding steps toward home. Not for twenty paces did I realize that this was a desperate mistake.

Gail didn't know where I lived. She couldn't have told them. They didn't know the facts about Elizabeth; they thought she was a rich woman who would divorce me. *They picked me up this morning outside the* Blaze. . . . At the same weary pace I turned right at the next crossing.

If the man in the black homburg didn't know where I lived, the raincoat would be following to find out. Around the next corner I stopped and looked back through the thick branches of a may bush, and there he was, hurrying. I went on slowly as before, heading imperceptibly toward Fleet Street.

The Homburg Hat had been bluffing. He couldn't tell Elizabeth about Gail, because he didn't know where to find her. Ex-directory telephone. My address in none of the reference books. By sheer luck I twice hadn't led them straight to my own front door.

All the same, it couldn't go on forever. Even if I fooled them until after the Lamplighter, one day, somehow, they would tell her what I'd done.

First they buy you, then they blackmail, Bert Checkov had said. Buy Gail, blackmail me. All of a piece. I thought about blackmail for three long miles back to the *Blaze*.

Luke-John and Derry were surprised to see me back. They made no comment on a change in my appearance. I supposed the inner turmoil didn't show.

"Have any of the crime reporters a decent pull with the police?" I asked.

Derry said, "Jimmy Sienna might have. What do you want?"

"To trace a car number."

"Someone bashed that ancient van of yours?" Luke-John asked uninterestedly.

"Hit and run," I agreed with distant accuracy.

"We can always try," Derry said with typical helpfulness. "Give me the number, and I'll go and ask him."

I wrote down for him the registration number of Homburg Hat's Silver Wraith.

"A London number," Derry remarked. "That might make it easier." He took off across the room to the crime desk and consulted a mountainous young man with red hair.

I strolled over to the deserted news desk and, with a veneer of unconcern over a thumping heart, dialed the number Homburg Hat had told me to ring at seven. It was three-eighteen. More than two hours gone out of six.

A woman answered, sounding surprised.

"Are you sure you have the right number?" she said.

I read it out to her.

"Yes, that's right. How funny."

"Why is it funny?"

"Well, this is a public phone box. I had just shut the door and was going to make a call when the phone started ringing. . . . Are you *sure* you have the right number?"

"I can't have," I said. "Where is this phone box, exactly?"

"It's one of a row in Picadilly underground station."

I thanked her and rang off. Not much help.

Derry came back and said Jimmy Sienna was doing what he could; good job it was Tuesday, he was bored and wanted something to pass the time with.

I remembered that I had left my copy of *Tally* and Elizabeth's apple cake on the floor of the Rolls. Debated whether or not to get replacements. Decided there was no harm in it, and went out and bought them. I didn't see Raincoat, but that didn't mean he wasn't there, or that they hadn't swapped him for someone I wouldn't know.

Derry said Jimmy Sienna's police friend was checking the registration number but would use his discretion as to whether it was suitable to pass on to the *Blaze*. I sat on the side of Derry's desk and bit my nails.

Outside, the fog which had been threatening all day slowly cleared right away. It would. I thought about unobserved exits under the bright Fleet Street lights.

At five Luke-John said he was going home, and Derry apologetically followed. I transferred myself to Jimmy Sienna's desk and bit my nails there instead. When he, too, was lumbering to his feet to leave, his telephone finally rang. He listened, thanked, scribbled.

"There you are," he said to me. "And good luck with the insurance. You'll need it."

I read what he'd written. The Silver Wraith's number had been allocated to an organization called Hire Cars Lucullus.

I left the *Blaze* via the roof. *Tally*, apple cake, and mending ribs complicated the journey, but after circumventing ventilation shafts and dividing walls I walked sedately in through the fire door of the next-door newspaper, a popular daily in the full flood of going to press.

No one asked me what I was doing. I went down in the lift to the basement and out to the huge garage at the rear where rows of yellow vans stood ready to take the wet-ink bundles off to the trains. I knew one of the drivers slightly, and asked him for a lift.

"Sure, if you want Paddington."

"I do." I wanted anywhere he was going.

"Hop in, then."

I hopped in, and after he was loaded he drove briskly out of the garage, one indistinguishable van among a procession. I stayed with him to Paddington, thanked him, and backtracked home on the underground, as certain as I could be that no one had followed.

I beat Mrs. Woodward to six by two minutes but had no heart for the game.

From six-thirty to seven I sat in the armchair holding a glass of whiskey and looking at Elizabeth, trying to make up a beleaguered mind.

"Something's worrying you, Ty," she said, with her ultra-sensitive feeling for trouble.

"No, honey."

The hands galloped around the clock. At seven o'clock precisely I sat absolutely still and did nothing at all. At five past I found I had clenched my teeth so hard that I was grinding them. I imagined the telephone box in Piccadilly Circus, with Homburg Hat or Raincoat or the chauffeur waiting inside it. Tiddely Pom was nothing compared with Elizabeth's peace of mind, and yet I didn't pick up the receiver. From seven onward the clock hands crawled.

At half past Elizabeth said again, with detectable fear, "Ty, there *is* something wrong. You never look so—so bleak."

I made a great effort to smile at her as usual, but she wasn't convinced. I looked down at my hands and said with hopeless pain, "Honey, how much would it hurt you if I went—and slept with a girl?"

There was no answer. After an unbearable interval I dragged my head up to look at her. Tears were running down her cheeks. She was swallowing, trying to speak.

From long, long habit I pulled a tissue out of the box and wiped her eyes, which she couldn't do for herself.

"I'm sorry," I said uselessly. "I'm sorry."

"Ty . . ." She never had enough breath for weeping. Her mouth strained open in her need for more air.

"Honey, don't cry. Don't cry. Forget I said it. You know I love you, I'd never leave you. Elizabeth, honey, dear Elizabeth, don't cry."

I wiped her eyes again and cursed the whim which had sent me down to the Huntersons' for *Tally.* I could have managed without Gail. Without anyone. I had managed without for most of eleven years.

"Ty." The tears had stopped. Her face looked less strained. "Ty." She gulped, fighting for more breath. "I can't bear to think about it."

I stood beside her, holding the tissue, wishing she didn't have to.

"We never talk about sex," she said. The Spiroshell heaved up her chest, let it drop, rhythmically. "I don't want it any more . . . you know that . . . but sometimes I remember . . . how you taught me to like it. . . ." Two more tears welled up. I wiped them away. She said, "I haven't ever asked you . . . about girls. . . . I couldn't, somehow."

"No," I said slowly.

"I've wondered sometimes . . . if you ever have, I mean . . . but I didn't really want to know. . . . I know I would be too jealous. . . . I decided I'd never ask you . . . because I wouldn't want you to say yes . . . and yet I know that's selfish. . . . I've always been told men are different, they need women more . . . is it true?"

"Elizabeth," I said helplessly.

"I didn't expect you ever to say anything . . . after all these

years. . . . Yes, I would be hurt, if I knew. . . . I couldn't
help it. . . . Why did you ask me? I wish you hadn't."

"I would never have said anything," I said with regret, "but
someone is trying to blackmail me."

"Then . . . you *have*. . . ."

"I'm afraid so."

"Oh." She shut her eyes. "I see."

I waited, hating myself. The tears were over. She never cried
for long. She physically couldn't. If she progressed into one of
her rare bursts of rebellious anger, she would utterly exhaust
herself. Most wives could scream or throw things. Elizabeth's
furies were the worse for being impotent. It must have been
touch and go, because when she spoke her voice was low, thick,
and deadly quiet.

"I suppose you couldn't afford to be blackmailed."

"No one can."

"I know it's unreasonable of me to wish you hadn't told me.
To wish you hadn't done it at all. Any man who stays with a
paralyzed wife ought to have *something*. . . . So many of them
pack up and leave altogether. . . . I know you say you never
will and I do mostly believe it, but I must be such an unbearable
burden to you. . . ."

"That," I said truthfully, "is just not true."

"It must be. Don't tell me . . . about the girl."

"If I don't, the blackmailer will."

"All right . . . get it over quickly. . . ."

I got it over quickly. Briefly. No details. Hated myself for
having to tell her, and knew that if I hadn't, Homburg Hat
wouldn't have stopped his leverage with the whereabouts of
Tiddely Pom. Blackmailers never did. Don't sell your soul, Bert
Checkov said. Don't sell your column. Sacrifice your wife's
peace instead.

"Will you see her again?" she asked.

"No."

"Or . . . anyone else?"

"No."

"I expect you will," she said. "Only if you do . . . don't tell me. . . . Unless of course someone tries to blackmail you again. . . ."

I winced at the bitterness in her voice. Reason might tell her that total lifelong celibacy was a lot to demand, but emotion had practically nothing to do with reason, and the tearing emotions of any ordinary wife on finding her husband unfaithful hadn't atrophied along with her muscles. I hadn't expected much else. She would have to have been a saint or a cynic to have laughed it off without a pang, and she was neither of those things, just a normal human being trapped in an abnormal situation. I wondered how suspicious she would be in future of my most innocent absences; how much she would suffer when I was away. Reassurance, always tricky, was going to be doubly difficult.

She was very quiet and depressed all evening. She wouldn't have any supper, wouldn't eat the apple cake. When I washed her and did the rubs and the other intimate jobs, I could almost feel her thinking about the other body my hands had touched. Hands, and much else. She looked sick and strained and, for almost the first time since her illness, embarrassed. If she could have done without me that evening, she would have.

I said, meaning it, "I'm sorry, honey."

"Yes." She shut her eyes. "Life's just bloody, isn't it."

Eleven

The uncomfortable coolness between Elizabeth and myself persisted in the morning. I couldn't go on begging for a forgiveness she didn't feel. At ten I said I was going out, and saw her make the first heart-rending effort not to ask where.

Hire Cars Lucullus hung out in a small plushy office in Stratton Street, off Piccadilly. Royal-blue Wilton carpet, executive-type acre of polished desk, tasteful prints of vintage cars on dove-gray walls. Along one side, a wide gold upholstered bench for wide gold upholstered clients. Behind the desk, a deferential young man with Uriah Heep eyes.

For him I adopted a languid voice and my best imitation of the Homburg Hat manners. I had, I explained, left some property in one of his firm's cars, and I hoped he could help me get it back.

We established gradually that no, I had not hired one of their cars, and no, I did not know the name of the man who had; he had merely been so kind as to give me a lift. Yesterday.

Ah. Then had I any idea which car. . . ?

A Rolls-Royce, a Silver Wraith.

They had four of those. He briefly checked a ledger, though I suspected he didn't need to. All four had been out on hire yesterday. Could I describe the man who had given me a lift?

"Certainly. Tallish, blondish, wearing a black homburg. Not English. Possibly South African."

"Ah. Yes." He had no need to consult the ledger this time. He put his spread fingertips carefully down on the desk. "I regret, sir, I cannot give you his name."

"But surely you keep records?"

"This gentleman puts great store on privacy. We have been instructed not to give his name or address to anyone."

"Isn't that a bit odd?" I said, raising eyebrows.

He considered judicially. "He is a regular customer. We would, of course, give him any service he asked for, without question."

"I suppose it wouldn't be possible to—um—purchase the information?"

He tried to work some shock into his deference. It was barely skin-deep.

"Was your lost property very valuable?" he asked.

Tally and apple cake. "Very," I said.

"Then I am sure our client will return it to us. If you would let us have your own name and address, perhaps we could let you know?"

"I said the first name I thought of, which nearly came out as Kempton Park. "Kempton Jones. 31 Cornwall Street."

He wrote it down carefully on a scratch pad. When he had finished, I waited. We both waited.

After a decent interval he said, "Of course, if it is really important, you could ask in the garage. . . . They would let you know as soon as the car comes in, whether your property is still in it."

"And the garage is where?" The only listed number and address of the Lucullus cars had been the office in Stratton Street.

He studied his fingertips. I produced my wallet and resignedly sorted out two fivers. The twenty-five for the book-

maker's clerk's information about Charlie Boston's boys I had
put down to expenses and the *Blaze* had paid. This time I could
be on my own. Ten pounds represented six weeks' whiskey, a
month's electricity, three and a half days of Mrs. Woodward,
one and a half weeks' rent.

He took it greedily, nodded, gave me a hypocritical obsequi-
ous smile, and said, "Radnor Mews, Lancaster Gate."

"Thanks."

"You do understand, sir, that it's more than my job is worth
to give you our client's name?"

"I understand," I said. "Principles are pretty things."

Principles were luckily not so strongly held in Radnor Mews.
The foreman sized me up and another tenner changed hands.
Better value for money this time.

"The chauffeur comes here to collect the car, see? We never
deliver it or supply a driver. Unusual, that. Still, the client is
always right, as long as he pays for it, I always say. This
foreigner, see, he likes to travel in style when he comes over
here. Course, most of our trade is like that. Americans, mostly.
They hire a car and a driver for a week, two weeks, maybe
three. We drive them all over, see, Stratford, Broadway, the
Cotswold run most often, and Scotland a good deal, too. Never
have all the cars in here at once; there'd hardly be room, see,
four Silver Wraiths for a start, and then two Austin Princesses,
and three Bentleys and a couple of large Wolseleys."

I brought him back gently to the Silver Wraith in question.

"I'm telling you, aren't I?" he protested. "This foreign chap,
he takes a car—always a Rolls, mind you, though of course not
always the same one—whenever he's over here. Started coming
just over a year ago, I'd say. Been back several times, usually
just for three or four days. Longer this time, I'd say. Let's see,
the chauffeur came for a car last week. I could look it up. . . .

Wednesday. Yes, that's right. What they do, see, is the chauffeur flies over first, picks up the car, and then drives out to Heathrow to fetch his gent off the next flight. Neat, that. Shows money, that does."

"Do you know where they fly from?"

"From? Which country? Not exactly. Mind, I think it varies. I know once it was Germany. But usually further than that, from somewhere hot. The chauffeur isn't exactly chatty, but he's always complaining how cold it is here."

"What is the client's name?" I asked patiently.

"Oh, sure, hang on a minute. We always put the booking in the chauffeur's name, see; it's easier, being Ross. His gent's name is something chronic. I'll have to look back."

He went into his little boarded cubicle of an office and looked back. It took him nearly twenty minutes, by which time he was growing restive. I waited, making it plain I would wait all day. For ten pounds he could keep on looking. He was almost as relieved as I was when he found it.

"Here it is, look." He showed me a page in a ledger, pointing to a name with a black-rimmed fingernail. "That one."

There was a pronunciation problem, as he'd said.

Vjoersterod.

"Ross is easier," the foreman repeated. "We always put Ross."

"Much easier," I agreed. "Do you know where I could find them, or where they keep the car while they're in England?"

He sniffed meditatively, shutting the ledger with his finger in the page.

"Can't say as I do, really. Always a pretty fair mileage on the clock, though. Goes a fair way in the three or four days, see? But then that's regular with our cars, most times. Mind you, I wouldn't say that this Ross and his gent go up to Scotland, not as far as that."

"Birmingham?" I suggested.

"Easily. Could be, easily. Always comes back immaculate, I'll say that for Ross. Always clean as a whistle. Why don't you ask in the front office, if you want to find them?"

"They said they couldn't help me."

"That smarmy crumb," he said disgustedly. "I'll bet he knows, though. Give him his due, he's good at that job, but he'd sell his grandmother if the price was right."

I started to walk in the general direction of Fleet Street, thinking. Vjoersterod had to be the real name of Homburg Hat. Too weird to be an alias. Also, the first time he had hired a Silver Wraith from Hire Cars Lucullus he would have to have produced cast-iron references and a passport at least. The smarmy crumb was no fool. He wouldn't let five thousand pounds' worth of machinery be driven away without being certain he would get it back.

Vjoersterod. South African of Afrikaner stock.

Nothing like Fleet Street if one wanted information. The only trouble was, the man who might have heard of Vjoersterod worked on the racing page of a deadly rival to the *Blaze*. I turned in to the first telephone box and rang his office. Sure, he agreed cautiously, he would meet me in the Devereux for a pint and a sandwich. He coped manfully with stifling any too open speculation about what I wanted. I smiled, and crossed the road to catch a bus. A case of who pumped who. He would be trying to find out what story I was working on, and Luke-John would be slightly displeased if he was successful and scooped the *Blaze*.

Luke-John and Derry were both among the crowd in the Devereux. Not so, Mike de Jong. I drank a half pint while Luke-John asked me what I planned to write for Sunday.

"An account of the Lamplighter, I suppose."

"Derry can do that."

I lowered my glass, shrugging. "If you like."

"Then you," said Luke-John, "can do another follow-up to the Tiddely Pom business. Whether he wins or loses, I mean. Give us a puff for getting him to the starting gate."

"He isn't there yet," I pointed out.

Luke-John sniffed impatiently. "There hasn't been a vestige of trouble. No reaction at all. We've frightened them off, that's what's happened."

I shook my head, wishing we had. Asked about the reports on Tiddely Pom and the Roncey children.

"All O.K.," said Derry cheerfully. "Everything going smoothly."

Mike de Jong appeared in the doorway, a quick dark intense man with double-strength glasses and a fringe of black beard outlining his jaw. Caution rolled over him like a sea mist when he saw who I was with, and most of the purposefulness drained out of his stride. It took much maneuvering to get Luke-John and Derry to go into the further bar to eat without me, and Luke-John left looking back over his shoulder with smoldering suspicion, wanting to know why.

Mike joined me, his sharp face alight with appreciation. "Keeping secrets from the boss, eh?"

"Sometimes he's butterfingered with other people's TNT."

Mike laughed. The cogs whirred around in his high-speed brain. "So what you want is private? Not for the *Blaze*?"

I dodged a direct answer. "What I want is very simple. Just anything you may have heard about a fellow countryman of yours."

"Who?" His accent was a carbon copy, clipped and flat.

"A man called Vjoersterod."

There was a tiny pause while the name sank in, and then he

choked on his beer. Recovered, and pretended someone had jogged his elbow. Made a playing-for-time fuss about brushing six scattered drops off his trouser leg. Finally he ran out of alibis and looked back at my face.

"Vjoersterod?" His pronunciation was subtly different from mine. The real thing.

"That's right," I agreed.

"Yes. . . . Well, Ty—why do you ask me about him?"

"Just curiosity."

He was silent for thirty seconds. Then he said carefully again, "Why are you asking about him?" Who pumped who.

"Oh, come on," I said in exasperation. "What's the big mystery? All I want is a bit of gen on a harmless chap who goes racing occasionally."

"*Harmless?* You must be mad."

"Why?" I sounded innocently puzzled.

"Because he's—" He hesitated, decided I wasn't on to a story, and turned thoroughly helpful. "Look here, Ty, I'll give you a tip, free, gratis, and for nothing. Just steer clear of anything to do with that man. He's poison."

"In what way?"

"He's a bookmaker, back home. Very big business, with branches in all the big cities and a whole group of them round Johannesburg. Respectable enough on the surface. Thousands of perfectly ordinary people bet with him. But there have been some dreadful rumors. . . ."

"About what?"

"Oh, blackmail, extortion, general high-powered thuggery. Believe me, he is not good news."

"Then why don't the police. . . ?" I suggested tentatively.

"Why don't they? Don't be so naïve, Ty. They can't find anyone to give evidence against him, of course."

I sighed. "He seemed so charming."

Mike's mouth fell open and his expression became acutely anxious.

"You've *met* him?"

"Yeah."

"Here . . . in England?"

"Well, yes, of course."

"Ty, for God's sake, keep away from him."

"I will," I said with feeling. "Thanks a lot, Mike. I'm truly grateful."

"I'd hate anyone I liked to tangle with Vjoersterod," he said, the genuine friendship standing out clear in his eyes, unexpectedly affecting. Then, with a born newspaperman's instinct for the main chance, a look of intense curiosity took over.

"What did he want to talk about with you?" he asked.

"I don't really know," I said, sounding puzzled.

"Is he going to get in touch with you again?"

"I don't know that, either."

"Hmm. . . . Give me a ring if he does, and I'll tell you something else."

"Tell me now." I tried hard to make it casual.

He considered, shrugged, and friendship won again over journalism. "All right. It's nothing much. Just that I, too, saw him here in England; must have been nine or ten months ago, back in the spring." He paused.

"In that case," I said, "whyever were you so horrified when I said I'd met him?"

"Because when I saw him he was in the buffet bar on a race train, talking to another press man. Bert Checkov."

With an enormous effort, I kept my mildly puzzled face intact.

Mike went on without a blink. "I warned Bert about him

later, just like I have you. In here, actually. Bert was pretty drunk. He was always pretty drunk after that."

"What did he say?" I asked.

"He said I was three months too late."

Mike didn't know any more. Bert had clammed up after that one indiscretion and had refused to elaborate or explain. When he fell out of the window, Mike had wondered. Violent and often unexplained deaths among people who had had dealings with Vjoersterod were not unknown, he said. When I said I had met Vjoersterod, it had shocked him. He was afraid for me. Afraid I could follow Bert down onto the pavement.

I put his mind at rest. After what he'd told me, I would be forewarned, I said.

"I wonder why he got his hooks into Bert," Mike said, his eyes on the middle distance, all the cogs whirring.

"I've no idea," I said, sighing, and distracted his attention to another half pint and a large ham sandwich. Luke-John's thin freckled face loomed over his shoulder, and he turned to him with a typical bounce, as if all his body were made of springs.

"So how's the Gospel Maker? What's cooking on the *Blaze*?"

Luke-John gave him a thin smile. He didn't care for his Fleet Street nickname, or for puns in general. Or, it seemed, for Mike de Jong's puns in particular. Mike received the message clearly, sketched me a farewell, and drifted over to another group.

"What did he want?" Luke-John asked sharply.

"Nothing," I said mildly. "Just saying hello."

Luke-John gave me a disillusioned look, but I knew very well that if I told him at that stage about Vjoersterod he would dig until he stumbled on the blackmail, dig again quite ruthlessly to find out how I could have been blackmailed, and then proceed to mastermind all subsequent inquiries with a stunning absence of discretion. Vjoersterod would hear his steamroller approach clean across the country. Luke-John was a brilliant sports editor. As a field marshal his casualty list would have been appalling. He and Derry drank around to closing time at three, by which time the crowd had reduced to Sunday writers only. I declined their invitation to go back with them to the doldrums of the office, and on reflection telephoned to the only member of the racing authorities I knew well enough for the purpose.

Eric Youll at thirty-seven was the youngest and newest of the three Stewards of the National Hunt Committee, the ruling body of steeplechasing. In two years, by natural progression, he would be Senior Steward. After that, reduced to the ranks until re-elected for another three-year term. As a Steward he made sense because until recently he had himself ridden as an amateur, and knew at first hand all the problems and mechanics of racing. I had written him up in the *Blaze* a few times and we had been friendly acquaintances for years. Whether he either could or would help me now was nonetheless open to doubt.

I had a good deal of trouble getting through to him, as he was a junior sprig in one of the grander merchant banks. Secretaries with bored voices urged me to make an appointment.

"Right now," I said, "will do very well."

After the initial shock the last voice conceded that right now Mr. Youll could just fit me in. When I got there, Mr. Youll was busily engaged in drinking a cup of tea and reading the *Sporting Life*. He put them both down without haste, stood up, and shook hands.

"This is unexpected," he said. "Come to borrow a million?"

"Tomorrow, maybe."

He smiled, told his secretary on the intercom to bring me some tea, offered me a cigarette, and leaned back in his chair, his manner throughout one of indecision and uncertainty. He was wary of me and of the purpose of my visit. I saw that uneasy expression almost every day of my life: the screen my racing friends erected when they weren't sure what I was after, the barrier that kept their secrets from publication. I didn't mind that sort of withdrawal. Understood it. Sympathized. And never printed anything private, if I could help it. There was a very fine edge to be walked when one's friends were one's raw material.

"Off the record," I assured him. "Take three deep breaths and relax."

He grinned and tension visibly left his body. "How can I help you, then?"

I waited until the tea had come and been drunk, and the latest racing news chewed over. Then, without making much of it, I asked him if he'd ever heard of a bookmaker called Vjoersterod.

His attention pinpointed itself with a jerk.

"Is that what you've come to ask?"

"For openers."

He drummed his fingers on the desk. "Someone showed me your column last week and the week before. . . . Stay out of it, Ty."

"If you racing bigwigs know what's going on and who is doing it, why don't you stop him?"

"How?"

The single word hung in the air, cooling. It told me a lot about the extent of their knowledge. They should have known how.

"Frankly," I said at last, "that's your job, not mine. You could of course ban all antepost betting, which would knock the fiddle stone dead."

"That would be highly unpopular with the Great British Public. Anyway, your articles have hit the antepost market badly enough as it is. One of the big firms was complaining to me bitterly about you a couple of hours ago. Their Lamplighter bets are down by more than twenty per cent."

"Then why don't they do something about Charlie Boston?"

He blinked. "Who?"

I took a quiet breath. "Well, now. . . . Just what do the Stewards know about Vjoersterod?"

"Who is Charlie Boston?"

"You first," I said.

"Don't you trust me?" He looked hurt.

"No," I said flatly. "You first."

He sighed and told me that all the Stewards knew about Vjoersterod was hearsay, and scanty at that. None of them had ever actually seen him, and wouldn't know him if they did. A member of the German horse-racing authorities had sent them a private warning that Vjoersterod was suspected of stage-managing a series of nonstarting antepost favorites in big races in Germany, and that they had heard rumors he was beginning to operate in England. Pursuit had almost cornered him in Germany. He was now moving on. The British Stewards had noted the alarming proportion of nonstarters in the past months and were sure the German authorities were right, but although they had tried to find out the facts from various owners and trainers, they had been met with only a brick wall of silence everywhere.

"It's a year since Vjoersterod came here first," I remarked. "A year ago he bought out Charlie Boston's string of betting shops round Birmingham and started raking in the dough. He also found a way to force Bert Checkov to write articles which persuaded antepost punters to believe they were on to a good thing. Vjoersterod chose a horse, Checkov wrote it up, Vjoersterod stopped it running, and, bingo, the deed was done."

His face was a mixture of astonishment and satisfaction. "Ty, are you sure of your facts?"

"Of course I am. If you ask me, both the bookmakers and the authorities have been dead slow on the trail."

"And how long exactly have you been on it?"

I grinned, conceding the point. I said, "I met Vjoersterod yesterday. I referred to Charlie Boston being his partner and he told me he owned Charlie Boston. Vjoersterod wanted to know where Tiddely Pom was."

He stared. "Would you—um—well, if necessary, testify to that?"

"Certainly. But it would be only my word against his. No corroboration."

"Better than anything we've had before."

"There might be a quicker way to get results, though."

"How?" he asked again.

"Find a way to shut Charlie Boston's shops, and you block off Vjoersterod's intakes. Without which there is no point in him waiting around to stop any favorites. If you can't get him convicted in the Courts, you might at least freeze him out, back to South Africa."

There was another long pause, during which he thought complicated thoughts. I waited, guessing what was in his mind. Eventually, he said it.

"How much do you want for your help?"

"An exclusive for the *Blaze*."

"As if I couldn't guess. . . ."

"It will do," I said, "if the *Blaze* can truthfully claim to have made the antepost market safe for punters to play in. No details. Just a few hints that but for the libel laws, all would and could be revealed."

"Whyever do you waste your time with that dreadful rag?" he exclaimed in exasperation.

"Good pay," I said. "It's a good paper to work for. And it suits me."

"I'll promise you one thing," he said, smiling. "If through you personally we get rid of Vjoersterod, I'll take it regularly."

From Eric Youll's bank, I went home. If the youngest Steward did his stuff, Vjoersterod's goose was on its way to the oven and would soon be cooked. He might of course one day read the *Blaze* and send someone to carve up the chef. It didn't trouble me much. I didn't believe it would happen.

Elizabeth had had Mrs. Woodward put her favorite rose-pink, white-embroidered sheets on the bed. I looked at her searchingly. Her hair had been done with particular care. Her make-up was flawless.

"You look pretty," I said tentatively.

Her expression was a mixture of relief and misery. I understood with a sudden rocking wince what had led her to such scenery painting: the increased fear that if she was bitchy I would leave her. No matter if I'd earned and deserved the rough side of her tongue; I had to be placated at all costs, to be held by the best she could do to appear attractive, to be obliquely invited, cajoled, entreated to stay.

"Did you have a good day?" Her voice sounded high and near to cracking point.

"Quite good. . . . How about a drink?"

She shook her head, but I poured her one all the same, and fixed it in the clip.

"I've asked Mrs. Woodward to find someone to come and sit with me in the evenings," she said. "So that you can go out more."

"I don't want to go out more," I protested.

"You must do."

"Well, I don't." I sat down in the armchair and took a hefty mouthful of nearly neat whiskey. At best, I thought, in an unbearable situation alcohol offered postponement. At worst, aggravation. And anyway it was too damned expensive, nowadays, to get drunk.

Elizabeth didn't answer. When I looked at her, I saw she was quietly crying again. The tears rolled down past her ears and into her hair. I took a tissue out of the box and dried them. Had she but known it, they were harder for me to bear than any amount of fury.

"I'm getting old," she said. "And you still look so young. You look . . . strong . . . and dark . . . and young."

"And you look pale and pretty and about fifteen. So stop fretting."

"How old is . . . that girl?"

"You said you didn't want to hear about her."

"I suppose I don't, really."

"Forget her," I said. "She is of no importance. She means nothing to me. Nothing at all." I sounded convincing, even to myself. I wished it were true. In spite of the scope of her betrayal, in a weak inner recess I ached to be able to sleep with her again. I sat with the whiskey glass in my hand and thought about her on the white rug and in her own bed and in the hotel, and suffered dismally from the prospect of the arid future.

After a while I pushed myself wearily to my feet and went to fix the supper. Fish again. Mean little bits of frozen plaice. I cooked and ate them with aversion and fed Elizabeth when her wrist tired on the gadget. All evening she kept up the pathetic attempt to be nice to me, thanking me exaggeratedly for every tiny service, apologizing for needing me to do things for her which we had both for years taken for granted, trying hard to

keep the anxiety, the embarrassment, and the unhappiness out
of her eyes and voice, and nowhere near succeeding.

She couldn't have punished me more if she had tried.

Late that evening Tiddely Pom developed violent colic.

Norton Fox couldn't get hold of Luke-John or Derry, who
had both long gone home. The *Blaze* never divulged home
addresses, however urgent the inquiry. Norton didn't know my
telephone number, either; didn't know anyone who did.

In a state of strong anxiety, and on his vet's advice, he rang
up Victor Roncey and told him where his horse was, and what
they were doing to save its life.

Twelve

I heard about it in the morning. Roncey telephoned at ten-thirty, when I was sitting in the writing room looking vacantly at the walls and trying to drum up some preliminary gems for my column on Sunday. Mrs. Woodward had gone out to the launderette, and Elizabeth called me to the telephone with two rings on the bell over my head: two rings for come at once but not an emergency. Three rings for 999. Four for panic.

Roncey had calmed down from the four-ring stage he had clearly been in the night before. He was calling, he said, from Norton Fox's house, where he had driven at once after being given the news. I sorted out that he had arrived at 2 A.M. to find that the vet had got Tiddely Pom over the worst, with the stoppage in the horse's gut untangling into normal function. Norton Fox had given Roncey a bed for the rest of the night, and he had just come in from seeing Tiddely Pom walk and trot out at morning exercise. The horse was showing surprisingly few ill effects from his rocky experience, and it was quite likely he would be fit enough to run in the Lamplighter on Saturday.

I listened to his long, brisk, detailed saga with uncomfortable alarm. There were still two whole days before the race. Now that Roncey knew where he was, Tiddely Pom's safety was halved. When he had come to the end of the tale, I asked him whether anyone had tried to find out from him at home where his horse had gone.

"Of course they did," he said. "Exactly as you said. Several other newspapers wanted to know. Most of them telephoned. Three or four actually turned up at the farm, and I know they asked Peter and Pat as well as me. Some of their questions were decidedly tricky. I thought at the time you'd been quite right, we might have let it slip if we'd known ourselves."

"When did these people come to the farm? What did they look like?"

"They didn't look like anything special. Just nondescript. One of them was from the *Evening Peal,* I remember. All the inquiries were on Sunday and Monday, just after your article came out."

"No one turned up in a Rolls?" I asked.

He laughed shortly. "They did not."

"Were any of your visitors tallish, thickish, blondish, with a faintly yellow skin and a slightly foreign accent?"

"None that I saw were like that. One or two saw only the boys, because they called while I was in Chelmsford. You could ask them, if you like."

"Maybe I will," I said. "No one tried any threats?"

"No. I told your sports editor that. No one has tried any pressure of any sort. To my mind, all your elaborate precautions have been a waste of time. And now that I know where Tiddely Pom is, you may as well tell me where my family is, too."

"I'll think about it," I said. "Would you ask Norton Fox if I could have a word with him?"

He fetched Norton, who apologized for busting open the secrecy, but said he didn't like the responsibility of keeping quiet when the horse was so ill.

"Of course not. It can't be helped," I said. "As long as it goes no further than Roncey himself, it may not be too bad, though I'd prefer—"

"His sons know, of course," Norton interrupted. "Though I don't suppose that matters."

"*What?*" I said.

"Roncey told one of his sons where he was. He telephoned to him just now. He explained to me that he couldn't remember your telephone number, but he'd got it written down somewhere at home, from having rung you up before sometime. So he rang his son—Pat, I think he said—and his son found it for him. I think he, the son, asked Roncey where he was calling from, because Roncey said that as everyone had stopped inquiring about where the horse was, he didn't see any harm in his son knowing, so he told him."

"Damn it," I said. "The man's a fool."

"He might be right."

"And he might be wrong," I said bitterly. "Look, Norton, I suppose there was no question of Tiddely Pom's colic being a misjudged case of poisoning?"

"For God's sake, Ty . . . no. It was straightforward colic. How on earth could he have been poisoned? For a start, no one knew then who he was."

"And now?" I asked. "How many of your lads know now that he is Tiddely Pom?"

There was a brief supercharged silence.

"All of them," I said flatly.

"Some of them knew Roncey by sight," he explained. "And they'd all read the *Blaze*. So they put two and two together."

One of them would soon realize he could earn a fiver by ringing up a rival newspaper. Tiddely Pom's whereabouts would be as secret as the Albert Memorial. Tiddely Pom, at that moment, was a certain nonstarter for the Lamplighter Gold Cup.

Even if Victor Roncey thought that the opposition had backed out of the project, I was certain they hadn't. In a man like Vjoersterod, pride would always conquer discretion. He wouldn't command the same respect in international criminal circles if he turned out and ran just because of a few words in the *Blaze*. He wouldn't, therefore, do it.

At the four-day declaration stage, on the Tuesday, Roncey had confirmed with Weatherbys that his horse would be a definite runner. If he now withdrew him, as he could reasonably do because of the colic, he would forfeit his entry fee, a matter of fifty pounds. If he left his horse at Norton's, still intending to run, he would forfeit a great deal more.

Because I was certain that if Tiddely Pom stayed where he was, he would be lame, blind, doped, or dead by Saturday morning.

Norton listened in silence while I outlined these facts of life.

"Ty, don't you think you are possibly exaggerating?"

"Well," I said with a mildness I didn't feel, "how many times will you need to have Brevity—or any other of your horses—taken out of the Champion Hurdle at the last moment without any explanation before you see any need to do something constructive in opposition?"

There was a short pause. "Yes," he said. "You have a point."

"If you will lend me your horse box, I'll take Tiddely Pom off somewhere else."

"Where?"

"Somewhere safe," I said noncommittally. "How about it?"

"Oh, all right." He sighed. "Anything for a quiet life."

"I'll come as soon as I can."

"I'll repel boarders until you do." The flippancy in his voice told me how little he believed in any threat to the horse. I felt a great urge to leave them to it, to let Roncey stew in his own indiscretion, to let Vjoersterod interfere with the horse and stop it running, just to prove I was right. Very childish urge indeed. It didn't last long, because in my way I was as stubborn as Vjoersterod. I wasn't going to turn and run from him, either, if I could help it.

When I put the telephone receiver back in its special cradle, Elizabeth was looking worried with a more normal form of anxiety.

"That Tiddely Pom," I said lightly, "is more trouble than a busload of eleven-year-old boys. As I expect you gathered, I'll have to go and shift him off somewhere else."

"Couldn't someone else do it?"

I shook my head. "Better be me."

Mrs. Woodward was still out. I filled in the time until her return by ringing up Luke-John and giving him the news that the best-laid plan had gone astray.

"Where are you taking the horse, then?"

"I'll let you know when I get there."

"Are you sure it's necessary—" He began.

"Are you," I interrupted, "sure the *Blaze* can afford to take any risk, after boasting about keeping the horse safe?"

"Hmm." He sighed. "Get on with it, then."

When Mrs. Woodward came back, I took the van and drove to Berkshire. With me went Elizabeth's best effort at a fond wifely farewell. She had even offered her mouth for a kiss, which she did very rarely, as mouth-to-mouth kissing interfered with her frail breathing arrangements and gave her a feeling of suffocation. She liked to kiss and be kissed on the cheek or forehead, and never too often.

I spent most of the journey worrying whether I should not after all have allowed myself to be blackmailed, whether any stand against pressure was a luxury when compared with the damage I'd done to Elizabeth's weak hold on happiness. After all the shielding, which had improved her physical condition, I'd laid into her with a bulldozer. Selfishly. Just to save myself from a particularly odious form of tyranny. If she lost weight or fretted to breakdown point, it would be directly my fault; and either or both seemed possible.

A hundred and fifty guineas, plus expenses, less tax. A study in depth. *Tally* had offered me the deeps. And in I'd jumped.

On the outskirts of London I stopped to make a long and involved telephone call, arranging a destination and care for Tiddely Pom. Norton Fox and Victor Roncey were eating lunch when I arrived at the stables, and I found it impossible to instill into either of them enough of a feeling for urgency to get them to leave their casseroled beef.

"Sit down and have some," Norton said airily.

"I want to be on my way."

They didn't approve of my impatience and proceeded to gooseberry crumble and biscuits and cheese. It was two o'clock before they agreed to amble out into the yard and see to the shifting of Tiddely Pom.

Norton had at least had his horse box made ready. It stood in the center of the yard with the ramp down. As public an exit as possible. I sighed. The horse-box driver didn't like handing over to a stranger and gave me some anxious instructions about the idiosyncratic gear change.

Sandy Willis led Tiddely Pom across the yard, up the ramp, and into the center stall of the three-stall box. The horse looked worse than ever, no doubt because of the colic. I couldn't see him ever winning any Lamplighter Gold Cup. Making sure he ran in it seemed a gloomy waste of time. Just as well, I reflected, that it wasn't to Tiddely Pom himself that I was committed, but to the principle that if Roncey wanted to run

Tiddely Pom he should. Along the lines of "I disagree that your horse has the slightest chance, but I'll defend to the death your right to prove it."

Sandy Willis finished tying the horse into his stall and took over where the box driver left off. Her instructions on how Tiddely Pom was to be managed were detailed and anxious. In her few days with the horse she had already identified herself with its well-being. As Norton had said, she was one of the best of his lads. I wished I could take her, too, but it was useless expecting Norton to let her go, when she also looked after Zig Zag.

She said, "He will be having proper care, won't he?"

"The best," I assured her.

"Tell them not to forget his eggs and beer."

"Right."

"And he hates having his ears messed about with."

"Right."

She gave me a long searching look, a half smile, and a reluctant farewell. Victor Roncey strode briskly across to me and unburdened himself along similar lines.

"I want to insist that you tell me where you are taking him."

"He will be safe."

"Where?"

"Mr. Roncey, if you know where, he is only half as safe. We've been through all this before."

He pondered, his glance darting about restlessly, his eyes not meeting mine. "Oh, very well," he said finally, with impatience. "But it will be up to you to make sure he gets to Heathbury Park in good time on Saturday."

"The *Blaze* will arrange that," I said. "The Lamplighter is at three. Tiddely Pom will reach the racecourse stables by noon, without fail."

"I'll be there," he said. "Waiting."

I nodded. Norton joined us, and the two of them discussed this arrangement while I shut up the ramp with the help of the hovering box driver.

"What time do you get Zig Zag to Heathbury?" I asked Norton, pausing before I climbed into the cab.

"Midday," he said. "It's only thirty-two miles. He'll be setting off at about eleven."

I climbed into the driving seat and looked out of the window. The two men looked back, Roncey worried, Norton not. To Norton I said, "I'll see you this evening when I bring the horse box back." To Roncey, "Don't worry, he'll be quite safe. I'll see you on Saturday. Ring the *Blaze,* as before, if you'd like to be reassured tonight and tomorrow."

I shut the window, sorted out the eccentric gears, and drove Tiddely Pom gently out of the yard and up the land to the village. An hour later than I had intended, I thought in disgust. Another hour for Mrs. Woodward. My mind shied away from the picture of Elizabeth waiting for me to come back. Nothing would be better. Nothing would be better for a long time to come. I felt the first stirrings of resentment against Elizabeth and at least had the sense to realize that my mind was playing me a common psychological trick. The guilty couldn't stand the destruction of their self-esteem involved in having to admit they were wrong, and wriggled out of their shame by transforming it into resentment against the people who had made them feel it. I resented Elizabeth because I had wronged her. Of all the ridiculous injustices. And of all the ridiculous injustices, one of the most universal.

I maneuvered the heavy horse box carefully through the small village and set off northeastward on the road over the Downs, retracing the way I had come from London. Wide rolling hills with no trees except a few low bushes leaning sideways from the prevailing wind. No houses. A string of pylons. Black furrows in a mile of plow. A bleak early December sky, a high sheet of steel-gray cloud. Cold, dull, mood-matching landscape.

There was very little traffic on the unfenced road, which served only Norton's village and two others beyond. A blue-gray Cortina appeared on the brow of the next hill, coming toward me, traveling fast. I pulled over to give him room, and he rocked past at a stupid speed for the space available.

My attention was so involved with Elizabeth that it was several seconds before the calamity got through. With a shattering jolt the casually noticed face of the Cortina's driver kicked my memory to life. It belonged to one of Charlie Boston's boys from the train. The big one. With the brass knuckles.

December weather couldn't stop the prickly sweat that broke out on my skin. I put my foot on the accelerator and felt Tiddely Pom's weight lurch behind me from the sudden spurt. All I could hope for was that the big man had been too occupied judging the width of his car to look up and see me.

He had, of course, had a passenger.

I looked in the driving mirror. The Cortina had gone out of sight over the hill. Charlie Boston's boys hurrying toward Norton Fox's village was no wild coincidence; but Tiddely Pom's whereabouts must have been transmitted with very little delay for them to be here already, especially if they had had to come from Birmingham. Just who, I wondered grimly, had told who where Tiddely Pom was to be found? Not that it mattered much at that moment. All that mattered was to get him lost again.

I checked with the driving mirror. No Cortina. The horse box was pushing sixty-five on a road where forty would be wiser.

Tiddely Pom's hoofs clattered inside his stall. He didn't like the swaying. He would have to put up with it until I got him clear of the Downs road, which was far too empty and far too visible from too many miles around.

When I next looked in the mirror, there was a pale speck on the horizon two hills behind. It might not be them, I thought. I looked again. It was them. I swore bitterly. The speedometer needle crept to sixty-eight. That was the lot. My foot was down on the floor boards. And they were gaining. Easily.

There was no town close enough to get lost in, and once on my tail they could stay there all day, waiting to find out where I took Tiddely Pom. Even in a car it would have been difficult to lose them: in a lumbering horse box impossible. Urgent appraisal of a depressing situation came up with only a hope that Charlie Boston's boys would again be propelled by more aggression than sense.

They were. They came up fast behind me, leaning on the horn. Maybe they thought I hadn't had time to see *them* as they went past me the other way, and wouldn't know who wanted to pass.

If they wanted to pass, they didn't want to follow. I shut my teeth. If they wanted to pass, it was now, it was here, that they meant to make certain that Tiddely Pom didn't run in the Lamplighter. What they intended to do about me was a matter which sent me and my mending ribs into a tizzy. I swallowed. I didn't want another hammering like the last time, and this time they might not be so careful about what they did or didn't rupture.

I held the horse box in the center of the road so that there wasn't room enough for their Cortina to get by. They still went on blowing the horn. Tiddely Pom kicked his stall. I took my foot some way off the accelerator and slowed the proceedings down to a more manageable forty-five. They would guess I knew who they were. I didn't see that it gave them any advantage.

A hay lorry appeared around a hill ahead with its load overhanging the center of the road. Instinctively I slowed still further, and began to pull over. The Cortina's nose showed sharply in the wing mirror, already up by my rear axle. I swung the horse box back into the center of the road, which raised flashing headlights from the driver of the advancing hay lorry. When I was far too close to a radiator-to-radiator confrontation, he started blowing his horn furiously as well. I swung back to my side of the road when he was almost stationary from standing rigidly on his brakes, and glimpsed a furious face and a shaking fist as I swerved past. Inches to spare. Inches were enough.

The Cortina tried to get past in the short second before the horse box was re-established on the crown of the road. There was a bump, this time, as I cut across its bows. It dropped back ten feet, and stayed there. It would only stay there, I thought despairingly, until Charlie Boston's boys had got what they came for.

Less than a mile ahead lay my likely Waterloo, in the shape of a crossroads. A halt sign. It was I who would have to halt. Either that or risk hitting a car speeding legitimately along the major road, risk killing some innocent motorist, or his wife, or his child. . . . Yet if I stopped, the Cortina with its faster acceleration would pass me when I moved off again, whether I turned right, as I had intended to, or left, back to London, or went straight on, to heaven knew where.

There wouldn't be anyone at the crossroads to give me any help. No police car sitting there waiting for custom. No A.A. man having a smoke. No lifesaving bystander of any sort. No troop of United States cavalry to gallop up in the nick of time.

I changed down into second to climb a steepish hill and forgot Norton's box driver's instructions. For a frightening moment the gears refused to mesh and the horse box's weight dragged it almost to a standstill. Then the cogs slid together, and with a regrettable jolt we started off again. Behind me, Charlie Boston's boys still wasted their energy and wore out their battery by almost nonstop blasts on their horn.

The horse box trundled to the top of the hill, and there already, four hundred yards down the other side, was the crossroads.

I stamped on the accelerator. The horse box leaped forward. Charlie Boston's boy had time to take in the scene below, and to realize that I must be meaning not to halt at the sign. In the wing mirror, I watched him accelerate to keep up, closing enough to stick to me whatever I did at the crossroads.

Two hundred yards before I got there, I stood on the brake pedal as if the road ended in an abyss ten yards ahead. The reaction was more than I'd bargained for. The horse box shuddered and rocked and began to spin. Its rear slewed across the road, hit the verge, rocked again. I feared the whole high-topped structure would overturn. Instead, there was a thudding crunching anchoring crash as the Cortina bounced on and off at the rear.

The horse box screeched and slid to a juddering stop. Upright. Facing the right way.

I hauled on the hand brake and was out of the cab onto the road before the glass from the Cortina had stopped tinkling on the tarmac.

The blue-gray car had gone over onto its side and was showing its guts to the wind. It lay a good twenty yards behind the horse box, and from the dented look of the roof it had rolled completely over before stopping. I walked back toward it, wishing I had a weapon of some sort, and fighting an inclination just to drive off and leave without looking to see what had happened to the occupants.

There was only one of them in the car. The big one, the driver. Very much alive, murderously angry, and in considerable pain from having his right ankle trapped and broken among the pedals. I turned my back on him and ignored his all too audible demands for assistance. Revenge, I decided, would overcome all else if I once got within reach of his hands.

The second Boston boy had been flung out by the crash. I found him on the grass verge, unconscious and lying on his face. With anxiety I felt for his pulse; but he, too, was alive. With extreme relief I went back to the horse box, opened the side door, and climbed in to take a look at Tiddely Pom. He calmly swiveled a disapproving eye in my direction and began to evacuate his bowels.

"Nothing much wrong with you, mate," I said aloud. My voice came out squeaky with tension. I wiped my hand around my neck, tried to grin, felt both like copying Tiddely Pom's present action and being sick.

The horse really did not seem any the worse for his highly unorthodox journey. I took several deep breaths, patted his rump, and jumped down again into the road. Inspection of the damage at the back of the horse box revealed a smashed rear light and a dent in the sturdy off-rear fender no longer than a soup plate. I hoped that Luke-John would agree to the *Blaze* paying for the repairs. Charlie Boston wouldn't want to.

His unconscious boy was beginning to stir. I watched him sit up, put his hands to his head, begin to remember what had happened. I listened to his big colleague still shouting furiously from inside the car. Then with deliberate non-haste I climbed

back into the cab of the horse box, started the engine, and drove
carefully away.

I had never intended to go far. I took Tiddely Pom to the
safest place I could think of: the racecourse stables at Heathbury Park. There he would be surrounded by a high wall and
guarded by a security patrol at night. Everyone entering racecourse stables had to show a pass; even owners were not allowed in unless accompanied by their trainers.

Willy Ondroy, consulted on the telephone, had agreed to
take in Tiddely Pom, and to keep his identity a secret. The
stables would in any case be open from midday and the guards
would be on duty from then on; anytime after that, he said,
Tiddely Pom would be just one of a number of horses arriving
for the following day's racing. Horses which came from more
than a hundred miles away normally traveled the day before
their race and stayed overnight in the racecourse stables. A
distant stable running one horse on Friday and another on Saturday would send them both down on Thursday and leave them
both at the racecourse stables for two nights, or possibly even
three. Tiddely Pom's two nights' stay would be unremarkable
and inconspicuous. The only oddity about him was that he had
no lad to look after him, an awkward detail to which Willy
Ondroy had promised to find a solution.

He was looking out for me and came across the grass outside
the stable block to forestall me from climbing down from the
cab. Instead, he opened the door on the passenger side and
joined me.

"Too many of these lads know you by sight," he said waving
an arm to where two other horse boxes were unloading. "If they
see you they will know you would not have brought any other
horse but Tiddely Pom. And as I understand it, you don't want

to land us with the security headache of a bunch of crooks trying to injure him. Right?"

"Right," I agreed thankfully.

"Drive down this road, then. First left. In through the white gateposts, fork left, park outside the rear door of my house. Right?"

"Right," I said again, and followed his instructions, thankful for his quick grasp of essentials and his jet-formation pilot's clarity of decision.

"I've had a word with the racecourse manager," he said. "The stables and security are his pigeon, really. Had to enlist his aid. Hope you don't mind. He's a very sound fellow, very sound indeed. He's fixing up a lad to look after Tiddely Pom. Without telling him who the horse is, naturally."

"That's good," I said with relief.

I stopped the horse box and we both disembarked. The horse, Willy Ondroy said, could safely stay where he was until the racecourse manager came over for him. Meanwhile would I care for some tea? He looked at his watch. Three-fifty. He hesitated. Or a whiskey, he added.

"Why a whiskey?" I asked.

"I don't know. I suppose because you look as though you need it."

"You may be right," I said, dredging up a smile. He looked at me appraisingly, but how could I tell him that I'd just risked killing two men to bring Tiddely Pom safe and unfollowed to his door. That I had been extremely lucky to get away with merely stopping them. That only by dishing out such violence had I avoided a second beating of proportions I couldn't contemplate. It wasn't really surprising that I looked as if I needed a whiskey. I did. It tasted fine.

Thirteen

Norton Fox was less than pleased when I got back.

He heard me rumble into the yard and came out of his house to meet me. It was by then full dark, but there were several external lights on, and more light flooded out of open stable doors as the lads bustled around with the evening chores. I parked, climbed stiffly down from the cab, and looked at my watch. Five-fifty. I'd spent two hours on a roundabout return journey to fool the box driver over the distance I'd taken Tiddely Pom. Heathbury Park and back was probably the driver's most beaten track: he would know the mileage to a hundred yards, recognize it instantly if he saw it on the clock, know for a certainty where the horse was, and make my entire afternoon a waste of time.

"You're in trouble, Ty," Norton said, reaching me and frowning. "What in God's name were you thinking of? First the man delivering my hay gets here in a towering rage and says my horse box drove straight at him with some maniac at the wheel and that there'd be an accident if he was any judge, and the next thing is we hear there has been an accident over by Long Barrow crossroads involving a horse box and I've had the police here making inquiries."

"Yes." I said. "I'm very sorry, Norton. Your horse box has a dent in it, and a broken rear light. I'll apologize to the hay-lorry driver. And I guess I'll have to talk to the police."

Dangerous driving. Putting it mildly. Very difficult to prove it was a case of self-preservation.

Norton looked near to explosion. "What on earth were you *doing?*"

"Playing cowboys-and-Indians," I said tiredly. "The Indians bit the dust."

He was not amused. His secretary came out to tell him he was wanted on the telephone, and I waited by the horse box until he came back, gloomily trying to remember the distinction between careless, reckless, and dangerous, and the various penalties attached. Failing to stop. Failing to report an accident. How much for those?

Norton came back less angry than he went. "That was the police," he said abruptly. "They still want to see you. However, it seems the two men involved in the crash have vanished from the casualty department in the hospital and the police have discovered that the Cortina was stolen. They are less inclined to think that the accident was your fault, in spite of what the hay-lorry driver told them."

"The men in the Cortina were after Tiddely Pom," I said flatly, "and they damn nearly got him. Maybe you could tell Victor Roncey that there is some point to our precautions, after all."

"He's gone home," he said. I began to walk across the dark stable yard to where I'd left my van, and he followed me, giving me directions about how to find the police station.

I stopped him. "I'm not going there. The police can come to me. Preferably on Monday. You tell them that."

"Why on Monday?" He looked bewildered. "Why not now?"

"Because," I spelled it out, "I can tell them roughly where to find those men in the Cortina and explain what they were up to. But I don't want the police issuing any warrants before Monday; otherwise the whole affair will be *sub judice* and I won't be able to get a squeak into the *Blaze*. After all this trouble, we've earned our story for Sunday."

"You take my breath away," he said, sounding as if I had. "And the police won't like it."

"For God's sake, don't tell them," I said in exasperation. "That was for your ears only. If and when they ask you where I am, simply say I will be getting in touch with them, that you don't know where I live, and that they can reach me through the *Blaze* if they want me."

"Very well," he agreed doubtfully. "If you're sure. But it sounds to me as though you're landing yourself in serious trouble. I wouldn't have thought Tiddely Pom was worth it."

"Tiddely Pom, Brevity, Polyxenes, and all the rest—individually none of them was worth the trouble. That's precisely why the racket goes on."

His disapproving frown lighted into a half smile. "You'll be telling me next that the *Blaze* is more interested in justice than sensationalism."

"It says so. Often," I agreed sardonically.

"Huh," said Norton. "You can't believe everything you read in the papers."

I drove home slowly, tired and depressed. Other times, trouble had been a yeast lightening the daily bread. A positive plus factor. Something I needed. But other times trouble hadn't bitterly invaded my marriage or earned me such a savage physical attack.

This time, although I was fairly confident that Tiddely Pom would start in his race, the successful uncovering and extermination of a racing scandal was bringing me none of the usual upsurging satisfaction. This time, dust and ashes. This time, present grief and a gray future.

I stopped on the way and rang the *Blaze.* Luke-John had left for the day. I got him at home.

"Tiddely Pom is in the racecourse stables at Heathbury," I said. "Guarded by an ex-policeman and a large Alsatian. The Clerk of the Course and the racecourse manager both know who he is, but no one else does. O.K.?"

"Very, I should think." He sounded moderately pleased, but no more. "We can take it as certain now that Tiddely Pom will start in the Lamplighter. It's made a good story, Ty, but I'm afraid we exaggerated the danger."

I disillusioned him. "Charlie Boston's boys were three miles from Norton Fox's stable by two-thirty this afternoon."

"Christ," he said. "So it's really true. . . ."

"You've looked at it so far as a stunt for the *Blaze*."

"Well. . . ."

"Well, so it is," I agreed. "Anyway, Charlie Boston's boys had a slight accident with their car, and they are now back to square one, as they don't know where I took Tiddely Pom."

"What sort of accident?"

"They ran into the back of the horse box. Careless of them. I put the brakes on rather hard, and they were following a little too close."

A shocked silence. Then he said, "Were they killed?"

"No. Hardly bent." I gave him an outline of the afternoon's events. Luke-John's reaction was typical and expected, and the enthusiasm was alive again in his voice.

"Keep away from the police until Sunday."

"Sure thing."

"This is great, Ty."

"Yeah," I said.

"Knock out a preliminary version tonight and bring it in with you in the morning," he said. "Then we can discuss it tomorrow, and you can phone in the final touches from Heathbury after the Lamplighter on Saturday."

"All right."

"Oh, and give Roncey a ring, would you, and tell him the horse is only safe thanks to the *Blaze*."

"Yes," I said. "Maybe I will."

I put down the receiver and felt like leaving Roncey severely alone. I was tired and I wanted to go home. And when I got home, I thought drearily, there would be no let-off, only another dose of self-hate and remorse.

Roncey answered the telephone at the first ring and needed no telling. Norton Fox had already been through.

"Tiddely Pom is safe and well looked after," I assured him.

"I owe you an apology," he said abruptly.

"Be my guest," I said.

"Look here, there's something worrying me. Worrying me badly." He paused, swallowing a great deal of pride. "Do you— I mean, have you any idea—how those men appeared so quickly on the scene?"

"The same idea as you," I said. "Your son Pat."

"I'll break his neck," he said with real and unfatherly viciousness.

"If you've any sense, you'll let him ride your horses in all their races, not just the unimportant ones."

"What are you talking about?"

"About Pat's outsize sense of grievance. You put up anyone except him, and he resents it."

"He's not good enough," he protested.

"And how will he ever be if you don't give him the experience? Nothing teaches a jockey faster than riding a good horse in a good race."

"He might lose," he sad pugnaciously.

"He might win. When did you ever give him the chance?"

"But to give away the secret of Tiddely Pom's whereabouts. . . . What would he expect to gain?"

"He was getting his own back, that's all."

"*All!*"

"There's no harm done."

"I hate him."

"Then send him to another stable. Give him an allowance to live on and let him see if he's going to ride well enough to turn professional. That's what he wants. If you stamp on people's ambitions too hard, it's not frantically astonishing if they bite back."

"It's a son's duty to work for his father. Especially a farmer's son."

I sighed. He was half a century out of date, and no amount of telling from me was going to change him. I said I'd see him on Sunday, and disconnected.

Like his father, I took no pleasure at all in Pat Roncey's vengeful disloyalty. Understood, maybe. Admired, far from it.

One of the men who came to inquire at Roncey's farm must have sensed Pat's obvious disgruntlement and have given him a telephone number to ring if he ever found out where Tiddely Pom had gone, and wanted to revenge himself on his father. One might give Pat the benefit of enough doubt to suppose that he'd thought he was only telling a newspaperman from one of the *Blaze*'s rivals; but even so he must have known that a rival paper would spread the information to every corner of the country. To the ears which waited to hear. Exactly the same in the end. But because of the speed with which Charlie Boston's boys had reached Norton Fox's village, it must have been Raincoat or the chauffeur, or even Vjoersterod himself who had talked to Pat at the farm.

It had to be Pat. Norton Fox's stable lads might have passed the word on to newspapers, but they couldn't have told Vjoersterod or Charlie Boston because they didn't know they wanted to know, and probably didn't even know they existed.

I drove on, back to London. Parked the van in the garage downstairs. Locked up. Walked slowly and unenthusiastically up to the flat.

"Hi," said Elizabeth brightly.

"Hi yourself." I kissed her cheek.

It must have looked, to Mrs. Woodward, a normal greeting. Only the pain we could read in each other's eyes said it wasn't.

Mrs. Woodward put on her dark blue coat and checked the time again to make sure it was ten to, not ten after. She'd had three hours extra, but she wanted more. I wondered fleetingly if I could charge her overtime to the *Blaze*.

"We've had our meal," Mrs. Woodward said. "I've left yours ready to warm up. Just pop it in the oven, Mr. Tyrone."

"Thanks."

"Night, then, luv," she called to Elizabeth.

"Night."

I opened the door for her and she nodded briskly, smiled, and said she'd be there on the dot in the morning. I thanked her appreciatively. She would indeed be there on the dot. Kind, reliable, necessary Mrs. Woodward. I hoped the *Tally* check wouldn't be too long coming.

Beyond that first greeting Elizabeth and I could find little to say to each other. The most ordinary inquiries and remarks seemed horribly brittle, like a thin sheet of glass over a pit.

It was a relief to both of us when the doorbell rang.

"Mrs. Woodward must have forgotten something," I said. It was barely ten minutes since she had left.

"I expect so," Elizabeth agreed.

I opened the door without a speck of intuition. It swung inward with a rush, weighted and pushed by a heavy man in black. He stabbed a solid leather-gloved fist into my diaphragm and, when my head came forward, chopped down with something hard on the back of my neck.

On my knees, coughing for breath, I watched Vjoersterod appear in the doorway, take in the scene, and walk past me into the room. A black-booted foot kicked the door shut behind him. There was a soft whistling swish in the air and another terrible thump high up between my shoulder blades. Elizabeth cried out. I staggered to my feet and tried to move in her direction. The heavy man in black—Ross, the chauffeur—slid his arm under mine and twisted and locked my shoulder.

"Sit down, Mr. Tyrone," Vjoersterod said calmly. "Sit there." He pointed to the tapestry-covered stool Mrs. Woodward liked to knit on, as there were no arms or back to get in the way of her busy elbows.

"Ty!" Elizabeth's voice rose high with fear. "What's happening?"

I didn't answer. I felt stupid and sunk. I sat down on the stool when Ross released my arm, and tried to work some control into the way I looked at Vjoersterod.

He was standing near Elizabeth's head, watching me with swelling satisfaction.

"So now we know just where we are, Mr. Tyrone. Did you really have the conceit to think you could defy me and get away with it? No one does, Mr. Tyrone. No one ever does."

I didn't answer. Ross stood beside me, a pace to the rear. In his right hand he gently swung the thing he had hit me with, a short elongated pear-shaped truncheon. Its weight and crushing power made a joke of Charlie Boston's boys' knuckle-dusters. I refrained from rubbing the aching places below my neck.

"Mr. Tyrone," Vjoersterod said conversationally, "where is Tiddely Pom?"

When I still didn't answer immediately, he half turned, looked down, and carefully put the toe of his shoe under the switch of the electric outlet. From there the cable led directly to Elizabeth's breathing pump. Elizabeth turned her head to follow my eyes and saw what he was doing.

"No!" she said. It was high-pitched, terrified. Vjoersterod smiled.

"Tiddely Pom?" he said to me.

"He's in the racecourse stables at Heathbury Park."

"Ah." He took his foot away, put it down on the floor. "You see how simple it is? It's always a matter of finding the right lever. Of applying the right pressure. No horse, I find, is ever worth a really serious danger to a loved one."

I said nothing. He was right.

"Check it," Ross said from behind me.

Vjoersterod's eyes narrowed. "He couldn't risk a lie."

"He wouldn't be blackmailed. He was out to get you, and no messing. Check it." There was advice in Ross's manner, not authority. More than a chauffeur. Less than an equal.

Vjoersterod shrugged but stretched out a hand and picked up the receiver. Telephone inquiries. Heathbury Park racecourse. The Clerk of the Course's house? That would do very well.

Willy Ondroy himself answered. Vjoersterod said, "Mr. Tyrone asked me to call you to check if Tiddely Pom had settled in well. . . ."

He listened to the reply impassively, his pale yellow face immobile. It accounted for the fact, I thought inconsequentially, that his skin was unlined. He never smiled, seldom frowned. The only wrinkles were around his eyes, which I supposed he screwed up against his native sun.

"Thank you so much," he said. His best Foreign Office voice, courteous and charming.

"Ask him which box the horse is in," Ross said. "The number."

Vjoersterod asked. Willy Ondroy told him.

"Sixty-eight. Thank you. Good night."

He put the receiver carefully back in its cradle and let a small silence lengthen. I hoped that since he had got what he came for he would decently go away again. Not a very big hope to start with, and one which never got off the ground.

He said, studying his fingernails, "It is satisfactory, Mr. Tyrone, that you do at least see the need to cooperate with me." Another pause. "However, in your case I would be foolish to think that this state of affairs would last very long if I did nothing to convince you that it must."

I looked at Elizabeth. She didn't seem to have followed Vjoersterod's rather involved syntax. Her head lay in a relaxed way on the pillow and her eyes were shut. She was relieved that I had told where the horse was; she thought that everything was now all right.

Vjoersterod followed my glance and my thought. He nodded. "We have many polio victims on respirators in my country. I understand about them. About the importance of electricity. The importance of constant attendance. The razor edge between life and death. I understand it well."

I said nothing. He said, "Many men desert wives like this. Since you do not, you would care if harm came to her. Am I right? You have, in fact, just this minute proved it, have you not? You wasted so little time in telling me correctly what I wanted to know."

I made no comment. He waited a fraction, then went smoothly on. What he said, as Dembley had found out, was macabrely at variance with the way he said it.

"I have an international reputation to maintain. I simply

cannot afford to have pip-squeak journalists interfering with my enterprises and trying to hold me up to ridicule. I intend to make it clear to you once and for all, to impress upon you indelibly, that I am not a man to be crossed."

Ross moved a pace at my side. My skin crawled. I made as good a job as I could of matching Vjoersterod's immobility of expression.

Vjoersterod had more to say. As far as I was concerned, he could go on all night. The alternative hardly beckoned.

"Charlie Boston reports to me that you have put both his men out of action. He, too, cannot afford such affronts to his reputation. Since all you learned from his warning attentions on the train was to strike back, we will see if my chauffeur can do any better."

I tucked one foot under the stool, pivoted on it, and on the way to my feet struck at Ross with both hands, one to the stomach, one to the groin. He bent over, taken by surprise, and I wrenched the small truncheon out of his hand, raising it to clip him on the head.

"Ty!" Elizabeth's voice rose in an agonized wail. I swung around with the truncheon in my hand and met Vjoersterod's fiercely implacable gaze.

"Drop it."

He had his toe under the switch. Three yards between us.

I hesitated, boiling with fury, wanting above anything to hit him, knock him out, get rid of him—out of my life and most particularly out of the next hour of it. I couldn't risk it. One tiny jerk would cut off the current. I couldn't risk not being able to reach the switch again in time, not with Vjoersterod in front of it and Ross behind me. Under the weight of the Spiroshell she would suffocate almost immediately. If I resisted any more, I could kill her. He might really do it. Let her die. Leave me to explain her death and maybe even be accused of slaughtering her myself. The unwanted-wife bit. . . . He didn't know I knew his name or anything about him. He would think he could kill Elizabeth with reasonable safety. I simply couldn't risk it.

I put my arm down slowly and dropped the truncheon on the carpet. Ross, breathing heavily, bent and picked it up.

"Sit down, Mr. Tyrone," Vjoersterod said. "And stay sitting down. Don't get up again. Do I make myself clear?"

He still had his toe under the switch. I sat down, seething inside, rigid outside, and totally apprehensive. Twice in a fortnight was definitely too much.

Vjoersterod nodded to Ross, who hit me solidly with the truncheon on the back of the shoulder. It sounded horrible. Felt worse.

Elizabeth cried out. Vjoersterod looked at her without pity and told Ross to switch on the television. They both waited while the set warmed up. Ross adjusted the volume to medium loud and changed the channel from a news magazine to song and dance. No neighbors, unfortunately, would call to complain about the noise. The only ones who lived near enough were out working in a night club.

Ross had another go with his truncheon. Instinctively I started to stand up, to retaliate, to escape, heaven knows what.

"Sit down," Vjoersterod said.

I looked at his toe. I sat down. Ross swung his arm and that time I fell forward off the stool onto my knees.

"Sit," Vjoersterod said. Stiffly I returned to where he said.

"Don't," Elizabeth said to him in a wavering voice. "Please don't."

I looked at her, met her eyes. She was terrified. Scared to death. And something else. Beseeching. Begging me. With a flash of blinding understanding I realized she was afraid I wouldn't take any more, that I wouldn't think she was worth it, that I would somehow stop them hurting me even if it meant switching off her pump. Vjoersterod knew I wouldn't. It was ironic, I thought mordantly, that Vjoersterod knew me better than my own wife.

It didn't last a great deal longer. It had anyway reached the stage where I no longer felt each blow separately but rather as a crushing addition to an intolerable whole. It seemed as though I had the whole weight of the world across my shoulders. Atlas wasn't even in the race.

I didn't see Vjoersterod tell Ross to stop. I had the heels of my hands against my mouth and my fingertips in my hair. Some nit on the television was advising everyone to keep their sunny side up. Ross cut him off abruptly in mid-note.

"Oh God," Elizabeth said. "Oh God."

Vjoersterod's smooth voice dryly comforted her. "My dear Mrs. Tyrone, I assure you that my chauffeur knows how to be a great deal more unpleasant than that. He has, I hope you realize, left your husband his dignity."

"Dignity," Elizabeth said faintly.

"Quite so. My chauffeur used to work in the prison service in the country I come from. He knows about humiliation. It would not have been suitable, however, to apply certain of his techniques to your husband."

"Russia?" she asked. "Do you come from Russia?"

He didn't answer her. He spoke to me.

"Mr. Tyrone, should you try to cross me again, I would allow my chauffeur to do anything he liked. Anything at all. Do you understand?"

I was silent. He repeated peremptorily, "Do you understand?"

I nodded my head.

"Good, that's a start. But only a start. You will also do

something more positive. You will work for me. You will write for me in your newspaper. Whatever I tell you to write, you will write.

I detached my hands slowly from my face and rested my wrists on my knees.

"I can't," I said dully.

"I think you will find that you can. In fact you will. You must. And neither will you contemplate resigning from your paper." He touched the electric switch with his brown polished toecap. "You cannot guard your wife adequately every minute for the rest of her life."

"Very well," I said slowly. "I will write what you say."

"Ah."

Poor old Bert Checkov, I thought drearily. Seven floors down to the pavement. Only I couldn't insure myself for enough to compensate Elizabeth for having to live forever in a hospital.

"You can start this week," Vjoersterod said. "You can say on Sunday that what you have written for the last two weeks turns out to have no foundation in fact. You will restore the situation to what it was before you started interfering."

"Very well."

I put my right hand tentatively over my left shoulder. Vjoersterod watched me and nodded.

"You'll remember that," he said judiciously. "Perhaps you will feel better if I assure you that many who have crossed me are now dead. You are more useful to me alive. As long as you write what I say, your wife will be safe and my chauffeur will not need to attend to you."

His chauffeur, did he but know it, had proved to be a pale shadow of the Boston boys. For all my fears, it now seemed to me that the knuckle-dusters had been worse. The chauffeur's work was a bore, a present burden, yet not as crippling as be-

fore. No broken ribs. No all-over weakness. This time I would
be able to move.

Elizabeth was close to tears. "How can you?" she said. "How
can you be so . . . so . . . beastly?"

Vjoersterod remained unruffled. "I am surprised you care so
much for your husband after his behavior with that colored
girl."

She bit her lip and rolled her head away from him on the
pillow. He stared at me calmly. "So you told her."

There was no point in saying anything. If I'd told him where
Tiddely Pom had been on Tuesday, when he first tried to make
me, I would have saved myself a lot of pain and trouble. I
would have saved Elizabeth from knowing about Gail. I would
have spared her all this fear. Some of Bert Checkov's famous
last words floated up from the past: "It's the ones who don't
know when to give in who get the worst clobbering . . . in the
ring, I mean. . . ."

I swallowed. The ache from my shoulders was spreading
down my back. I was dead tired of sitting on that stool. Mrs.
Woodward could keep it, I thought. I wouldn't want it in the flat
any more.

Vjoersterod said to Ross, "Pour him a drink."

Ross went over to where the whiskey bottle stood on its tray
with two glasses and the Malvern water. The bottle was nearly
half full. He unscrewed the cap, picked up one of the tumblers,
and emptied into it all the whiskey. It was filled to the brim.

Vjoersterod nodded. "Drink it."

Ross gave me the glass. I stared at it.

"Go on," Vjoersterod said. "Drink it."

I took a breath to protest. He moved his toe toward the
switch. I put the glass to my lips and took a mouthful. Jump
through hoops when the man said.

"All of it," he said. "Quickly."

I had eaten little or nothing in the last twenty-four hours. Though I had a natural tolerance, a tumblerful of alcohol on an empty stomach was not my idea of fun. I had no choice. Loathing Vjoersterod, I drank it all.

"He seems to have learned his lesson," Ross said.

Fourteen

They stood in silence for nearly fifteen minutes, watching me. Then Vjoersterod said, "Stand up."

I stood.

"Turn round in a circle."

I turned. Lurched. Staggered. Swayed on my feet.

Vjoersterod nodded in satisfaction. "That's all, Mr. Tyrone. All for today. I expect to be pleased by what you write in the paper on Sunday. I had better be pleased."

I nodded. A mistake. My head swam violently. I overbalanced slightly. The whiskey was being absorbed into my bloodstream at a disastrous rate.

Vjoersterod and Ross let themselves out unhurriedly and without another word. As soon as the door closed behind them, I turned and made tracks for the kitchen, Behind me Elizabeth's voice called in a question, but I had no time to waste and explain. I pulled the tin of salt from the shelf, poured two inches of it into a tumbler, and splashed in an equal amount of water.

Stirred it with my fingers. No time for a spoon. Seconds counted. Drank the mixture. It tasted like the Seven Seas rolled into one. Scorched my throat. An effort to get more than one mouthful down. I was gagging over the stuff even before it did its work and came up again, bringing with it whatever of the whiskey hadn't gone straight through my stomach wall.

I leaned over the sink, retching and wretched. I had lurched for Vjoersterod more than was strictly necessary, but the alcohol had in fact taken as strong and fast a hold as I had feared it would. I could feel its effects rising in my brain, disorganizing coordination, distorting thought. No possible antidote except time.

Time. Fifteen minutes, maybe, since I had taken the stuff. In ten minutes more, perhaps twenty, I would be thoroughly drunk.

I didn't know whether Vjoersterod had made me drink for any special purpose or just from bloody-mindedness. I did know that it was a horrible complication to what I had planned to do.

I rinsed my mouth out with clean water and straightened up. Groaned as the heavy yoke of bruises across my shoulders reminded me I had other troubles besides drink. Went back to Elizabeth concentrating on not knocking into the walls and doors, and picked up the telephone.

A blank. Couldn't remember the number.

Think.

Out it came. Willy Ondroy answered.

"Willy," I said. "Move that horse out of box sixty-eight. That was the opposition you were talking to earlier. Put on all the guards you can, and move the horse to another box. Stake out sixty-eight and see if you can catch any would-be nobblers in the act."

"Ty! Will do."

"Can't stop, Willy. Sorry about this."

"Don't worry. We'll see no one reaches him. I think like you, that it's essential he should be kept safe until the race."

"They may be determined."

"So am I."

I put the receiver back in its cradle with his reassurance shoring me up, and met Elizabeth's horrified gaze.

"Ty," she said faintly, "what are you doing?"

I sat down for a moment on the arm of the chair. I felt terrible. Battered, sick, and drunk.

I said, "Listen, honey. Listen well. I can't say it twice. I can't put things back to where they were before I wrote the articles."

"You told him you would," she interrupted in bewilderment.

"I know I did. I had to. But I can't. I've told the Stewards about him. I can't go back on that. In fact I won't. He's utter poison, and he's got to be stopped."

"Let someone else do it."

"That's the classic path to oppression."

"But why you?" A protesting wail, but a serious question.

"I don't know. . . . Someone has to."

"But you gave in to him . . . You let him . . ." She looked at me with wide appalled eyes, struck by sudden realization. "He'll come back."

"Yes. When he finds out that Tiddely Pom has changed boxes and the whole stable is bristling with guards, he'll guess I warned them, and he'll come back. So I'm moving you out of here. Away. At once."

"You don't mean now?"

"I do indeed."

"But, Ty . . . all that whiskey. . . . Wouldn't it be better to leave it until the morning?"

I shook my head. The room began spinning. I held on to the chair and waited for it to stop. In the morning I would be sore and ill, much worse than at that moment; and the morning might be too late anyway. Heathbury and back would take less than three hours in a Rolls.

"Ring up Sue Davis and see if Ron can come along to help. I'm going downstairs to get the van out. O.K.?"

"I don't want to go."

I understood her reluctance. She had so little grasp on life that even a long-planned daytime move left her worried and insecure. This sudden bustle into the night seemed the dangerous course to her, and staying in a familiar warm home the safe one. Whereas they were the other way around.

"We must," I said. "We absolutely must."

I stood up carefully and concentrated on walking a straight path to the door. Made it with considerable success. Down the stairs. Opened the garage doors, started the van, and backed it out into the mews. A new set of batteries for Elizabeth's pump was in the garage. I lifted them into the van and put them in place. Waves of giddiness swept through me every time I bent my head down. I began to lose hope that I could retain any control of my brain at all. Too much whiskey sloshing about in it. Too much altogether.

I went upstairs again. Elizabeth had the receiver to her ear and her eyes were worried.

"There isn't any reply. Sue and Ron must be out."

I swore inwardly. Even at the best of times it was difficult to manage the transfer to the van on my own. This was far from the best of times.

I took the receiver out of the cradle, disconnected the Davis's vainly ringing number, and dialed that of Antonio Perelli. To my bottomless relief, he answered.

"Tonio, will you call the nursing home and tell them I'm bringing Elizabeth over?"

"Do you mean now, tonight?"

"Almost at once, yes."

"Bronchial infection?" He sounded brisk, preparing to be reassuring, acknowledging the urgency.

"No. She's well. It's a different sort of danger. I'll tell you later. Look—could you possibly down tools and come over here and help me with her?"

"I can't just now, Ty. Not if she isn't ill."

"But life and death, all the same," I said with desperate flippancy.

"I really can't, Ty. I'm expecting another patient."

"Oh. Well, just ring the nursing home, huh?"

"Sure," he said. "And—er—bring Elizabeth here on the way. Would you do that? It isn't much of a detour. I'd like just to be sure she's in good shape. I'll leave my patient for a few minutes, and just say hello to her in the van. All right?"

"All right," I said. "Thanks, Tonio."

"I'm sorry. . . ."

"Don't give it a thought," I said. "Be seeing you."

The room whirled when I put the receiver down. I held on to the bedstead to steady myself, and looked at my watch. Couldn't focus on the dial. The figures were just a blur. I made myself see. Concentrated hard. The numbers and the hands came back sharp and clear. Ten-thirty-seven. As if it mattered.

Three more trips to make up and down the stairs. Correction: five. Better start, or I'd never finish. I took the pillows and blankets off my bed, folded them as I would need them in the van, and took them down. When I'd made up the stretcher bed ready for Elizabeth, I felt an overpowering urge to lie down on it myself and go to sleep. Dragged myself back to the stairs instead.

Ridiculous, I thought. Ridiculous to try to do anything in the state I was in. Best to unscramble the eggs and go to bed. Wait till morning. Go to sleep. Sleep.

If I went to sleep, I would sleep for hours. Sleep away our margin of safety. Put it into the red time-expired section. Cost us too much.

I shook myself out of it. If I walked carefully, I could stop the world spinning around me. If I thought slowly, I could still think. There was a block now somewhere between my brain and

my tongue, but if the words themselves came out slurred and
wrong, I still knew with moderate clarity what I had intended
them to be.

"Honey," I said to Elizabeth. "I'm going to take the pump
down first. Then you and the Shiro—Spiro."

"You're drunk," she said miserably.

"Not surprising," I said. "Now, listen, love. You'll have to
breathe on your own. Four minutes. You know you can do it
eash—easily." She did four minutes every day, while Mrs.
Woodward gave her a bed bath.

"Ty, if you drop the pump—"

"I won't," I said. "I won't . . . drop . . . the pump."

The pump was the only one we had. There was no replace-
ment. Always we lived in the shadow of the threat that one day
its simple mechanism would break down. Spares were almost
impossible to find, because respirators were an uneconomical
item to the manufacturers, and they had discontinued making
them. If the pump needed servicing, Mrs. Woodward and I
worked the bellows by hand while it was being done in the flat.
Tiring for an hour. Impossible for a lifetime. If I dropped the
pump and punctured the bellows, Elizabeth's future could be
precisely measured.

Four minutes.

"We'd better," I said, considering, "pack some things for you
first. Clean nightdress, f'rinstance."

"How long . . . how long will we be going for?" She was
trying hard to keep the fear out of her voice, to treat our flight
on a rational sensible basis. I admired her, understood her
effort, liked her for it, loved her, had to make and keep her
safe. . . . And I'd never do it, I thought, if I let my mind
dribble on in that silly way.

How long? I didn't know how long. Until Vjoersterod had

been jailed or deported. Even then, it would be safer to find another flat.

"A few days," I said.

I fetched a suitcase and tried to concentrate on what she needed. She began to tell me, item by item, realizing I couldn't think.

"Washing things. Hairbrush. Make-up. Bedsocks. Hot-water bottle. Cardigans. Pills. . . ." She looked with longing at the Possum machine and all the gadgets.

"I'll come soon—come back soon for those," I promised. With company, just in case.

"You'll need some things yourself," she said.

"Hmm?" I squinted at her. "Yeah."

I fetched toothbrush, comb, electric razor. I would sleep in the van, dressed, on the stretcher bed. Better take a clean shirt. And a sweater. Beyond that, I couldn't be bothered. Shoved them into a grip. Packing done.

"Could you leave a note for Mrs. Woodward?" she asked. "She'll be so worried if we aren't here in the morning."

A note for Mrs. Woodward. Found some paper. Ball-point pen in my pocket. Note for Mrs. Woodward. "Gone away for few days. Will write to you." Didn't think she would be much less worried when she read that, but didn't know what else to put. The writing straggled upward, as drunk as I felt.

"All set," I said.

The packing had postponed the moment we were both afraid of. I looked at the pump. Its works were encased in a metal cabinet about the size of a bedside table, with a handle at each side for carrying. Like any large heavy box, it was easy enough for two to manage, but difficult for one. I'd done it often enough before, but not with a whirling head and throbbing bruises. I made a practice shot at picking it up, just to find out.

I found out.

Elizabeth said weakly, "Ty . . . you can't do it."

"Oh, yes, I can."

"Not after. . . . I mean, it's hurting you."

"The best thing about being drunk," I said carefully, "is that what you feel you don't feel, and even if you feel it you don't care."

"What did you say?"

"Live now, hurt later."

I pulled back her sheets and my fingers fumbled on the buckle which unfastened the Spiroshell. That wouldn't do, I thought clearly. If I fumbled the buckle, I'd never have a chance of doing the transfer in four minutes. I paused, fighting the chaos in my head. Sometimes in my youth I'd played a game against alcohol, treating it like an opponent, drinking too much of it and then daring it to defeat me. I knew from experience that if one concentrated hard enough it was possible to carry out quite adequately the familiar jobs one did when sober. This time it was no game. This time for real.

I started again on the buckle, sharpening every faculty into that one simple task. It came undone easily. I lifted the Spiroshell off her chest and laid it over her knees, where it hissed and sucked at the blankets.

Switched off the electricity. Unplugged the lead. Wound it into the lugs provided. Disconnected the flexible tube which led to the Spiroshell.

Committed now. I tugged the pump across the floor pulling it on its rocky old casters. Opened the door. Crossed the small landing. The stairs stretched downward. I put my hand on the wall to steady myself and turned around to go down backward.

Step by step. One foot down. Lift the pump down one step. Balance it. One foot down. Lift the pump. Balance. . . .

Normally, if Ron or Sue or Mrs. Woodward was not there to

help, I simply carried it straight down. This time if I did that, I would fall. I leaned against the wall. One foot down. Lift the pump down. Balance it. . . . It overhung the steps. Only its back two casters were on the ground, the others out in space. If it fell forward, it would knock me down the stairs with it. . . .

Hurry. Four minutes. Halfway down it seemed to me with an uprush of panic that the four minutes had already gone by. That I would be still on the stairs when Elizabeth died. That I would never, never get it to the bottom unless I fell down there in a tangled heap.

Step by deliberate step, concentrating acutely on every movement, I reached the ground below. Lugged the pump across the small hall, lifted it over the threshold onto the street. Rolled it to the van.

The worst bit. The floor of the van was a foot off the ground. I climbed in, stretched down, grasped the handles, and tugged. I felt as if I'd been torn apart, like the old Chinese torture of the two trees. The pump came up, in through the door, onto the floor of the van. The world whirled violently around my head. I tripped over the end of the stretcher and fell backward still holding the pump by one handle. It rocked over, crashed on its side, broke the glass over the gauge which showed the pressures and respirations per minute.

Gasping, feeling I was clamped into a hopeless nightmare, I bent over the pump and lifted it upright. Shoved it into its place. Fastened the straps which held it. Pushed the little wedges under its wheels. Plugged in the leads to and from the batteries. Couldn't believe I had managed it all, and wasted several seconds checking through again.

If it didn't work. . . . If some of the broken glass was inside . . . If it rubbed a hole in its bellows . . . I couldn't think straight, didn't know what to do about it, hoped it would be all right.

Up the stairs. Easy without the pump. Stumbled over half the steps, reached the landing on my knees.

Elizabeth was very frightened, her eyes wide and dark, looking at death because I was drunk. When she had to do her own breathing, she had no energy or air left for talking, but this time she managed one desperate word.

"Hurry."

I remembered not to nod. Picked her up, one arm under her knees, one arm around her shoulders, pulling her toward me so that she could rest her head against my shoulder. As one carries a baby.

She was feather light, but not light enough. She looked at my face and did my moaning for me.

"Hush," I said. "Just breathe."

I went down the stairs leaning against the wall, one step at a time, refusing to fall. Old man alcohol was losing the game.

The step up into the van was awful. More trees. I laid her carefully on the stretcher, putting her limp limbs straight.

Only the Spiroshell now. Went back for it, up the stairs. Like going up a down escalator, never ending, moving where it should have been still. Picked up the Spiroshell. The easiest burden. Very nearly came to grief down the stairs through tripping over the long concertina connecting tube. Stumbled into the van and thrust it much too heavily onto Elizabeth's knees.

She was beginning to labor, the tendons in her neck standing out like strings under her effort to get air.

I couldn't get the tube to screw into its connection in the pump. Cursed, sweated, almost wept. Took a deep breath, choked down the panic, tried again. The tricky two-way nut caught and slipped into a crossed thread, caught properly at last, fastened down firmly. I pressed the battery switch on the pump. The moment of truth.

The bellows nonchalantly swelled and thudded. Elizabeth gave the smallest sound of inexpressible relief. I lifted the Spiroshell gently onto her chest, slipped the strap underneath her, and couldn't do up the buckle because my fingers were finally trembling too much to control. I just knelt there holding the ends tight so that the Spiroshell was close enough for its vacuum to work. It pulled her chest safely up and down, up and down, filling her lungs with air. Some of the agonized apprehension drained out of her face, and some fragile color came back.

Sixteen life-giving breaths later I tried again with the buckle. Fixed it after two more attempts. Sat back on the floor of the van, rested my elbows on my bent knees, and my head on my hands. Shut my eyes. Everything spun in a roaring black whirl. At least, I thought despairingly, at least I had to be nearly as drunk as I was going to get. Which, thanks to having got some of the stuff up, might not now be passing-out drunk.

Elizabeth said with effortful calm, "Ty, you aren't fit to drive."

"Never know what you can do till you try."

"Wait a little while. Wait till you're better."

"Won't be better for hours." My tongue slipped on the words, fuzzy and thick. It sounded terrible. I opened my eyes, focused carefully on the floor in front of me. The swimming gyrations in my head gradually slowed down to manageable proportions. Thought about the things I still had to do.

"Got to get the shoot—suitcases."

"Wait, Ty. Wait a while."

She didn't understand that waiting would do no good. If I didn't keep moving, I would go to sleep. Even while I thought it, I could feel the insidious languor tempting me to do just that. Sleep. Sleep deadly sleep.

I climbed out of the van, stood holding on to it, waiting for some sort of balance to come back.

"Won't be long," I said. Couldn't afford to be long. She couldn't be left alone. In case.

Coordination had again deteriorated. The stairs proved worse than ever. I kept lifting my feet up far higher than was necessary, and half missing the step when I put them down. Stumbled upward, banging into the walls. In the flat, propped up the note for Mrs. Woodward so she couldn't miss it. Tucked Elizabeth's hot-water bottle under my arm, carried the suitcases to the door, switched off the light, let myself out. Started down the stairs and dropped the lot. It solved the problem of carrying them, anyway. To prevent myself following them, I finished the journey sitting down, lowering myself from step to step.

I picked up the hot-water bottle and took it out to Elizabeth. "I thought . . . Did you fall?" She was acutely anxious.

"Dropped the cases." I felt an insane urge to giggle. "'S all right." Dropped the cases, but not the pump, not Elizabeth. Old man alcohol could stuff it.

I fetched the bags and put them on the floor of the van. Shut the doors. Swayed around to the front and climbed into the driving seat. Sat there trying very hard to be sober. A losing battle, but not yet lost.

I looked at Elizabeth. Her head was relaxed on the pillows, her eyes shut. She'd reached the stage, I supposed, when constant fear was too much of a burden and it was almost a relief to give up hope and surrender to disaster. She'd surrendered for nothing, if I could help it.

Eyes front. Method needed. Do things by numbers, slowly. Switched off the light inside the van. Suddenly very dark. Switched it on again. Not a good start. Start again.

Switched on the side lights. Much better. Switch on ignition.

Check fuel. Pretty low after the run to Berkshire, but enough for five miles. Pull out the choke. Start engine. Turn out light inside van.

Without conscious thought I found the gear and let out the clutch. The van rolled forward up the mews.

Simple.

Stopped at the entrance, very carefully indeed. No one walking down the pavement, stepping out in front of me. Turned my head left and right, looking for traffic. All the lights in the road swayed and dipped. I couldn't see anything coming. Took my foot off the clutch. Turned out into the road. Gently accelerated. All clear so far.

Part of my mind was stone cold. In that area, I was sharply aware that to drive too slowly was as obvious a giveaway as meandering all over the road. To drive too fast meant no margin for a sudden stop. My reaction times were a laugh. Hitting someone wouldn't be.

As long as I kept my head still and my eyes front, it wasn't impossible. I concentrated fiercely on seeing pedestrian crossings, stationary cars, traffic lights. Seeing them in time to do something about them. I seemed to be looking down a small cone of clarity: everything in my peripheral vision was a shimmering blur.

I stopped without a jerk at some red lights. Fine. Marvelous. They changed to green. A sudden hollow void in my stomach. I couldn't remember the way. Knew it well, really. The man in the car behind began flashing his headlights. Thought of the old joke. . . . What's the definition of a split second? The interval between the lights going green and the man behind hooting or flashing. Couldn't afford to sit there doing nothing. Let in the clutch and went straight on, realizing that if I strayed off course and got lost I would be sunk. The small print on my maps was for other times. Couldn't ask anyone the way; they might turn me over to the police. Breathalizers, and all that. I'd turn the crystals black.

Ten yards over the crossing I remembered the way to Welbeck Street. I hadn't gone wrong. A vote of thanks to the unconscious mind. Hip, hip, hooray. For God's sake, mind that taxi. Making U turns in front of drunken drivers ought to be banned. . . .

Too much traffic altogether. Cars swimming out of side roads like shiny half-seen fish with yellow eyes. Cars with orange rear-direction blinkers as blinding as the sun. Buses charging across to the curb and pulling up in six feet at the stops. People running where they shouldn't cross, saving the seconds and risking the years.

Fight them all. Defeat the inefficiency of crashing. Stamp on the enemy in the blood, beat the drug confusing the brain. . . . Stop the world spinning, hold tight to a straight and steady twenty miles an hour through an imaginary earthquake. Keep death off the roads. Arrive alive. Fasten your safety belts. London welcomes careful drivers. . . .

I wouldn't like to do it again. Apart from the sheer physical exertion involved in keeping control of my arms and legs, there was also a surging recklessness trying to conquer every care I took. An inner voice saying, "Spin the wheel largely; go on, you can straighten out fine round the bend," and an answer flicker saying faintly, "Careful, careful, careful, careful. . . ."

Caution won. Mainly, I imagine, through distaste at what would happen to me if I were caught. Only pulling up safely at the other end could possibly justify what was to all intents a crime. I knew that, and clung to it.

Welbeck Street had receded since I went there last.

Fifteen

Tonio must have been looking out for us, because he opened the front door and came out onto the pavement before I had climbed out of the van. True, I had been a long time climbing out of the van. The waves of defeated intoxication had swept in as soon as I'd put on the brakes. Not defeated after all. Just postponed.

I finally made it onto the road, put one foot in front of the other around the front of the van, and leaned against the nearside fender.

Tonio peered at me with absolute incredulity.

"You're drunk."

"You're so right."

"Elizabeth . . ." he said anxiously.

I nodded my head toward the van and wished I hadn't. Hung on to the wing mirror. Still liable for drunk in charge, even on his pavement.

"Ty," he said, "for God's sake, man. Pull yourself together."

"You try," I said. "I can't."

He gave me a withering look and went around to the back of the van to open the doors. I heard him inside, talking to Elizabeth. Tried hard not to slither down the fender and fold up into the gutter. Remotely watched a man in a raincoat get out of a taxi away down the street and cross into a telephone box. The taxi waited for him. Knew I couldn't drive any farther, would have to persuade Tonio to do it, or get someone else. No use

210

thinking any more that one could remain sober by will power. One couldn't. Old bloody man alcohol sneaked up on you just when you thought you'd got him licked.

Tonio reappeared at my elbow.

"Get in the passenger seat," he said. "And give me the keys, so that you can't be held to be in charge. I'll drive you to the nursing home. But I'm afraid you'll have to wait ten minutes or so, because I still have that patient with me and there's a prescription to write. . . . Are you taking in a word I say?"

"The lot."

"Get in, then." He opened the door for me, and put his hand on my arm when I rocked. "If Elizabeth needs me, blow the horn."

"Right."

I sat in the seat, slid down, and put my head back. Sleep began to creep in around the edges.

"You all right?" I said to Elizabeth.

Her head was behind me. I heard her murmur quietly, "Yes."

The pump hummed rhythmically, aiding and abetting the whiskey. The sense of urgency drifted away. Tonio would drive us. . . . Elizabeth was safe. My eyelids gave up the struggle. I sank into a pit, whirling and disorientated. Not an unpleasant feeling if one didn't fight it.

Tonio opened the door and shook me awake.

"Drink this," he said. A mug of coffee, black and sweet. "I'll be with you in a minute."

He went back into the house, propping the door open with a heavy wrought-iron facsimile of the Pisa Tower. The coffee was too hot. With exaggerated care I put the mug down on the floor. Straightened up wishing the load of ache across my shoulders would let up and go away, but was much too full of the world's oldest anesthetic to feel it very clearly.

I had been as drunk as that only once before, and it wasn't
the night they told me Elizabeth would die, but four days later
when they said she would live. I'd downed uncountable double
whiskeys and I'd eaten almost nothing for a week. It was odd to
remember the delicious happiness of that night because of
course it hadn't after all been the end of an agony but only the
beginning of the years of pain and struggle and waste. . . .

I found myself staring vacantly at the off side wing mirror. If
I conshen—well, concentrated—very hard, I thought be-
musedly, I would be able to see what it reflected. A pointless
game. It simply irritated me that I couldn't see clearly if I
wanted to. Looked obstinately at the mirror and waited for the
slowed-down focusing process to come right. Finally, with a
ridiculous smile of triumph, I saw what it saw down the street.
Nothing much. Nothing worth the trouble. Only a silly old taxi
parked by the curb. Only a silly man in a raincoat getting into it.

Raincoat.

Raincoat.

The alarm bells rang fuzzily in my sluggish head. I opened
the door and fumbled my way onto the pavement, kicking the
coffee over in the process. Leaned against the side of the van
and looked down toward the taxi. It was still parked. By the
telephone box. Where the man in the raincoat had been ringing
someone up.

They say sudden overwhelming disaster sobers you, but it
isn't true. I reeled across the pavement and up the step to
Tonio's door. Forgot all about blowing the car horn. Banged
the solid knocker on his door, and called him loudly. He appeared at the top of the stairs which led to his consulting room
on the first floor and his flat above that.

"Shut up, Ty," he said. "I won't be long."

"Shome—someone's followed us," I said. "It's dangerous."

He wouldn't understand, I thought confusedly. He wouldn't know what I was talking about. I didn't know where to start explaining.

Elizabeth, however, must have told him enough.

"Oh. All right, I'll be down in one minute." His head withdrew around the bend in the stairs and I swiveled unsteadily to take another look down the street. Taxi still there, in the same place. Light out, not for hire. Just waiting. Waiting to follow us again if we moved. Waiting to tell Vjoersterod where we'd gone.

I shook with futile rage. Vjoersterod hadn't after all been satisfied that Ross's truncheon and the threats against Elizabeth had been enough to insure a permanent state of docility. He'd left Raincoat outside to watch. Just in case. I hadn't spotted him. Had been much too drunk to spot anything. But there he was. Right on our tail.

I'll fix him, I thought furiously. I'll fix him properly.

Tonio started to come down the stairs, escorting a thin bent elderly man whose breath rasped audibly through his open mouth. Slowly they made it to the bottom. Tonio held his arm as they came past me, and helped him over the threshold and down the step to the pavement. An almost equally elderly woman emerged from the Rover parked directly behind my van. Tonio handed him over, helped him into the car, came back to me.

"He likes to come at night," he explained. "Not so many fumes from the traffic, and easier parking."

"Lord Fore—Fore something," I said.

"Forlingham," Tonio nodded. "Do you know him?"

"Used to go racing. Poor old thing." I looked woozily up the street. "See that taxi?"

"Yes."

"Following us."

"Oh."

"So you take 'Lizabeth on to the nursing home. I'll stop the taxi." A giggle got as far as the first ridiculous note. "What's worse than raining cats and dogs? I'll tell you—hailing taxis."

"You're drunk," Tonio said. "Wait while I change my coat." He was wearing formal consultant's dress and looked young and glamorous enough to be a pop singer. "Can we wait?"

I swung out a generous arm in a wide gesture. "The taxi," I said owlishly, "is waiting for *us*."

He went to change his coat. I could hear Elizabeth's pump thudding safely away; wondered if I ought to go and reassure her; thought that in my state I probably couldn't. The Forling-hams started up and drove away. The taxi went on waiting.

At first I thought what I saw next was on the pink-elephant level. Not really there. Couldn't be there. But this time no hallucination. Edging smoothly around the corner, pulling gently into the curb, stopping behind the taxi, one Silver Wraith, property of Hire Cars Lucullus.

Raincoat emerged from the taxi and reported to the Rolls. Two minutes later he returned to the taxi, climbed in, and was driven away.

Tonio ran lightly down the stairs and came to a halt beside me in a black sweater instead of a coat.

"Let's get going," he said.

I put my hand clumsily on his arm.

"Shee—I mean, see that Rolls down there, where the taxi was."

"Yes."

"In that," I said carefully, "is the man who—oh God, why can't I think—who said he would . . . kill . . .'Lizabeth if I didn't do what he wanted. . . . Well . . . he might . . . he might not . . . but can't rish—risk it. Take her. . . . Take her. I'll stop . . . him following you."

"How?" Tonio said unemotionally.

I looked at the Tower of Pisa holding the door open.

"With that."

"It's heavy," he objected, assessing my physical state.

"Oh for God's sake, stop arguing," I said weakly. "I want her to go where they can't find her. Please—please get going. . . . Go on, Tonio. And drive away slowly."

He hesitated, but finally showed signs of moving. "Don't forget," he said seriously, "that you are no use to Elizabeth dead."

"S'pose not."

"Give me your coat," he said suddenly. "Then they'll think it's still you in the van."

Behind the van I took off my coat obediently, and he put it on. He was shorter than me. It hung on him. Same dark head, though. They might mistake us from a distance.

Tonio gave a rip-roaring impression of my drunken walk, reeling right around the back of the van on his way to the driving seat. I laughed. I was that drunk.

He started the van and drove slowly away. I watched him give one artistic weave across the road and back. Highly intelligent fellow, Tonio Perelli.

Down the road, the Silver Wraith began to move. Got to stop him, I thought fuzzily. Got to stop him smashing up our lives, smashing up other people's lives. Someone, somewhere, had to stop him. In Welbeck Street, with a doorstop. Couldn't think clearly beyond that one fact. Had to stop him.

I bent down and picked up the Leaning Tower by its top two stories. As Tonio had said, it was heavy. Bruised-muscle tearingly heavy. Tomorrow its effects would be awful. Fair enough.

Tomorrow would be much more awful if I put it down again—
or if I missed.

The Rolls came toward me as slowly as Tonio had driven
away. If I'd been sober, I'd have had all the time in the world.
As it was, I misjudged the pace and all but let him go cruising by.

Down one step. Don't trip. Across the pavement. Hurry.
Swung the wrought-iron tower around with both hands as if I
were throwing the hammer and forgot to let go. Its weight and
momentum pulled me after it; but although at the last moment
Ross saw me and tried to swerve away, the heavy metal base
crashed exactly where I wanted it. Drunks' luck. Dead center of
the windscreen.

Scrunch went the laminated glass in a radiating star. Silver
cracks streaked across Ross's vision. The huge car swerved
violently out into the center of the road and then in toward the
curb as Ross stamped on the brakes. A screech of tires, a scraping jolt. The Rolls stopped abruptly at a sharp angle to the
pavement with its rear end inviting attention from the police.
No police appeared to pay attention. A great pity. I wouldn't
have minded being scooped in for being drunk and disorderly
and disturbing the peace.

I had rebounded off the smooth side of the big car and fallen
in a heap in the road. The Rolls had stopped, and that was that.
Job done. No clear thought of self-preservation spearheaded its
way through the mist in my head. I didn't remember that
Tonio's solid front door stood open only a few yards away. Jelly
had taken over from bone in my legs. Welbeck Street had
started revolving around me and was taking its time over
straightening out.

It was Ross who picked me up. Ross with his truncheon. I
was past caring much what he did with it; and what he intended
I don't know, because this time I was saved by the bell in the

shape of a party of people in evening dress who came out into
the street from a neighboring house. They had cheerful gay
voices full of a happy evening, and they exclaimed in instant
sympathy over the plight of the Rolls.

"I say, do you need any help. . . ?"

"Shall we call anyone—the police, or anything?"

"Can we give you a lift. . . ?"

"Or call a garage?"

"No, thank you," said Vjoersterod in his most charming
voice. "So kind of you . . . but we can manage."

Ross picked me to my feet and held on grimly to my arm.
Vjoersterod was saying, "We've been having a little trouble
with my nephew. I'm afraid he's very drunk. Still, once we get
him home everything will be all right."

They murmured sympathetically. Began to move away.

"It's not true!" I shouted. "They'll prob'ly kill me." My voice
sounded slurred and much too melodramatic. They paused,
gave Vjoersterod a group of sympathetic, half-embarrassed
smiles, and moved off up the street.

"Hey," I called. "Take me with you."

Useless. They didn't even look back.

"What now?" Ross said to Vjoersterod.

"We can't leave him here. Those people would remember."

"In the car?"

While Vjoersterod nodded, Ross shoved me toward the Rolls,
levering with his grasp on my right arm. I swung at him with
the left, and missed completely. I could see two of him, which
made it difficult. Between them they more or less slung me into
the back of the car and I sprawled there face down, half on and
half off the seat, absolutely furious that I still could not climb
out of that crippling alcoholic stupor. There was a ringing in
my head like the noise of the livid green corridors of gas at the

dentist's. But no stepped-up awakening to daylight and the taste of blood. Just a continuing extraordinary sensation of being conscious and unconscious, not alternately but both at once.

Ross knocked out a few of the worst-cracked pieces of the windscreen and started the car.

Vjoersterod, sitting beside him, leaned over the back of his seat and said casually, "Where to, Mr. Tyrone? Which way to your wife?"

"Round and round the mulberry bush," I mumbled indistinctly. "And good night to you, too."

He let go with four-letter words which were much more in keeping with his character than his usual elevated chat.

"It's no good," Ross said disgustedly. "He won't tell us unless we take him to pieces, and even then—if we did get it out of him—what good would it do? He'll never write for you. Never."

"Why not?" said Vjoersterod obstinately.

"Well, look at it this way. We threatened to kill his wife. Does he knuckle under? Yes, as long as we're there. The moment our backs are turned, first thing he does is to move her out. We follow, find her, he shifts her off again. That could go on and on. All we can do more is actually kill her, and if we do that we've no hold on him anyway. So he'll never write for you, whatever we do."

Full marks, I said to myself fatuously. Masterly summing up of the situation. Top of the class.

"You didn't hit him hard enough," Vjoersterod said accusingly, sliding out of the argument.

"I did."

"You can't have."

"If you remember," Ross said patiently, "Charlie Boston's boys made no impression either. They either do or don't respond to the treatment. This one doesn't. Same with the threats. Same with the drink. Usually one method is enough. This time we use all three, just to make sure. And where do we get? We get nowhere at all. Just like Gunther Braunthal last year."

Vjoersterod grunted. I wondered remotely what had become of Gunther Braunthal. Decided I didn't really want to know.

"I can't afford for him to get away with it," Vjoersterod said.

"No," Ross said.

"I don't like disposals in England," Vjoersterod went on in irritation. "Too much risk. Too many people everywhere."

"Leave it to me," Ross said calmly.

I struggled up into a sitting position, propping myself up on my hands. Looked out of the side window. Lights flashing past, all one big whirl. We weren't going very fast, on account of the broken windscreen, but the December night air swept into the car in gusts, freezing me in my cotton shirt. In a minute, when my head cleared a fraction, I would open the door and roll out. We weren't going very fast. If I waited for a bit of main street, with people. . . . Couldn't wait too long. Didn't want Ross attending to my disposal.

Vjoersterod's head turned my way. "You've only yourself to thank, Mr. Tyrone. You shouldn't have crossed me. You should have done what I said. I gave you your chance. You've been very stupid, Mr. Tyrone. Very stupid indeed. And now, of course, you'll be paying for it."

"Huh?" I said.

"He's still drunk," Ross said. "He doesn't understand."

"I'm not so sure. Look what he's done in the past hour. He's got ahead like a bullet."

My eyes suddenly focused on something outside. Something I knew, that everyone knew. The aviary in Regent's Park, pointed

angular wire opposite the main entrance to the Zoo. Been there
before with Vjoersterod. He must be staying somewhere near
there, I thought. Must be taking me to where he lived. It didn't
matter that it was near the Zoo. What did matter was that this
was also the way to the nursing home where Tonio had taken
Elizabeth. It was less than a mile ahead.

I thought for one wild horror-stricken moment that I must
have told Vjoersterod where to go; then remembered and knew
I hadn't. But he was much too close. Much too close. Supposing
his way home took him actually past the nursing home, and he
saw the van—saw them unloading Elizabeth, even. . . . He
might change his mind and kill her and leave me alive . . .
which would be unbearable, totally and literally unbearable.

Distract his attention.

I said with as much clarity as my tongue would allow:
"Vjoersterod and Ross. Vjoersterod and Ross."

"*What?*" said Vjoersterod.

The shock to Ross resulted in a swerve across the road and a
jolt on the brakes.

"Go back to South Africa before the bogies get you."

Vjoersterod had twisted round and was staring at me. Ross
had his eyes too much on the mirror and not enough on the
road. All the same, he started his indicator flashing for the right
turn which led over the bridge across Regent's Canal and then
out of the park. Which led straight past the nursing home, half
a mile ahead.

"I told the Stewards," I said desperately. "I told the Stewards
—all about you. Last Wednesday. I told my paper. . . . It'll all
be there on Sunday. So you'll remember me, too, you'll remember. . . ."

Ross turned the wheel erratically, sweeping wide to the turn.
I brought my hands around with a wholly uncoordinated swing

and clamped them hard over his eyes. He took both his own hands off the wheel to try and detach mine, and the car rocked straight halfway through the turn and headed across the road at a tangent, taking the shortest distance to the bank of the canal.

Vjoersterod shouted frantically and pulled with all his strength at my arm, but my desperation was at least the equal of his. I hauled Ross's head back toward me harder still, and it was their own doing that I was too drunk to care where or how the car crashed.

"Brake!" Vjoersterod screamed. "Brake, you stupid fool!"

Ross put his foot down. He couldn't see what he was doing. He put his foot down hard. On the accelerator.

The Rolls leaped across the pavement and onto the grass. The bank sloped gently and then steeply down to the canal, with saplings and young trees growing here and there. The Rolls scrunched sideways into one trunk and ricocheted into a sapling which it mowed down like corn.

Vjoersterod grabbed the wheel, but the heavy car was now pointed downhill and going too fast for any change of steering. The wheel twisted and lurched out of his hand under the jolt of the front wheel hitting another tree and slewing to the side. Branches cracked around the car and scraped and stabbed at the glossy coachwork. Vjoersterod fumbled on the glove shelf and found the truncheon, and twisted around in his seat and began hitting my arm in panic-stricken fury.

I let go of Ross. It was far too late for him both to size up the situation and to do anything useful about it. He was just beginning to reach for the hand brake when the Rolls crashed down over the last sapling and fell into the canal.

The car swung convulsively on impact, throwing me around like a rag doll in the back and tumbling Vjoersterod and Ross together in the front. Black water immediately poured through the broken windscreen and with lethal speed began filling the car.

How to get out. . . . I fumbled for a door handle in the sudden dark, couldn't find one, and didn't know what I had my feet on, didn't know which way up I was. Didn't know if the car was on its back or its nose. Didn't know anything except that it was sinking.

Vjoersterod began screaming as the water rose up his body. His arm was still flailing about and knocking into me. I felt the truncheon still in his hand. Snatched it from him and hit it hard against where I thought the rear window must be. Connected only with material. Felt around wildly with my hand, found glass above my head and hit at that.

It cracked. Laminated and tough. Cursed Rolls-Royce for their standards. Hit again. Couldn't get a decent swing. Tried again. Crunched a hole. Water came through it. Not a torrent, but too much. The window was under the surface. Not far under. Tried again. Bash, bash. Made a bigger hole but still not enough . . . and water fell through it and over me, and from the front of the car the icy level was rising past my waist.

Great to die when you're dead drunk, I thought. And when I die don't bury me at all, just pickle my bones in alcohol. . . . Crashed the truncheon against the hole. Missed. My arm went right up through it. Felt it up there in the air, out of the water. Stupid. Silly. Drowning in less than an inch of Regent's Canal.

Pulled my arm back and tried again. Absolutely no good. Too much water, too much whiskey. One outside, one in. No push in my battered muscles and not much comprehension in my mind. Floating off on the river of death. . . . Sorry, Elizabeth. . . .

Suddenly there were lights shining down over me. Hallucinations, I thought. Hallelujah hallucinations. Death was a blinding white light and a crashing noise in the head and a shower of water and glass and voices calling and arms grasping and pulling and raising one up . . . up . . . into a free cold wind. . . .

"Is there anyone else in the car?" a voice said. A loud urgent voice, speaking to me. The voice of earth. Telling me I was alive. Telling me to wake up and do something. I couldn't adjust. Blinked at him stupidly.

"Tell us," he said. "Is there anyone else in the car?" He shook my shoulder. It hurt. Brought me back a little. He said again, "Is there anyone else?"

I nodded weakly. "Two."

"Christ," he muttered. "What a hope."

I was sitting on the grass on the canal bank, shivering. Someone put a coat around my shoulders. There were a lot of people and more coming, black figures against the reflection on the dark water, figures lit on one side only by the headlights of the car which had come down the path plowed by the Rolls. It was parked there on the edge, with its lights on the place where the Rolls had gone. You could see the silver rim of the rear window shimmering just below the surface, close to the bank. You could see the water sliding shallowly through the gaping hole my rescuers had pulled me through. You could see nothing inside the car except darkness and water.

A youngish man had stripped to his underpants and was proposing to go through the rear window to try to rescue the others. People tried to dissuade him, but he went. I watched in a daze, scarcely thinking, scarcely feeling. His head came back through the window into the air, and several hands bent over to help him.

They pulled Vjoersterod out and laid him on the bank.

"Artificial respiration," one said. "Kiss of life."

Kiss Vjoersterod. . . . If they wanted to, they were welcome.

The diver went back for Ross. He had to go down twice. A very brave man. The Rolls could have toppled over onto its side at any moment and trapped him inside. People, I thought groggily, were amazing.

They put Ross beside Vjoersterod, and kissed him, too. Neither of them responded.

Cold was seeping into every cell of my body. From the ground I sat on it rose, from the wind it pierced, from my wet clothes it clung clammily to my skin. Bruises stiffen fast in those conditions. Everything started hurting at once, climbing from piano to fortissimo. The noises in my head were deafening. A fine time for the drink to begin dying out on me, I thought. Just when I needed it most.

I lay back on the grass, and someone put something soft under my head. Their voices sprayed over me, questioning and solicitous.

"How did it happen?"

"We've sent for an ambulance. . . ."

"What he needs is some good hot tea. . . ."

"We're so sorry about your friends. . . ."

"Can you tell us your name?"

I didn't answer them. Didn't have enough strength. Could let it all go now. Didn't have to struggle any more. Old man alcohol could have what was left.

I shut my eyes. The world receded rapidly.

"He's out cold," a tiny faraway voice said.

It wasn't true at that moment. But a second later it was.

Sixteen

I was in a dim long room with a lot of bodies laid out in white. I, too, was in white, being painfully crushed in a cement sandwich. My head, sticking out of it, pulsed and thumped like a steam hammer.

The components of this nightmare gradually sorted themselves out into depressing reality. Respectively, a hospital ward, a savage load of bruises, and an emperor-sized hangover.

I dragged my arm up and squinted at my watch. Four-fifty. Even that small movement had out-of-proportion repercussions. I put my hand down gently on top of the sheets and tried to duck out by going to sleep again.

Didn't manage it. Too many problems. Too many people would want too many explanations. I'd have to edit the truth here and there, juggle the facts a little. Needed a clear head for it, not a throbbing dehydrated morass.

I tried to sort out into order exactly what had happened the evening before, and wondered profitlessly what I would have done if I hadn't been drunk. Thought numbly about Vjoersterod and Ross being pulled from the wreck. If they were dead, which I was sure they were, I had certainly killed them. The worst thing about that was that I didn't care.

If I shut my eyes, the world still revolved and the ringing noise in my head grew more persistent. I thought wearily that people who poisoned themselves with alcohol for pleasure had to be crazy.

At six they woke up all the patients, who shook my tender brain with shattering decibels of coughing, spitting, and brushing of teeth. Breakfast was steamed haddock and weak tea. I asked for water and something for a headache, and thought sympathetically about the man who said he didn't like Alka-Seltzers because they were so noisy.

The hospital was equipped with telephone trolleys, but for all my urging I couldn't get hold of one until nine-thirty. I fed it with coins salvaged from my now-drying trousers and rang Tonio. Caught him luckily in his consulting room after having insisted his receptionist tell him I was calling.

"Ty! *Deo gratias.* Where the hell have you been?"

"Swimming," I said. "I'll tell you later. Is Elizabeth O.K.?"

"She's fine. But she was extremely anxious when you didn't turn up again last night. Where are you now? Why haven't you been to find out for yourself how she is?"

"I'm in University College Hospital. At least, I'm here for another few hours. I got scooped in here last night, but there's not much damage."

"How's the head?"

"Lousy."

He laughed. Charming fellow.

I rang the nursing home and talked to Elizabeth. There was no doubt she was relieved to hear from me, though from the unusual languor in her voice it was clear they had given her some sort of tranquilizer. She was almost too calm. She didn't ask me what had happened when Tonio had driven her away; she didn't want to know where I was at that moment.

"Would you mind staying in the nursing home for a couple of days?" I asked. "Just till I get things straight."

"Sure," she said. "Couple of days. Fine."

"See you soon, honey."

"Sure," she said again vaguely. "Fine."

After a little while I disconnected and got through to Luke-John. His brisk voice vibrated loudly through the receiver and sent javelins through my head. I told him I hadn't written my Sunday column yet because I'd been involved in a car crash the night before, and held the receiver six inches away while he replied.

"The car crash was yesterday afternoon."

"This was another one."

"For God's sake, do you make a habit of it?"

"I'll write my piece this evening and come in with it in the morning before I go to Heathbury for the Lamplighter. Will that do?"

"It'll have to, I suppose," he grumbled. "You weren't hurt in the second crash, were you?" He sounded as if an affirmative answer would be highly unpopular.

"Only bruised," I said, and got a noncommittal unsympathetic grunt.

"Make that piece good," he said. "Blow the roof off."

I put down the receiver before he could blow the roof off my head. It went on thrumming mercilessly. Ross's target area also alternately burned and ached and made lying in bed draggingly uncomfortable. The grim morning continued. People came and asked me who I was. And who were the two men with me who had both drowned in the car? Did I know their address?

No, I didn't.

And how had the accident happened?

"The chauffeur had a blackout," I said.

A police sergeant came with a notebook and wrote down the uninformative truth I told him about the accident. I didn't know Mr. Vjoersterod well; he was just an acquaintance. He had insisted on taking me in his car to the nursing home where my wife was at present a patient. The chauffeur had had a blackout and the car had run off the road. It had all happened very quickly. I couldn't remember clearly, because I was afraid I had had a little too much to drink. Mr. Vjoersterod had handed me something to smash our way out of the car with, and I had done my best. It was very sad about Mr. Vjoersterod and the chauffeur. The man who had fetched them out ought to have a medal. The sergeant said I would be needed for the inquest, and went away.

The doctor who came to examine me at midday sympathized with my various discomforts and said it was extraordinary sometimes how much bruising one could sustain through being thrown about in a somersaulting car. I gravely agreed with him and suggested I go home as soon as possible.

"Why not?" he said. "If you feel like it."

I felt like oblivion. I creaked into my rough-dried crumpled shirt and trousers and left my face unshaven, my hair unbrushed, and my tie untied, because lifting my arms up for those jobs was too much trouble. Tottered downstairs and got the porter to ring for a taxi, which took me the short distance to Welbeck Street and decanted me on Tonio's doorstep. Someone had picked up the Leaning Tower and put it back in place. There wasn't a mark on it. More than could be said for the Rolls. More than could be said for me.

Tonio gave me one penetrating look, an armchair, and a medicine glass of disprin and nepenthe.

"What's this made of?" I asked when I'd drunk it.

"Nepenthe? A mixture of opium and sherry."

"You're joking."

He shook his head. "Opium and sherry wine. Very useful stuff. How often do you intend to turn up here in dire need of it?"

"No more," I said. "It's finished."

He wanted to know what had happened after he had driven Elizabeth away, and I told him, save for the one detail of my having blacked out the chauffeur myself. He was no fool, however. He gave me a twisted smile of comprehension and remarked that I had behaved like a drunken idiot.

After that he fetched my jacket from his bedroom and insisted on driving me and the van back to the flat, on the basis that Elizabeth needed me safe and sound, not wrapped around one of the lampposts I had miraculously missed the night before. I didn't argue. Hadn't the energy. He put the van in the garage for me and walked away up the mews to look for a taxi, and I slowly went up the stairs to the flat feeling like a wet dishcloth attempting the Matterhorn.

The flat was stifling hot. I had left all the heaters on the night before and Mrs. Woodward hadn't turned them off. There was a note from her on the table. "Is everything all right? Have put milk in fridge. Am very anxious. Mrs. W."

I looked at my bed. Nothing on it but sheets. Remembered all the blankets and pillows were still downstairs on the stretcher in the van. Going down for them was impossible. Pinched Elizabeth's. Spread one pink blanket roughly on the divan, lay down on it still dressed, pulled another over me, put my head down gingerly on the soft cool pillow.

Bliss.

The world still spun. And otherwise far too little to put out flags for. My head still manufactured its own sound track. And in spite of the nepenthe the rest of me still felt fresh from a cement mixer. But now there was luxuriously nothing more to do except drift over the edge of a precipice into a deep black heavenly sleep. . . .

The telephone bell rang sharply, sawing the dream in half. It was Mrs. Woodward, Lancashire accent very strong under stress, sounding touchingly relieved that no unbearable disaster had happened to Elizabeth.

"It's me that's not well," I said. "My wife's spending a couple of days in the nursing home. If you'll ring again, I'll let you know when she'll be back. . . ."

I put the receiver down in its cradle and started across to my bed. Took two steps, yawned, and wondered if I should tell Victor Roncey to go fetch Madge and the boys. Wondered if I should tell Willy Ondroy to slacken the ultra-tight security. Decided to leave things as they were. Only twenty-four more hours to the race. Might as well be safe. Even with Vjoersterod dead, there was always Charlie Boston.

Not that Tiddely Pom would win. After all the trouble to get him there his chances were slender, because the bout of colic would have taken too much out of him. Charlie Boston would make his profit, just as if they'd nobbled him as planned.

I retraced the two steps back to the telephone and after a chat with inquiries put through a personal call to Birmingham.

"Mr. Boston?"

"Yers."

"This is James Tyrone."

There was a goggling silence at the other end punctuated only by some heavy breathing.

I asked, "What price are you offering on Tiddely Pom?"

No answer except a noise halfway between a grunt and a growl.

"The horse will run," I commented.

"That's all you know," he said. A rough bad-tempered voice. A rough bad-tempered man.

"Don't rely on Ross or Vjoersterod," I said patiently. "You won't be hearing from them again. The poor dear fellows are both dead."

I put down the receiver without waiting for the Boston reactions. Felt strong enough to take off my jacket. Made it back to bed and found the friendly precipice still there waiting. Didn't keep it waiting any longer.

A long while later I woke up thirsty and with a tongue which felt woolly and grass green. The nepenthe had worn off. My shoulders were heavy, stiffly sore, and insistent. A bore. All pain was a bore. It was dark. I consulted my luminous watch. Four o'clock, give or take a minute. I'd slept twelve hours.

I yawned. Found my brain no longer felt as if it were sitting on a bruise and remembered with a wide-awakening shock that I hadn't written my column for the *Blaze*. I switched on the light and took a swig of Tonio's mixture and, after it had worked, went to fetch a notebook and pencil and a cup of coffee. Propped up the pillows, climbed back between the blankets, and blew the roof off for Luke-John.

"The lawyers will have a fit," he said.

"As I've pointed out, the man who ran the racket died this week, and the libel laws only cover the living. The dead can't sue. And no one can sue for them. Also you can't accuse or try the dead. Not in this world, anyway. So nothing they've done can be *sub judice*. Right?"

"Don't quote *Blaze* dictums to me, laddie. I was living by them before you were weaned." He picked up my typed sheets as if they would burn him.

"Petrified owners can come out of the caves," he read aloud. "The reign of intimidation is over and the scandal of the non-starting favorites can be fully exposed."

Derry lifted his head to listen, gave me a grin, and said, "Our trouble shooter loosing the big guns again?"

"Life gets tedious otherwise," I said.

"Only for some."

Luke-John eyed me appraisingly. "You look more as if you'd been the target. I suppose all this haggard-eyed stuff is the result of a day spent crashing about in cars." He flicked his thumbs against my article. "Did you invent this unnamed villain, or did he really exist? And if so, who was he?"

If I didn't tell, Mike de Jong in his rival newspaper might put two and two together and come up with a filling-in-the-gaps story that Luke-John would never forgive me for. And there was no longer any urgent reason for secrecy.

I said, "He was a South African called Vjoersterod, and he died the night before last in the second of those car crashes."

Their mouths literally fell open.

"Dyna . . . *mite*," Derry said.

I told them most of what had happened. I left Gail and Ross's truncheon out altogether but put in the threat to Elizabeth. Left out the drunken driving and the hands over Ross's eyes. Made it bald and factual. Left out the sweat.

Luke-John thought through the problem and then read my article again.

"When you know what you've omitted, what you've included seems pale. But I think this is enough. It'll do the trick, tell everyone the pressure's off and that they can safely bet antepost again, thanks entirely to investigations conducted by the *Blaze*. That's, after all, what we wanted."

"Buy the avenging *Blaze*," said Derry only half sardonically. "Racket-smashing a specialty."

Luke-John gave him a sour look for a joke in bad taste. I asked him if he would ring up a powerful bookmaking friend of his and ask him the present state of the Lamplighter market, and with raised eyebrows but no other comment he got through. He asked the question, listened with sharpening attention to the answer, and scribbled down some figures. When he had finished, he gave a soundless whistle and massaged his larynx.

"He says Charlie Boston's main Birmingham office has been trying to lay off about fifty thousand on Tiddely Pom since yesterday afternoon. Everyone smells a sewer full of rats because of your articles and the *Blaze's* undertaking to keep the horse safe, and they're in a tizzy whether to take the bets or not. Only one or two of the biggest firms have done so."

I said, "If Boston can't lay off and Tiddely Pom wins, he's sunk without trace, but if Tiddely Pom loses he'll pocket all Vjoersterod's share of the loot as well as his own and be better off than if we'd done nothing at all. If he manages to lay off and Tiddely Pom wins, he'll be smiling, and if he lays off and Tiddely Pom loses, he'll have thrown away everything the crimes were committed for."

"A delicate problem," said Derry judicially. "Or what you might call the antlers of a dilemma."

"Could he know about the colic?" Luke-John asked.

We decided after picking it over that as he was trying to lay off he probably couldn't know. Luke-John rang back to his bookmaker friend and advised him to take as much of the Boston money as he could.

"And after that," he said gloomily as he put down the receiver, "every other bloody horse will fall, and Tiddely Pom will win."

Derry and I went down to Heathbury Park together on the race train. The racecourse and the sponsors of the Lamplighter had been smiled on by the day. Clear, sunny, still, frosty: a perfect December morning. Derry said that fine weather was sure to bring out a big crowd, and that he thought Zig Zag would win. He said he thought I looked ill. I said I felt better

than yesterday. We completed the journey in our usual relationship of tolerant acceptance and I wondered inconsequentially
why it had never solidified into friendship.

He was right on the first count. Heathbury Park was bursting
at the seams. I went first to Willy Ondroy's office beside the
weighing room and found a scattered queue of people wanting
a word with him, but he caught my eye across the throng and
waved a beckoning hand.

"Hey," he said, swinging around in his chair to talk to me
behind his shoulder. "Your wretched horse has caused me more
bother. . . . That Victor Roncey, he's a bloody pain in the
neck."

"What's he been doing?"

"He arrived at ten this morning all set to blow his top if the
horse arrived a minute after twelve, and when he found he was
there already he blew his top anyway and said he should have
been told."

"Not the easiest of characters," I agreed.

"Anyway, that's only the half of it. The gateman rang me at
about eight this morning to say there was a man persistently
trying to get in. He'd offered him a bribe and then increased it
and had tried to slip in unnoticed while he, the gateman, was
having an argument with one of the stable lads. So I nipped
over from my house for a recky, and there was this short stout
individual walking along the back of the stable block looking
for an unguarded way in. I marched him round to the front and
the gateman said that was the same merchant, so I asked him
who he was and what he wanted. He wouldn't answer. Said he
hadn't committed any crime. I let him go. Nothing else to do."

"Pity."

"Wait a minute. My racecourse manager came toward us as
the man walked away, and the first thing he said to me was
"What's Charlie Boston doing here?""

"What?"

"Ah. I thought he might mean something to you. But he was extraordinarily clumsy if he was after Tiddely Pom."

"No brains and no brawn," I agreed.

He looked at me accusingly. "If Charlie Boston was the sum total of the threat to Tiddely Pom, haven't you been overdoing the melodrama a bit?"

I said dryly, "Read the next thrilling instalment in the *Blaze*."

He laughed and turned back decisively to his impatient queue. I wandered out into the paddock thinking of Charlie Boston and his futile attempt to reach the horse. Charlie Boston who thought with his muscles. With other people's muscles, come to that. Having his boys on the sick list and Vjoersterod and Ross on the dead, he was as naked and vulnerable as an opened oyster.

He might also be desperate. If he was trying to lay off fifty thousand pounds, he had stood to lose at least ten times that—upward of half a million—if Tiddely Pom won. A nose dive of epic proportions. A prospect to induce panic and recklessness in ever-increasing intensity as the time of the race drew near.

I decided that Roncey should share the care of his horse's safety, and began looking out for him in the throng. I walked around the corner with my eyes scanning sideways and nearly bumped into someone standing by the Results at Other Meetings notice board. The apology was halfway to my tongue before I realized who it was.

Gail.

I saw the pleasure which came first into her eyes, and the uncertainty afterward. Very likely I was showing her exactly the same feeling. Very likely she, like me, felt a thudding shock at meeting. Yet if I'd considered it at all, it was perfectly reasonable that she should come to see her uncle's horse run in the Lamplighter.

"Ty?" she said tentatively, with a ton less than her usual poise.

"Surprise, surprise." It sounded more flippant than I felt.

"I thought I might see you," she said. Her smooth black hair shone in the sun and the light lay along the bronze lines of her face, touching them with gold. The mouth I had kissed was a rosy pink. The body I had liked naked was covered with a turquoise coat. A week today, I thought numbly. A week today I left her in bed.

"Are Harry and Sarah here?" I said. Social chat. Hide the wound which hadn't even begun to form scar tissue. I'd no right to be wounded in the first place. My own fault. Couldn't complain.

"They're in the bar," she said. Where else?

"Would you like a drink?"

She shook her head. "I want to—to explain. I see that you know. . . . I have to explain."

"No need. A cup of coffee, perhaps?"

"Just listen."

I could feel the rigidity in all my muscles and realized it extended even into my mouth and jaw. With a conscious effort I loosened them and relaxed.

"All right."

"Did she— I mean, is she going to divorce you?"

"No."

"Ohhhh." It was a long sigh. "Then I'm sorry if I got you into trouble with her. But why did she have you followed if she didn't want to divorce you?"

I stared at her. The wound half healed in an instant.

"What's the matter?" she said.

I took a deep breath. "Tell me what happened after I left you. Tell me about the man who followed me."

"He came up and spoke to me in the street just outside the hotel."

"What did he look like?"

"He puzzled me a bit. I mean, he seemed too—I don't know—civilized, I suppose is the word, to be a private detective. His clothes were made for him, for instance. He had an accent of some sort and a yellowish skin. Tall. About forty, I should think."

"What did he say?"

"He said your wife wanted a divorce and he was working on it. He asked me for—concrete evidence."

"A bill from the hotel?"

She nodded, not meeting my eyes. "I agreed to go in again and ask for one."

"Why, Gail?"

She didn't answer.

"Did he pay you for it?"

"God, Ty," she said explosively. "Why not? I needed the money. I'd only met you three times and you were just as bad as me, living with your wife just because she was rich."

"Yes," I said. "Well, how much?"

"He offered me fifty pounds, and when I'd got used to the idea that he was ready to pay I told him to think again; with all your wife's money she could afford more than that for her freedom."

"And then what?"

"He said . . . if I could give him full and substantial facts, he could raise the payment considerably." After a pause, in a mixture of defiance and shame, she added, "He agreed to a thousand pounds, in the end."

I gave a gasp which was half a laugh.

"Didn't your wife tell you?" she asked.

I shook my head. "He surely didn't have that much money on him? Did he give you a check?"

"No. He met me later, outside the art school, and gave me a brown carrier bag. Beautiful new notes, in bundles. I gave him the bill I'd got, and told him—everything I could."

"I know," I said.

"Why did she pay so much, if she doesn't want a divorce?" When I didn't answer at once, she went on. "It wasn't really only the money. I thought if she wanted to divorce you, why the hell should I stop her? You said you wouldn't leave her, but if she sort of left *you*, then you would be free, and maybe we could have more than a few Sundays. . . ."

I thought that one day I might appreciate the irony of it.

I said, "It wasn't my wife who paid you that money. It was the man himself. He wasn't collecting evidence for a divorce, but evidence to blackmail me with."

"Ohh." It was a moan. "Oh, no, Ty. Oh God, I'm so sorry." Her eyes widened suddenly. "You must have thought— I suppose you thought—that I sold you out for *that*."

"I'm afraid so," I apologized. "I should have known better."

"That makes us about quits, then." All her poise came back at one bound. She said, with some concern but less emotional disturbance, "How much did he take you for?"

"He didn't want money. He wanted me to write my column in the *Blaze* every week according to his instructions."

"How extraordinary. Well, that's easy enough."

"Would you design dresses to dictation by threat?"

"Oh."

"Exactly. Oh. So I told my wife about you myself. I had to."

"What—what did she say?"

"She was upset," I said briefly. "I said I wouldn't be seeing you again. There'll be no divorce."

She slowly shrugged her shoulders. "So that's that."

I looked away from her, trying not to mind so appallingly much that that was that. Tomorrow was Sunday. Tomorrow was Sunday and I could be on my own, and there was nothing on earth that I wanted so much as to see her again in her smooth warm skin and hold her close and tight in the half dark. . . .

She said thoughtfully, "I suppose if that man was a black-mailer it explains why I thought he was so nasty."

"Nasty? He was usually fantastically polite."

"He spoke to me as if I'd crawled out of the cracks. I wouldn't have put up with it—except for the money."

"Poor Gail," I said sympathetically. "He was South African."

She took in the implication and her eyes were furious. "That explains it. A beastly Afrikaner. I wish I'd never agreed—"

"Don't be silly," I interrupted. "Be glad you cost him so much."

She calmed down and laughed. "I've never even been to Africa. I didn't recognize his accent or give it a thought. Stupid, isn't it?"

A man in a check tweed suit came and asked us to move, as he wanted to read the notices on the board behind us. We walked three or four steps away, and paused again.

"I suppose I'll see you sometimes at the races," she said.

"I suppose so."

She looked closely at my face and said, "If you really feel like that, why—*why* don't you leave her?"

"I can't."

"But we could. . . . You want to be with me. I know you do. Money isn't everything."

I smiled twistedly. I did after all mean something to her, if she could ever say that.

"I'll see you sometimes," I repeated emptily. "At the races."

Seventeen

I caught Victor Roncey coming out of the luncheon room and told him that the danger to Tiddely Pom was by no means over.

"He's here, isn't he?" he said squashingly.

"He's here thanks to us," I reminded him. "And there are still two hours to the race."

"What do you expect me to do? Hold his hand?"

"It wouldn't hurt," I said flatly.

There was the usual struggle between aggressive independence and reasonable agreement. He said grudgingly, "Peter can sit outside his box over in the stables."

"Where is Peter now?"

He waved a hand behind him. "Finishing lunch."

"You'll have to take him in yourself, if he hasn't got a stable lad's pass."

He grumbled and agreed, and went back to fetch his son. I walked over to the stables with them and checked with the man on the gate, who said he'd had the usual number of people trying to get in, but not the man he'd turned away in the morning. Wing Commander Ondroy had told him to sling that man in the storeroom and lock him in if he came sniffing around again.

I smiled appreciatively and went in with Roncey to look at the horse. He stood patiently in his box, propped on one hip, resting a rear leg. When we opened the door, he turned his head lazily and directed at us an unexcited eye. A picture of a racehorse not on his toes, not strung up by the occasion, not looking ready to win Lamplighter Gold Cups.

"Is he always like this before a race?" I said. "He looks doped."

Roncey gave me a horrified glance and hurried to his horse's head. He looked in his mouth and eyes, felt his neck and legs, and kicked open and studied a small pile of droppings. Finally he shook his head.

"No dope that I can see. No signs of it."

"He never has nerves," Peter observed. "He isn't bred for it."

He looked bred for a milk cart. I refrained from saying so. I walked back into the paddock with Roncey and got him to agree to saddle up his horse in the stables, not in the saddling boxes, if the Stewards would allow it.

The Stewards, including Eric Youll, didn't hesitate. They said only that Tiddely Pom would have to walk the three stipulated times around the parade ring for the public to see him before the jockey mounted, but were willing for him to walk six feet in from the rails and be led and guarded by Peter and myself.

"All a waste of time," Roncey muttered. "No one will try anything here."

"Don't you believe it," I said. "You'd try anything if you stood to lose half a million you hadn't got."

I watched the first two races from the press box and spent the time in between aimlessly wandering about in the crowd trying to convince myself that I wasn't really looking out for another glimpse of Gail.

I didn't see her. I did see Dermot Finnegan. The little Irish jockey walked in front of me and gave me a huge gap-toothed grin. I took in, as I was supposed to, that he was dressed in colors, ready to ride in a race. The front of his jacket was carefully unbuttoned. I added up the purple star on the pink and white horizontal stripes and he laughed when he saw my astonishment.

"Bejasus, and I'm almost as staggered as yourself," he said. "But there it is, I've got my big chance on the Governor's first string, and if I make a mess of it may God have mercy on my soul, because I won't."

"You won't make a mess of it."

"We'll see," he said cheerfully. "That was a grand job you made of me in *Tally*, now. Thank you for that. I took that when it came and showed it to the Governor, but he'd already seen it, he told me. And you know I wouldn't be certain that it wasn't the magazine that put him in mind of putting me up on Rockville, when the other two fellows got hurt on Thursday. So thank you for that, too."

When I told Derry about it in the press box during the second race, he merely shrugged. "Of course he's riding Rockville. Don't you read the papers?"

"Not yesterday."

"Oh. Well, yes, he's got as much as he can chew this time. Rockville's a difficult customer, even with the best of jockeys, and our Dermot isn't that." He was busy polishing the lenses of his race glasses. "Luke-John's bookmaker friend must have accepted a good deal of Boston's fifty thousand, because the price on Tiddely Pom has come crashing down like an express lift from a hundred to eight to only four to one. That's a stupid price for a horse like Tiddely Pom, but there you are."

I did a small sum. If Boston had taken bets at 10 or 12 to 1 and had only been able to lay them off at 4 to 1, that left him a large gap of 6 or 8 to 1. If Tiddely Pom won, that would be the rate at which he would have to pay, which added up still to more than a quarter of a million pounds and meant that he would have to sell off the string of betting shops to pay his debts. Dumb Charlie Boston, trying to play with the big boys and getting squeezed like a toothpaste tube.

There was no sign of him in the paddock. Roncey saddled his horse in the stables and brought him straight into the parade ring very shortly before the time for the jockeys to mount. Peter led him around and I walked along by his quarters; but no one leaned over the rails to squirt him with acid. No one tried anything at all.

"Told you so," Roncey muttered. "All this fuss." He put up his jockey, slapped Tiddely Pom's rump, and hurried off to get a good position on the trainers' stand. Peter led the horse out onto the course and let him go, and Tiddely Pom cantered off unconcernedly with the long lolloping stride so unlike his appearance. I sighed with relief and went up to join Derry in the press box to watch the race.

"Tiddely Pom's favorite," he said. "Then Zig Zag, then Rockville. Zig Zag should have it in his pocket." He put his race glasses to his eyes and studied the horses milling around at the start. I hadn't taken my own glasses, as I'd found the carry strap pressed too heavily on tender spots. I felt lost without them, like a snail without antennae. The start for the Lamplighter was a quarter of a mile down the course from the stands. I concentrated on sorting out the colors with only force-four success.

Derry exclaimed suddenly, "What the devil!"

"Tiddely Pom," I said fearfully. Not now. Not at the very post. I should have foreseen . . . should have stationed someone down there. . . . But it was so public. So many people walked down to watch the start. Anyone who tried to harm a horse there would have a hundred witnesses.

"There's someone hanging on to his reins. No, he's been

pulled off. Great God!" Derry started laughing incredulously.
"I can't believe it. I simply can't believe it."

"What's happening?" I said urgently. All I could see was a
row of peacefully lining-up horses, which miraculously included Tiddely Pom, and some sort of commotion going on in
the crowd on the far side of the rails.

"It's Madge. . . . Madge Roncey. It must be. No one else
looks like that. . . . She's rolling about on the grass with a fat
little man . . . struggling. She pulled him away from Tiddely
Pom. . . . Arms and legs are flying all over the place. . . ."
He stopped, laughing too much. "The boys are with her. . . .
They're all piling onto the poor little man in a sort of Rugger
scrum. . . ."

"It's a pound to a penny the poor little man is Charlie
Boston," I said grimly. " And if it's Madge and not the *Blaze*
who's saved the day, we'll never hear the end of it from Victor
Roncey."

"Damned Victor Roncey," Derry said. "They're off."

The line of horses bounded forward, heading for the first
jump. Seventeen runners, three and a half miles, and a gold
trophy and a fat check to the winner.

One of them crumpled up over the first. Not Tiddely Pom,
whose scarlet and white chevrons bobbed in a bunch at the rear.
Not Zig Zag, already positioned in the fourth place, from
where he usually won. Not Egocentric, leading the field up past
the stands to give the Huntersons their moment of glory. Not
Rockville, with Dermot Finnegan fighting for his career in a
battle not to let the horse run away with him.

They jumped the water jump in front of the stands. A gasp
from the crowd as one of them splashed his hind legs right into
it. The jockey in orange and green was dislodged and rolled.

"That horse always makes a balls of the water," Derry said

dispassionately. "They should keep it for hurdles." No tremor of excitement in his voice or hands. It had cost him nothing to get Tiddely Pom onto the track. It had cost me too much.

They swept around the top bend and started out around the circuit. Twice around the course to go. I watched Tiddely Pom all the way, expecting him to fall, expecting him to drop out at the back and be pulled up, expecting him to be too weak from colic to finish the trip.

They came around the bottom bend and up over the three fences in the straight toward the stands. Egocentric was still in front. Zig Zag still fourth. Dermot Finnegan had Rockville in decent control somewhere in the middle, and Tiddely Pom was still there and not quite last.

Over the water. Zig Zag stumbled, recovered, raced on. Not fourth any more, though. Sixth or seventh. Tiddely Pom scampered over it with none of the grace of Egocentric but twice the speed. Moved up two places.

Out they went again into the country. Derry remarked calmly, "Tiddely Pom has dropped his bit."

"Damn," I said. The jockey was working with his arms, urging the horse on. Hopeless. And half the race still to run.

I shut my eyes. Felt the fatigue and illness come swamping back. Wanted to lie down somewhere soft and sleep for a week and escape from all the problems and torments and disillusionments of weary life. A week alone, to heal in. A week to give a chance for some energy for living to come creeping back. I needed a week at least. If I were lucky, I'd have a day.

"There's a faller at that fence." The race commentator's amplified voice jerked my eyes open. "A faller among the leaders. I think it was Egocentric. . . . Yes, Egocentric is down. . . ."

Poor Huntersons. Poor Harry, poor Sarah.

Gail.

I didn't want to think about her. Couldn't bear to, and couldn't help it.

"He's still going," Derry said. "Tiddely Pom."

The red and white chevrons were too far away to be clear.

"He's made up a bit," Derry said. "He's taken a hold again."

They jumped the last fence on the far side and began the sweeping bend around into the straight, very strung out now, with great gaps between little bunches. One or two staggered fifty yards in the rear. There was a roar from the crowd and the commentator's voice rose above it: "And here is Zig Zag coming to the front, opening up a commanding lead. . . ."

"Zig Zag's slipped them," Derry said calmly. "Caught all the others napping."

"Tiddely Pom?" I asked.

"He's well back. Still plodding on, though. Most we could expect."

Zig Zag jumped the first fence in the straight five seconds clear of the rest of the field.

"Nothing will catch him," Derry said. I forgave him the satisfaction in his voice. He had tipped Zig Zag in his column. It was nice to be right. "Tiddely Pom's in the second bunch. Can you see him? Even if he hasn't won, he's not disgraced."

Zig Zag jumped the second-last fence well ahead, chased after an interval by four horses more or less abreast. After these came Tiddely Pom, and behind him the other half dozen still standing. If we had to settle for that, at least the antepost punters had had some sort of run for their money.

It was clear twenty yards from the last fence that Zig Zag was meeting it wrong. The jockey hesitated fatally between pushing him on to lengthen his stride and take off sooner or shortening the reins to get him to put in an extra one before he jumped. In the end he did neither. Simply left it to the horse to sort himself out. Some horses like to do that. Some horses like to be told what to do. Zig Zag went into the fence like a rudderless ship, took off too late and too close, hit the fence hard with his forelegs, slewed around in midair, crashed down in a tangle of hoofs, and treated his rider to a well-deserved thump on the turf.

"Stupid *bastard*," Derry said, furiously lowering his glasses. "An apprentice could have done better."

I was watching Tiddely Pom. The four horses ahead of him jumped the last fence. One of them swerved to avoid Zig Zag and his supine jockey and bumped heavily into the horse next to him. Both of them were thoroughly unbalanced and the jockey of one fell off. When Tiddely Pom came away from the fence to tackle the straight, he was lying third.

The crowd roared. "He's got a chance!" Derry yelled. "Even now."

He couldn't quicken. The low lolloping stride went on at the same steady pace and all the jockey's urging was having no constructive effect. But one of the two in front of him was tiring and rolling about under pressure. Tiddely Pom crept up on him yard by yard, but the winning post was coming nearer and there was still one more in front. . . .

I looked at the leader, taking him in for the first time. A jockey in pink and white stripes, riding like a demon on a streak of brown straining hard-trained muscle. Dermot Finnegan on Rockville, with all his future in his hands.

While I watched he swept conclusively past the post, and even from the stands one could see that Irish grin bursting out like the sun.

Three lengths behind, Tiddely Pom's racing heart defeated the colic and put him second. A genuine horse, I thought thankfully. Worth all the trouble. Or, at least, worth some of it.

"All we need now," said Derry, "is an objection."

He wrapped the strap around his race glasses, put them in their case, and hurriedly made for the stairs. I followed him more slowly down and edged gingerly through the crowd milling around the unsaddling enclosure until I reached the clump of other press men waiting to pick up something to print. There was a cheer as Rockville was led through into the winner's place. Another cheer for Tiddely Pom. I didn't join in. Had nothing to contribute but a dead feeling of anticlimax.

All over. Tiddely Pom hadn't won. What did I expect?

The crowd parted suddenly like the Red Sea and through the gap struggled a large untidy earth mother surrounded by planets. Madge Roncey and her sons.

She walked purposefully across the comparatively empty unsaddling enclosure and greeted her husband with a gentle pat on the arm. He was astounded to see her and stood stock-still with his mouth open and Tiddely Pom's girth buckles half undone. I went across to join them.

"Hullo," Madge said. "Wasn't that splendid?" The faraway look in her eyes had come a few kilometres nearer since fact had begun to catch up on fantasy. She wore a scarlet coat a shade too small. Her hair floated in its usual amorphous mass. She had stockings on. Laddered.

"Splendid," I agreed.

Roncey gave me a sharp look. "Still fussing?"

I said to Madge, "What happened down at the start?"

She laughed. "There was a fat little man there going absolutely berserk and screaming that he would stop Tiddely Pom if it was the last thing he did."

Roncey swung around and stared at her. "He started hanging

on to Tiddely Pom's reins," she went on, "and he wouldn't let go when the starter told him to. It was absolutely crazy. He was trying to kick Tiddely Pom's legs. So I just ducked under the rails and walked across and told him it was our horse and would he please stop it, and he was frightfully rude." A speculative look came into her eye. "He used some words I didn't know."

"For God's sake," said Roncey irritably. "Get on with it."

She went on without resentment: "He still wouldn't let go so I put my arms round him and lifted him up and carried him off and he was so surprised he dropped the reins, and then he struggled to get free and I let him fall down on the ground and rolled him under the rails, and then the boys and I sat on him."

I said, trying to keep a straight face, "Did he say anything after that?"

"Well, he hadn't much breath," she admitted judiciously. "But he did say something about killing you, as a matter of fact. He didn't seem to like you very much. He said you'd smashed everything and stopped him getting to Tiddely Pom, and as a matter of fact he was so hysterical he was jolly nearly in tears."

"Where is he now?" I asked.

"I don't know exactly. When I let him get up, he ran away."

Roncey gave me a mean look. "So it took my wife to save my horse, not the *Blaze*."

"Oh, no, dear," she said placidly. "If Mr. Tyrone hadn't been looking after him, the little man would have been able to reach him sooner, and if I hadn't come back from the Isle of Wight because I thought it would be quite safe if no one knew, and we all wanted to see the race, if I hadn't been there at the starting gate, someone else would have taken the little man away. Lots of people were going to. It was just that I got to him first." She gave me a sweet smile. "I haven't had so much fun for years."

The day fragmented after that into a lot of people saying things to me that I didn't really hear. Pieces still stick out: Dermot Finnegan being presented with a small replica of the Lamplighter Gold Cup and looking as if he'd been handed the Holy Grail. Willy Ondroy telling me that Charlie Boston had been slung off the racecourse, and Eric Youll outlining the Stewards' plan for warning him off permanently, which would mean the withdrawal of his betting license and the closing of all his shops.

Derry telling me he had been through to Luke-John, whose bookmaker friend had taken all of Charlie Boston's fifty thousand and was profoundly thankful Tiddely Pom hadn't won.

Colly Gibbons asking me to go for a drink. I declined. I was off drink. He had his wife with him, and not an American colonel in sight.

Pat Roncey staring at me sullenly, hands in pockets. I asked if he'd passed on my telephone number along with the whereabouts of Tiddely Pom. Belligerently he tried to justify himself: the man had been even more keen to know where I lived than where the horse was. What man? The tall yellowish man with some sort of accent. From the *Guardian*, he'd said. Didn't Pat know that the *Guardian* was the one paper with no racing page? Pat did not.

Sandy Willis walking past leading Zig Zag, giving me a worried smile. Was the horse all right, I asked. She thought so, poor old boy. She muttered a few unfeminine comments on the jockey who had thrown the race away. She said she'd grown quite fond of Tiddely Pom; she was glad he'd done well. She'd won a bit on him, as he'd come in second. Got to get on, she said; Zig Zag needed sponging down.

The Huntersons standing glumly beside Egocentric while their trainer told them their raffle horse had broken down badly and wouldn't run again for a year, if ever.

That message got through to me razor sharp and clear. No Egocentric racing, no Huntersons at the races. No Gail at the races. Not even that.

I'd had enough. My body hurt. I understood the full meaning of the phrase "sick at heart." I'd been through too many mangles, and I wasn't sure it was worth it. Vjoersterod was dead, Bert Checkov was dead, the nonstarter racket was dead . . . until someone else tried it, until the next wide boy came along with his threats and his heavies. Someone else could bust it next time. Not me. I'd had far far more than enough.

I wandered slowly out onto the course and stood beside the water jump, looking down into the water. Couldn't go home until the race train went, after the last race. Couldn't go home until I'd phoned in to Luke-John for a final check on what my column would look like the next day. Nothing to go home to anyway, except an empty flat and the prospect of an empty future.

Footsteps swished toward me through the grass. I didn't look up. Didn't want to talk.

"Ty," she said.

I did look then. There was a difference in her face. She was softer; less cool, less poised. Still extraordinarily beautiful. I badly wanted what I couldn't have.

"Ty, why didn't you tell me about your wife?"

I shook my head. Didn't answer.

She said, "I was in the bar with Harry and Sarah, and someone introduced us to a Major Gibbons and his wife, because he had been in your *Tally* article, too, like Harry and Sarah. They were talking about you. . . . Major Gibbons said it was such a tragedy about your wife. I said, what tragedy, and he told us. . . ."

She paused. I took a deep difficult breath: said nothing.

"I said it must be some help that she was rich, and he said

what do you mean rich; as far as I know she hasn't a bean, because Ty is always hard up with looking after her, and he'd be reasonably well off if he put her in a hospital and let the country pay for her keep instead of struggling to do it himself. . . ."

She turned half away from me and looked out across the course. "Why didn't you tell me?"

I swallowed and loosened my mouth. "I don't like—I didn't want—consolation prizes."

After a while she said, "I see." It sounded as if she actually did.

There was a crack in her cool voice. She said, "If it was me you'd married, and I'd got polio. . . . I can see that you must stay with her. I see how much she needs you. If it had been me—and you left me. . . ." She gave a small laugh which was half a sob. "Life sure kicks you in the teeth. I find a man I don't want to part with—a man I'd live on crumbs with—and I can't have him—even a little while, now and then."

Eighteen

I spent Sunday alone in the flat, mostly asleep. Part of the time I pottered around tidying things up, trying to put my mind and life into order along with my house. Didn't have much success.

On Monday morning I went to fetch Elizabeth. She came home in an ambulance, with two fit uniformed men to carry her and the pump upstairs. They laid her on the bed I had made up freshly for her, checked that the pump was working properly, helped replace the Spiroshell on her chest, accepted cups of coffee, agreed that the weather was raw and cold but what could you expect in December, and eventually went away.

I unpacked Elizabeth's case and made some scrambled eggs for lunch, and fed her when her wrist packed up, and fixed another mug of coffee into the holder.

She smiled and thanked me. She looked tired, but very calm. There was a deep difference in her, but for some time I couldn't work out what it was. When I finally identified it, I was surprised. She wasn't anxious any more. The long-established deep-rooted insecurity no longer looked out of her eyes.

"Leave the dishes, Ty," she said. "I want to talk to you."

I sat in the armchair. She watched me. "It still hurts . . . what that man did."

"A bit," I agreed.

"Tonio told me they were both killed that night . . . trying to find me again."

"He did, did he?"

She nodded. "He came to see me yesterday. We had a long talk. A long, long talk. He told me a lot of things."

"Honey," I said, "I—"

"Shut up, Ty. I want to tell you . . . what he said."

"Don't tire yourself."

"I won't. I am tired, but it feels different from usual. I feel just ordinarily tired, not . . . not *worried* tired. Tonio did that. And you. I mean, he made me understand what I saw on Thursday, that you would let yourself be smashed up . . . that you would drive when you were drunk and risk going to prison . . . that you would do anything, however dangerous . . . to keep me safe. . . . He said, if I'd seen that with my own eyes, why did I doubt . . . why did I ever doubt that you would stay with me? . . . It was such a relief. . . . I felt as if the whole world were lighter. . . . I know you've always told me . . . but now I do believe it, through and through."

"I'm glad," I said truthfully. "I'm very glad."

She said, "I talked to Tonio about . . . that girl."

"Honey—"

"Hush," she said. "I told him about the blackmail. We talked for ages. . . . He was so understanding. He said of course I would be upset, anyone would, but that I shouldn't worry too much. . . . He said you were a normal healthy man and if I had any sense I would see that the time to start worrying would be if you *didn't* want to sleep with someone." She smiled. "He said if I could face it, we would both be happier if I didn't mind if sometimes . . . He said you would always come home."

"Tonio said a great deal."

She nodded. "It made such sense. I haven't been fair to you."

"Elizabeth," I protested.

"No. I really haven't. I was so afraid of losing you I couldn't see how much I was asking of you. But I understand now that

the more I can let you go, the easier you will find it to live with
me . . . and the more you will want to."

"Tonio said that?"

"Yes, he did."

"He's very fond of you," I said.

She grinned. "He said so. He also said some pretty ear-
burning things about you, if you want to know." She told me
some of them, her mouth curving up at the corners and the new
security gleaming in her eyes.

"Exaggeration," I said modestly.

She laughed. A breathy giggle. Happy.

I got up and kissed her on the forehead and on the cheek. She
was the girl I'd married. I loved her very much.

On Tuesday morning, when Mrs. Woodward came back, I
went out along the mews, around the corner and into the
telephone box, and dialed the number of the Western School of
Art.

SLAYRIDE

One

COLD GRAY WATER lapped the flimsy-looking sides of the fiber-glass dinghy, and I shivered and thought of the five hundred feet straight down to the seabed underneath.

An hour out of Oslo with the outboard motor stilled and my friend Arne Kristiansen taking all afternoon to answer some simple questions.

A gray day, damp, not far from rain. The air sang in my ears with stinging chill. My feet were congealing. The October temperature down the fjord was giving the land a twenty-degree lead toward zero, and of the two of us only Arne was dressed for it.

I was wearing a showerproof jacket over an ordinary suit and no hat. He had come equipped with the full bit: a red padded cap with ear flaps fastened by a strap under his chin, blue padded trousers tucked into short wide-legged rubber boots, and a red padded jacket fastened up the front with silver-colored press studs. A glimpse of black and yellow at the neck spoke of other warm layers underneath.

He had arranged on the telephone to meet me at the statue in Rådhusplassen, the huge square by the harbor, brushing aside my suggestion that he should come to the Grand Hotel, where I was staying. Even in those wide-open spaces, he had gone on muttering about being overheard by long-range bugging machines (his words) and had finally insisted on taking to the dinghy. Knowing from past experience that in the end the quickest way to deal with his perennial mild persecution complex was to go along with it, I had shrugged and followed him onto the quay where the small, pale green craft bobbed beside a flight of steps.

I had forgotten that it is always very much colder out on open water. I flexed the stiffening fingers inside my pockets and repeated my last question.

"How would you smuggle sixteen thousand stolen kroner out of the country?"

For the second time, I got no answer. Arne produced answers as prodigally as tax collectors offer rebates.

He blinked, the dropping of the eyelids marking some intermediary stage in the chesslike permutations going on in his head. He was no doubt, as always, considering every foreseeable consequence: if answer A might produce any one of five responses, and answer B led on to six subsidiary questions, wouldn't it be wiser to answer C? In which case, though . . .

It made conversation with him a trifle slow.

I tried a little prompting. "You said it was all in coins and used notes of small denominations. How bulky? Enough to fit in a small-sized suitcase?"

He blinked again.

"Do you think he just walked out with it through the customs?"

He blinked.

"Or do you think he is still somewhere in Norway?"

Arne opened his mouth and said grudgingly, "No one knows."

I tried some more. "When a foreigner stays in one of your hotels, he has to fill in a form and show his passport. These forms are for the police. Have your police checked those forms?"

Pause.

"Yes," he said.

"And?"

"Robert Sherman did not fill in any form."

"None at all? What about when he arrived from England?"

"He did not stay in a hotel."

Patience, I thought. Give me patience.

"Where, then?"

"With friends."

"What friends?"

He considered. I knew he knew the answer. He knew he was
eventually going to tell me. I suppose he couldn't help the way
his mind worked, but this, God help us, was supposed to be an
investigator.

What was more, I had taught him myself. "Think before you
answer any question," I'd said. So now he did.

In the three months he had spent in England learning how
the Jockey Club ran its investigation department, we had
grown to know each other well. Some of the time he had stayed
in my flat, most of the time we had traveled together to the
races, all of the time he had asked and listened and blinked as
he thought. That had been three years ago. Two minutes had
been enough to resuscitate the old warm feelings of tolerant
regard. I liked him, I thought, more because of the mild eccentric kinks than despite.

"He stayed with Gunnar Holth," he said.

I waited.

After ten seconds he added, "He is a racehorse trainer."

"Did Bob Sherman ride for him?"

This dead simple question threw him into a longer-than-ever
session of mental chess, but finally he said, "Bob Sherman rode
the ones of his horses which ran in hurdle races while Bob
Sherman was in Norway. *Ja.* He did not ride the horses of
Gunnar Holth, which ran in flat races while he was in Norway."

God give me strength.

Arne hadn't actually finished. "Robert Sherman rode horses for the racecourse."

I was puzzled. "How do you mean?"

He consulted his inner man again, who evidently said it was O.K. to explain.

"The racecourse pays appearance money to some foreign jockeys, to get them to come to Norway. It makes the racing more interesting for the racegoers. So the racecourse paid Robert Sherman to ride."

"How much did they pay him?"

A rising breeze was stirring the fjord's surface into proper little wavelets. The fjord just below Oslo is not one of those narrow canyon jobs on the "Come to Scenic Norway" posters, but a wide expanse of sea dotted with rocky islands and fringed by the sprawling suburbs of the city. A coastal steamer surged past half a mile away and tossed us lightly in its wake. The nearest land looked a lot farther off.

"Let's go back," I said abruptly.

"No, no." He had no patience for such weak suggestions. "They paid him fifteen hundred kroner."

"I'm cold," I said.

He looked surprised. "It is not winter yet."

I made a noise which was half laugh and half teeth beginning to chatter. "It isn't summer, either."

He looked vaguely all around. "Robert Sherman had made six visits to race in Norway," he said. "This was his seventh."

"Look, Arne, tell me about it back at the hotel, huh?"

He attended to me seriously. "What is the matter?"

"I don't like heights," I said.

He looked blank. I took one frozen mitt out of its pocket, hung it over the side of the boat, and pointed straight down. Arne's face melted into comprehension and a huge grin took the place of the usual tight careful configuration of his mouth.

"David, I am sorry. The water to me, it is home. Like snow. I am sorry."

He turned at once to start the outboard, and then paused to say, "He could simply have driven over the border to Sweden. The customs, they would not search for kroner."

"In what car?" I asked.

He thought it over. "Ah, yes." He blinked a bit. "Perhaps a friend drove him."

"Start the engine," I said encouragingly.

He shrugged and gave several small nods of the head, but turned to the outboard and pressed the necessary knobs. I had half expected it to prove as lifeless as my fingers, but the spark hit the gas in an orderly fashion and Arne pointed the sharp end back toward hot coffee and radiators.

The dinghy slapped busily through the little waves and the crosswind flicked spray onto my left cheek. I pulled my jacket collar up and made like a tortoise.

Arne's mouth moved as he said something, but against the combined noises of the engine and the sea and the rustle of gabardine against my ears, I couldn't hear any words.

"What?" I shouted.

He started to repeat whatever it was, but louder. I caught only snatches like "ungrateful pig" and "dirty thief," which I took to be his private views of Robert Sherman, British steeplechase jockey. Arne had had a bad time since the said Bob Sherman disappeared with the day's take from the turnstiles of Øvrevoll, because Arne Kristiansen, besides being the Norwegian Jockey Club's official investigator, was also in charge of racecourse security.

The theft, he had told me on the outward chug, was an insult, first to himself, and secondly to Norway. Guests in a foreign country should not steal. Norwegians were not criminals, he said, and quoted jail statistics per million of population to prove it. When the British were in Norway, they should keep their hands to themselves.

Commiserating, I refrained from drawing his country's raids on Britain to his attention: they were, after all, a thousand or so years in the past, and the modern Vikings were less likely to burn, rape, pillage, and plunder than to take peaceable photographs of Buckingham Palace. I felt, moreover, a twinge of national shame about Bob Sherman: I had found myself apologizing, of all things, for his behavior.

Arne was still going on about it: unfortunately on that subject he needed no prompting. Phrases like "put me in an intolerable position" slid off his tongue as if he had been practicing them for weeks—which, on reflection, of course he had. It was three weeks and four days since the theft: and forty-eight hours since the Chairman of the racecourse had telephoned and asked me to send over a British Jockey Club investigator to see what he could do. I had sent (you will have guessed) myself.

I hadn't met the Chairman yet, nor seen the racecourse, nor ever before been to Norway. I was down the fjord with Arne because Arne was the devil I knew.

Three years earlier, the hair now closely hidden under the red padded hood had been a bright blond fading at the temples to gray. The eyes were as fierce a blue as ever, the wrinkles around them as deep, and the bags below a good deal heavier. The spray blew onto skin that was weather-beaten but not sun-burned, thick-looking impervious yellowish-white skin lumped and pitted by forty-something winters.

He was still breaking out in bursts of aggrieved half-heard monologue, trudging along well-worn paths of resentment. I gave up trying to listen. It was too cold.

He stopped in midsentence and looked with raised eyebrows at some distant point over my left shoulder. I turned. A large speedboat, not very far away, was slicing down the fjord in our general direction with its bow waves leaping out like heavy silver wings.

I turned back to Arne. He shrugged and looked uninterested, and the outboard chose that moment to splutter and cough and choke to silence.

"Fanden," said Arne loudly, which was nothing at all to what I was saying in my head.

"Those people will help us," he announced, pointing at the approaching speedboat, and without hesitation he stood up, braced his legs, and waved his scarlet-clad arms in wide sweeps above his head.

Twisting on my bench seat, I watched the speedboat draw near.

"They will take us on board," Arne said.

The speedboat did not seem to be slowing down. I could see its shining black hull and its sharp cutting bow, and the silver wings of wave looked as high and full as ever.

If not higher and fuller.

I turned to Arne with the beginnings of apprehension.

"They haven't seen us," I said.

"They must have." Arne waved his arms with urgent acceleration, rocking the dinghy precariously.

"Hey," Arne shouted to the speedboat. "Look out!" And after that he screamed at it in Norwegian.

The wind blew his words away. The helmsman of the speedboat didn't hear, didn't see. The sharp hard shining black prow raced straight toward us at forty knots.

"Jump!" yelled Arne; and he jumped. A flash of scarlet streaking into the sea.

I was slow. Thought perhaps that the unimaginable wouldn't happen, that the bow wave would toss the dinghy clear as it would a swan, that the frail craft would bob away as lightly as a bird.

I tumbled over the side into the water about one second before the bow split the fiberglass open like an eggshell. Something hit me a colossal bang on the shoulder while I was still gasping from the shock of immersion, and I went down under the surface into a roaring buffeting darkness.

People who fall off boats die as often from the propellers as from drowning, but I didn't remember that until the twin screw had churned past and left me unsliced. I came sputtering and gulping to the daylight in the jumbled frothing wake and saw the back of the speedboat tearing away unconcernedly down the fjord.

"Arne!" I shouted, which was about as useless as dredging for diamonds in the Thames. A wave slapped me in the open mouth and I swallowed a double salt water, neat.

The sea seemed much rougher at face level than it had done from above. I floundered in high choppy waves with ruffles of white frothing across their tops and blowing into my eyes, as I shouted again for Arne. Shouted with intensifying concern for him and fear for myself; but the wind tore the words away and battered them to bits.

There was no sign of the dinghy. My last impression was that it had been cut clean into two pieces, which were now, no doubt, turning over and over in a slow sink down to the faraway seabed.

I shuddered as much from imagination as from cold.

There was no sign anywhere of Arne. No red padded head, no red waving arms above the waves, no cheerful smile coming to tell me that the sea was home to him and that safety and hot muffins were *this* way, just over here.

Land lay visible all around me in grayish misty heights. None of it was especially near. About two miles away, I guessed, whichever way I looked.

Treading water, I began to pull my clothes off, still looking desperately for Arne, still, still expecting to see him.

There was nothing but the rough slapping water. I thought about the speedboat's propellers and I thought about Arne's wide-legged rubber boots, which would fill with water in the first few seconds. I thought finally that if I didn't accept that

Arne was gone and get started shoreward, I, too, was very likely
going to drown on that spot.

I kicked off my shoes and struggled with the zipper of my
raincoat. Ripped open the buttons of my suit jacket underneath
and shrugged out of both coats together. I let go of them, then
remembered my wallet, and although it seemed crazy I took it
out of my jacket pocket and shoved it inside my shirt.

The two coats, waterlogged, floated briefly away and started
to go down out of sight. I slid out of my trousers, and let them
follow.

Pity, I thought. Nice suit, that had been.

The water was very cold indeed.

I began to swim. Up the fjord. Toward Oslo. Where else?

I was thirty-three and hardy and I knew more statistics than
I cared to. I knew, for instance, that the average human can live
less than an hour in water of thirty-three degrees Fahrenheit.

I tried to swim unhurriedly in long undemanding strokes,
postponing the moment of exhaustion. The water in Oslo fjord
was not one degree above freezing, but at least five. Probably
not much colder than the stuff buffeting the English beach at
Brighton at that very moment. In water five degrees above
freezing, one could last . . . well, I didn't actually know *that*
statistic. Had to take it on trust. Long enough to swim something over two miles, anyway.

Bits of distant geography lessons made no sense. "The Gulf
Stream warms the coast of Norway. . . ." Good old Gulf Stream.
Where had it gone?

Cold had never seemed a positive force to me before. I suppose I had never really been *cold*, just chilled. This cold dug
deep into every muscle and ached in my gut. Feeling had gone
from my hands and feet, and my arms and legs felt heavy. The
best long-distance swimmers had a nice thick insulating layer of
subcutaneous fat: I hadn't. They also covered themselves with

water-repelling grease and swam alongside comfort boats which fed them hot cocoa through tubes on demand. The best long-distance swimmers were, of course, usually going twenty miles or so farther than I was.

I swam.

The waves seemed frighteningly big. I couldn't see where I was aiming unless I lifted my head right up and trod water, and that wasted time and energy.

The nearest-looking land seemed to my salt-stinging eyes to be as far away as ever. And surely Oslo fjord should be a Piccadilly Circus of boats? But I couldn't see a single one.

Dammit, I thought. I'm bloody well not going to drown. I'm bloody well *not*.

I swam.

Daylight was slowly fading. Sea, sky, and distant mountains were all a darker gray. It began to rain.

I traveled, it seemed, very slowly. The land I was aiming for never appeared to be nearer. I began to wonder if some current was canceling out every yard I swam forward, but when I looked back, the land behind was definitely receding.

I swam mechanically, growing tired.

Time passed.

A long way off, straight ahead, pinpricks of light sprang out against the fading afternoon. Every time I looked, there were more. The city was switching on in the dusk.

Too far, I thought. They are too far for me. Land and life all around me, and I couldn't reach them.

An awful depth beneath. And I never did like heights.

A cold lonely death, drowning.

I swam. Nothing else to do.

When another light shone out higher up and to the left, it took at least a minute for the news to reach my sluggish brain. I trod water and wiped the rain and sea out of my eyes as best I could and tried to make out where it came from: and there, a great deal nearer than when I'd last looked, was the solid gray shape of land.

Houses, lights, and people. All there, somewhere, on that rocky hump.

Gratefully I veered fifteen degrees left and pressed on faster, pouring out the carefully hoarded reserves of stamina like a penitent miser. And that was stupid, because no shelving beach lay ahead. The precious land, when I reached it, proved to be a smooth sheer cliff dropping perpendicularly into the water. Not a ledge, not a cranny, to offer even respite from the effort of staying afloat.

The last quarter mile was the worst. I could *touch* the land if I wanted to, and it offered nothing to cling to. There had to be a break somewhere, if I went far enough, but I had practically nothing left. I struggled feebly forward through the slapping waves, wishing in a hazy way that I could surge through warm calm water like Mark Spitz and make a positive touchdown against a nice firm rail, with my feet on the bottom. What I actually did was a sort of belly flop onto a small boat slipway bordered with large rock slabs.

I lay half in and half out of the water, trying to get back breath I didn't know I'd lost. My chest heaved. I coughed.

It wasn't dark; just the slow Northern twilight. I wouldn't have minded if it had been three in the morning: the cold wet concrete beneath my cheek felt as warm and welcoming as goose feathers.

Footsteps crunched rhythmically along the quay at the head of the slipway and then suddenly stopped.

I did a bit toward lifting my head and flapping a numb hand.

"*Hvem er det?*" he said; or something like it.

I gave a sort of croak and he walked carefully, crabwise, down the slipway toward me, a half-seen well-wrapped figure in the rainy gloom.

He repeated his question, which I still didn't understand.

"I'm English," I said. "Can you help me?"

Nothing happened for a few seconds. Then he went away.

So what, I thought tiredly. At least from the waist up I was safe in Norway. Didn't seem to have the energy to drag myself uphill till my feet were out of the water, not just for a minute or two. But I would, I thought, given time.

The man came back, and brought a friend. Ungrateful of me to have misjudged him.

The companion peered through the rain and said, "You are English? Did you say you are English?" His tone seemed to suggest that being English automatically explained such follies as swimming in October in shirt and underpants and lying about on slipways.

"Yes," I said.

"You fell off a ship?"

"Sort of."

I felt his hand slide under my armpit.

"Come. Out of the water."

I scraped myself onto the slipway and with their help more or less crawled to the top. The quay was edged with railings and posts. I sat on the ground with my back against one of the posts and wished for enough strength to stand up.

They consulted in Norwegian. Then the English-speaking one said, "We will take you to my house, to dry and get warm."

"Thank you," I said, and by God I meant it.

One of them went away again and came back with a battered old van. They gave me the front passenger seat, though I offered to drip in the back, and whisked me about a quarter of a mile to a small wooden house standing near two or three others. There was no village, no shops, no telephone.

"This is an island," my rescuer explained. "One kilometer long, three hundred meters across." He told me its name, which seemed to me like "gorse."

His living room was small and bright, and warmed by the huge stove which took up at least a sixth of the floor space. Seen clearly in the light, he himself was a short friendly man of middle age, with hands that were used for work. He shook his head over me and produced first a blanket and then, after some rummaging, a thick woolen shirt and a pair of trousers.

"You are not a sailor," he said matter-of-factly, watching me fumble off my shirt and pants.

"No," I agreed.

My wallet fell on the floor. I was surprised it was still there; had forgotten it. The Norwegian-only rescuer politely picked it up and handed it to me, smiling broadly. He looked very like his friend.

Between hopeless bouts of shivering, I told them what had happened and asked them how I could get back to the city. While I dressed they talked to each other about it, first with a lot of shaking of heads but finally with a few nods.

"When you are warmer, we will take you by boat," said the English-speaker. He looked at the wallet, which lay now on a polished pine table. "We ask only that you will pay for the fuel. If you can."

Together we took out my sodden money and spread it on the table. I asked them to take whatever they liked, and after debate they chose a fifty-kroner note. I urged them to double it. It wouldn't cost so much, they protested, but in the end they put two notes aside and dried the rest for me quickly on the stove so that the edges curled. After more consultation, they dug in a cupboard and brought out a bottle of pale gold liquid. One small glass followed, and a moderate tot was poured into it. They handed it to me.

"*Skål,*" they said.

"*Skål,*" I repeated.

They watched interestedly while I drank. Smooth fire down the throat, heat in the stomach, and soon a warm glow along all the frozen veins.

They smiled.

"*Akevitt,*" said my host, and stored the precious bottle away, ready for the next needy stranger who swam to their doorstep.

They suggested I should sit for a while on the one comfort-
able-looking chair. Since various muscles were still trembling
with weakness, this seemed a good idea, so I rested while they
busied themselves putting out businesslike sets of oilskins, and
by the time they were kitted up, my skin had returned from a
nasty bluish purplish white to its more usual shade of sallow.

"D'you feel better?" my host asked, smiling.

"I do."

They nodded, pleased, and held out a spare set of oilskins for
me to put on. They took me in a big smelly fishing boat back
up the twinkle-edged fjord to the city, and it rained all the way.
I spent the journey calculating that I had been in the water for
about two hours, which didn't prove anything in particular
about the current in the fjord or the inefficiency of my swimming or the distance I had traveled, but did prove pretty conclusively that the temperature was more than one degree above
freezing.

Two

THEY WAITED while I changed at the Grand, so that they could take back the lent clothes. We parted with warm handshakes and great camaraderie, and it was only after they had gone that I realized I didn't know their names.

I would have liked nothing better than to go to bed and sleep for half a century, but the thought of Arne's wife waiting for him to come home put a damper on that. So I spent the next couple of hours with various Norwegian authorities, reporting what had happened.

When the police finished taking notes and said they would send someone to tell Mrs. Kristiansen, I suggested that I should go, too. They agreed. We went in an official car and rang the bell of Flat C on the first floor of a large timber house in a prosperous road not far from the city center.

The girl who opened the door looked inquiringly out at us from clear gray eyes in a firm, friendly, thirtyish face. Behind her the flat looked warm and colorful, and the air was thick with Beethoven.

"Is Mrs. Kristiansen in?" I asked.

"Yes," she said. "I am Mrs. Kristiansen."

Not in the least what I would have expected. Oddballs like Arne shouldn't turn out to have slender young wives with thick pale blond hair falling in loose curls on their shoulders. She looked away from my less striking face to the policeman behind me, and the eyes widened.

"I'm David Cleveland," I said. "I was with Arne this afternoon. . . ."

"Oh, were you?" she exclaimed. "Oh, do come in. I'm *so* glad. . . ."

She held the door wider and turned to call over her shoulder.

"Arne," she said. "Arne, see who's here."

He stepped into the hall. Very much alive.

We stared at each other in consternation. My own face must have mirrored the surprise and shock I saw on his, and then he was striding forward with his hand outheld and his face creasing into the most gigantic smile of all time.

"David! I don't believe it. I have reported you drowned." He clasped my hands in both of his and shook them warmly. "Come in, come in, my dear fellow, and tell me how you were saved. I have been so grieved. . . . I was telling Kari."

His wife nodded, as delighted as he was.

The policeman behind me said, "It would seem Mr. Kristiansen wasn't drowned after all, then," which seemed in our high state of relief to be extremely funny. We all laughed. Even the policeman smiled.

"I was picked up by some fisherman near Nesodden," Arne told him. "I reported the accident to the police there. They said they would send a boat to look for Mr. Cleveland, but they weren't very hopeful of finding him. I'd better call them."

"Thank you," said the policeman. "That would be helpful," and he smiled once more at us all and went away.

Kari Kristiansen shut the front door and said, "Do come in, we must celebrate," and led me through into the living room. Beethoven was thundering away in there, and Kari switched him off. "Arne always plays loud music when he's upset," she said.

Out in the hall, Arne busied himself with the telephone, and in his explanatory flow of Norwegian I caught my name spoken with astonishment and relief.

"It is wonderful," he said, coming into the room and rubbing his hands together. "Wonderful." He gestured to me to sit on a deep comfortable sofa near a cheerful wood-burning fire. "The Nesodden police say they sent a boat out to search for you, but it was too dark and raining and they could see nothing."

"I'm sorry they had the trouble," I said.

"My dear fellow"—he spread his fingers—"it was nothing. And now, a drink, eh? To celebrate."

He filled glasses with red wine from a bottle standing already open on a side table.

"Arne has been so depressed all evening," Kari said. "It is truly a miracle that you were both saved."

We exchanged stories. Arne had torn off the red clothes and kicked his boots off instantly (I suppose I should have known that a man at home on the sea would wear *loose* rubber boots), but although he had called my name and searched around for some minutes he had caught no sign of me.

"When I last saw you," he said apologetically, "you were still in the dinghy, and I thought the speedboat must have hit you directly, so when I could not see you I thought that you must be already dead."

He had started swimming, he said; and, knowing a lot more than I did about tides and winds, had taken almost the opposite direction. He had been picked up near the coast by a small home-going fishing boat which was too low on fuel to go out into the fjord to look for me. It had, however, landed him in the small town where he reported my loss, and from there he had returned by hired boat to the city.

My story was so much the same that it could be told in two sentences: I swam to an island. Two men brought me back in a boat.

Arne searched among an untidy pile of papers and triumphantly produced a map. Spreading it out, he pointed to the widest part of the fjord and showed both Kari and me where we had been sunk.

"The worst possible place," Kari exclaimed. "Why did you go so far?"

"You know me," said Arne, folding the map up again. "I like to be moving."

She looked at him indulgently. "You don't like to be followed, you mean."

Arne looked a little startled, but that complex of his stood out like Gulliver in Lilliput.

I said, "The police asked me if I saw the name of that speed-boat."

"Did you?" asked Arne.

I shook my head. "No. Did you?"

He blinked through one of those maddening pauses into which the simplest question seemed to throw him, but in the end all he said was "No. I didn't."

"I don't think there was any name to see," I said.

They both turned their faces to me in surprise.

"There must have been," Kari said.

"Well . . . I've no impression of one. No name, no registration number, no port of origin. Perhaps you don't have things like that in Norway."

"Yes, we do," Kari said, puzzled. "Of course we do."

Arne considered lengthily, then said, "It was going too fast . . . and straight toward us. It must have had a name. We simply didn't see it." He spoke with finality, as if the subject could hold no more interest. I nodded briefly and let it go, but I was certain that on that thundering black hull there had been nothing to see but black paint. How were they off for smugglers, I wondered, in this neck of the North Sea?

"It's a pity," I said, "because you might have got compensation for your dinghy."

"It was insured," he said. "Do not worry."

Kari said, "It's disgraceful he did not stop. He must have felt the bump. Even a big heavy speedboat, like Arne says it was, could not crush a dinghy without feeling it."

Hit and run, I thought flippantly. Happens on the roads, why not on the water?

"Arne was afraid you could not swim."

"Up and down a pool or two," I said. "Never tried such long-distance stuff before."

"You were lucky," she said seriously.

"Arne, too." I looked at him thoughtfully, for I was younger by a good ten years and I had been near to exhaustion.

"Oh, no. Arne's a great swimmer. A great sportsman, all round. Very fit and tough." She smiled ironically, but the wifely pride was there. "He used to win cross-country ski races."

I had noticed several sets of skis stacked casually in an alcove in the hall, along with squash rackets, fishing rods, mountain walking boots, and half a dozen anoraks like the lost red one. For a man who liked to keep moving, he had all the gear.

"Have you eaten?" Kari asked suddenly. "Since your swim, I mean? Did you think of eating?"

I shook my head.

"I suppose I was worried about Arne."

She stood up, smiling. "Arne had no appetite for his supper." She looked at the clock. Ten minutes before ten. "I will bring something for you both," she said.

Arne fondly watched her back view disappearing toward the kitchen.

"What do you think of her, eh? Isn't she beautiful?"

Normally I disliked men who invited admiration of their wives as if they were properties like cars, but I would have forgiven Arne a great deal that evening.

"Yes," I said, more truthfully than on many similar occasions; and Arne positively smirked.

"More wine," he said, getting up restlessly and filling both our glasses.

"Your house, too, is beautiful," I said.

He looked over his shoulder in surprise. "That is Kari as well. She . . . It is her job. Making rooms for people. Offices, hotels. Things like that."

Their sitting room was a place of natural wood and white paint, with big parchment-shaded table lamps shedding a golden glow on string-colored upholstery and bright scattered cushions. A mixture of the careful and the haphazard, overlaid with the comfortable debris of a full life. Ultra-tidy rooms always oppressed me: the Kristiansens' was just right.

Arne brought back my filled glass and settled himself opposite, near the fire. His hair, no longer hidden, was now more gray than blond, longer than before, and definitely more distinguished.

"Tomorrow," I said, "I'd like to see the racecourse Chairman, if I could."

He looked startled, as if he had forgotten the real purpose of my visit.

"Yes." He blinked a bit. "It is Saturday tomorrow. It is the Grand National meeting on Sunday. He will be at the racecourse on Sunday."

Don't let a thieving jockey spoil the man's day off, Arne meant, so I shrugged and said Sunday would do.

"I'll maybe call on Gunnar Holth tomorrow, then."

For some reason, that didn't fill Arne with joy, either, but I discovered, after a long pause on his part, that this was because he, Arne, wished to go fishing all day and was afraid I would want him with me, instead.

"Does Gunnar Holth speak English?" I asked.

"Oh, yes."

"I'll go on my own, then."

He gave me the big smile and jumped up to help Kari, who was returning with a laden tray. She had brought coffee and open sandwiches of prawns and cheese and pineapple, which we ate to the last crumb.

"You must come another evening," Kari said. "I will make you a proper dinner."

Arne agreed with her warmly and opened some more wine.

"A great little cook," he said proprietorially.

The great little cook shook back her heavy blond hair and stretched her elegant neck. She had a jawline in the same class and three small brown moles like dusty freckles high on one cheekbone.

"Come anytime," she said.

I got back to the Grand by taxi at one in the morning, slept badly, and woke at seven feeling like Henry Cooper's punching bag.

Consultation with the bathroom looking glass revealed a plate-sized bruise of speckled crimson over my left shoulder blade, souvenir of colliding boats. In addition, every muscle I possessed was groaning with the morning-after misery of too much strain. David Cleveland, it seemed, was no Matthew Webb.

Bath, clothes, and breakfast didn't materially improve things, nor on the whole did a telephone call to Gunnar Holth.

"Come if you like," he said. "But I can tell you nothing. You will waste your time."

As all investigators waste a lot of time listening to people with nothing to tell, I naturally went. He had a stable yard adjoining the racecourse and a belligerent manner.

"Questions, questions," he said. "There is nothing to tell."

I paid off my taxi driver.

"You shouldn't have sent him away," Gunnar Holth said. "You will be going soon."

I smiled. "I can go back on a tram."

He gave me a grudging stare. "You don't look like a Jockey Club official."

"I would appreciate it very much," I said, "if you would show

me your horses. Arne Kristiansen says you have a good lot, that
they've been winning big prizes this year."

He loosened, of course. He gestured toward a large barn on
the other side of an expanse of mud. We made our way there,
he in his boots showing me I shouldn't have come in polished
shoes. He was short, wiry, middle-aged, and a typical stableman,
more at home with his horses, I guessed, than with their owners;
and he spoke English with an Irish accent.

The barn contained two rows of boxes facing into a wide
central passage. Horses' heads showed over most of the half
doors, and three or four lads were carrying buckets of water and
haynets.

"They've just come in from exercise," Holth said. "We train
on the sand track on the racecourse." He turned left and
opened the door of the first box. "This fellow runs tomorrow in
the Grand National. Would you look at his shoulders, now—isn't
that a grand sort of horse?"

"Bob Sherman won a race on him the day he disappeared,"
I said.

He gave me a sharp wordless glance and went in to pat a
strong-looking character with more bone than breeding. He felt
the legs, looked satisfied, and came back to join me.

"How do you know?" he said.

No harm in telling him. "Arne Kristiansen gave me a list of
Bob Sherman's last rides in Norway. He said that this horse of
yours was likely to win the National, and if Sherman had had
any sense he would have come back for that race and then
stolen the National day takings, which would have been a better
haul all round."

Holth allowed himself a glint of amusement. "That's true."

We continued around the barn, admiring every inmate.
There were about twenty altogether, three-quarters of them
running on the flat, and although they seemed reasonable animals, none of them looked likely to take Epsom by storm. From

their coats, though, and general air of well-being, I surmised
that Holth knew his trade.

One end of the barn was sectioned off to form living quarters
for the lads, and Holth took me through to see them. Dormi-
tory, washroom, and kitchen.

"Bob stayed here, most times," he said.

I glanced slowly around the big main room, with its half-
dozen two-tiered bunk beds, its bare board floor, its wooden
table, wooden chairs. A big brown tiled stove and double-glazed
windows with curtains like blankets promised comfort against
future snow, and a couple of mild girlie calendars brightened
the walls, but it was a far cry from the Grand.

"Always?" I asked.

Holth shrugged. "He said it was good enough here, and he
saved the expense of a hotel. Nothing wrong there, now, is
there?"

"Nothing at all," I agreed.

He paused. "Sometimes he stayed with an owner."

"Which owner?"

"Oh . . . the man who owns Whitefire. Per Bjørn Sandvik."

"How many times?"

Holth said with irritation, "What does it matter? Twice, I
suppose. Yes, twice. Not the last time. The two times before
that."

"How often did he come over altogether?"

"Six, perhaps. Or seven . . . or eight."

"All this summer?"

"He didn't come last year, if that's what you mean."

"But he liked it?"

"Of course he liked it. All British jockeys who are invited,
they like it. Good pay, you see."

"How good?"

"Well," he said, "they get their fare over here, and a bit

toward expenses. And the fees for riding. And the appearance money."

"The racecourse pays the appearance money?"

"Not exactly. Well . . . the racecourse pays the money to the jockey but collects it from the owners who the jockey rode for."

"So an owner, in the end, pays everything—the riding fees, the winning percentage, a share of the fares, and a share of the appearance money?"

"That is right."

"What happens if after all that the jockey rides a stinking race?"

Holth answered with deadly seriousness. "The owner does not ask the jockey to come again."

We stepped out of the barn back into the mud. It hadn't actually rained that day, but the threat still hung in the cold misty air.

"Come into my house," suggested Holth. "Have some coffee before you catch the tram."

"Great," I said.

His house was a small wooden bungalow with lace curtains and geraniums in pots on every windowsill. The stove in the living room was already lit, with an orange metal coffeepot heating on top. Gunnar dug into a cupboard for two earthenware mugs and some sugar in a packet.

"Would the owners have asked Bob Sherman to come again?" I said.

He poured the coffee, stirring with a white plastic spoon.

"Per Bjørn Sandvik would. And Sven Wangen—that's the owner of that dappled mare on the far side." He pondered. "Rolf Torp, now. Bob lost a race the day he went. Rolf Torp thought he should have walked it."

"And should he?"

Holth shrugged. "Horses aren't machines," he said. "Mind you, I don't train Rolf Torp's horses, so I don't really know, do I?"

"Who trains them?"

"Paul Sundby."

"Will Rolf Torp be at the races tomorrow?"

"Naturally," Holth said. "He has the favorite in the National."

"And you," I said. "Would you have asked him to ride for you again?"

"Certainly," he said without hesitation. "Bob is a good jockey. He listens to what you say about a horse. He rides with his head. He would not have been asked so many times if he had not been good."

The door from the yard opened without warning and one of the lads poked his head in: he was about twenty-five, cheerful, and wore a woolen cap with a pompon.

"Gunny," he said, "will ye be takin' a look at that bleedin' mare now? She's a right cow, that one."

The trainer said he would look in a minute, and the head withdrew.

"He's Irish," I said, surprised.

"Sure. I've three Irish lads and one from Yorkshire. And three from here. There's a lot of British lads in Norwegian racing."

"Why is that?"

"They get a chance of riding in races here, see? More than they do at home."

We drank the coffee, which was well boiled and all the stronger for it.

I said, "What did Bob do for transport? Did he ever hire a car?"

"No. I don't think so. When he stayed here, he used to go with me over to the course."

"Did he ever borrow your car? Or anyone's?"

"He didn't borrow mine. I don't think he ever drove when he came."

"Did you take him anywhere except to the races the day he disappeared?"

"No."

I knew from a file of statements which had been awaiting my arrival at the hotel that Bob Sherman had been expected to leave the racecourse by taxi to catch the late flight to Heathrow. He had not caught it. The taxi driver who had been engaged for the trip had simply shrugged when his passenger didn't show, and had taken some ordinary racegoers back to the city instead.

That left public transport, all the taxi drivers who didn't know Bob by sight, and other people's cars. Plus, I supposed, his own two feet. It would have been all too easy to leave the racecourse without being seen by anyone who knew him, particularly if, as the collected notes implied, the last race had been run after dark.

I put down my empty coffee mug, and Gunnar Holth abruptly said, "Could you be doing something about Bob's wife, now?"

"His wife? I might see her when I go back if I find out anything useful."

"No." He shook his head. "She is here."

"Here?"

He nodded. "In Oslo. And she won't go home."

"Arne didn't mention it."

Holth laughed. "She follows him round like a dog. She asks questions, like you. Who saw Bob go, who did he go with, why does no one find him. She comes to every race meeting and asks and asks. Everyone is very tired of it."

"Do you know where she's staying?"

He nodded vigorously and picked up a piece of paper lying near on a shelf.

"The Norsland Hotel. Second class, away from the center. This is her telephone number. She gave it to me in case I could think of anything to help." He shrugged. "Everyone is sorry for her. But I wish she would go away."

"Will you telephone her?" I said. "Say I would like to ask her some questions about Bob. Suggest this afternoon."

"I've forgotten your name," he said without apology.

I smiled and gave him one of the firm's official cards. He looked at it and me in disbelief, but got the Norsland Hotel on the line. Mrs. Emma Sherman was fetched.

Holth said into the receiver, "A Mr. David Cleveland . . . come from England to try to find your husband." He read from the card, "Chief Investigator, Investigation Office, Jockey Club, Portman Square, London. He wants to see you this afternoon."

He listened to the reaction, then looked at me and said, "Where?"

"At her hotel. Three o'clock."

He relayed the news.

"She'll be waiting for you," he said, putting the receiver down.

"Good."

"Tell her to go home," he said.

Three

SHE WAS WAITING in the small lobby of the Norsland, sitting on the edge of a chair and anxiously scanning the face of every passing male. I watched her for a while through the glass doors to the street before going in. She looked small and pale and very very jumpy. Twice she half stood up, and twice, as the man she had focused on walked past without a sign, subsided slowly back to her seat.

I pushed through the doors into air barely warmer than the street, which in a completely centrally heated city spoke poorly of the management. Emma Sherman looked at me briefly and switched her gaze back to the door. I was not what she expected: the next man through, sixtyish and military-looking, had her again halfway to her feet.

He passed her without a glance on his way to collect his room key at the desk. She sat down slowly, looking increasingly nervous.

I walked over to her.

"Mrs. Sherman?"

"Oh." She stood up slowly. "Is there a message from Mr. Cleveland?"

"I am David Cleveland," I said.

"But," she said, and stopped. The surprise lingered on her face among the strain and tiredness, but she seemed past feeling anything very clearly. At close quarters, the nervousness resolved itself into a state not far from total breakdown.

Her skin looked almost transparent from fatigue, dark shadows around her eyes emphasizing the pebbly dullness of the eyes themselves. She was about twenty-two and should have been pretty: she had the bones and the hair for it, but they hadn't a chance. She was also, it seemed to me, pregnant.

"Where can we talk?" I asked.

She looked vaguely around the lobby, which contained three chairs, no privacy, and a rubber plant.

"Your room?" I suggested.

"Oh, no," she said at once, and then more slowly, in explanation, "it is small—not comfortable—nowhere to sit."

"Come along, then," I said. "We'll find a coffee shop."

She came with me out into the street and we walked in the general direction of the Grand.

"Will you find him?" she said. "Please find him."

"I'll do my best."

"He never stole that money," she said. "He didn't."

I glanced at her. She was trembling perceptibly and looking paler than ever. I stopped walking and put my hand under her elbow. She looked at me with glazing eyes, tried to say something else, and fell forward against me in a thoroughgoing swoon.

Even ninety-eight pounds of fainting girl is hard to support suddenly. Two passing strangers proved to have friendly faces but no English, and the third, who had the tongue, muttered something about the disgrace of being drunk at three in the afternoon and scurried away. I held her up against me with my arms under hers and asked the next woman along to call a taxi.

She, too, looked disapproving and backed away, but a boy of

about sixteen gave her a withering glance and came to the rescue.

"Is she ill?" he asked. His English was punctilious stuff, learned in school.

"She is. Can you get a taxi?"

"*Ja.* I will return. You will"—he thought, then found the word —"wait."

"I will wait," I agreed.

He nodded seriously and darted away round the nearest corner, a slim figure in the ubiquitous uniform of the young, blue jeans and a padded jacket. He came back, as good as his word, with a taxi, and helped me get the girl into it.

"Thank you very much," I said.

He beamed. "I learn English," he said.

"You speak it very well."

He waved as the taxi drew away: a highly satisfactory encounter to both parties.

She began to wake up during the short journey, which seemed to reassure the taxi driver. He spoke no English except one word which he repeated at least ten times with emphasis, and which was "doctor."

"*Ja,*" I agreed. "*Ja.* At the Grand Hotel."

He shrugged, but drove us there. He also helped me support her through the front doors and accepted his fare after she was safely sitting down.

"Doctor," he said as he left, and I said, "*Ja.*"

"No," said Bob Sherman's wife, in little more than a whisper. "What . . . happened?"

"You fainted," I said briefly. "And doctor or no doctor, you need to lie down. So up you come." I more or less lifted her to her feet, walked her to the lift, and took her up the one floor to my room. She flopped full length on the bed without question and lay there with her eyes closed.

"Do you mind if I feel your pulse?" I asked.

She gave no answer either way, so I put my fingers on her

wrist and found the slow heartbeat. Her arm was slippery with sweat, though noticeably cold, and all in all she looked disturbingly frail.

"Are you hungry?" I said.

She rolled her head on the pillow in a slow negative, but I guessed that what was really wrong with her, besides strain, was simple starvation. She had been too worried to take care of herself, and besides eating came expensive in Norway.

A consultation on the telephone with the hotel restaurant produced a promise of hot meat soup and some bread and cheese.

"And brandy," I said.

"No brandy, sir, on Saturday. Or on Sunday. It is the rule."

I had been warned, but had forgotten. Extraordinary to find a country with madder licensing laws than Britain's. There was a small refrigerator in my room, however, which stocked, among the orangeade and mineral waters, a quarter bottle of champagne. It had always seemed to me that bottling in quarters simply spoiled good fizz, but there's an occasion for everything. Emma said she couldn't, she shouldn't; but she did, and within five minutes was looking like a long-picked flower caught just in time.

"I'm sorry," she said, leaning on one elbow on my bed and sipping the golden bubbles from my tooth mug.

"You're welcome."

"You must think me a fool."

"No."

"It's just that no one seems to care anymore . . . where he's gone. They just say they can't find him. . . . They aren't even looking."

"They've looked," I began, but she wasn't ready to listen.

"Then Gunnar Holth said the Jockey Club had sent their chief investigator . . . and I've been hoping so hard all day that at last someone would find him, and then . . . and then . . . you . . ."

"I'm not the father figure you were hoping for," I said.

She shook her head. "I didn't think you'd be so young."

"Which do you want most," I asked, "a father figure or some-one to find Bob?" But it was too soon to expect her to see that the two things didn't necessarily go together. She needed the comfort as much as the search.

"He didn't steal that money," she said.

"How do you know?"

"He just wouldn't." She spoke with conviction, but I won-dered if the person she most wanted to convince was herself.

A waiter knocked on the door, bringing a tray, and Emma felt well enough to sit at the table and eat. She started slowly, still in a weak state, but by the end it was clear she was fiercely hungry.

As she finished the last of the bread, I said, "In about three hours we'll have dinner."

"Oh, no."

"Oh, yes. Why not? Then you'll have plenty of time to tell me about Bob. Hours and hours. No need to hurry."

She looked at me with the first signs of connected thought and almost immediately glanced around the room. The aware-ness that she was in my bedroom flashed out like neon in the North Pole.

I smiled. "Would you prefer the local nick? One each side of a table in an interview room?"

"Oh! I . . . suppose not." She shuddered slightly. "I've had quite a lot of that, you see. In a way. Everyone's been quite kind, really, but they think Bob stole that money and they treat me as if my husband was a crook. It's—it's pretty dreadful."

"I understand that," I said.

"Do you?"

The meal had done nothing for her pallor. The eyes still looked hollowed and black-smudged, and the strain still vi-brated in her manner. It was going to take more than cham-pagne and soup to undo the knots.

"Why don't you sleep for a while?" I suggested. "You look very tired. You'll be quite all right here . . . and I've some reports which I ought to write. I'd be glad to get them out of the way."

"I can't sleep," she said automatically, but when I determinedly took papers out of my briefcase, spread them on the table, and switched on a bright lamp to see them by, she stood up and hovered a bit and finally lay down again on the bed. After five minutes, I walked over to look and she was sound asleep, her cheeks sunken and pale blue veins in her eyelids.

She wore a camel-colored coat, which she had relaxed as far as unbuttoning, and a brown-and-white checked dress underneath. With the coat falling open, the bulge in her stomach showed unmistakably. Could be about five months, I thought.

I pushed the papers together again and returned them to the briefcase. They were the various statements and accounts relating to her husband's disappearance, and I had no report to write on them. I sat instead in one of the Grand's comfortable armchairs and thought about why men vanished.

In the main, they either ran *to* something or *from* something: occasionally a combination of both. To a woman; from a woman. To the sunshine; from the police. To political preference; from political oppression. To anonymity; from blackmail.

Sometimes they took someone else's money with them to finance the future. Bob Sherman's sixteen thousand kroner didn't seem, at first sight, to be worth what he'd exchanged for it. He earned five times as much every year.

So what had he gone *to?*

Or what had he gone *from?*

And how was I to find him by Monday afternoon?

She slept soundly for more than two hours, with periods of peaceful dreaming, but after that she went into a session which was distressing her. She moved restlessly and sweat appeared on her forehead, so I touched her hand and called her out of it.

"Emma. Wake up. Wake up, now, Emma."

She opened her eyes fast and wide with the nightmare pictures still in them. Her body began to tremble.

"Oh," she said. "Oh, God . . ."

"It's all right. You were dreaming. It was only a dream."

Her mind finished the transition to consciousness, but she was neither reassured nor comforted.

"I dreamed he was in jail. . . . There were bars, and he was trying to get out—frantically—and I asked him why he wanted to get out, and he said they were going to execute him in the morning. . . . And then I was talking to someone in charge and I said what had he done, why were they going to execute him, and this man said he'd stolen the racecourse, and the law said that if people stole racecourses they had to be executed."

She rubbed a hand over her face.

"It's so silly," she said. "But it seemed so real."

"Horrid," I said.

She said with desolation, "But where is he? Why doesn't he write to me? How can he be so cruel?"

"Perhaps there's a letter waiting at home."

"No. I telephone . . . every day."

I said, "Are you—well—are you happy together?"

"Yes," she said firmly, but after five silent seconds the truer version came limping out. "Sometimes we have rows. We had one the day he came here. All morning. And it was over such a little thing—just that he'd spent a night away when he didn't have to. . . . I'd not been feeling well and I told him he was selfish and thoughtless, and he lost his temper and said I was too damn demanding. . . . And I said then I wouldn't go with him to Kempton, and he went silent and sulky because he was going to ride the favorite in the big race and he always likes to have me there after something like that; it helps him unwind." She stared into a past moment she would have given the world to change. "So he went on his own. And from there to Heathrow for the six-thirty to Oslo, same as usual. Only usually I went with him, to see him off and take the car home."

"And meet him again Sunday night?"

"Yes. On Sunday night, when he didn't come back at the right time, I was worried sick that he'd had a fall in Norway and hurt himself, and I telephoned to Gunnar Holth. . . . But he said Bob hadn't fallen; he'd ridden a winner and got round in the other two races, and as far as he knew he'd caught the plane as planned. So I rang the airport again. I'd rung them before, and they said the plane had landed on time. . . . And I begged them to check and they said there was no Sherman on the passenger list." She stopped and I waited, and she went on in a fresh onslaught of misery, "Surely he knew I didn't really mean it? I love him. . . . Surely he wouldn't just leave me, without saying a word?"

It appeared, however, that he had.

"How long have you been married?"

"Nearly two years."

"Children?"

She glanced down at the brown-and-white checked mound and gestured toward it with a flutter of slender fingers. "This is our first."

"Finances?"

"Oh . . . all right, really."

"How really?"

"He had a good season last year. We saved a bit then. Of course he does like good suits and a nice car. . . . All jockeys do, don't they?"

I nodded. I also knew more about her husband's earnings than she seemed to, as I had access to the office which collected and distributed jockeys' fees; but it wasn't so much the reasonable income that was significant as the extent to which they lived within it.

"He does get keen on schemes for making money quickly, but we've never lost much. I usually talk him out of it. I'm not a gambler at all, you see."

I let a pause go by. Then, "Politics?"

"How do you mean?"

"Is he interested in Communism?"

She stared. "Good heavens, no."

"Militant in any way?"

She almost laughed. "Bob doesn't give a damn for politics or politicians. He says they're all the same, hot air and hypocrisy. Why do you ask such an extraordinary question?"

I shrugged. "Norway has a common frontier with Russia."

Her surprise was genuine on two counts: she didn't know her geography and she did know her husband. He was not the type to exchange good suits and a nice car and an exciting job for a dim existence in a totalitarian state.

"Did he mention any friends he had made here?"

"I've seen nearly everyone I can remember him talking about. I've asked them over and over—Gunnar Holth, and his lads, and Mr. Kristiansen, and the owners. . . . The only one I haven't met is one of the owners' sons, a boy called Mikkel. Bob mentioned him once or twice. He's away at school now, or something."

"Was Bob in any trouble before this?"

She looked bewildered. "What sort?"

"Bookmakers?"

She turned her head away and I gave her time to decide on her answer. Jockeys were not allowed to bet, and I worked for the Jockey Club.

"No," she said indistinctly.

"You might as well tell me," I said. "I can find out. But you would be quicker."

She looked back at me, perturbed. "He only bets on himself, usually," she said defensively. "It's legal in a lot of countries."

"I'm only interested in his betting if it's got anything to do with his disappearance. Was anyone threatening him for payment?"

"Oh." She sounded forlorn, as if the one thing she did not

want to be given was a good reason for Bob to steal a comparatively small sum and ruin his life for it.

"He never said. . . . I'm sure he would have told me." She gulped. "The police asked me if he was being blackmailed. I said no, of course not. . . . But if it was to keep me from knowing something . . . how can I be sure? Oh, I do wish, I do wish he'd write to me."

Tears came in a rush and spilled over. She didn't apologize, didn't brush them away, and in a few seconds they had stopped. She had wept a good deal, I guessed, during the past three weeks.

"You've done all you can here," I said. "Better come back with me on Monday afternoon."

She was surprised and disappointed. "You're going back so soon? But you won't have found him."

"Probably not. But I've a meeting in London on Tuesday that I can't miss. If it looks like being useful, I'll come back here afterward, but for you it's time now to go home."

She didn't answer at once, but finally, in a tired, quiet, defeated voice, said, "All right."

Four

ARNE WAS HAVING DIFFICULTY with his complex, constantly looking over his shoulder to the extent of making forward locomotion hazardous. Why he should find any threat in the cheerful frostbitten-looking crowd which had turned up at Øvrevoll for the Norsk Grand National was something between him and his psychiatrist, but as usual his friends were suffering from his affliction.

He had refused, for instance, to drink a glass of wine in a comfortable available room with a king-sized log fire. Instead we were marching back and forth outside, he, I, and Per Bjørn Sandvik, wearing out shoe leather and turning blue at the ears, for fear of bugging machines. I couldn't see how overhearing our present conversation could possibly benefit anyone, but then I wasn't Arne. And at least this time, I thought philosophically, we would not be mowed down by a speedboat.

As before, he was ready for the outdoor life: a blue padded hood joined all in one to his anorak. Per Bjørn Sandvik had a felt hat. I had my head. Maybe one day I would learn.

Sandvik, one of the Stewards, was telling me again at first hand what I'd already read in the statements: how Bob Sherman had had access to the money.

"It's collected into the officials' room, you see, where it is checked and recorded. And the officials' room is in the same building as the jockeys' changing room. Right? And that Sunday, Bob Sherman went to the officials' room to ask some question or other, and the money was stacked there, just inside the door. Arne saw him there himself. He must have planned at once to take it."

"What was the money contained in?" I asked.

"Canvas bags. Heavy double canvas."

"What color?"

He raised his eyebrows. "Brown."

"Just dumped on the floor?"

He grinned. "There is less crime in Norway."

"So I've heard," I said. "How many bags?"

"Five."

"Heavy?"

He shrugged. "Like money."

"How were they fastened?"

"With leather straps and padlocks."

Arne cannoned into a blonde who definitely had the right of way. She said something which I judged from his expression to be unladylike, but it still didn't persuade him to look where he was going. Some enemy lay behind, listening: he was sure of it.

Sandvik gave him an indulgent smile. Sandvik was a tall, pleasant, unhurried man of about fifty, upon whom authority sat as lightly as fluff. Arne had told me he was "someone at the top in oil," but he had none of the usual aura of big business: almost the reverse, as if he derived pleasure from leaving an impression of no power, no aggression. If so, he would be a boardroom opponent as wicked as a mantrap among the daisies. I looked at him speculatively. He met my eyes. Nothing in his that shouldn't be.

"What was going to be done with the bags if Sherman hadn't nicked them?" I asked.

"Lock them in the safe in the officials' room until Monday morning, when they would go to the bank."

"Guarded," Arne said—eyes front, for once—"by a night watchman."

But by the time the night watchman had clocked in, the booty had vanished.

"How did the officials all happen to desert the room at once, leaving the money so handy?" I asked.

Sandvik spread his thickly gloved hands. "We have discussed this endlessly. It was accidental. The room can only have been empty for five minutes or less. There was no special reason for them all being out at one time. It just happened."

He had a high-register voice with beautifully distinct enunciation, but his almost perfect English sounded quite different from the home-grown variety. I worked it out after a while: it was his "l"s. The British pronounce "l" with their tongue lolling back in the throat; the Norwegians say theirs with the tongue tight up behind the teeth. Retaining the Norwegian "l" gave Sandvik's accent a light, dry, clear-voweled quality which made everything he said sound logical and lucid.

"No one realized, that evening, that the money had been stolen. Each of the officials took it for granted that another had put the bags in the safe, as they were no longer to be seen. It was the next day, when the safe was opened for the money to be banked, that it was found to be missing. And then, of course, we heard from Gunnar Holth that Sherman had disappeared as well."

I thought a moment. "Didn't Gunnar Holth tell me that Bob Sherman stayed with you once or twice?"

"Yes, that's right." Sandvik briefly pursed his well-shaped mouth. "Twice. But not the time he stole the money, I'm glad to say."

"You liked him, though?"

"Oh, yes, well enough, I suppose. I asked him out of politeness. He had ridden several winners for me, and I know what Gunnar's bunk room is like." He grinned slightly. "Anyway, he came. But we had little of common interest except horses, and I think he really preferred Gunnar's, after all."

"Would you have expected him to steal?"

"It never crossed my mind. I mean, it doesn't, does it? But I didn't know him well."

Arne could not bear the close quarters of the crowd on the stands, so we watched the first race, a hurdle, from rising ground just past the winning post. The racecourse, forming the floor of a small valley, was surrounded by hillsides of spruce and birch, young trees growing skyward like the Perpendicular period come to life. The slim dark evergreens stood in endless broken vertical stripes alternating with the yellow-drying leaves and silver trunks of the birch, and the whole backdrop, that afternoon, was hung along the skyline with fuzzy drifts of misty low cloud.

The light was cold gray, the air cold damp. The spirits of the crowd sunny Mediterranean. An English jockey won the race on the favorite and the crowd shouted approval.

It was time, Sandvik said, to go and see the Chairman, who had not been able to meet us sooner because he was entertaining a visiting Ambassador at lunch. We went into the Secretariat Building adjoining the grandstand, up some sporting-print-lined stairs, and into a large room containing not only the Chairman but five or six supporting Stewards. Per Bjørn Sandvik walked in first, then I, then Arne pushing his hood back. The Chairman went on looking inquiringly at the door, still waiting for me, so to speak, to appear. I sometimes wondered if it would help if I were fat, bald, and bespectacled: if premature aging might produce more confidence and belief than the thin-six-feet-with-brown-hair job did. I'd done a fair amount of living, one way or another, but it perversely refused to show.

"This is David Cleveland," Sandvik said, and several pairs of eyes mirrored the same disappointment.

"How do you do," I murmured gently to the Chairman, and held out my hand.

"Er . . ." He cleared his throat and recovered manfully. "So glad you have come."

I made a few encouraging remarks about how pleasant I found it in Norway; and I wondered if any of them knew that Napoleon had been promoted to General at twenty-four. The Chairman, Lars Baltzersen, was much like his letters to my office: brief, polite, and effective. It took him approximately ten seconds to decide I wouldn't have been given my job if I couldn't do it, and I saw no need to tell him that my boss had died suddenly eighteen months earlier and left the manager-elect in charge a lot sooner than anyone intended.

"You sound older on the telephone," he said simply, and I said I'd been told so before, and that was that.

"Go anywhere you like on the racecourse," he said. "Ask anything. . . . Arne can interpret for those who do not speak English."

"Thank you."

"Do you need anything else?"

Second sight, I thought; but I said, "Perhaps, if possible, to see you again before I go at the end of the afternoon."

"Of course. Of course. We'll want to hear of your progress. We'll all gather here after the last race."

Heads nodded dubiously, and I fully expected to justify their lowly expectations. Either briefed or bored or merely busy, they drifted away through the door, leaving only Arne and the Chairman behind.

"Some beer?" suggested Baltzersen.

Arne said yes and I said no. Despite the glow from a huge stove, it was a cold day for hops.

"How far is it to the Swedish border?" I asked.

"By road, about eighty kilometers," Baltzersen said.

"Any formalities there?"

He shook his head. "Not for Scandinavians in their own cars.

There are few inspections or customs. But none of the frontier posts remember an Englishman crossing on that evening."

"I know. Not even as a passenger in a Norwegian car. Would he have been spotted if he'd gone across crouching under a rug on the floor behind the driver's seat?"

They pondered. "Very probably not," Baltzersen said, and Arne agreed.

"Can you think of anyone who might have taken him? Anyone he was close to here, either in business or friendship?"

"I do not know him well enough," the Chairman said regretfully, and Arne blinked a little and said Gunnar Holth, or maybe some of the lads who worked for him.

"Holth says he drove him only round to the races," I said: but he would have had plenty of time to drive into Sweden and back before Emma Sherman had rung him up.

"Gunnar tells lies whenever it suits him," Arne said.

Lars Baltzersen sighed. "I'm afraid that is true."

He had gray hair, neatly brushed, with a tidy face and unimaginative clothes. I was beginning to get the feel of Norwegian behavior patterns, and he came into the very large category of sober, slightly serious people who were kind, efficient, and under little stress. Get-up-and-go was conspicuously absent, yet the job would clearly be done. The rat race taken at a walk. Very civilized.

There were other types, of course.

"The people I hate here," Emma Sherman had said, "are the drunks."

I'd taken her to dinner in the hotel the evening before, and in the end had listened for several hours to details of her life with Bob, her anxieties, and her experiences in Norway.

"When I first came," she said, "I used to have dinner in the dining room, and all these men used to come and ask if they could share my table. They were quite polite, but very very persistent. They wouldn't go away. The headwaiter used to get rid of them for me. He told me they were drunk. They didn't really look it. They weren't rolling or anything."

I laughed. "Considering the price of alcohol here, you wouldn't think they could."

"No," she had said. "Anyway, I stopped having dinner. I needed to make my money go as far as possible and I hated eating on my own."

Arne tapped my shoulder. "Where do you want to go first?"

Arne belonged to a third group: the kinks. You find them everywhere.

"Weighing room, I should think."

They both nodded in agreement. Arne pulled his hood back over his head and we went down into the raw outdoors. The crowd had swelled to what Arne described as "very big," but there was still plenty of room. One of the greatest advantages of life in Norway, I guessed, was the small population. I had not so far in its leisurely capital seen a queue or a crush or anyone fighting to get anywhere first: as there always seemed to be room for all, why bother?

The officials checking tickets at the gates between different enclosures were all keen young men of about twenty, most of them blond, all with blue armbands on their anoraks. They knew Arne, of course, but they checked my pass even though I was with him, the serious faces hardly lightening as they nodded me through. Lars Baltzersen had given me a three-by-five card stamped all over with *"adgang paddock," "adgang stallomadet," "adgang indre bane,"* and one or two other *"adgang"*s, and it looked as if I wouldn't get far if I lost it.

The weighing room—black wood walls, white paint, red tiled roof—lay on the far side of the parade ring, where the jockeys were already out for the second race. Everything looked neat, organized, and pleasing, and despite an eye trained to spot trouble at five hundred paces in a thick fog, I couldn't see any. Even in racing, good nature prevailed. Several of the lads leading the horses around wore sweaters in the owners' colors, matching the jockeys; a good and useful bit of display I'd seen nowhere else. I commented on it to Arne.

"*Ja,*" he said. "Many of the private stables do that now. It helps the crowd to know their colors."

Between the paddock and the U-shaped weighing-room buildings, and up into the U itself, there was a grassy area planted thickly with ornamental bushes. Everyone walking between weighing room and paddock had to detour either to one side or the other along comparatively narrow paths: it made a change from the rolling acres of concrete at home but took up a lot of apology time.

Once inside the weighing room, Arne forgot about bugging machines and introduced me rapidly to a stream of people— like the Secretary, the Clerk of the Course, and the Clerk of the Scales—without once looking over his shoulder. I shook hands and chatted a bit, but although they all knew I was looking for Bob Sherman, I couldn't see anyone feeling twitchy about my presence.

"Come this way, David," Arne said, and took me down a side passage with an open door at the end leading out to the racecourse. A step or two before this door, Arne turned smartly right, and we found ourselves in the officials' room from which the money had been stolen. It was just an ordinary businesslike room: wooden walls, wooden floor, wooden tables acting as desks, wooden chairs. (With all those forests, what else?) There were pleasant red checked curtains, first-class central heating, and in one corner a no-nonsense safe.

Apart from us, there was no one there.

"That's all there is," Arne said. "The money bags were left there on the floor"—he pointed—"and the lists of totals from each collecting point were put there on that desk, same as usual. We still have the lists."

It had struck me several times that Arne felt no responsibility for the loss of the money, nor did anyone seem in the remotest way to blame him, but by even the most elementary requirements of a security officer, he'd earned rock-bottom marks.

"Do you still have the same system with the bags?" I asked.

Arne gave me a look somewhere between amusement and hurt.

"No. Since that day, the bags are put immediately into the safe."

"Who has the keys?"

"I have some, and the Secretary, and the Clerk of the Course."

"And each of you three thought one of the other two had stowed the money away safely?"

"That is right."

We left the room and stepped out into the open air. Several jockeys, changed into colors for later races but with warm coats on at the moment, came along the passage and out through the same door, and they, Arne, and I climbed an outside staircase onto a small open stand attached to the side of the weighing-room buildings. From there, a furlong or more from the winning post, we watched the second race.

Arne had begun looking apprehensively around again, though there were barely twenty on the stand. I found I had begun doing it myself: it was catching. It netted, however, the sight of Rinty Ranger, an English jockey who knew me, and as everyone after the finish poured toward the stairs, I arranged to fetch up beside him. Arne went on down the steps, but the jockey stopped when I touched his arm, and was easy to keep back.

"Hallo," he said in surprise. "Fancy seeing you here."

"Came about Bob Sherman," I explained.

I'd found that if I said straight out what I wanted to know, I got better results. No one wasted time wondering what I suspected them of, and if they weren't feeling on the defensive they talked more.

"Oh. I see. Found the poor bugger, then?"

"Not yet," I said.

"Let him go, why don't you?"

Rinty Ranger knew Bob Sherman as well as anyone who'd been associated with him in the same small professional group for five years, but they were not especially close friends. I took this remark to be a general statement of sympathy for the fox, and asked if he didn't think stealing the money had been a bloody silly thing to do.

"Too right," he said. "I'll bet he wished he hadn't done it five minutes after. But that's Bob all over, smack into things without thinking."

"Makes him a good jockey," I said, remembering how he flung his heart over fences regardless.

Rinty grinned, his thin sharp face looking cold above his sheepskin coat. "Yeah. Done him no good this time, though."

"What else has he done that was impulsive?"

"I don't know. . . . Always full of get-rich-quick schemes like buying land in the Bahamas or backing crazy inventors, and I even heard him on about pyramid selling once, only we told him not to be such a bloody fool. I mean, it's hard enough to earn the stuff, you don't actually want to throw it down the drain."

"Were you surprised when he stole the money?" I asked.

"Well, of course I was, for Chrissakes. And even more by him doing a bunk. I mean, why didn't he just stash away the loot and carry on with business as usual?"

"Takes nerve," I said, but of course that was just what Bob Sherman had. "Also the money was in heavy canvas bags which would take a lot of getting into. He wouldn't have had time to do that and catch his flight home."

Rinty thought a bit but came up with nothing useful.

"Stupid bugger," he said. "Nice wife, kid coming, good job— you'd think he'd have more sense." And I'd got as far as that myself.

"Anyway, he's done me a favor," Rinty said. "I've got his ride in this here Grand National." He opened his sheepskin a fraction to show me the colors underneath. "The owner, fellow called Torp, isn't best pleased with Bob on any account. Says he should've won at a canter that last day he was here. Says he threw it away, left it too late, came through too soon, should've taken the outside, didn't put him right at the water—you name it, Bob did it wrong."

"He got another English jockey, though."

"Oh, sure. D'you know how many homebred jump jocks there are here? About fifteen, that's all, and some of those are English or Irish. Lads, they are mostly. You don't get many self-employed chaps, like us. There isn't enough racing here for that. You get them going to Sweden on Saturdays—they race there on Saturdays. Here Thursdays and Sundays. That's the lot. Mind you, they don't keep the jumpers to look at. They all run once a week at least, and as there are only four or five jump races—all the rest are flat—it makes life interesting."

"Were you and Bob often over here together?"

"This year, three or four trips, I suppose. But I came last year, too, which he didn't."

"How long is a trip?"

He looked surprised. "Only a day, usually. We race in England Saturday afternoon, catch the six-thirty, race here Sunday, catch the late plane back if we can, otherwise the eight-fifteen Monday morning. Sometimes we fly here Sunday morning, but it's cutting it a bit fine. No margin for holdups."

"Do you get to know people here well in that time?"

"I suppose it sort of accumulates. Why?"

"Has Bob Sherman made any friendships here, would you say?"

"Good God. Well, no, not that I know of, but then likely as not I wouldn't know if he did. He knows a lot of trainers and owners, of course. Do you mean girls?"

"Not particularly. Were there any?"

"Shouldn't think so. He likes his missus."

"Do you mind thinking fairly hard about it?"

He looked surprised. "If you like."

I nodded. He lengthened the focus of his gaze in a most satisfactory manner and really concentrated. I waited without pressure, watching the crowd. Young, it was, by British standards: at least half under thirty, half blond, all the youth dressed in anoraks of blue, red, orange, and yellow in the sort of colorful haphazard uniformity that stage designers plan for the chorus.

Rinty Ranger stirred and brought his vision back to the present.

"I don't know. . . . He stayed with Mr. Sandvik a couple of times, and said he got on better with his son than the old man. . . . I met him once—the son, that is—with Bob when they were chatting at the races, but I wouldn't say they were great friends or anything."

"How old is he, roughly?"

"The son? Sixteen, seventeen. Eighteen, maybe."

"Anyone else?"

"Well . . . One of the lads at Gunnar Holth's. An Irish lad, Paddy O'Flaherty. Bob knows him well, because Paddy used to work for old Tasker Mason, where Bob was apprenticed. They were lads together, one time, you might say. Bob likes staying at Gunnar Holth's on account of Paddy, I think."

"Do you know if Paddy has a car?"

"Haven't a clue. Why don't you ask him? He's bound to be here."

"Were you here the day Bob disappeared?" I asked.

" 'Fraid not."

"Well . . . Mm . . . anything you can think of which is not what you'd've expected?"

"What bloody questions! Let's see. . . . Can't think of anything . . . except that he left his saddle here."

"Bob?"

"Yes. It's in the changing room. And his helmet. He must have known, the silly sod, that he'd never be able to race anywhere in the world again; otherwise he'd never have left them."

I moved toward the stairs. Rinty hadn't told me a great deal, but if there had been much to tell, the police of one country or the other would have found Bob long ago. He followed me down, and I wished him good luck in the National.

"Thanks," he said. "Can't say I wish you the same, though. Let the poor bastard alone."

At the bottom of the steps, Arne was talking to Per Bjørn Sandvik. With smiles they turned to include me, and I asked the offensive question with as much tact as possible.

"Your son, Mikkel, Mr. Sandvik . . . Do you think he could've driven Bob Sherman away from the races? Without knowing, of course, that he had the money with him?"

Per Bjørn reacted less violently than many a father would to the implication that his son, having entertained a thief even if unawares, had nonetheless kept quiet about it. Scarcely a ripple went through him.

He said smoothly, "Mikkel cannot drive yet. He is still at school. . . . His seventeenth birthday was six weeks ago."

"That's good," I said in apology; and I thought, That's that.

Per Bjørn said, "Excuse me," without noticeable resentment, and walked away. Arne, blinking furiously, asked where I wanted to go next. To see Paddy O'Flaherty, I said, so we went in search and found him in the stables getting Gunnar Holth's runner ready for the Grand National. He turned out to be the lad in the wooly cap with uncomplimentary opinions of a mare, and described himself as "Gunny's head lad, so I am."

"What did I do after the races?" he repeated. "Same as I always do. Took the runners home, squared 'em up, and saw to their scoff."

"And after that?"

"After that, same as always, down to the local hop. There's a good little bird there, d'you see?"

"Do you have a car?" I asked.

"Well, sure I have, now, but the tires are as thin as a stockpot on Thursday, and I wouldn't be after driving on them anymore at all. And there's the winter coming on, so there's my car up on bricks, d'you see?"

"When did you put it on bricks?"

"The police stopped me about those tires, now. . . . Well, there's the canvas peeping through one or two, if you look close. Sure it's all of six weeks ago now."

After that we drifted around while I took in a general view of what went on, and then walked across the track to watch a race from the tower. This looked slightly like a small airfield control tower, two stories high with a glass-walled room at the top. In this aerie during races sat two keen-eyed men with fierce race glasses clamped to their eyes: they were nonautomatic patrol cameras, and never missed a trick.

Arne introduced me. Feel free to come up into the tower at any time, they said, smiling. I thanked them and stayed to watch the next race from there, looking straight down the narrow elongated oval of the track. Sixteen hundred meters for staying two-year-olds: they started almost level with the tower, scurried a long way away, rounded the fairly sharp bottom bend, and streamed up the long straight to finish at the winning post just below where we stood. There was a photo finish. The all-seeing eyes unstuck themselves from their race glasses, nodded happily, and said they would be back for the next race.

Before following them down the stairs, I asked Arne which way the Grand National went, as there seemed to be fences pointing in every direction.

"Round in a figure of eight," he said, sweeping a vague arm. "Three times round. You will see when they go." He seemed to want to be elsewhere fairly promptly, but when we had hurried back over to the paddock, it appeared merely that he was hungry and had calculated enough eating time before the Norsk St. Leger. He magicked some huge open sandwiches on about a foot of French loaf, starting at one end with prawns and proceeding through herring, cheese, pâté, and egg to beef at the far end, adorned throughout by pickled cucumber, mayon-

naise, and scattered unidentified crispy bits. Arne stayed the
course, but I blew up in the straight.

We drank wine: part of a bottle. We would come back later,
Arne said, and finish it. We were in the big warm room he had
shunned earlier, but the listeners weren't troubling him at that
moment.

"If you're going home tomorrow, David," he said, "come to
supper with us tonight."

I hesitated. "There's Emma Sherman," I said.

"That girl," he exclaimed. He peered around, though there
were barely six others in the room. "Where is she? She's usually
on my heels."

"I talked to her yesterday. Persuaded her not to come today
and to go back to England tomorrow."

"Great. Great, my friend." He rubbed his hands together.
"She'll be all right, then. You come to supper with us. I will
telephone to Kari."

I thought of Kari's hair and Kari's shape. Everything stacked
as I liked it best. I imagined her in bed. Very likely I should have
allowed no such thoughts, but you might as well forbid fish to
swim. A pity she was Arne's, I thought. To stay away would
make it easier on oneself.

"Come," Arne said.

Weak, that's what I am. I said, "I'd love to."

He bustled off instantly to do the telephoning and soon returned beaming.

"She is very pleased. She says we will give you cloudberries;
she bought some yesterday."

We went out to the raw afternoon and watched the big flat
race together, but then Arne was whisked off on official business
and for a while I wandered around alone. Though the organization and upkeep were clearly first class, it was not on British
terms a big racecourse. Plenty of room, but few buildings. Everyone could see: no one was pushed, rushed, or crushed. Space
was the ultimate luxury, I thought, as I strolled past a small

oblong ornamental pond with a uniformed military band playing full blast beside it. Several children sat in bright little heaps around the players' feet, and one or two were peering interestedly into the quivering business ends of trombones.

Øvrevoll, someone had told me, was a fairly new racecourse, the only one in Norway to hold ordinary flat and jump races. Most racing, as in Germany, was trotting, with sulkies.

For the Grand National itself I went back up the tower, which I found stood in the smaller, top part of the figure eight; the larger part lay in the main part of the course, inside the flat track. Twenty runners set off at a spanking pace to go three and a half times around, which set the binocular men in the tower rotating like gyros. Soon after the start, the horses circled the tower, cut closer across beside it, and sped toward the water jump and the farther part of the course, took the bottom bend, and returned toward the start. In the top part of the course, near the tower, lay a large pond with a couple of swans swimming in stately unison across from two small devoted black and white ducks. Neither pair took the slightest notice of the throng of horses thundering past a few feet from home.

Rinty Ranger won the race, taking the lead at the beginning of the last circuit and holding off all challengers, and I saw the triumphant flash of his teeth as he went past the post.

The misty daylight had already faded to the limit for jumping fences safely, but the two races still to come, in a card of ten altogether, were both on the flat. The first was run in peering dusk and the second in total darkness, with floodlights from the tower illuminating just the winning line, bright enough to activate the photo finish. Eleven horses sped up the dark track, clearly seen only for the seconds it took them to flash through the bright patch, but cheered nonetheless by a seemingly undiminished crowd.

So they literally did race in the dark. I walked thoughtfully back toward the officials' room to meet with Arne. It really *had* been night-black when Bob Sherman left the racecourse.

There was bustle in the officials' room and a lot of grins and
assurances that the takings this day were safe in the safe. Arne
reminded several of them that the Chairman had said they
could come to the progress-report meeting if they liked: he said
it in English in deference to me, and in English they answered.
They would come, except for one or two who would wait for the
night watchman. A right case of bolting stable doors.

The Chairman's room had too many people in it, as far as I
was concerned. Fifteen besides myself. Every chair filled up,
coffee and drinks circulated, and the eyes waited. Lars Baltzersen raised his eyebrows in my direction to tell me I was on,
and shushed the low-key chatter with a single smooth wave of
his hand.

"I think you've all met Mr. Cleveland at some time today."
He turned directly to me and smiled forgivingly. "I know we
have asked the impossible. Sherman left no traces, no clues. But
is there any course of action you think we might take which we
have not so far done?"

He made it so easy.

"Look for his body," I said.

Five

It seemed that that was not what they expected.

Per Bjørn Sandvik said explosively, in his high distilled English, "We know he is a thief. Why should he be *dead?*" and someone else murmured, "I still think he is in the South of France, living in the sun."

Rolf Torp, owner of the Grand National winner, lit a cigar and said, "I do not follow your reasoning." Arne sat shaking his head and blinking as if he would never stop.

Lars Baltzersen gave me a long stare and then invited me to explain.

"Well," I said, "take first the mechanics of the theft. Everyone agrees that the officials' room was empty for a very few minutes, and that no one could have predicted when it would be empty, or that it would be empty at all. Everyone agrees that Bob Sherman simply saw the money lying handy, was overcome with sudden temptation, and swiped it. Sorry," I said as I saw their puzzlement; "stole it."

Heads nodded all around. This was well-worn ground.

"After that," I said, "we come to a few difficulties. That money was enclosed in five hefty—er, bulky—canvas bags fastened with straps and padlocks. Now, a one-hundred-and-thirty-three-pound jockey couldn't stow five such bags out of sight under his coat. Anyone, however big, would have found it awkward to pick all of them up at once. To my mind, if Sherman's first impulse was to steal, his second would instantly be to leave well enough alone. He had no way of knowing how much the bags contained. No way of judging whether the theft would be worthwhile. But in fact there is no evidence at all to suggest that he felt any impulse to steal, even if he saw the bags on the floor when he went earlier to ask some question or other. There is no evidence whatsoever to prove that Bob Sherman stole the money."

"Of course there is," Rolf Torp said. "He disappeared."

"How?" I asked.

There were several puzzled frowns, one or two blank faces, and no suggestions.

"This must have been a spur-of-the-moment theft," I said, "so he could have made no preparations. Well, say for argument he had taken the bags: there he is staggering around with the swag —the stolen goods—in full view. What does he do? Even with a sharp knife, it would have taken some time to slit open those bags and remove the money. But we can discount that he did this on the racecourse, because the bags in fact have never been found."

Some heads nodded. Some were shaken.

"Bob Sherman had a small overnight grip with him, which I understand from his wife was not big enough to contain five canvas bags, let alone his clothes as well. No one has found his clothes lying around, so he could not have packed the money in his grip."

Lars Baltzersen looked thoughtful.

"Take transport," I said. "He had ordered a taxi to take him to Fornebu airport, but he didn't turn up. The police could find no taxi driver who took one single Englishman anywhere. Gunnar Holth says he drove him round to the racecourse at midday, but not away. Because the theft has to be unpremeditated, Sherman could not have hired himself a getaway car, and the police could trace no such hiring, anyway. He did not steal a car to transport the money: no cars were stolen from here that day. Which leaves friends . . ." I paused. "Friends who could be asked to take him, say, to Sweden and keep quiet afterward."

"They would be also guilty," said Rolf Torp disbelievingly.

"Yes. Well . . . he had been to Norway seven times but only for a day or two each time. The only friends I can find who might conceivably have known or liked him well enough to get themselves into trouble on his account are Gunnar Holth's head lad, Paddy O'Flaherty, and perhaps—if you'll forgive me, sir—Mikkel Sandvik."

He was much more annoyed this time, but protested no further than a grim stare.

"But Paddy O'Flaherty's car has been up on bricks for six weeks," I said. "And Mikkel Sandvik cannot drive yet. Neither of them had wheels—er, transport—ready and waiting for Sherman's unexpected need."

"What you are saying is that once he'd stolen the money, he couldn't have got it away," Baltzersen said. "But suppose he hid it, and came back for it later?"

"He would still have much the same transport problem, and also the night watchmen to contend with. No . . . I think if he had stolen and hidden the money, he would not have gone back for it, but just abandoned it. Sense would have prevailed. Because there are other things about that cash. . . . To you, it is familiar. It is *money*. To Bob Sherman, it was foreign currency. All British jockeys riding abroad have enough trouble changing currency as it is: they would not leap at stealing bagfuls of something they could not readily spend. And don't forget, a large proportion of it was in coins, which are both heavy and even more difficult to exchange in quantity than notes, once they are out of Norway."

Per Bjørn Sandvik was studying the floor and looking mild again. Arne had blinked his eyes to a standstill and was now holding them shut. Rolf Torp puffed his cigar with agitation, and Lars Baltzersen looked unhappy.

"But that still does not explain why you think Sherman is dead," he said.

"There has been no trace of him from that day to this. . . . No one even thinks they might have seen him. There have been no reports from anywhere. His pregnant wife has had no word of reassurance. All this is highly unusual in the case of a thief on the run, but entirely consistent with the man being dead."

Baltzersen took his bottom lip between his teeth.

I said, "It is usually fairly easy to account for a man's abrupt disappearance. . . . During an investigation, his motive emerges pretty strongly. But there seems to have been no factor in Bob Sherman's life likely to prompt him into impulsive and irreversible flight. No one would exchange a successful career for an unknown but not huge amount of foreign currency unless some secondary force made it imperative. Neither your police nor the British police nor his wife nor Arne Kristiansen nor I have found any suggestion, however faint or unlikely, that there was any such force at work."

Arne opened his eyes and shook his head.

"Suppose," I said, "that someone else stole the money, and Bob Sherman saw him."

The Stewards and officials looked startled and intensely gloomy. No one needed to have it spelled out that anyone caught red-handed might have had too much to lose, and from there it was a short step to imagine the thief desperate enough to kill Bob Sherman to keep him quiet.

"Murder." Baltzersen spoke the word slowly, as if it were strange on his tongue. "Is that what you mean?"

"It's possible," I said.

"But not certain."

"If there were any clear pointers to murder," I said, "your police would have already found them. There is no clarity any-where. But if there are no answers at all to the questions where he went, why he went, and how he went, I think one should then ask *whether* he went."

Baltzersen's strained voice reflected their faces: they did not want me to be right. "You surely don't think he is still *here?* On the racecourse?"

Rolf Torp shook his head impatiently. He was a man most unlike the Chairman, as quick-tempered as Baltzersen was steady. "Of course he doesn't. There are people here every day training their horses, and we have held eight race meetings since Sherman disappeared. If his body had been *here*, it would have been found at once."

Heads nodded in unanimous agreement, and Baltzersen said regretfully, "I suppose he could have been driven away from here unconscious or dead, and hidden—buried—later, somewhere else."

"There's a lot of deep water in Norway," I said.

My thoughts went back to our little junket on the fjord, and I missed some lightning reaction from someone in that room. I knew that a shift had been made, but because of that gap in concentration I couldn't tell who had made it. Fool, I thought, you got a tug on the line and you didn't see which fish, and even the certainty that a fish was there was no comfort.

The silence lengthened, until finally Per Bjørn Sandvik looked up from the floor with a thoughtful frown. "It would seem, then, that no one can ever get to the truth of it. I think David's theory is very plausible. It fits all the facts—or, rather, the lack of facts—better than any explanation we have discussed before."

The heads nodded.

"We will tell our police here what you have suggested," Baltzersen said, in a winding-up-the-meeting voice, "but I agree with Per. . . . After so long a time, and after so much fruitless investigation, we will never really know what happened either to Sherman or to the money. We are all most grateful that you took the trouble to come over, and I know that for most of us, on reflection, your answer to the puzzle will seem the one most likely to be right."

They gave me a lot of worried half smiles and some more nods. Rolf Torp stubbed out his cigar vigorously and everyone shifted on his chair and waited for Baltzersen to stand up.

I thought about the two graceful swans and the two little black and white ducks swimming around quietly out there on the dark side of the tower.

"You could try the pond," I said.

The meeting broke up half an hour later, after it had been agreed with a certain amount of horror that the peaceful little water should be dragged the following morning.

Arne had some security jobs to see to, which he did with painstaking slowness. I wandered aimlessly around, listening to the Norwegian voices of the last of the crowd going home. A good hour after the final race, and still a few lights, still a few people. Not the most private place for committing murder.

I went back toward the weighing room and stood beside the clump of ornamental bushes on the grass outside. Well . . . they were thick enough and dark enough to have hidden a body temporarily, until everyone had gone. A jockey and his over- night grip, and five bags of stolen money. Plenty of room in these bushes for the lot. There were lights outside the weighing room, but the bushes threw heavy shadows and one could not see to their roots.

Arne found me there and exclaimed with passionate cer- tainty, "He can't be in those, you know. Someone would have seen him long ago."

"And smelled him," I said.

Arne made a choking noise and said, "Christ."

I turned away. "Have you finished now?"

He nodded, one side of his face brightly lit, the other in shadow. "The night watchman is here and everything is as it should be. He will make sure all the gates are locked for the night. We can go home."

He drove me in his sturdy Swedish Volvo back toward the city and around to his leafy urban street. Kari greeted us with roaring logs on the fire and tall glasses of frosty thirst-quenching white wine. Arne moved restlessly about the apartment like a bull and switched Beethoven on again fortissimo.

"What's the matter?" Kari asked him, raising her voice. "For God's sake, turn it down."

Arne obliged, but the sacrifice of his emotional safety valve clearly oppressed him.

"Let him rip," I told him. "We can stand it for five minutes."

Kari gave me a gruesome look and vanished into the kitchen as Arne with great seriousness took me at my word. I sat resignedly on the sofa, while the stereophonics shook the foundations, and admired the forbearance of his neighbors. The man who lived alone below my flat in London had ears like stethoscopes and was up knocking on my door at every dropped pin.

The five minutes stretched to nearly twenty before Arne stopped pacing around and turned down the volume.

"Great stuff, great stuff," he said.

"Sure," I agreed, because it was, in its place, which was somewhere the size of the Albert Hall.

Kari returned from exile with little wifely indulgent shakes of the head. She looked particularly disturbing in a copper-colored silky trouser suit which did fantastic things for the hair, the coloring, and the eyes, and nothing bad for the rest of her. She refilled our glasses and sat on some floor cushions near the fire.

"How did you enjoy the races?" she asked.

"Very much," I said.

Arne blinked a bit, said he had some telephone calls to make, and removed himself to the hall. Kari said she had watched the Grand National on television but rarely went to the races herself.

"I'm an indoors person," she said. "Arne says the outdoor life is healthier, but I don't enjoy being cold or wet or cut up by the wind, so I let him go off doing all those rugged things like skiing and sailing and swimming, and me, I just make a warm room for him to come back to."

She grinned, but I caught the faintest of impressions that, wifely though she might thoroughly appear to be, she had feelings for Arne which were not wholehearted love. Somewhere deep lay an attitude toward the so-called manly pursuits which was far from admiration; and a basic antipathy to an activity nearly always extended, in my experience, to anyone who went in for it.

Arne's voice floated in from the hall, speaking Norwegian.

"He is talking about dragging a pond," Kari said, looking puzzled. "What pond?"

I told her what pond.

"Oh, dear, his poor little wife. . . . I hope he isn't in there. How would she bear it?"

Better, I thought, on the whole than believing he was a thief who had deserted her. I said, "It's only a possibility. But it's as well to make sure."

She smiled. "Arne has a very high opinion of you. I expect you are right. Arne said when he came back from England that he would never want to be investigated by you; you seemed to know what people were thinking. When the Chairman asked for someone to find Bob Sherman and Arne heard that you were coming yourself, he was very pleased. I heard him telling someone on the telephone that you had the eyes of a hawk and a mind like a razor." She grinned ironically, the soft light gleaming on her teeth. "Are you flattered?"

"Yes," I said. "I wish it were true."

"It must be true if you are in charge when you are so young."

"I'm thirty-three," I said. "Alexander the Great had conquered the world from Greece to India by that time."

"You look twenty-five," she said.

"It's a great drawback."

"A what?"

"A disadvantage."

"No woman would think so."

Arne came back from the hall looking preoccupied.

"Everything all right?" she asked.

"Oh—er, *ja.*" He blinked several times. "It is all arranged.
Nine o'clock tomorrow morning, they drag the pond." He
paused. "Will you be there, David?"

I nodded. "And you?"

"*Ja.*" The prospect did not seem to please him; but then I was
not wildly excited about it myself. If Bob Sherman were indeed
there, he would be the sort of unforgettable object you wished
you had never seen, and my private gallery of those was already
too extensive.

Arne piled logs on the fire as if to ward off demons, and Kari
said it was time to eat. She gave us reindeer steaks in a rich dark
sauce and after that the promised cloudberries, which turned
out to be yellow brown and to taste of caramel.

"They are very special," Arne said, evidently pleased to be
able to offer them. "They grow in the mountains, and are only
in season for about three weeks. There is a law about picking
them. One can be prosecuted for picking them before the right
date."

"You can get them in tins," Kari said. "But they don't taste
the same as these."

We ate in reverent silence.

"No more until next year," Arne said regretfully, putting
down his spoon. "Let's have some coffee."

Kari brought the coffee and with amusement declined halfhearted offers from me to help with the dishes.

"You do not want to. Be honest."

"I do not want to," I said truthfully.

She laughed. A highly feminine lady with apparently no ban-
ners to wave about equality in the kitchen. Between her and

Arne the proposition that everything indoors was her domain,
and everything outside his seemed to lead only to harmony. In
my own sister, it had led to resentment, rows, and a broken
marriage. Kari, it seemed to me, expected less, settled for less,
and achieved more.

I didn't stay late. I liked looking at Kari just a shade too much,
and Arne, for all his oddnesses, was an investigator. I had taught
myself how to notice where people were looking, because
where their eyes were, their thoughts were, as often as not.
Some men felt profound gratification when others lusted after
their wives, but some felt a revengeful anger. I didn't know
what Arne's reaction would be, and I didn't aim to find out.

Six

MONDAY MORNING. Drizzle. Daylight slowly intensifying over Øvrevoll racecourse, changing anthracite clouds to flannel gray. The dark green spruce and yellow birch stood around in their dripping thousands, and the paper debris from the day before lay soggily scattered across the wet tarmac.

On the lower end of the track, Gunnar Holth and one or two other trainers were exercising their strings of racehorses, but the top part, by and above the winning post, had been temporarily railed off.

Shivering from depression more than cold, I was sitting up in the observation tower with Lars Baltzersen, watching the dragging of the pond down below. Hands in pockets, shoulders hunched, rain dripping off hat brims, Arne and two policemen stood at the water's edge, peering morosely at the small boat going slowly, methodically, backward and forward from bank to bank.

The pond was more or less round, approximately thirty yards in diameter, and apparently about six feet deep. The boat contained two policemen with grappling hooks and a third, dressed in a black rubber scuba suit, who was doing the rowing. He wore flippers, gloves, hood, and goggles, and had twice been over the side with an underwater torch to investigate when the

323

grapples caught. Both times he had returned to the surface and shaken his head.

The swans and the black and white ducks swam around in agitated circles. The water grew muddier and muddier. The boat moved slowly on its tenth traverse, and Lars Baltzersen said gloomily, "The police think this is a waste of time."

"Still," I said, "they did come."

"They would, of course."

"Of course," I said.

We watched in silence.

A grapple caught. The swimmer went over the side, submerged for a full minute, came up, shook his head, and was helped back into the boat. He took up the oars; rowed on. One each side of the boat, the men swung the three-pronged grapples into the water again, dragging them slowly across the bottom.

"They considered emptying the pond," Baltzersen said. "But the technical difficulties are great. Water drains into it from all the top part of the racecourse. They decided on dragging."

"They are being thorough enough," I said.

He looked at me soberly. "If they do not find Sherman, then, will you be satisfied that he is not there?"

"Yes," I said.

He nodded. "That is reasonable."

We watched for another hour. The swimmer made two more trips into the water, and came up with nothing. The boat finished its journey, having missed not an inch. There was no body. Bob Sherman was not in the pond.

Beside me, Baltzersen stood up stiffly and stretched, his chair scraping loudly on the wooden boards.

"That is all, then," he said.

"Yes."

I stood and followed him down the outside staircase, to be met at the bottom by Arne and the policeman in charge.

"No one is there," he said to me in English, implying by his tone that he wasn't surprised.

"No. But thank you for finding out."

He, Baltzersen, and Arne spoke together for some time in Norwegian, and Baltzersen walked across to thank the boatmen personally. They nodded, smiled, shrugged, and began to load their boat onto a trailer.

"Never mind, David," said Arne with sympathy. "It was a good idea."

"One more theory down the drain," I agreed philosophically.

"Not the first, by a long way."

"Will you go on looking?"

I shook my head. The fjords were too deep. Someone in the Chairman's room had reacted strongly to my mention of water, and if Bob Sherman wasn't in the pond he was somewhere just as wet.

Baltzersen, Arne, the senior policeman, and I trudged back across the track and into the paddock enclosure, on our way to the cars parked beside the main entrance. Baltzersen frowned at the rubbish lying around—mostly dropped race cards and old Tote tickets—and said something to Arne. Arne replied in Norwegian and then repeated it in English.

"The manager thought it better that the refuse collectors should not be here to see the police drag the pond. Just in case, you see . . . Anyway, they are coming tomorrow instead."

Baltzersen nodded. He had taken the morning off from his timber business and looked as though he regretted it.

"I'm sorry to have wasted your time," I said.

He made a little movement of his head to acknowledge that I was more or less forgiven. The persistent drizzle put a damper on anything warmer.

In silence we passed the stands, the ornamental pond (too shallow) and the Secretariat, and it was probably because the only noise was the crunch of our feet that we heard the child.

He was standing near a corner of the Tote Building, sobbing. About six, soaked to the skin, with hair plastered to his forehead in forlorn-looking spikes. The policeman looked across to him and beckoned, and in a kind enough voice said what must have been "Come here."

The boy didn't move, but he said something which halted my three companions in mid-step. They stood literally immobile, as if their reflexes had all stopped working. Their faces looked totally blank.

"What did he say?" I asked.

The boy repeated what he had said before, and if anything the shock of my companions deepened.

Baltzersen loosened his jaw with a visible effort, and translated.

"He said, 'I have found a hand.'"

The child was frightened when we approached, his big eyes looking frantically around for somewhere to run to, but whatever the policeman said reassured him, and when we reached him he was just standing there, wet, terrified, and shivering.

The policeman squatted beside him, and they went into a longish quiet conversation. Eventually the policeman put out his hand, and the child gripped it, and after that the policeman stood up and told us in English what he'd said.

"The boy came to look for money. The racing crowd often drop coins and notes, especially after dark. He says he always squeezes through a hole in the fence, before the rubbish collectors come, to see if he can find money. He says he always finds some. This morning he found twenty kroner before the men came. He means before the police came. But he is not supposed to be here, so he hid. He hid behind the stands, up there." The policeman nodded across the tarmac. "He says that behind the stands he found a hand lying on the ground."

He looked down at the child clutching his own hand like a lifeline, and asked Arne to go across to his men, who had packed up all their gear and were on the point of leaving, to ask them to come over at the double. Arne gave the child a sick look and did as he was asked, and Baltzersen himself slowly returned to businesslike efficiency.

The policeman had difficulty transferring the boy's trust to one of his men, but finally disengaged himself, and he, two of his men, Baltzersen, Arne, and I walked up to and around the stands to see the hand which was lying on the ground.

The child was not mistaken. Waxy-white and horrific, it lay back on the tarmac, fingers laxly curled up to meet the rain.

What the child had not said, however, was that the hand was not alone.

In the angle between the wall and the ground lay a long mound covered by a black tarpaulin. Halfway along its length, visible to the wrist, the hand protruded.

Wordlessly the senior policeman took hold of a corner of the tarpaulin and pulled it back.

Arne took one look, bolted for the nearest bushes, and heaved up whatever Kari had given him for breakfast. Baltzersen turned gray and put a shaking hand over his mouth. The policemen themselves looked sick, and I added another to the unwanted memories.

He was unrecognizable, really: it was going to be a teeth job for the inquest. But the height and clothes were right, and his overnight grip was lying there beside him, still with the initials "R.T.S." stamped on it in black.

A piece of nylon rope was securely knotted around the chest, and another halfway down the legs, and from each knot, one over the breastbone, one over the knees, hung a loose piece of rope with a frayed end.

One of the policemen said something to his chief, and Baltzersen obligingly translated for me.

"That is the man who was diving," he said. "He says that in the pond the grapples caught on a cement block. He did not think anything of it at the time, but he says there were frayed ends of rope coming from the cement. He says it looked like the same rope as this."

The policeman in charge pulled the tarpaulin back over the tragic bundle and started giving his men instructions. Arne stood several yards away, mopping his face and mouth with a large white handkerchief and looking anywhere but at the black tarpaulin. I walked over and asked if he was all right. He was trembling, and shook his head miserably.

"You need a drink," I said. "You'd better go home."

"No." He shuddered. "I'll be all right. So stupid of me. Sorry, David."

He came with me around to the front of the stands and we walked over to where Baltzersen and the top policeman had rejoined the little boy. Baltzersen adroitly drew me aside a pace or two, and said quietly, "I don't want to upset Arne again. . . . The child says the hand was not showing at first. He lifted the tarpaulin a little to see what was underneath—you know what children are like—and he saw something pale and tried to pull it out. It was the hand. When he saw what it was, he ran away."

"Poor little boy," I said.

"He shouldn't have been here," he said, meaning, by his tone, it served him right.

"If he hadn't been, we wouldn't have found Bob Sherman."

Lars Baltzersen looked at me thoughtfully. "I suppose whoever took him out of the pond meant to return with transport and get rid of him somewhere else."

"No, I shouldn't think so," I said.

"He must have done. If he didn't mind him being found, he would have left him in the pond."

"Oh, sure. I just meant, why take him anywhere else? Why not straight back into the pond as soon as it was dark? That's the one place no one would ever look for Bob Sherman again."

He gave me a long considering stare, and then unexpectedly, for the first time that morning, he smiled.

"Well . . . you've done what we asked," he said.

I smiled faintly back and wondered if he yet understood the significance of that morning's work. But catching murderers was a matter for the police, not for me. I was only catching the two-five to Heathrow, with little enough margin for what I still had to do first.

I said, "Anytime I can help," in the idle way that one does, and shook hands with him, and with Arne, and left them there with their problem, in the drizzle.

I picked up Emma Sherman at her hotel, as I had arranged, and took her up to my room in the Grand. I had been going to give her lunch before we set off to the airport, but instead I asked the restaurant to bring hot soup upstairs. Still no brandy. Not until three o'clock, they said. Next time, I thought, I'd pack a gallon.

Champagne was emotionally all wrong for the news I had to give her, so I stirred it around with some orange juice and made her drink it first. Then I told her, as gently as I could, that Bob had died at the time of his disappearance. I told her he was not a thief and had not deserted her. I told her he had been murdered.

The desperately frail look came back to her face, but she didn't faint.

"You did . . . find him, then."

"Yes."

"Where is he?"

"At the racecourse."

She stood up, swaying a bit. "I must go and see him."

"No," I said firmly, holding her elbow. "No, Emma, you must not. You must remember him alive. He doesn't look the same now, and he would hate you to see him. He would beg you not to see him."

"I must see him. . . . Of course I must."

I shook my head.

"Do you mean"—it began to dawn on her—"that he looks
. . . *horrible?*"

"I'm afraid so. He's been dead a month."

"Oh, God."

She sat down with weak knees and began to cry. I told her
about the pond, the ropes, the cement. She had to know sometime, and it couldn't be much worse than the agony of spirit she
had suffered through four long weeks.

"Oh, my poor Bob," she said. "Oh, darling . . . oh, darling . . ."

The floodgates of all that misery were opened and she wept
with a fearful outpouring intensity, but at least and at last it was
a normal grief, without the self-doubt and humiliating shame.

After a while, still shaking with sobs, she said, "I'll have to get
my room back at the hotel."

"No," I said. "You're coming home to England today with me,
as we planned."

"But I can't."

"Indeed you can, and indeed you will. The last place for you
now is here. You need to go home, to rest, recover, and look
after that baby. The police here will do everything necessary,
and I'll see that the Jockey Club—and the Injured Jockeys
Fund, perhaps—organizes things from the English end. In a
little while we can have Bob brought home to England, if that's
what you would like. But for today, it's you that matters. If you
stay here, you will be ill."

She listened, took in barely half, but in fact raised no more
objections. Maybe the police would not be overjoyed at her
leaving, I thought, but they'd had her around for a month, and
there couldn't be much she hadn't already told them. We
caught the flight on schedule, and she stared out the window all
the way home with tears running intermittently down her
cheeks.

Her grandfather, alerted from Oslo, met her at Heathrow.
Tall, thin, stooping, and kind, he greeted her with a small kiss
and many affectionate pats: her parents, she had told me, had

died during her school days, leaving her and a brother to be shuttled between relays of other relations. She liked her mother's widowed father best, and wanted him most in her troubles.

He shook my hand.

"I'll see she's looked after," he said.

He was a nice scholarly man. I gave him my private address and telephone number, in case she needed an inside edge on official help.

Seven

TUESDAY MORNING from nine to ten I spent in the office finding out that everyone had been doing just fine in my absence and would undoubtedly continue to do so if I disappeared altogether. On my desk lay neat reports of finished inquiries: the man we had suspected of running a retired high-class steeplechaser under a hunter's name in a point-to-point had in fact done so and was now in line for a fraud prosecution, and an applicant for a trainer's license in the Midlands had been found to have totally unsuitable training facilities.

Nothing to make the hair curl. Nothing like weighted bodies in Norwegian ponds.

The whole of the rest of the day was spent with two opposite numbers from the New York Racing Commission who had come to discuss the viability of a worldwide racing investigatory linkup, something along the lines of Interpol. It was one of a series of talks I'd had with officials of many countries, and the idea seemed to be staggering very slowly toward achievement. As usual, the chief stumbling block to any rapid progress seemed to be my apparent youth: I supposed that by the time I was sixty, when I'd run out of steam, they would begin to nod while they listened.

I talked my throat dry, gave away sheaves of persuasive literature, took them to dinner at Inigo Jones, and hoped the seed hadn't fallen on stony ground. At farewell time, the older of them asked a question I was by then well used to.

"If you succeed in setting this thing up, do you expect to be head of it yourself?"

I smiled. I knew very well that if the baby was born it would very smartly be found to be not mine after all.

"Once it's set up," I said, "I'll move on."

He looked at me curiously.

"Where to?"

"Don't know yet."

They shook their heads and tut-tutted slightly, but gripped hands with cordiality as we separated into a couple of homeward taxis. It was after midnight when I reached the house where I lived behind the Brompton Road, but as usual the lights were still on in the rooms below my small flat. The street door banged if you let it go, reverberating through the walls, and perhaps that, I thought, as I shut it gently, explained the ground floor tenant's hypersensitivity. He was a self-contained man, grayish, in his fifties, very neat and precise. Our acquaintanceship, after six months of living stacked one over the other, extended simply to his trips to my door urging an instant lessening of decibels on the television. Once I had asked him in for a drink, but he had politely declined, preferring solitude downstairs. Hardly the *entente cordiale* of the century.

I went up, opened my own door, and shut that quietly also. The telephone bell, starting suddenly in all that noble silence, made me jump.

"Mr. Cleveland?" The voice was hurried, practically incoherent. "Thank goodness you're back at last. . . . This is William Romney, Emma's grandfather. She didn't want me to ring you so late, but I must. Two men were searching her house when she went in and they hit her. Mr. Cleveland, she needs your help."

"Stop a minute," I said. "First thing you need is the police."

He calmed down a fraction. "They've been here. Just left. I called them."

"And a doctor for Emma?"

"Yes, yes. He's gone, too."

"What time did all this happen?"

"About seven this evening. We drove over from my house just to fetch some things for her, and there was a light on—and she went in first and they jumped on her. They hit us both. ... I do wish—well, to tell you the truth, I think we're both still frightened."

I stifled a sigh. "Where exactly are you?"

"At Emma's house, still."

"Yes, but—"

"Oh, I see. Near Newbury. You go down the M. 4 ..." He gave me details of the journey, certain in his own mind that I would hurry to their aid. He made it impossible for me to say take a tranquilizer and I'll come in the morning, and anyway by the sound of his voice nothing short of a full anesthetic was going to give him any rest.

At least it was a fast straightforward journey at night; so I took the M.G.B. and got there in fifty minutes flat. The Shermans' house proved to be a modernized pair of farm cottages down an uninhabited lane, a nerve-testing isolation at the best of times.

Lights were on in every window, and at the sound of my car William Romney's anxious figure appeared in the doorway.

"Thank goodness, thank goodness," he said agitatedly, coming down the short path to meet me. "I don't know what we would have done if you hadn't been coming."

I refrained from saying that I thought they should have gone back to his house or otherwise stayed in a hotel, and once through the door I was glad I hadn't because it wouldn't have helped. Shock prevents people from leaving the scene of personal disaster of their own accord, and of the scope and depth of their shock there could be no doubt.

The house was a shambles. Pictures had been torn from the walls, curtains from the windows, carpets from the floor. Furniture was not merely turned inside out, but smashed. Lamps, vases, ornaments lay in pieces. Papers and books scattered the wreckage like autumn leaves.

"It's all like this," Romney said. "The whole house. All except the spare bedroom. That's where they were when we interrupted them. The police say so. . . ."

Emma herself was in the spare bedroom, lying awake with eyes like soot smudges. Both her cheeks were swollen and puffy, with red marks showing where blows had landed. Her lower lip had been split, and one eyebrow ended in a raw skinned patch.

"Hullo," I said inadequately, and pulled up a chair so that I could sit beside her. Her grandfather hovered around making fussing noises, obviously freshly worried by the darkening bruises and tiring Emma beyond bearing. He looked more upset than ever when I asked him if I could speak to her alone, but in the end he reluctantly returned to the devastation below.

I held her hand.

"David . . ."

"Wait a bit," I said. "Then tell me."

She nodded slightly. She was lying on the blankets of the unmade bed, still wearing the brown-and-white checked dress, her head supported by two coverless pillows, a flowered quilt over her from the waist down.

The room was hot with a pulsating gas fire, but Emma's hand was cold.

"I told the police I think they were Norwegians," she said.

"The two men?"

She nodded. "They were big. . . . They had thick sweaters and rubber gloves. . . . They talked with accents."

"Start at the beginning," I said.

She loosened her mouth, obviously troubled by the split and swelling lip.

"We came over to get me some different clothes. I was begin-

ning to feel better. . . . There was a light on upstairs but I
thought Mrs. Street, who has been looking after the house, had
left it on . . . but when I unlocked the front door and went into
the hall they jumped on me. . . . They switched all the lights on.
I saw the mess. . . . One of them hit me in the face and I
screamed for Granddad. When he came in, they knocked him
over . . . so easily, it was awful . . . and they kicked him. One
of them asked me where Bob would hide papers, and when I
didn't answer at once he just went on . . . punching me in the
face . . . with his fists. . . . I didn't answer because I didn't know.
Bob doesn't hide things—didn't— Oh, God . . ."

Her fingers curled tight around mine.

"All right, all right, Emma," I said, meaning nothing except
that I understood. "Wait a bit."

We waited until some of the tension left her body; then she
swallowed and tried again.

"The telephone rang then, and it seemed to worry them.
They talked to each other, and then suddenly they just threw
me into a chair, and they went away . . . through the front door.
. . . Granddad got up off the floor, but the telephone stopped
before he reached it. But anyway he called the police."

The tired voice stopped. I said, "Did the men wear masks of
any sort?"

"No."

"Would you know them again?"

"The police asked . . . they want me to look at photographs,
but I don't know. . . . I was trying to avoid being hurt. I tried
to put my hands in front of my face and I shut my eyes. . . ."

"How about your grandfather?"

"He says he might know them. But it was over so quickly,
really."

"I suppose they didn't tell you what papers they were looking
for?"

She shook her head miserably. "The police asked me that,
over and over."

"Never mind," I said. "How does your face feel now?"

"Awfully stiff. Dr. West gave me some pills, though. He says he'll look in again tomorrow."

"Here?"

"Yes. I didn't want to go back to Granddad's. This—this is home."

"Do you want the bed made properly?"

"No, thank you. I'm comfortable like this—too tired to move."

"I'll go down, then, and give your grandfather a hand."

"All right." Anxiety flooded her suddenly. "But you won't go, will you?"

I promised her, and in fact I slept in trousers and shirt on the sofa in the sitting room on a cleared oasis amid the rubble. William Romney, taxed almost too far, snored gently—the effect of a strong sedative—on the double bed in the Shermans' room, and from three o'clock to five the cottage was dark and quiet.

I awoke suddenly with a soft wail in my ears like the sound of a lamb in a snowstorm.

"David . . ."

It was Emma's voice from upstairs, urgent and quavery.

I tossed off the rug, stood up, and beat it up there fast. I'd left her door open and the fire on, and as I went in I could see the ultimate disaster looking out of her great dark eyes.

"David . . ." Her voice filled with unconsolable desolation. "David . . . I'm bleeding."

She lost the baby and very nearly her life. I went to see her three days after she'd been whisked away in a bell-ringing ambulance (three days because no one was allowed in sooner) and was surprised to discover that she could and did look even paler than she had in Oslo. The swellings had gone down in her face, though the bruises showed dark in patches. Her eyes were dulled, which seemed a mercy.

The five-minute visit passed on the surface.

"Nice of you to come," she said.

"Brought you some grapes."

"Very kind."

"Sorry about the baby."

She nodded vaguely, but some sort of drug was dealing with that pain also.

"Hope you'll soon be better."

"Oh, yes. Yes, I will."

William Romney shook with fury, stamping up and down my office with outrage.

"Do you realize that it is a week tomorrow since we were attacked and no one has done *anything?* People can't just vanish into thin air. Those men must be somewhere. Why can't the police find them? It isn't right that thugs should just walk into a defenseless girl's house and tear things to pieces and hurt her so much that she nearly dies of it. . . . It's *disgraceful* that the police haven't found those despicable *bastards.*"

The word was a strong one for him: he looked almost surprised that he'd used it, and nothing could have more clearly stated the fierceness of his feelings.

"I believe neither you nor Emma could identify the men from police photographs," I said, having checked via a friendly police contact that this was so.

"They weren't there. There weren't any pictures of them. Can't say that's surprising. . . . Why don't the police get photographs of *Norwegian* crooks for us to look at?"

"It would probably mean your going to Norway," I said. "And Emma's in no state, physical or emotional, to do that."

"I'll go, then," he said belligerently. "I'll go, at my own expense. Anything—*anything* to see those men punished for what they've done to Emma."

His thin face was flushed with the strength of his resentment. I wondered if part of his fury sprang from unnecessary guilt that he hadn't been young and strong enough to defend or rescue her from two aggressive toughs. Amends in the shape of effort and expense were what he was offering, and I saw no reason to dissuade him from a journey which would bring him mental ease even if no concretely helpful results.

"I'll fix it for you, if you like," I said.

"What?"

"To go to Norway and look at the mug shots."

His resolution took shape and hardened. He straightened his stooping shoulders, calmed his voice, and stopped wearing out so much of the Jockey Club's carpet.

"Yes. Please do that. I'll go as soon as I can."

I nodded. "Sit down," I said. "Do you smoke? And how's Emma?"

He sat down, declined a desk box of cigarettes, and said that last evening, when he'd seen her, Emma was very much stronger.

"She says she'll be out of hospital in two or three days."

"Good."

He didn't look as if it were good. He said, in recurring worried anger, "What on earth is that poor girl going to do? Her husband murdered, her home wrecked. . . . I suppose she can live with me, but—"

"I'm sure she'll live in her own house," I said. "For a while, at least. Best if she does. Get her grieving done properly."

"What an extraordinary thing to say."

"When can you go?" I said, reaching for the telephone.

"At once."

"Right."

Øvrevoll racecourse answered in the shape of the manager, who gave me the home and office telephone numbers of Lars Baltzersen. He answered from his office, and I explained the situation. Of course, he said in dismay, of course he could arrange it with the police. For tomorrow? Certainly. Poor Mrs. Sherman, he said, please give her my condolences. I said I would, and asked if there had been any recent progress.

"None at all, I'm afraid," he said. He hesitated for several seconds, and then went on, "I have been thinking. . . . I suppose if the police don't solve this crime that you wouldn't come back yourself, and see what you can do?"

I said, "I'm not experienced in murder investigation."

"It must in essence be the same as any other sort."

"Mm . . . My masters here might not be willing for me to take the time."

"If I asked them myself, as an international favor? After all, Bob Sherman was a British jockey."

"Wouldn't Norway prefer to ship him home and forget about the whole nasty incident?"

"No, Mr. Cleveland," he said severely. "A murder has been done, and justice should follow."

"I agree."

"Then you'll come?"

I thought. "Wait another week. Then if neither your police nor ours have found any new leads, and if you still want me to —well, maybe I can. But . . . don't expect too much, will you?"

"No more than before," he said dryly, and disconnected.

William Romney had adjusted by then to the prospect of traveling the next day, and began to fuss mildly about tickets, currency, and hotels. I shooed him out because he could do all that for himself, and I had a good deal of work on hand to start with, and more still if I had to clear time for another trip to Oslo. The police, I hoped, would quickly dig down to the roots themselves and save me from proving to the world that I couldn't.

William Romney went to Norway, spent two full days there, and returned depressed. The Norwegian police did not have photographs of the intruders, or if they did, Romney did not recognize them.

Emma left the hospital and went home to put her house straight. An offer from me to help her do that was declined; one to come down and take her out to lunch was accepted.

"Sunday?" I suggested.

"Fine."

Sunday found the carpets flat on the floors, the pictures back on the walls, the broken mess cleared away, and the curtains bundled up for the cleaners. The house looked stark and un-lived-in, but its mistress had come a long way back to life. For the first time since I had known her, she was wearing lipstick. Her hair was newly washed, her clothes neat, her manner composed. The pretty girl lurked not far away now, just below the still over-pale skin, just behind the still unhappy eyes.

"It's his funeral on Thursday," she said.

"Here?"

She nodded. "In the church in the village. Thank you for doing everything about bringing him home."

I had delegated the whole job. "I only got it done," I said.

"Anyway . . . thanks."

The October day was calm and sunny and crisp around the edges. I took her to a Thames-side pub where pointed yellow willow leaves floated slowly past on gray water and anglers flicked maggots on hooks to wily fish. We walked along the bank; slowly, because she was still weak from hemorrhage.

"Have you any plans?" I asked.

"I don't know. . . . I've thought a lot, of course, while I've been in hospital. I'll go on living in the cottage for a while, I think. It feels right, somehow. In the end, I suppose I'll sell it, but not yet."

"How are the finances?"

She produced a flicker of smile. "Everyone is being fantastic. Really marvelous. Did you know the owners Bob rode for in Norway clubbed together and sent me a check? How kind people are."

Conscience money, I thought sourly, but I didn't say so.

"Those two men who broke into your house—do you mind if we talk about them?"

She sighed. "I don't mind."

"Describe them."

"But—"

"Yes, I've read what you told the police. You didn't look at them, you shut your eyes, you only saw their sweaters and their rubber gloves."

"That's right."

"No. What you told the police was all you could bear to remember, and you would have shut out even that if they hadn't pressed you for answers."

"That's nonsense."

"Try it another way. Which one hit you?"

She said instantly, "The bigger one with the—" Her voice stopped uncertainly.

"With the what?"

"I was going to say, with the reddish hair. How odd. I didn't remember until now that one of them had reddish hair."

"What about the other?"

"Brown. Brown hair. He was kicking Granddad."

"The one who was hitting you—what was he saying?"

"Where does your husband keep secret papers? Where does he hide things? Tell us where he hides things."

"Good English?"

"Ye-es. Pretty good. He had an accent."

"What were his eyes like while he was hitting you?"

"Fierce . . . frightful . . . like an eagle . . . sort of black and yellow . . . very angry."

There was a small silence; then she said, "Yes, I do remember, like you said. I shut it out."

"Look back now at his face."

After a few seconds, "He was quite young, about the same as you. His mouth was very tight . . . his lips were stiff . . . his face looked hard . . . very angry."

"How tall?"

"Same as you, about. Broader, though. Much heavier. Big thick shoulders."

"Big shoulders in a thick sweater. What sort of thick sweater? Did it have a pattern?"

"Well, yes, that was why—" She stopped again.

"Why what?"

"Why I thought at once that he was Norwegian—before he even spoke. Because of the patterns in his sweater. They were sort of white patterns—two colors, though, I think—all over a brown sweater. I'd seen dozens like it in the shops in Oslo." She looked puzzled. "Why didn't I think of that before?"

"Memories often work like that. Sort of delayed action."

She smiled. "I must say it's easier remembering things quietly here by the river than in all that mess with my face hurting and policemen asking me questions from all sides and bustling about."

We went indoors for a drink and a good lunch, and over coffee I asked her other things.

"You said Bob never hid papers. Are you sure?"

"Oh, yes. He wasn't secretive. Never. He was more careless, really, than anything else, when it came to papers and documents and things like that."

"It seems quite extraordinary that two men should come all the way from Norway to search your house for papers."

She frowned. "Yes, it does."

"And to search it so violently, so destructively, so thoroughly."

"And they were so angry, too."

"Angry, I expect, because they'd worked hard and hadn't found what they'd come for."

"But what *did* they come for?"

"Well," I said slowly, "something to do with Norway. What papers did Bob ever have that had anything to do with Norway?"

She shook her head. "Nothing much. A few receipts, for the accounts. Race cards, sometimes. A cutting from a Norwegian paper with a picture of him winning a race. Nothing, honestly, that anyone could want."

I drank my coffee, considering. I said, "Look at it the other way round. Did he ever take any papers *to* Norway?"

"No. Why should he?"

"I don't know. I just wondered. Because those men might have been looking for something he hadn't taken to Norway, not for something he had brought away."

"You do think some weird things."

"Mm . . ."

I paid the bill and drove her home. She was silent most of the way, but thoughtful, and the fruit of that was a plum.

"I suppose . . . Well, it's stupid, really, but it couldn't have anything to do with blue pictures?"

"What sort of blue pictures?" I asked.

"I don't know. I didn't see them. Only Bob said that's what they were."

I pulled up outside her gate but made no move to leave the car.

"Did he get them in Norway?"

She was surprised. "Oh, no. It was like you said. He was taking them over there with him. In a brown envelope. It came by hand the night before he went. He said they were blue pictures which a chap in Oslo wanted him to bring over."

"Did he say what chap?"

She shook her head. "No. I hardly listened. I'd forgotten all about it until you said—"

"Did you see the brown envelope? How big was it?"

"I must have seen it. I mean, I know it was brown." She frowned, concentrating. "Fairly big. Not an ordinary letter. About the size of a magazine."

"Was it marked 'Photographs,' or anything like that?"

"I don't think so. I can't remember. It's more than six weeks ago." Her eyes filled suddenly with tears. "He put it in his overnight grip at once, so as not to forget to take it." She sniffed twice, and found a handkerchief. "So he did take it to Norway. It wasn't in the house for those men to find. If that's what they were looking for, they did all that for nothing." She put the handkerchief to her mouth and stifled a sob.

"Was Bob interested in blue pictures?" I asked.

"Like any other man, I suppose," she said through the handkerchief. "He'd look at them."

"But he wouldn't collect them himself?"

She shook her head.

I got out of the car, opened the door on her side, and went with her into the cottage. She looked at the racing pictures of Bob which hung in the hall.

"They tore all those photographs out of the frames," she said. "Some of them were ruined."

Many of the prints were about ten inches by eight. A magazine-sized brown envelope would have held them easily.

I stayed another hour simply to keep her company, but for the evening ahead she insisted that she would be all right alone. She looked around at the bareness of the sitting room and smiled to herself. She obviously found the place friendly, and maybe Bob was there, too.

When I went, she gave me a warm kiss on the cheek and said, "I can't thank you enough—" and then broke off and opened her eyes wide.

"Golly," she said. "That was the second lot."

"What of?"

"Blue pictures. He took some before. Oh—months ago. Back in the summer." She shook her head in fresh frustration. "I can't remember. I just remember him saying blue pictures."

I kissed her in return.

"Take care of yourself," I said.

"You, too."

Eight

A LITTLE MATTER of doping-to-win took me to Plumpton races in Sussex the following day, but I saw no harm in some extra spadework on the side. Rinty Ranger, busy in the second and fifth races, was comparatively easy to pin down between the third and the fourth.

"What did you say?" he repeated in exaggerated amazement. "Take pornography to Scandinavia? Christ, that's like wasting pity on bookmakers. They don't need it, mate. They don't bloody need it."

"Bob Sherman told his wife he was taking blue pictures to Norway."

"And she believed it?"

"The point is, did he?"

"He never said a word about it to me."

"Do me a favor," I said. "Find out in the changing room here today if anyone ever asked any jockey to act as a messenger— a carrier—of any papers of any sort from Britain to Norway."

"Are you serious?"

"Bob Sherman's dead."

"Yes." He thought. "O.K."

He gave me a noncommittal wave as he walked out to the fifth, in which he rode a bright, tight, tactical race to be beaten half a length by a better horse, but he came straight out of the weighing room after he had changed and put an end to my easy theory.

"None of them who have ridden in Norway has ever been asked to take over any papers or pictures or anything like that."

"Would they say if they had?"

He grinned. "Depends how much they'd been paid to forget."

"What do you think yourself?"

"Hard to tell. But they all seemed surprised. There weren't any knowing looks, sort of, if you see what I mean."

"Carry on asking, would you? Tomorrow and so on. Say they can tell me hush-hush, if they like. No kickbacks if they've been fiddling currency."

He grinned again. "Some copper you are. Bend the rules like curling tongs."

That evening I telephoned Baltzersen at his home. There was no news, he said. He had consulted his friends in the police, and they would raise no objections if I joined the hunt. On the contrary, they would, as before, let me see what they'd got, to save me replowing their furrows.

"So, Mr. Cleveland, will you come?"

"I guess so," I said.

With flattering relief he said, "Good, good," explosively, and added, "Come tomorrow."

" 'Fraid I can't. I have to give evidence in court tomorrow, and the case may last two days. Soonest would be Thursday morning."

"Come straight to the racecourse, then. We have a meeting on Thursday and another on Sunday, but I fear they may be the last this year. It's a little colder now, and we have had frost."

I wrote "warm clothes" in large letters on my memo pad and said I'd see him at the races.

"By the way," I said. "You know I told you the people who

broke into the Shermans' house were looking for papers? Mrs. Sherman now remembers that Bob took with him to Norway a packet which had been entrusted to him, which he believed contained blue pictures. Did anyone mention to you, or to the police, or to Arne, in all those preliminary investigations into his disappearance, anything at all about his bringing such a packet with him, or delivering it?"

There was an unexpectedly long silence on the other end of the line, but in the end he only said uncertainly, "Blue pictures . . . what are those?"

"Pornography."

"I see." Another pause. "Please explain a little."

I said, "If the package reached its destination, then it cannot be that particular package that the men were searching for. So I could stop chasing after innocent blue pictures and start looking elsewhere."

"*Ja.* I see." He cleared his throat. "I haven't heard of any such package, but perhaps Arne or the police have done. I will ask them. Of course, you know it is unlikely that anyone would need to bring pornography secretly into this country?"

"It would have to be special," I said, and left it at that.

All Tuesday and Wednesday morning I spent in court giving evidence for the prosecution in an insurance swindle involving grievous cruelty to horses, and Wednesday afternoon I sat in the office juggling six jobs at once like some multi-armed Siva. Looking for Bob Sherman's murderer had meant advancing myself a week's leave when I was too busy to take one, and by seven o'clock when I locked up and left, I was wishing he'd got himself bumped off at any other time.

I went home on tube and foot, thinking comforting thoughts about a large Scotch indoors followed by a stroll around to a local grill for a steak. I shut the street door without letting it bang, put one foot in front of the other up the carpeted stairs, unlocked the door to my own flat, and switched on the lights;

and it was at that point that the day stopped operating according to schedule.

I heard, felt, maybe assimilated by instinct, a charge in the air behind me. Nothing as definite as a noise. More a current. Undoubtedly a threat.

All those useful dormant jungle reactions came to my rescue before a thought process based on reason had time to get off the ground. So I was already whipping around to face the stairs and pushing farther through my own doorway when the man with the knife did his best to send me early to the cemetery.

He did not have reddish hair, angry yellow eagle eyes, or a Norwegian sweater. He did have rubber gloves, a stocky muscular body, a lot of determination, and a very sharp blade.

The stab which had been supposed to stop my heart from the back ripped instead through some decent Irish tweed, through a blue cotton shirt below that, and down half a dozen inches of skin on my chest.

He was surprised that at first he hadn't succeeded, but he'd heard all about try try again. He crowded through my door after me with the knife already rising for another go, as I backed through the tiny hall and into the sitting room, unable to take my eyes off his intentions long enough to find any household object to fight him off with.

He came on with a feint and a slice at my middle region and as I sidestepped I got another rip in my jacket and a closer look at some narrowed and murderous eyes.

He tried next a sort of lunging jump, the point of the knife coming in fast and upward. I tried to leap away backward, tripped on a rug, fell on my back, and found my hand hitting the base of the standard lamp. One wild clutch and I'd pulled it over, knocking him off his aim just when he thought he finally had me. The lamp hit him with a crash, and while he was off balance I got both my hands on his knife arm; but it was then that I discovered the rocklike muscles. And also, unfortunately, that he was more or less ambidextrous.

He shifted the knife like lightning from his right hand to his left, and I avoided the resulting stab only by a sort of swinging jump over an armchair, using his arm as a lever. The blade hit a cushion and feathers floated up like snowflakes.

I threw a cigarette box at him and missed, and after that a vase, which hit but made no difference. As long as I kept the armchair between us, he couldn't reach me, but neither did he give me much chance of getting past him to the still open door to the stairs.

Behind me on a wide shelf stood my portable television. I supposed it might stop him if I threw it at him, but on the other hand . . . I stretched out backward without losing sight of his knife, found the on-off switch, and turned the volume up to maximum.

The din when it started took him totally by surprise and gave me a fractional chance. I pushed the armchair viciously forward at his knees and he overbalanced, twisting as he tried to get his feet under him. He went down as far as one knee, partially recovered, and toppled altogether when I shoved again with the chair. But it was nothing permanent. He was rolling back to his feet like a cat before I had time to get around the big chair and step on some of his tender bits.

Up until that point, he had said not a word and now if he did I wouldn't hear: the television literally vibrated with the intense noise of some pop star or other's Special Spectacular; and if that didn't bring the U.S. cavalry, nothing would.

He came. Looking cross. Ready to blow like a geyser. And stood there in consternation in my open door.

"Fetch the police!" I yelled, but he didn't hear. I slapped off the switch.

"Fetch the police!" I yelled again, and my voice bounced off the walls in the sudden silence.

The man with the knife turned to see, gave himself fresh instructions, and went for my friend from downstairs. I did a sort of sliding rugger tackle, throwing myself feet first at his legs. He stumbled over my shoes and ankles and went down on his side. I swept one leg in an arc and by sheer good luck kicked him on the wrist. The knife flew out of his hand at least ten feet, and fell nearer to me than to him, and only at that point did he think of giving up.

He scrambled to his feet, looked at me with the first sign of uncertainty, then made up his mind, turned on his heel, crashed past my neighbor, and jumped down the stairs in two giant strides. The front door slammed behind him with a force that shook the building, and from the window I saw him running like the Olympics under the streetlamps.

I looked breathlessly at the mess in my sitting room and at my man from downstairs.

"Thanks," I said.

He took a tentative step into the sitting room.

"You're bleeding," he said.

"But not dying."

I picked up the standard lamp.

"Was he a burglar?" he asked.

"A murderer," I said. "Enter a murderer."

We looked at each other in what was no doubt professional curiosity on both sides, because all he said next was "Sit down, you're suffering from shock."

It was advice I'd given pretty often to others, and it made me smile. All the same, there was a perceptible tremble somewhere around my knees, so I did as he said.

He looked around the room, looked at the knife still lying where it had fallen, and took it all in quietly.

"Shall I carry out your instructions, or were they principally a diversion?"

"Hm?"

"Fetch the police."

"Oh . . . It can wait a bit."

He nodded, considered a moment, and then said, "If you'll excuse me asking, why was he trying to kill you?"

"He didn't say."

My neighbor's name was Stirling. C. V. Stirling, according to the neat white card beside his bell push. He had gray patches neatly brushed back over his ears and nostrils pinched into an expression of distaste for bad smells. His hands looked excessively clean and well manicured, and even in these bizarre circumstances he wore a faint air of exasperated patience. A man used to being the brightest person around, I guessed, with the power to make it felt.

"Did he need to?"

"It would have been helpful," I said.

He came a pace nearer.

"I could do something about that bleeding, if you like."

I looked down at the front of my shirt, which had changed color pretty thoroughly from blue to red.

"Could you?"

"I'm a surgeon," he said. "Ear, nose, and throat, actually. Other areas by arrangement."

I laughed. "Stitch away, then."

He nodded, departed downstairs, and returned with a neat flat case containing the tools of his trade. He used clips, not needles. The slice through my skin was more gory than deep, bleeding away persistently like a shaving cut. When he'd finished, it was a thin red line under a sticking plaster.

"You were lucky," he said.

"Yes, I was."

"Do you do this sort of thing often? Fight for your life, I mean."

"Very rarely."

"My fee for professional services rendered is a little more chat."

I smiled wryly.

"O.K. I'm an investigator. I don't know why I was attacked, unless there's someone around who particularly does not want to be investigated."

"Good God." He stared at me curiously. "A private eye? Philip Marlowe, and all that?"

"Nothing so fancy. I work in racing; for the Jockey Club. Looking into small frauds, most of the time."

"This"—he waved at my chest and the knife and the scattered cushion feathers—"doesn't look like a small fraud."

It didn't. It didn't look, either, like a severe warning-off. It looked like a ruthless all-out push for a final solution.

I changed my clothes and took him around to the grill for the overdue steak. His name was Charles, he said, and we walked back home as friends. When I let myself in upstairs and reviewed the general untidiness, it occurred to me that in the end I had never called in the police. It seemed a little late to bother, so I didn't.

Nine

I CAUGHT the eleven-twenty-five to Norway the next morning with the knife wrapped in polythene in my sponge bag—or, rather, the black zippered leather case which did that duty. It was a hunter's knife, the sort of double-sided blade used for skinning and disjointing game. The cutting edges had been sharpened like razors and the point would have been good as a needle. A professional job: no amateur could have produced that result with a few passes over a carborundum.

The handle was of horn of some sort, but workmanlike, not tourist-trap stuff. Between handle and blade protruded a short silver bar for extra leverage with the fingers. There were no fingerprints on it anywhere, and no blood. Punched into the blade near the hilt were the words "Norsk Stål."

Its owner hadn't, of course, intended to leave it behind. Just one dead body neatly disposed inside its own front door, out of sight and undiscovered for a minimum of twenty-four hours.

He hadn't followed me into the house: he'd been there before I came, waiting higher up the stairs for me to come home.

At breakfast time, I'd knocked on the doors of the other three tenants—the one in the basement, the one above me, and the one above that—and asked them if they'd seen my visitor on the stairs or let him in through the front door. I got negatives all around, but as one of them said, we were hardly a matey lot, and if the visitor entered boldly while one of the tenants was leaving, no one would have stopped him. None of them remembered him, but the basement man observed that as the laundry van had called that day, a stranger could easily have walked in with the man who collected and delivered the boxes from the hall.

There had been nothing suspicious or memorable about my visitor's appearance. His face was a face: hair brown, skin sallow, eyes dark. Age, about thirty. Clothes, dark gray trousers, navy close-fitting sweater, neat shirt and tie showing at the neck. Entirely the right rig for the neighborhood. Even a little formal.

B.E.A. landed on time at Fornebu and I took a taxi straight out to the racecourse. Nothing much had changed in the two and a half weeks I'd been away, not even the weather or the runners in the races, and within the first half hour I had spotted all the same faces, among them Gunnar Holth, Paddy O'Flaherty, Per Bjørn Sandvik, Rolf Torp, and Lars Baltzersen. Arne greeted me with a beaming smile and an invitation to spend as much time with Kari and him as I could.

I walked around with him for most of the afternoon, partly from choice, partly because Baltzersen was busy being Chairman. Arne said that whereas he personally was pleased to see me, many of the racecourse committee had opposed Baltzersen in the matter of bringing me back.

"Lars told us at the Tuesday committee meeting that you were definitely coming today, and that caused quite a row. You should have heard it. Lars said that the racecourse would be paying your fare and expenses like last time, and half of them said it was unjustifiable to spend so much."

He broke off rather suddenly, as if he had decided not to repeat what had actually been said.

"I could easily have been persuaded to stay at home," I said.

But by words, I reflected. Not knives.

"Several of the committee said Lars had no right to act with-out taking a vote."

"And Lars?"

Arne shrugged. "He wants Bob Sherman's death explained. Most of them just want to forget."

"And you?" I asked.

He blinked. "Well," he said, "I would give up more easily than Lars or you. Which is no doubt why"—he grinned—"Lars is Chairman and you are the chief investigator, and I am only a security officer who lets the racecourse takings be stolen from under his nose."

I smiled. "No one blames you."

"Perhaps they should."

I thought in my intolerant way that they definitely should, but I shook my head and changed the subject.

"Did Lars tell you about the attack on Emma Sherman, and about her losing her baby?"

"Yes," he said. "Poor girl." There was more lip service in his voice than genuine regret. I supposed that no one who hadn't seen her as I had could properly understand all that she'd suf-fered; and I knew that it was in great part because of Emma that I was back in Norway. No one should be allowed to inflict such hurt on another human being, and get away with it. The fact that the same agency had murdered Bob and tried to see me off was in a curious way secondary: it was possible future victims who had to be saved. If you don't dig ground elder out of the flower beds, it can strangle the garden.

Rolf Torp was striding about in a bad temper. His horse, he said, had knocked itself that morning and his trainer had omit-ted to tell him it couldn't run. He had taken the afternoon off from his mining office, which he wouldn't have done if he'd known, on account of being indispensable and nothing con-structive ever being achieved in his absence.

After he had delivered himself of that little lot, he adjusted his sights more specifically on me.

"I was against bringing you back. I'll tell you that myself. I told the committee. It is a waste of our money."

His name was on the list Emma had given me of the contributors to the solidly worthwhile check the Norwegian owners had sent. If he thought that any available cash should only be spent on the living, perhaps it was a valid point of view; but he wasn't paying my expenses out of his own private pocket.

He was a man of less than average height and more than average aggressiveness: a little bull of a man with a large black mustache that was more a statement than an adornment. Difficult to please and difficult to like, I thought, but sharp of eye and brain as well as tongue.

His voice boomed as heavily as a bittern in the reed beds, and although his English was as comprehensive as most well-educated Norwegians', he spoke it unlovingly, as if he didn't care too much for the taste.

I said without heat, "As a miner, you'll understand that surveys are a legitimate expense even when they don't strike ore."

He gave me a hard look. "As a miner, I understand that I would not finance a survey to find slime."

Klonk. One over the head for D. Cleveland. I grinned appreciatively, and slowly, unwillingly, the corners of his mouth twitched.

I made the most of it. "May I come and see you in your office?" I asked. "Just for a few questions. I might as well try my best to earn what you're paying me, now that I'm here."

"Nothing I can tell you will be of any help," he said, as if believing made it so.

"Still . . ."

The vestiges of smile disappeared, but finally, grudgingly, he nodded.

"Very well. Tomorrow afternoon. Four o'clock." And he

went so far as to tell me how to find him.

As he walked away, Arne said, "What are you going to ask him?"

"Don't know yet. I just want to see his background. You can't tell what people are really like if you only meet them at the races."

"But," he said, blinking furiously, "why Rolf Torp?"

"Not especially Rolf Torp," I said. "Everyone who knew Bob Sherman."

"David!" He looked staggered. "It will take you months."

I shook my head. "Several days, that's all. Bob didn't know so many people here as all that."

"But he could have been killed by a total stranger. I mean, if he saw someone stealing the money and didn't know him—"

"It's possible," I said, and asked him if he had ever heard Bob talking about bringing any sort of package from England to Norway.

Arne wrinkled his forehead and darted a compulsive look over his shoulder. No one there, of course.

"Lars mentioned this mysterious package on Tuesday night. No one knew anything about it."

"What did Lars actually ask?"

"Just said you wanted to know if anyone had received a package from Bob Sherman."

"And no one had?"

"No one who was there, anyway."

"Could you write me a list of those who were there?"

"Yes," he said with surprise. "If you want it. But I can't see what it could possibly have to do with Bob's death."

"I'm a great one for collecting useless information," I said, smiling, and Arne gave me a look which said oh, yeah, plain as plain.

The races proceeded the same as before, except that the watching crowd was a good deal thinner than on Grand National day. The birch trees had dropped most of their yellow leaves and looked silver, the daylight was colder and grayer than ever, and a sharp wind whipped around every corner. But this time I had come prepared with a skiing cap with ear flaps, and only my nose, like everyone else's, was turning blue.

Gunnar Holth saddled two for the hurdle race, hurrying busily from one to the other and juggling both sets of owners with anxious dexterity. One of his runners was the dappled mare with the uncertain temper, whose owner, Sven Wangen, was on Emma's list. Arne confirmed that the big young man assiduously hopping out of the way every time the mare presented her heels was indeed Sven Wangen, and added that the brunette sneering at him from a safe distance was his wife.

The jockey mounted warily and the mare bucked and kicked every inch to the start. Arne said that, like all mean bad-tempered females, she would get her own way in the end, and went off to invest a little something on the Tote.

Wise move. She won. Arne beamed and said what did I tell you, when she comes here bitching she always wins. Was she ever docile, I asked, and Arne said sure, but those were her off days. We watched her being unsaddled in the winner's enclosure, with Gunnar Holth and Sven Wangen both tangoing smartly out of her way.

I told Arne I would like to meet Sven Wangen, because Bob had ridden a winner for him on that last day. Arne showed reservations, so I asked him why.

He pursed his mouth. "I don't like him. That's why."

"What's wrong with him?"

"Too much money," Arne said reprovingly. "He behaves as if everyone ought to go on their knees when they talk to him. He has done nothing himself. The money was his father's. His father was a rich man. Too rich."

"In what way too rich?"

Arne raised his eyebrows at what evidently was to him a nonsensical question, because from the tone of his reply it seemed he held great wealth to be morally wrong.

"He was a millionaire."

"Don't you have millionaires in Norway?"

"Very few. They are not popular."

I persuaded him, however, to introduce me to the unpopular Sven Wangen, whose father had made a million out of ships: and I saw at once why Arne didn't like him.

Perhaps two inches taller than I, he looked down his nose as if from a great height: and it was clear that this was no accidental mannerism but the manifestation of deep self-importance. Still probably in his twenties, he was bulky to the point of fatness and used his weight for throwing about. I didn't take to his manner, his small mouth, or his unfriendly light amber eyes: nor, in fact, to his wife, who looked as if she could beat the difficult mare's temper by a couple of lengths.

Arne introduced me, and Sven Wangen saw no reason at all why I should call upon him at any time to ask him questions. He had heavy rust-brown hair growing long over his ears, and a small flat cap which made his big head look bigger.

I said I understood he was a member of the racecourse committee which had asked me to come.

"Lars Baltzersen asked you," he said brusquely. "I was against it. I said so on Tuesday."

"The sooner I get the questions answered, the sooner I'll go home," I said. "But not until."

He looked at me with intense disfavor. "What do you want, then?"

"Half an hour in your house," I said. "Any time that would suit you except for tomorrow afternoon."

He settled in irritation for Sunday morning. His elegantly thin wife manufactured a yawn, and they turned away without any pretense of politeness.

"See what I mean?" Arne said.

"I do indeed. Very unusual, wouldn't you say?"

"Unusual?"

"The rich don't usually behave like that."

"Do you know so many rich people?" Arne asked with a touch of sarcasm.

"Meet them every day of the week," I said. "They own race-horses."

Arne conceded that the rich weren't necessarily all beast-ly and went off on some official tasks. I tracked down Paddy O'Flaherty and found him with five minutes to spare between races.

"Brown envelope of blue pictures?" he repeated. "He never said a dicky-bird to me, now, about any blue pictures." He grinned, and then an uncertain memory floated back. "Wait now, I tell a lie. Back in the summer, he told me he had a good little tickle going for him, do you see? Always one for a chance at easy money, so he was. And there was this day, he winked at me like, and showed me the corner of an envelope in his over-night bag, and he said it would make our hair curl, so it would. So then I asked him for a look, do you see, but he said it was sealed some way so he couldn't steam it. I remember that, sure now I do."

"The last time he came, did he say anything about bringing an envelope?"

Paddy shook his head. "Like I said. Not a word."

I thought. "Did he come straight to your stable from the airport? Did he arrive on time, for instance?"

"I'll tell you something, now. No, he didn't." He concen-trated. "He was that late I thought he'd missed the flight and would come in the morning. Then, sure, a taxi rolls up and out he hops, large as life. He'd bought a bottle of brandy on the plane and there wasn't much left of that, now, before we went to bed."

"What did he talk about?"

"Bejasus, how do I know, after all this time?"

"You must have thought often about that night."

"Well, so I have, then." He sighed at my perseverance, but thought some more. "Horses, of course. We talked about horses.

I don't remember him saying why he was late, or anything like
that. And sure now I'd have thought it was the flight that was
late, that was all."

"I'll check," I said.

"Look, now, there was only one thing he said. . . . Later on,
when we'd maybe had a skinful, he said, Paddy, I think I've
been conned. That's what he said. Paddy, I think I've been
conned. So I asked him what he meant, but he didn't tell me."

"How insistently did you ask?"

"Insist? Bejasus, of course I didn't. Uh . . . there he was putting
his finger over his mouth and nodding. He was a bit tight, do
you see? So I just put my finger over my mouth like him and
I nodded just the same. Well, now, it seemed sensible enough
at the time, do you see?"

I did see. It was a miracle Paddy remembered that evening
at all.

The afternoon ambled on. Gunnar Holth won the steeplechase with Per Bjørn Sandvik's Whitefire, which displeased Rolf
Torp, whose horse was second. Per Bjørn, it appeared, had not
come to the meeting: he rarely did on Thursdays, because it set
a bad example to his staff.

It was Lars Baltzersen who told me this, with warm approval
in his voice. He himself, he said, had to leave his work only
because he was Chairman, and all his employees understood. As
one who had played lifelong truant at the drop of a starter's flag,
I found such noble standards a bit stifling, but one had to admire
them.

Lars and I crossed the track and climbed the tower and
looked down at the pond below. With its surface ruffled by the
breeze, it was far less peaceful than when I'd first seen it and
just as brownly muddy as the day it gave up its dead. The swans
and the ducks had gone.

"It will freeze soon," Lars said. "And snow will cover the
racecourse for three or four months."

"Bob Sherman is being buried today," I said. "In England."

He nodded. "We have sent a letter of regret to Mrs. Sherman."

"And a check," I said: because his name, too, was on the list. He made a disclaiming movement with his hands but seemed genuinely pleased when I told him how much Emma had appreciated their kindness.

"I'm afraid we were all a little annoyed with her while she was here. She was so persistent. But perhaps it was partly because of her that we asked you to come. Anyway, I am glad she is not bitter about the way we tried to avoid her continual questions. She would have a right to be."

"She isn't that sort of person."

He turned his head to look at me. "Do you know her well?" he asked.

"Only since all this started."

"I regret the way we treated her," he said. "I think of it often. Giving her money does not buy us off."

I agreed with him and offered no comfort. He looked away down the racecourse and I wondered if it was his guilty conscience that had driven him to persuade me back.

After the next race, a long-distance flat race, we walked across together to the weighing room.

I said, "You were in the officials' room that day when Bob Sherman poked his head in and could have seen the money lying on the floor."

"That's right," Lars said.

"Well . . . what was the question?"

He was puzzled. "What question?"

"Everyone's statement to the police was the same. You all said, 'Bob Sherman came to the door asking some question or other.' So what was the question?"

He looked deeply surprised. "It can't have had anything to do with his disappearance."

"What was it?"

"I can't remember. Nothing of the slightest importance, I assure you, or of course we would have told the police."

We rejoined Arne, and Lars asked him if he by any chance remembered what Bob had wanted. Arne looked just as surprised and said he had no idea; he'd been busy anyway and probably hadn't even heard. The racecourse manager, however, knew that he had known once, because it was he who had answered.

"Let me think," he said, frowning. "He came in . . . not his feet, just his head and shoulders. He looked down at the money, which was lying in front of him. I remember that distinctly. I told the police. But the question . . . it was nothing."

I shrugged. "Tell me if you ever remember?"

He said he would as if he thought it unlikely, but an hour later he sought me out.

"Bob Sherman asked if Mikkel Sandvik had already gone home, and I said I didn't know."

"Oh."

He laughed. "Well, we did tell you it was nothing important."

"And you were right." I sighed resignedly. "It was just a chance."

At the end of the afternoon, Lars took me up to his Chairman's room to give me the copies the police had provided of their Robert Sherman file. He stood in front of the big stove, a neat substantial figure in his heavy dark blue overcoat and ear-flapped astrakhan hat, blowing on his fingers.

"Cold today," he said.

I thought I probably knew him better than anyone else I'd met in Norway, but all the same I said, "May I call to see you in your office?"

He'd heard about my appointments and smiled wryly at being included. "Saturday, if you like. I'll be there until noon."

After declining a pressing invitation from Arne to dine with him and Kari, I ate early at the Grand and went upstairs to do my homework.

The police had been painstaking, but the net result, as Lars had said, was nil.

A long and immensely detailed autopsy report, filled with medical terms I only half understood, concluded that the deceased had died of three overlapping depressed fractures of the skull. Unconsciousness would have been immediate. Death followed a few minutes later: the exact interval could not be specified. Immersion was subsequent to death.

The nylon rope found on the deceased had been unraveled strand by strand, and an analysis had indicated it to be part of a batch manufactured the previous spring and distributed during the summer to countless shops and ships' chandlers throughout Greater Oslo.

The nylon rope found embedded in a cement block in the Øvrevoll pond was of identical composition.

The cement block itself was a sort of sandbag in widespread use for seawalling. The type in the pond was very common, and none of the contractors currently using it could remember having one stolen. The writer of the report added his personal opinion that no contractor would ever miss one single bag out of hundreds.

The properties of the bag were such that its ingredients were crumbly when dry, but solidified like rock under water. The nylon rope had been tied tightly around the cement bag while it had still been dry.

Extensive inquiries had produced no one who had heard or seen any activity around the pond on either the night of the deceased's disappearance or the night he had been removed from the water. The night watchman had proved a complete loss. There were lists of everything they had found in Bob Sherman's pockets and in his overnight bag. Clothes, watch, keys were all as they should be: it was papers I was interested in, and they, after a month submerged, were in a pretty pulpy state.

Passport and air ticket had been identified. Currency notes had been nearly all British: total value fifteen pounds sterling. There had been no Norwegian money to speak of, and certainly not five canvas bags of it.

The report made no mention of any papers or ruins of papers being found in the overnight bag. Nor of photographs: and photographic paper fared better than most under water.

I read everything through twice and drew no conclusions the police hadn't. Bob Sherman had had his head bashed in, and later he'd been roped to a cement bag and dumped in the pond. By person or persons unknown.

By person or persons who were doing their damnedest, also, to remain unknown.

I lifted the polythene-wrapped knife from my sponge case and propped it against the reading lamp; and immediately the slice down my chest took up throbbing where it had left off that morning. Why was it, I wondered irritably, that cuts only throbbed at night?

It was as well, though, to have that to remind me not to walk trustingly into hotel rooms or hail the first taxi that offered itself. Business had been meant in London, and I saw no safety in Oslo.

I smiled ruefully to myself. I was getting as bad as Arne about looking over my shoulder.

But there could be a lot more knives where that one came from.

Ten

IN THE MORNING, I took the knife along to the police and told them how I'd come by it. The man in charge of the case, the same policeman who had been overseeing the dragging of the pond, looked at me in a sort of startled dismay.

"We will try to trace it, as you ask. But this knife is not rare. There are many knives of this kind. In English, those words 'Norsk Stål' on the blade merely mean 'Norwegian Steel.' "

His name was Lund, his air that of long-term policemen everywhere: cautious, watchful, friendly, with reservations. It seemed to me that many policemen were only completely at ease with criminals; and certainly the ex-policemen who worked for the investigation branch of the Jockey Club always spoke of petty crooks more affectionately than of the general public.

Dedicated to catching criminals, policemen also admired them. They spoke the same language, used the same jargon. I knew from observation that if a crook and a detective who didn't know each other turned up at the same social gathering, they would unerringly seek each other out. Unless one of them happened to be chasing the other at that moment, they would get on well together—a fact which explained the apparently

extraordinary shared holidays which occasionally scandalized
the press.

Lund treated me with scrupulous fairness as a temporary
colleague. I thanked him warmly for letting me use his files, and
he offered help if I should need it.

I said at once that I needed a car with a driver I could trust,
and could he recommend one.

He looked at the knife lying on his desk.

"I cannot lend you a police car." He thought it over, then
picked up a telephone, gave some Norwegian instructions, put
down the receiver, and waited.

"I will ask my brother to drive you," he said. "He is an author.
His books make little money. He will be pleased to earn some
for driving, because he likes driving."

The telephone buzzed and Lund evidently put forward his
proposition. I gathered that it met with the author's approval
because Lund asked when I would like him to start.

"Now," I said. "I'd like him to collect me here."

Lund spoke into the phone, put down the receiver, and said,
"He will be here in half an hour. You will find him helpful. He
speaks English very well. He worked once in England."

I spent the half hour looking through mug shots, but my
London assailant was nowhere to be seen.

Lund's brother Erik was a bonus in every way.

He met me in the front hall with a vague distracted grin. A
tallish man of about fifty-five, he had sparse untidy blond hair,
a shapeless old sports jacket, and an air of being totally disorgan-
ized: and he drove, I soon discovered, as if other cars were
invisible.

He waved me from the police building to a small-sized cream
Volvo waiting at the curb. Dents and scratches of varying rust
vintages bore witness to long and sturdy service, and the trunk
was held shut by string. Upon opening the passenger-side door,

I found that most of the interior was already occupied by a very large Great Dane.

"Lie down, Odin," Erik said hopefully, but the huge dog understood no English, remained on his feet and slobbered gently down my neck.

"Where first?" Erik asked. His English, as his brother had said, was splendid. He settled himself in the driver's seat and looked at me expectantly.

"What did your brother tell you?" I asked.

"To drive you around and if possible make sure no one bumps you off." He said it as casually as if he'd been entrusted to see me onto the right train.

"What are you good at?" I said curiously.

"Driving, boxing, and telling tales out of school."

He had a long face, deeply lined around the eyes, smoother around mouth and chin: evidence of a nature more at home with a laugh than a scowl. In the course of the next few days, I learned that if it hadn't been for his highly developed sense of the ludicrous, he would have been a dedicated Communist. As it was, he held good radical left-wing views but found himself in constant despair over the humorlessness of his fellow travelers. He had worked on the gossip pages of newspapers throughout his youth, and had spent two years in Fleet Street; and he told me more about the people he was driving me to visit than I would have dug out in six weeks.

"Per Bjørn Sandvik?" he repeated when I told him our first destination. "The upright man of the oil fields?"

"I guess so," I said.

He took off into the traffic without waiting for a gap. I opened my mouth and shut it again: after all, if his brother was trusting him to keep me alive, the least I could do was let him get on with it. We swung around some hair-raising corners on two wheels but pulled up unscathed outside the main offices of

Norsk Oil Imports, Ltd. The Great Dane licked his great chops and looked totally unmoved.

"There you are," Erik said, pointing to an imposing double-door entrance into a courtyard. "Through there, turn left, big entrance with pillars."

"You know it?"

He nodded. "I know most places in Oslo. And most people." And he told me about his years on the newspapers.

"Tell me about Per Bjørn, then."

He smiled. "He is stuffy, righteous, and has given himself to big business. During the war, he wasn't like that at all. When we were all young, he was a great fighter against the Nazis, a great planner and saboteur. But the years go by and he has solidified into a dull lump, like the living core of a volcano pouring out and dying to dry gray pumice."

"He must have some fire left," I objected, "to be the head of an oil company."

He blew down his nostrils in amusement. "All the oil companies in Norway are tied hand and foot by government regulations, which is as it should be. There is no room for private speculation. Per Bjørn can only make decisions within a small area. For anything above ordering new ashtrays, he has to have permission from the government."

"You approve of that?"

"Naturally."

"What do you know about his family?" I asked.

His eyes glimmered. "He married a thoroughly boring plain girl called Ragnhild, whose dad just happened at that time to be the head man in Norsk Oil Imports."

I grinned and climbed out of the car, and told him I would be half an hour at least.

"I brought a book," he said equably, and pulled a tattered paperback of *The Golden Notebook* out of his jacket pocket.

The courtyard, tidily paved, had a stone-edged bed of frost-

bitten flowers in the center and distinguished pale yellow buildings all around the edge. The main entrance to the left was
imposing, and opposite, to the right, stood a similar entrance on
a much smaller scale. The wall facing the entrance from the
street was pierced with tall windows and decorated with shut-
ters, and the whole opulent little square looked more like a
stately home than an oil company's office.

It was, I found, both.

Per Bjørn's secretary fielded me from the main entrance,
shoveled me up one flight of carpeted stairs and into his office,
told me Mr. Sandvik was still at a meeting but would not be
long, and went away.

Although the building was old, the head man's room was
modern, functional, and highly Scandinavian, with thick double-glazed windows looking down into the courtyard. On the
wall hung a simple chart of a rock formation with layers labeled
"impermeable," "source," "permeable," and "reservoir"; a list
saying things like "spudded Oct. '71," "plugged and abandoned
Jan. '72"; and three brightly colored maps of the North Sea,
each of them showing a different aspect of the oil-drilling opera-
tions going on there.

In each map, the sea area was subdivided along lines of lati-
tude and longitude into small squares, each with its own identi-
fying number. Many of the squares were labeled "Shell,"
"Esso," "Sonoco," and so on, but although I looked carefully I
could see none marked Norsk Oil Imports.

The door opened behind me and Per Bjørn Sandvik came in,
as pleasant and easy as ever and giving every impression of
having got to the top without pushing.

"David," he said, in his high clear diction, "sorry to keep you
waiting."

"Just looking at your maps," I said.

He nodded, crossing to join me. "We're drilling there . . . and
there." He pointed to two areas which bore an entirely different

name. I commented on it, and he explained.

"We are part of a consortium. There are no private oil companies in Norway."

"What did Norsk Oil Imports do before anyone discovered oil under the North Sea?"

"Imported oil, of course."

"Of course."

I smiled and sat down in the square armchair he indicated.

"Fire away with the questions," he said.

"Did Bob Sherman bring you any papers or photographs from England?"

He shook his head. "No. Lars asked us this on Tuesday. Sherman did not bring any papers for anyone." He stretched out a hand toward his desk intercom. "Would you like some coffee?"

"Very much."

He nodded and asked his secretary to arrange it.

"All the same," I said, "he probably did bring a package of some sort with him, and he probably did pass it on. If anyone would admit to having received it, we might be able to take it out of consideration altogether."

He stared vaguely at his desk.

"For instance," I said, "if what he brought was straight pornography, it probably had nothing to do with his death."

He looked up.

"I see," he said. "And because no one has said they received it, you think it did not contain pornography?"

"I don't know what it contained," I said. "I wish I did."

The coffee arrived and he poured it carefully into dark brown crusty mugs.

"Have you discarded the idea that Bob Sherman was killed by whoever stole the money?"

"It's in abeyance," I said, refusing the offered cream and sugar. "Could you give me your impression of Bob Sherman as a man?"

He bunched his lips assessingly.

"Not overintelligent," he said. "Honest, but easily influenced. A good rider, of course. He always rode well for me."

"I gather Rolf Torp thought he rode a bad race for him that last day."

Sandvik delicately shrugged. "Rolf is sometimes hard to please."

We drank the coffee and talked about Bob, and after a while I said I would like very much to meet Per Bjørn's son, Mikkel. He frowned. "To ask him questions?"

"Well . . . some. He knew Bob comparatively well, and he's the one good contact I've not yet met."

He didn't like it. "I can't stop you, of course. Or, at least, I won't. But he has been very upset by the whole affair, first by thinking his friend was a thief, and now more since he knows he was murdered."

"I'll try not to worry him too much. I've read his short statement to the police. I don't expect to do much more than cover the same ground."

"Then why bother him at all?"

After a pause to consider it, I said, "I think I need to see him, to get the picture of Bob's visits complete."

He slowly sucked his lower lip but finally made no more objections.

"He's at boarding school now," he said. "But he'll be home here for the afternoon tomorrow. If you come at three, he'll be here."

"Here in your office?"

He shook his head. "In my house. The other side of the courtyard."

I stood up to go and thanked him for his time.

"I haven't been of much use," he said. "We've given you a pretty hopeless job."

"Oh, well," I said, and told myself that things sometimes broke if one hammered on long enough. "I'll do my best to earn your money."

He saw me to the top of the stairs and shook hands.

"Let me know if there's anything I can do."

"I will," I said. "And thank you."

I walked down the quiet stairs to the large empty hall. The only sounds of life seemed to come from behind a door at the back of the hall, so I walked over and opened it.

It led, I found, straight into the next-door building, one dedicated not to front offices but to getting the paper work done. Even there, however, things were going at a gentle pace without any feeling of pressure, and in the doorways of the row of small offices stretching away from me stood relaxed people in sweaters, drinking coffee and smoking and generally giving no impression that commercial life was rushing by.

I retreated through the hall, through the courtyard, and back to Erik Lund. He withdrew his eyes from his *Golden Notebook* as I climbed into the car, and appeared to be wondering who I was.

Recognition of sorts awoke. "Oh, yes," he said.

"Lunch, then?" I suggested.

He had few definite views on where to eat, but once we were installed in a decent restaurant, he lost no time in ordering something he called *gravlaks*. The price made me wince on behalf of the racecourse, but I had some, too, and it proved to be the most exquisite form of salmon, cured instead of smoked.

"Are you from Scotland Yard?" he asked after the last of the pink heaven had been dispatched.

"No. From the Jockey Club."

It surprised him, so I explained briefly why I was there.

"What's all this about being bumped off, then?"

"To stop me finding out what happened."

He gazed past me in thought. "Makes my brother, Knut, a dumb cluck, doesn't it? No one's tried to get rid of *him*."

"Knock down one policeman and six more pop up," I said.

"And there aren't six more of you?" he asked dryly.

"The racing cupboard's pretty bare."

He drank coffee thoughtfully. "Why don't you give it up while you're still whole?"

"Natural bloody obstinacy," I said. "What do you know about Rolf Torp?"

"Rolf Torp the terror of the ski slopes, or Rolf Torp who designs glass houses for pygmies?"

"Rolf Torp who owns racehorses and does something in mines."

"Oh. Him." He frowned, sniffed, and grimaced. "Another goddam capitalist exploiting the country's natural resources for private gain."

"Do you know anything about him personally?"

"Isn't that personal enough?"

"No."

He laughed. "You don't think moneygrubbing says anything about a man's soul?"

"Everything any man does says something about his soul."

"You wriggle out of things," he said.

"And things out of people."

"Well," he said, smiling, "I can't actually tell you much about that Rolf Torp. For one thing I've never met him, and for another capitalists make dull copy for gossip columns unless they're caught in bed with their secretaries and no pajamas."

Blue pictures for blackmail, I thought irrelevantly. Or black-and-white pictures for blackmail. Why not?

"Do you know anyone called Lars Baltzersen?" I asked.

"Sure. The Chairman of Øvrevoll? Every man's idea of a respectable pillar of society. Entertains Ambassadors and presents prizes. Often a picture on the sports pages, always beside the man of the moment. Mind you, our Lars was a live wire once himself. Did a lot of motor racing, mostly in Sweden. That was before banking finally smothered him, of course."

"Family?"

"Dutch wife, lots of solid children."

I paid the bill and we strolled back to the car. Odin stared out

the front window with his huge head close to the glass. Some
people who stopped to try "Isn't he a nice boy" noises got a big
yawn and a view down a cavernous throat.

Erik opened his door, gave the dog a shove, and said, *"Fanden ta dig."* The Dane shifted his bulk toward the back seat
without taking offense, and the journey continued.

"What did Lars do in the war?"

"He wasn't here," he said promptly. "He was in London,
reading the news in Norwegian on the radio."

"He didn't tell me he'd lived in London."

"He's quiet now. Another dead volcano. More pumice."

Erik crossed some traffic lights three seconds after they
turned red, and genuinely didn't seem to hear six other motor-
ists grinding their brake drums to screaming point. Odin gave
him an affectionate nudge in the neck, and Erik put out a hand
he needed on the gear shift and fondled the huge wet nose.

He pulled up in front of a modern square-built glass-and-slab
affair a mile out of the city center, a far cry from Sandvik's
architectural elegance.

"This is the address you gave me," Erik said dubiously.

"Fine," I said. "Would you like to wait inside?"

He shook his head, though the afternoon was cold and rapidly
growing dark. "Odin gives off heat like a nuclear reactor and I
don't like sitting in plastic lobbies being stared at."

"O.K."

I left them to their companionship and rode a lift up to Rolf
Torp's office, where, as I was early again, I was asked to wait.
This time not in Torp's own office, but in a small purposefully
decorated room overflowing with useful handouts about Torp-
Nord Associates.

The walls here also were hung with diagrams of rock forma-
tions, charts of progress, and maps showing areas being worked.
These maps were not of the North Sea but of the mainland, with
the thickest cluster of work tags to the west of Oslo, in the
mountains.

Someone had told me Rolf Torp's business was silver, but it wasn't, or no longer chiefly. He and his associates had switched to titanium.

Before he finally turned up (at four-twenty) for his four-o'clock appointment, I had learned a good deal I didn't especially want to know about titanium. For example, that it weighed only 0.163 pounds per cubic inch and in alloy form could reach a tensile strength of 200,000 pounds per square inch. Bully for titanium, I thought.

Rolf Torp was much like his product in tensile strength but couldn't match it for lightness. He made no effort to conceal that my visit was a nuisance: he burst into the waiting room, saying, "Come on, come on, then; I can give you ten minutes, that's all," and stomped off to his own office without waiting to see if I followed.

I did, of course. His office was much like Sandvik's: same type of furniture, fabrics, and carpet, a reflection of prevailing style but no clue to the occupant. The walls here were dotted with framed photographs of various stages of metal production, and another large map with thumbtacks took pride of place.

"How do you mine titanium?" I asked, and sat in the visitor's chair without being invited. Irritably he took his place behind half an acre of tidy desk and lit a cigarette.

"Like one?" he said belatedly, pushing a box toward me.

"No, thank you."

He flicked a lighter and inhaled the smoke deeply.

"You don't find titanium lying around like coal," he said. "Are you sure you want to use your ten minutes on this?"

"Might as well."

He gave me a puzzled look over the heavy black mustache, but seemed to find his own subject a lot less temper-disturbing than mine.

"Titanium is the ninth most common element on earth. It is found in ninety-eight percent of rocks and also in oil, coal, water, plants, animals, and stars."

"You can hardly dig it out of people."

"No. It is mostly mined as a mineral called ilmenite, which is one third titanium."

"Does your firm do the actual mining?"

He shook his head. "We survey, do first drillings, advise, and establish."

I looked vaguely at the photographs on the walls.

"Apart from high-speed aircraft, what's the stuff used for?"

He reeled off technical uses as if he'd been asked that once or twice before. Toward the end, slowing down, he included paint, lipstick, and smokescreens. There was little you couldn't do, it seemed, with the strength of the Titans.

"Did Bob Sherman bring you any photographs?"

I asked him casually without looking at him directly, but if it jerked him at all I couldn't tell, as he swept any involuntary movement into a quick gesture to flick off ash.

"No, he didn't."

"Did he ask your advice about anything?"

"Why should he?"

"People do need advice sometimes," I said.

He gave a laugh that was half a scowl. "I gave him some. He didn't ask. I told him to ride races better or stay in England."

"He didn't please you?"

"He should have won on my good horse. He went to sleep. He stopped trying to win, and he was beaten. Also he did not ride as I told him, all the way round."

"Do you think someone bribed him to lose?"

He looked startled. For all his bad-tempered criticism, it hadn't occurred to him, and to be fair, he didn't pounce on the idea.

"No," he said heavily. "He wanted to ride that horse in the Grand National. It started favorite and it won."

I nodded. "I saw the race."

"That's right. Bob Sherman wanted to ride it, but I would have got someone else, anyway. He rode it very badly."

I imagined that anytime Rolf Torp's jockey didn't win, he had automatically ridden badly. I stood up to go, which puzzled him again, and shook his hand.

"Coming here has been a waste of your time," he said.

"Of course not. . . . I'll let myself out."

He didn't stop me. I closed his door and did a brief exploration. More offices. More bustle than at Sandvik's. More impression of work being done, but nothing so earthy as a lump of ore.

Erik was not parked out front where I had left him. I went through the big glass entrance doors, peered briefly into the darkness, and ignominiously retreated. One thing I did not plan to do was walk around at night alone, making everything easy for assassins.

After ten minutes, I began to wonder if he'd simply forgotten about me and gone home, but he hadn't. The small cream Volvo returned at high speed and stopped outside in its own length. Its owner extricated himself from the quivering metal and strolled toward the building.

"Hullo," he said as I met him. "Hope you haven't been waiting. I had to get Odin's dinner. Forgot all about it."

In the car, Odin loomed hungrily over my head, dribbling. Just as well, I thought, that he was about to be fed.

Erik returned us to the Grand Hotel at tar-melting speed and seemed disappointed that I hadn't wanted any longer journeys.

Eleven

THE RECEPTIONISTS of the Grand Hotel considered me totally mad because I insisted on changing my room every day, but they would have thought me even madder if I'd told them the reason. I asked them just to allocate me the last empty room or, if there were several, to give me a random choice at bedtime. They did it with politely glazed eyes while I thankfully put my trust in unpredictability.

When Erik dropped me at the door and took his big friend home, I telephoned to Arne and Kari and asked them to dinner.

"Come here," Kari demanded warmly, but I said it was time I repaid their kindness, and after much demurring they agreed to the Grand. I sat in the bar and read a newspaper until they arrived, and thought about growing old.

It was strange, but away from her chosen setting Kari looked a different person. Not so young, not so domesticated, not so tranquil. This Kari, walking with assurance into the bar in a long black skirt and white ruffled shirt, was the woman who designed interiors as a business. This Kari, wearing perfect makeup, diamonds in her ears, and hair smoothly pinned up, looked at once cooler and more mature than the casual home girl. When she put a smooth sweet-smelling cheek forward for a kiss and gave me a pretty look from under her lashes, I found I liked her less and wanted her more, both of which reactions were disconcerting and no good.

Arne was Arne, the antithesis of a chameleon, his personality so concretely formed that it retained its own shape whatever the environment. He swept foursquare into the bar and gave it a quick suspicious survey to make sure no one could listen at his shoulder.

"Hallo, David," he said, shaking my hand vigorously. "What have you been doing all day?"

"Wasting time," I said, smiling. "And wondering what to do next."

We sat in a comfortable corner and drank (as, for once, it was the right hour on the right day) whiskey.

Arne wanted to know what progress I had made.

"Not much," I said. "You might practically say none."

"It must be very difficult," Kari said sympathetically, with Arne nodding in agreement. "How do you actually work things out?"

"You look. You listen. You think."

"So simple," she said ironically. "How do you know what to look for?"

"I don't often look for things. I look at what's there."

"All detectives look for things. Look for clues and follow trails. Of course they do."

"And trudge up dead ends and find red herrings," I said.

"Herrings are not red," Kari said in puzzlement.

Fifty-six varieties of herring in Norway, and not one of them red.

"A red herring is something that doesn't exist," Arne said, but had to explain it again to her in Norwegian.

She laughed, but returned to her questions. "How do you solve a crime?"

"Um . . . you think what you might have done if you'd been the crook, and then you look to see if that's what he did. And sometimes it is."

"No one else solves crimes like David," Arne said.

"Believe me," I said, "they do."

"What do you think the crook did this time?" Kari asked.

I looked at her clear gray eyes, asking the question I couldn't answer without freezing the evening in its tracks.

"There's more than one," I said neutrally. "Emma Sherman saw two."

We talked about Emma for a while. Arne had met her grandfather during his brief visit, and knew he had not been able to identify either of the intruders.

"And nobody knows what they were looking for," Kari said thoughtfully.

"The men knew," I said.

Arne's eyes stretched suddenly wide, which made a change from blinking. "So they did," he said.

"Of course they did," she said. "I don't see the point."

"It isn't really a point. Only that someone somewhere does know what is missing. Or what was missing, because it may have been found now."

Kari thought it over. "Why do you think they didn't search the Shermans' house at once, as soon as they'd killed Bob Sherman? Why wait a month?"

Arne went back to blinking fit to bust, but he left it to me to answer.

"I think," I said, "it was because Bob Sherman was found, and whatever it was that was missing wasn't found with him." I paused. "Say Mr. X kills Bob and dumps him in the pond, for a reason as yet unknown. Suppose this was after Bob delivered a package he had been bringing with him. Suppose also that Bob had opened the package and taken out some of the contents, but that Mr. X did not discover this until after he'd killed Bob and put him in the pond. O.K. so far? So then he has to guess whether Bob had the missing contents in his pockets or his overnight bag—in which case they, too, are safely in the pond—or whether he passed them on to someone else, or even posted them home to himself in England, before he was killed. Short of getting Bob out of the pond, Mr. X can't find out for certain, but the longer the missing contents don't turn up, the surer Mr. X becomes that they are with Bob. Right. But then Bob is found, and the missing contents are still missing. So a search party is sent to find out if Bob took them out of the package at home before he even left England, and Emma was unfortunate enough to choose just that moment to go back for some fresh clothes."

Kari's mouth had slowly opened. "Wow," she said. "And it seemed such a simple little question."

"I told you," Arne said. "Give him one fact and he guesses the rest."

"And a guess is all it is." I smiled. "I don't know why they took a month to start searching. Do you?"

Kari said, "But you must be right. It sounds so reasonable."

"Like the earth is flat."

"What?"

"Sounds reasonable until you know different."

We went in to dinner. There was an orchestra playing, and dancing, and later, with the coffee, a singer. In the end, it was all too much for Arne, who stood up abruptly, said he needed some air, and made a compulsive dash for the door.

We watched his retreating back.

"Has he always been like that?" I asked.

"Always since I've known him. Though lately, perhaps, it has been worse. He used not to worry about bugging machines."

"He used not to know they existed."

"Well . . . that's true."

"How did it start? His persecution complex, I mean."

"Oh—the war, I suppose. When he was a child. I wasn't born until after, but Arne was a child then. His grandfather was shot as a hostage, and his father was in the Resistance. Arne says he was always frightened when he was a child, but he wasn't always sure what he was frightened of. Sometimes his father sent

him to run with messages and told him to be sure not to be
followed. Arne says he was always terrified those times that he
would turn round and find a big man behind him."

"Poor Arne," I said.

"He has been to psychiatrists," Kari said. "He knows . . . but
he still can't help it." She looked away from me, at the couples
slowly circling on the square of polished floor. "He can't bear
dancing."

After a few seconds I said, "Would you like to?"

"I don't suppose he'd mind."

She stood up without hesitation and danced with natural
rhythm. She also knew quite well that I liked having her close:
I could see it in her eyes. I wondered if she'd ever been unfaithful to Arne, or ever would be. I wondered about the age-old
things. One can't help it, I find.

She smiled and moved forward until our bodies were touching at more points than not, and no woman ever did that unless
she meant to. What we were engaged in from that moment on
was an act of sex: upright, dancing, public, and fully clothed, but
an act of sex nonetheless. I knew theoretically that a woman
could reach a vivid orgasm without actual intercourse, that in
fact some could do it when all alone simply by thinking erotic
thoughts, but I had never before seen it happen.

It happened to Kari because she wanted it to. Because she
rubbed closely against me with every turn of the dance. Because I didn't expect it. Because I didn't push her off.

Her breathing grew slower and deeper and her eyes lost their
brightness. Her mouth was closed, half smiling. Head up, neck
straight, she looked more withdrawn and absent-minded than
passionately aroused. Then quite suddenly her whole body
flushed with heat, and behind her eyes and right through her
very deeply I was for almost twenty seconds aware of a gentle
intense throbbing.

After that she took a great deep gulping breath as if her lungs
had been cramped. Her mouth opened, the smile broadened,

and she unplastered herself from my front.

Her eyes grew bright as stars, and she laughed into mine.

"Thank you," she said.

She had finished with dancing. She broke away and walked back to the table, sitting down sociably as if nothing had happened. Oh, thanks very much, I thought, and where does that leave me? Dealing with an unscratchable itch and without the later comfort of doing it on my own as she had, because I'd never found that much fun.

"More coffee?" I said. One had to say something, I supposed. How about "Damn your eyes, you selfish little pig"?

"Thank you," she said.

The waiter brought more coffee. Civilization won the day.

Arne returned looking windblown and a little happier. Kari put her hand on his with wifely warmth and understanding, and I remembered ironically that I had wondered if she were ever unfaithful to him. She was and she wasn't: the perfect recipe for having it both ways.

They left shortly afterward, pressing me to spend another evening at their flat before I went home.

"See you on Sunday at Øvrevoll," Arne said. "If not before."

When they had gone, I collected my suitcase from the hall porter and took myself to the reception desk. There were five empty rooms to choose from, so I took a key at random and got myself a spacious double room with a balcony looking out toward the Parliament Building. I opened the well-closed double doors and let a blast from the arctic play havoc with the central heating. Then I shut them again and went coldly to bed, and lay awake for a long time thinking about a lot of things, but hardly at all about Kari.

Erik came to breakfast the next morning. He joined me with a grin, helped himself to half a ton of assorted pickled fish from the buffet, and ate as if there were no tomorrow.

"Where to?" he asked after two further bread rolls, four slices of cheese, and several cups of coffee.

"Øvrevoll," I said.

"But there's no racing today."

"I know."

"Well, if that's what you want, let's go."

Odin, in a friendly mood, sat centrally, with his rump wedged against the rear seat and his front paws and huge head burying the hand brake. When Erik gave him a nudge with his elbow, the dog lifted his chin long enough for his master to release the wheels. A double act of long standing, it seemed.

The journey was a matter of staring death in the face, but we got there. The main gates of the racecourse stood open, with various trade vans standing inside on the tarmac, so we simply drove in and stopped near the weighing room. Erik and Odin unfolded themselves and stretched their legs while I went on my short and abortive mission.

There were cleaners, a man and two women, in the weighing-room building, and none of them spoke English. I went outside and cajoled Erik, the easiest task on earth, to do my talking.

He asked, listened, and passed on the bad news.

"They say Bob Sherman's saddle was here for a long time. In the changing room, on the peg nearest the corner."

I had just looked all around the changing room. No saddles on any pegs and no trace of Bob Sherman's.

"They say it went at about the time the body was found in the pond. They don't know who took it."

"That's that, then."

We left the weighing-room building and strolled the few yards to the racecourse rails. The morning was icy, the wind fresh, the trees sighing. Winter on the doorstep, snow on the way.

Down the sand track, Gunnar Holth's string was starting a canter, and as we watched they came up fast toward us and swept past along to the winning post and around the top of the course where the pond lay. Paddy O'Flaherty, in his brilliant woolen cap, rode in front, giving a lead and setting the pace. With racing the next day, it was little more than a pipe-opener, and the string presently slowed to walk home.

"Next stop is Gunnar Holth's stable," I said.

We drew up in the yard as the horses came back from the track, steaming like kettles under their rugs. Gunnar Holth himself jumped down from Sandvik's Whitefire, patted him vigorously, and waited for me to open the game.

"Morning," I said.

"Morning."

"Can we talk?"

He nodded resignedly, led Whitefire off into the barn, returned, jerked his head toward his bungalow, and opened his door. Erik this time chose to stay in the car, for which Gunnar Holth, having spotted Odin, looked thankful.

"Coffee?"

Same orange pot on the stove. Same coffee, I dared say.

"I am looking for Bob Sherman's saddle," I said.

"His saddle? Didn't he leave it behind? I heard he did."

"I wondered if you knew who had it. I want to find it. . . . It belongs to his wife now."

"And saddles are worth money," he said, nodding. "I haven't seen it. I don't know who has it."

I asked him obliquely twice more in different ways but, in the end, was satisfied that he knew nothing helpful.

"I'll ask Paddy," I said. But Paddy, too, had few ideas.

"It was there, so it was, until they pulled the poor divil out of the water. Sure I saw it there myself on Grand National day. Then the next meeting, on the Thursday, it was gone."

"Are you sure of that?"

"As sure as I'm standing here."

I said mildly, "Why? Why are you so sure?"

His eyes flickered. "Well—as to that, now—"

"Paddy," I said. "Come clean."

"Uh . . ."

"Did you take it?"

"No," he said positively. "That I did not." The idea apparently outraged him.

"What, then?"

"Well, now then, do you see, he was after being a real mate of mine, Bob was. . . . Well, I was sure now, in my own mind, that he would want me to do it—" He ran down and stopped.

"To do what?"

"Look, now, it wasn't stealing or anything like that."

"Paddy, what did you do?"

"Well, there was my helmet, see, and there was his helmet, hanging there with his saddle. Well, now, my helmet had a strap broken, so it had, and Bob's was there, good as new, so I just swapped them over, do you see."

"And that was on Grand National day?"

"That's right. And the next race day, after Bob was found, his saddle was gone. And my helmet was gone with it, do you see."

"So Bob's helmet is here?"

"It is so. In my box, now, under my bunk."

"Will you lend it to me for a while?"

"Lend it?" He was surprised. "I thought you'd be taking it away altogether now, as by rights it belongs to his missus."

"I expect she'd be glad for you to keep it."

"It's a good helmet, so it is."

He went and fetched it and handed it over, an ordinary regulation jockey helmet with a chin strap. I thanked him, told him I'd let him have it back, waved goodbye to Gunnar Holth, and set off on the perilous passage back to central Oslo.

In between bounces, I pulled out the padded lining of the helmet and looked underneath. No photographs, papers, or other missing objects. Nothing but black regulation padding. I put it back into place.

"No good?" Erik said sympathetically, peering around Odin.

"All stones have to be turned."

"Which stone next, then?"

"Lars Baltzersen."

The route to his bank lay past the front door of the Grand, so I stopped off there and left Bob Sherman's helmet with the hall porter, who was already sheltering my newly repacked suitcase. He told me he would take good care of anything I left with him. I left three ten-krone notes with him, and with a smile he took good care of those.

Lars had almost given me up.

"Thought you'd changed your mind," he said, showing me into his office.

"Had to make a detour," I said, apologizing.

"Well, now that you are here . . ." He produced a bottle of red wine and two small glasses from a discreet cupboard, and poured for us both.

His room, like Sandvik's and Torp's, was standard Scandinavian, modern vintage. Commerce, I supposed, must be seen to be up-to-date, but as a source of personal information these interiors were a dead loss.

No maps on his walls. Pictures of houses, factories, office blocks, distant ports. When I asked him, he told me that his banking firm was chiefly concerned with the financing of industrial projects.

"Merchant banking," he said. "Also we run a building scheme very like an English building society. Except that here, of course, we lend at a much lower interest rate, so that mortgages are cheaper."

"Don't the investors complain?"

"They get almost the same return as British investors. It is just that Norwegian societies don't have to pay big taxes. It is the tax which puts up the British mortgage rate."

He told me that there were many small private banks in Norway running building schemes, but that his was one of the largest.

"There is a terrible shortage of building land round Oslo," he said. "Young couples find it very difficult to find a house. Yet far out in the country there are whole farms standing empty and derelict. The old people have died or are too weak to work the fields, and the young people have left the hard life and gone to the towns."

"Same everywhere," I said.

He liked wooden houses best, he said. "They breathe."

"How about fire?" I asked.

"It always used to be a fearful risk. Cities were burned sometimes. But now our fire services are so fast, so expert, that I am told if you want to burn your house for the insurance, you have to hose it down with gasoline. Otherwise the fire will be put out at the first puff of smoke."

We drank the wine and Lars smoked a cigarette. I asked him about his years in London and about his motor racing in Sweden, but he seemed to have no interest left in them.

"The past is over," he said. "It is banking and Øvrevoll which I think about now."

He asked me if I knew yet who had killed Bob Sherman. Such faith in the way he put it.

"Not yet," I said. "What's my limit on expenses?"

I couldn't pin him to an amount. It seemed that if I succeeded there was no limit. If I failed, I had already overspent.

"Have you any ideas?" he asked.

"Ideas aren't enough."

"You need proof as well, I suppose."

"Mm . . . I have to make like a poacher."

"What do you mean?"

"Set traps," I said. "And keep my feet out of other poachers' snares."

I stood up to go. He, too, said my visit had been a waste of time because he had told me nothing useful.

"You never know," I said.

Erik and I had lunch in a café not far from his brother's headquarters, because I wanted to call in afterward to see him.

He would be off duty at two o'clock, he said on the telephone; if that would do, he could see me before he went home.

Erik spent most of lunch explaining with chapter and verse how all revolutions ended in gloom because all revolutionaries were incapable of humor.

"If the activists knew how to be funny," he said, "the workers would have ruled the world long ago."

"Jokes should be taught in school," I suggested.

He looked at me suspiciously. "Are you taking the mickey?"

"I thought that was the point."

"Oh, God, yes." He laughed. "So it is. What makes you spend your life detecting?"

"Curiosity."

"Killed the cat."

"Shut up."

"Sorry," he said, grinning. "Anyway, you're still alive. How did you train for it? Is there a school for detectives?"

"Don't think so. I went to university. Tried industry, didn't like it. Didn't want to teach. Liked going racing, so got a job going racing."

"That's as smart a canter over the course as I've ever heard, and as a gossip columnist I've heard a lot. What did you read at which university?"

"Psychology at Cambridge."

"Ahah," he said. "Ah absolutely *hah.*"

He came with me up to Knut's office, leaving Odin in charge of the car. Knut was tired after an apparently frustrating spell of duty, yawning and rubbing his eyes when we walked in.

"I am sorry," he said. "But I have been awake since two o'clock this morning." He shook his head to clear it. "Never mind. How can I help you?"

"Not in detail today. Just in outline. Tell me how much scope you have. Tell me if your terms of reference would let you catch a rabbit if I enticed one out of a hole." I turned to Erik. "Explain to him. If I set a trap, can he help me to spring it? Is he allowed to, and would he personally want to?"

The brothers consulted in their own language, Knut neat, restrained, overtired, and Erik with undisciplined gestures, bohemian clothes, and wild wispy hair. Erik was older, but in him the life-force still flowed with generous vigor.

In the end, they both nodded. Knut said, "As long as it is not against the regulations, I will help."

"I'm very grateful."

He smiled faintly. "You are doing my work."

He collected his coat and cap and came down to the street with us. His car, it appeared, was along with Erik's in the side road running down by a small railed public garden.

Erik's car was a center of attention.

About ten feet away from it, ranged around in a semicircle, stood a dozen children and one uncertain-looking policeman. His face changed thankfully at the sight of Knut, and he saluted and began to shift his anxiety onto someone else.

Erik translated for me, looking puzzled.

"One of the children says a man told her not on any account to go near my car. He told her to run home as fast as she could."

I looked at the car. Odin was facing not toward the front window, as usual, but toward the back, and he was looking down, but not interestedly at the crowd. Something in the great dog's world seemed wrong to him. He was standing rigidly. Much too tense. And the trunk was no longer tied up with string.

"Oh, Christ," I said. "Get those children out of here. Make them run."

They simply stared at me and didn't move. But they hadn't been near the Old Bailey in London on March 8, 1973.

"It could be a bomb," I said.

Twelve

THE CHILDREN recognized the word, but of course they didn't believe it. The people in London hadn't believed it until flying glass ripped their faces.

"Tell them to run," I said to Knut.

He decided to take it seriously even if it were a false alarm. He said something unequivocal to the policeman, and then grabbed hold of Erik's arm.

He knew his brother. He must have loved him more than most. He grabbed him tight just as Erik took his first step toward the car, saying "Odin," half under his breath.

They more or less fought. Knut wouldn't let go and Erik grew frantic. Knut put a lock on Erik's arm which would have arrested a two-hundred-and-eighty-pound boxer with a skinful, and Erik's face crumpled into despair. The two of them, step by contested step, retreated from the car.

The policeman had chased the children away to a safe distance and was yelling to approaching pedestrians to get behind cover. No one paid any attention to me, so I nipped smartly along the pavement, put my hand on the handle, wrenched the door open, and sprinted.

Even then the wretched dog didn't come out at once. It took a screeching whistle from Erik to get results, and Odin came bounding after me down the pavement as if it were playtime. The bomb went off just as he drew level, twenty feet from the car. The blast slammed us both down in a heap, hitting like a fierce blow in the back, knocking all breath out, leaving us limp, weak, and shaken.

Not a big bomb by Irish standards. But this one had presumably not been meant to destroy the neighborhood. Just the occupants of a car. Two men and a dog.

Knut helped me to my feet and Erik took hold of Odin's collar, kneeling down and patting him solicitously. Odin slobbered all over him, as good as new.

"That was stupid," Knut said.

"Yes," I said.

"Are you hurt?"

"No."

"You deserve to be."

"It might not have gone off for hours."

"It might have gone off while you were beside it."

Erik's car was gutted. Windows blown out, interior torn to shreds, trunk burst wide open. I picked splinters of glass out of the hair on the back of my head and asked him if the car was insured.

"I don't know," he said vaguely. He rubbed his arm where Knut had locked it. "Knut wanted me to wait for an expert to come and see if it was a bomb, and if it was, to dismantle it."

"Knut was quite right."

"He didn't stop you."

"I'm not his brother. He had his hands full with you, and the bomb probably had my name on it in the first place."

"What a bloody awful way to die." He stood up and grinned suddenly, his whole face lighting up. "Thanks, anyway," he said. Which was pretty generous, considering the state of his Volvo.

Once the fireworks were over, the children came back, staring at the wreck with wide eyes. I asked Knut to find the little girl who'd been told to run home, and he said he'd already sent his policeman to bring her.

Apart from the car, there was little damage. The windows had been broken in a severe-looking building on the far side of the road, but neither the railings nor the shivering bushes in the little public garden near the Volvo seemed to have suffered. Cars parked several yards away fore and aft were slightly scratched with glass splinters but otherwise undamaged. If the bomb had gone off while we had been driving along a busy street, there would have been a lot more mess.

The little girl was blond, solemn, hooded, and zipped into a red anorak, and accompanied now by a scolding older child of about thirteen who had fallen down on the job of looking after her and was busy justifying herself. Knut, as with the boy on the racecourse, won the smaller girl's confidence by squatting down to her level and chatting along quietly.

I leaned against the railings and felt cold, and watched Erik smoothing Odin's sand-colored coat over and over, seeing him dissipate an overwhelming buildup of tension and release in small self-controlled gestures. Odin himself seemed to be enjoying it.

Knut stood up, holding the little girl's hand.

"Her name is Liv. She is four. She lives about half a mile away and she was playing in the park with her big sister. She came out of the gate down there and walked up the road here. Her sister had told her not to, but Liv says she doesn't do what her sister says."

"The sister's too damn bossy," Erik said unexpectedly. "Little Fascist."

"Liv says there was a man cutting some string at the back of the car and the big dog looking at him out the window. She stopped to watch. She was behind the man. He didn't see her or hear her. She says he took something out of his coat and put it inside the trunk, but she didn't see what shape it was. She says the man tried to shut the back of the car, but it wouldn't shut. Then he tried to tie the string where it had been before, but it was too short because he had cut it. He put the string in his pocket, and that was when he saw Liv. He told her to go away, but she seems to be a child who does the opposite of what she's told. She says she went up to the car and looked through the side window at the dog, but the dog went on looking out the back. Then the man shook her and told her to run home at once and not to play near the car. Then he went away."

Knut looked at the small crowd of children beginning to cluster again around Liv.

"She is one of those children who draw others to her. Like now. They came out of the park to join her, and she told them about the man cutting the string and trying to tie the trunk shut again. It was that which interested her most, it seemed. Then my policeman came along, on his way to start his afternoon duty, and he asked the children why they were standing there."

"Then we came?"

"Right."

"Has Liv said what the man looked like?"

"Big, she said. But all men are big to little girls."

"Could she see his hair?"

Knut asked her. She answered. Knut said, "He was wearing a woolen cap, like a sailor."

"What did his eyes look like?"

Knut asked. Her little voice rose clear, high, definite, and all the children looked interested.

"He had yellow eyes. Sharp, like a bird."

"Did he have gloves?"

Knut asked. "Yes," he reported.

"What sort of shoes?"

Back came the answer: big, soft, squashy shoes, like on a boat.

Children were the best witnesses on earth. Their eyes saw clearly, their memories were accurate, and their impressions weren't interpreted by probability or prejudice. So when Liv added something which made Knut and Erik and the older children laugh, I asked what she'd said.

"She must have been mistaken," Knut said.

"What did she say?"

"She said he had a butterfly on his neck."

"Ask her what sort of butterfly," I said.

"It's too late for butterflies," he said patiently. "Too cold."

"Ask her what it was like," I urged.

He shrugged, but he asked. The reply surprised him, because Liv described it with sharp positive little nods. She knew she'd seen a butterfly.

Knut said, "She says it was on the back of his neck. She saw it because his head was bent forward. It was between his wooly cap and his collar and it didn't move."

"What color?"

He consulted. "Dark red."

"Birthmark?"

"Could be," he agreed. He asked her one or two more questions and nodded to me. "I should think so," he said. "She says it had two wings lying open flat, but one was bigger than the other."

"So all we need now is a big man with yellow eyes and a butterfly birthmark."

"Or a small man," Erik said, "with the sun in his eyes and a dirty neck."

"No sun," I said. The iron-gray sky pressed down like an army blanket, without warmth. The shivers in my gut, however, had little to do with the cold.

Knut sent his policeman to fetch experts in fingerprints and explosives, and took the names and addresses of half the children. The crowd of watchers grew a bit, and Erik restively asked Knut when he could go home.

"What in?" said Knut pointedly, so we stamped around on the pavement for nearly another hour.

With darkness we returned to Knut's office. He took his coat and cap off and looked wearier than ever.

I borrowed his telephone and rang the Sandviks to apologize for my nonarrival. I spoke, in the event, to Mrs. Per Bjørn, who explained that her husband was out.

"Mikkel did wait for you, Mr. Cleveland," she said, in heavily accented English. "But after one hour he went away with some friends."

"Please tell him I'm very sorry."

"I will tell him."

"What school does he go to?"

"College of Gol," she said, and then thought better of it. "But I do not think that my husband would like—"

I interrupted, "I just wondered if I could see him this evening before he goes back."

"Oh . . . He is going straight back with the friends. They will have started by now."

"Never mind, then."

I put down the receiver. Knut was organizing coffee.

"Where is the College of Gol?" I asked.

"Gol is in the mountains, on the way to Bergen. It is a holiday ski town in the winter. The college is a boarding school for rich boys. Are you going all the way out there to see Mikkel Sandvik? He knows nothing about Bob Sherman's death. When I saw him, he was very upset about his friend dying like that. He would have helped me if he could."

"How upset? Crying?"

"No, not crying. Pale. Quite shocked. Trembling. Upset."

"Angry?"

"No. Why should he be angry?"

"People are usually furious when their friends are murdered. They feel like strangling the murderer, don't they?"

"Oh, that," he said, nodding. "No, I don't remember that Mikkel was especially angry."

"What is he like?" I asked.

"Just a boy. Sixteen. No, seventeen. Intelligent, but not outstanding. Average height, slim build, light brown hair, good manners. Nothing unusual about him. A nice boy. A little nervous, perhaps."

We sat around and drank the coffee. Odin had some, too, in a bowl, with a lot of sugar. Erik had recovered from almost

losing his companion and was beginning to think about his car.
"I'll need to hire one, I suppose," he said. "For driving David
around."

"You're not driving David anymore," Knut said positively.

"Of course I am."

"No," said Knut. "It's too dangerous."

There was a small meaningful silence. Anyone in future who
drove me must be presumed to be at risk. Which put me high
in the unpopularity stakes as a passenger.

"I'll manage," I said.

Erik said, "Where do you plan to go?"

"Tomorrow, to call on Sven Wangen, then to Øvrevoll. On
Monday . . . I don't know yet."

"I could do with another of those Grand Hotel breakfasts,"
Erik said.

"No," said Knut. They argued heatedly in private, and Knut
lost. He turned his grim face and compressed mouth to me.
"Erik says he never leaves a job unfinished."

Erik grinned and rubbed a hand over his straggly blond hair.
"Only dull ones."

Knut said crossly, "I suppose you realize that one of these
attempts will be successful? Two have failed, but—"

"Three," I said. "Someone tried to drown me in the fjord the
first day I came to Norway."

I told them about the black speedboat. Knut frowned and
said, "But that could have been an accident."

I nodded. "At the time, I thought it was. I don't think so any
longer." I got up to pour myself some more hot strong black
coffee. "I do rather agree with you that they will succeed in the
end, but I don't know what to do about it."

"Give up and go back to England," Knut said.

"Would you?"

He didn't answer. Nor did Erik. There wasn't an answer to
give.

Knut sent me back to the Grand in a police car, where, as the

bar was again shut (Saturday), I ate an early dinner, collected
my suitcases and Bob Sherman's helmet from the porter, picked
a room at random from those available, and spent the evening
upstairs alone, sitting in an armchair and contemplating several
unpalatable facts.

Such as, there was a limit to luck and little girls.

Such as, next time they could use a rifle, because sniping was
the surest way of killing.

Such as, tomorrow if I went to the races I would be scared to
death the whole bloody day.

Not much comfort in the hope that old yellow eyes with the
birthmark might be a lousy shot.

There were various other thoughts, chiefly that somewhere
there existed a particular way of discovering who had killed Bob
Sherman, and why. There had to be such a way, for if there
wasn't, no one would need to kill me. Knut hadn't found it.
Maybe he had looked the solution in the face and not recognized it, which was easy enough to do. Maybe I had also, but
could be expected to understand later what I had heard or seen.

Yellow eyes must have followed Erik's car, I thought. Erik's
breakneck driving and red-light jumping made it exceedingly
unlikely that anything except a fire engine could have tailed us
to Øvrevoll. But then I'd considerately returned to the Grand
to dump the helmet, and made it easy for a watcher to pick us
up again.

I hadn't spotted a follower, nor had Erik. But our trip to
Baltzersen's, and from there to where we parked for lunch, had
been comparatively short and in retrospect almost legal. Anyone risking a couple of head-on crashes could have kept us in
sight.

Yellow eyes was the man who had attacked Emma; and it
seemed likely that the man who kicked her grandfather was the
man who'd tried to knife me. Both, it seemed to me, were
mercenaries, paid to do a violent job, but were not the instiga-
tors. They hadn't the aura of principals.

To my mind, there were at least two others, one of whom I knew, one or more I didn't. To bring out the unknown, I had to bamboozle the known. The big snag was that when it came to setting traps, the only bait at present available was me, and the cheese could find itself eaten if it wasn't extremely careful.

It was easy to see that to bring out the big boys, yellow eyes and brown eyes would have to be decoyed away while, at the same time, a situation needing instant action was temptingly arranged elsewhere. How to do it was another matter. I stared at the carpet for ages and came up with nothing foolproof.

I wished there was a way of knowing what Bob Sherman had been bringing to Norway. Unlikely to be straight pornography, because Bob had told Paddy O'Flaherty that he, Bob, had been conned. If he had opened the packet and found that it did not contain ordinary pornography, he might well have thought that.

Suppose he had opened the packet and reckoned he was not being paid enough for what he was carrying.

Suppose he had removed something from the packet, meaning to use it to up the stakes.

But he couldn't have used it, because if he had, the enemy would have known he had taken it, and would not have killed him without getting it back.

So suppose simply opening the packet and seeing the contents was in itself a death warrant.

Suppose the enemy killed him for knowing the contents, and only discovered afterward that he had removed some of them.

It came back to that every time.

So . . . what the *hell* was in that packet?

Start another way.

When had he opened the packet?

Probably not at home. Emma had seen him put it in his overnight bag so as not to risk forgetting it. Yellow eyes and friend had subsequently smashed the place up looking for things from it, and hadn't found any. So it seemed reasonable to suppose that he had set off from home with the envelope intact.

He had had all day at Kempton races. Time enough if he'd urgently wanted to open it: but if he'd felt like that, he'd already had it available all night.

Not much time at Heathrow between arriving from Kempton and boarding the airplane. Hardly the opportunity for an impulsive bit of snooping.

He had turned up at Gunnar Holth's an hour or so later than expected. So he could have done his lethal bit of nosy-parkering either on the flight or in the first hour after he'd landed.

On the flight, I thought, was more likely.

A couple of drinks under his belt, an hour or so to while away, and a packet of blue pictures temptingly to hand.

Open the packet and see—what?

Suppose he had had perhaps half an hour before landing to come up with the idea of demanding a larger freight fee. Suppose he took something out of the envelope and hid it. . . . Where had he hidden it?

Not in his pockets or his overnight bag. Perhaps in his saddle, but doubtful, because for one thing his racing saddle was tiny, and for another he'd ridden three races on it the following day.

Not in his helmet: no papers or photographs lurked inside the padded headband.

Which left one unaccounted-for hour, during which he could have left an object at the reception desk of any hotel in Oslo, with a request to keep it for him until he returned.

In one hour, he could have hidden something in countless places.

I sighed. It was hopeless.

I stood up, stretched, unpacked a few things, undressed, brushed my teeth.

Bob's helmet lay on my bed. I picked it up and dangled it by the chin strap as I pulled back the quilt and pushed up the pillows as a backrest for reading before sleep. Sitting between the sheets, I turned the helmet idly over in my hands, scarcely looking at it, thinking about Bob and the last day he'd worn it.

I thought seriously about wearing it myself to Øvrevoll to protect my head, and of buying a bulletproof vest besides. I thought ungenerous thoughts about Emma's husband because I, too, could still die for what he'd done.

No papers. No photographs. I pulled the soft black padding out again. Nothing—still nothing tucked behind it.

In the crown there was just the small round centerpiece of black-covered padding suspended by straps fixed into the shell itself. A marvelous piece of engineering, designed to prevent a man falling on his nut at thirty miles an hour, off a galloping horse, from bashing his skull in. The central suspended piece of padding shielded the top of the head and stopped it crashing into the shell itself at concussion speed.

Underneath the central piece of padding there was no room at all for any papers or photographs or anything out of magazine-sized packets. I put my hand below it, just to make sure.

And there, in the roof of his helmet, Bob had left the key.

Literally, the key.

I felt it there with complete disbelief.

Fixed to the hard outer casing by two crossed strips of tape, unseen until one deliberately pushed the central piece of padding sidewise out of position, was a key.

I unstuck it from the helmet and pulled off the sticky tape. It was a Yale-type key, but with a small black tag bonded on instead of the usual round metal thumb plate. A small white letter and number, C 14, was stamped on the black plastic on the side that had been against the helmet's wall. The key itself, at first, second, third glance, had been unnoticeable: and Bob certainly could have ridden his races with it firmly and invisibly in place.

C 14.

It looked like a locker key. Very like those from the luggage lockers of any big airport or railway station in the world. Nothing at all to show which city, country, or continent it belonged to.

I thought.

If the key had been in the package, one would have expected it to be of extreme importance. Vital enough to be worth dragging the pond for, when it was found to be missing. Or searching for at once in the house in England.

The men searching the house in England had specifically mentioned papers. They had been looking for papers, not a key.

So suppose Bob had left the papers somewhere in a locker and this was the key to it.

Much easier. It cut out New York, Nairobi, and Outer Mongolia and narrowed the search to most of southern England or anywhere in Oslo.

The harmless-looking little key promised to be everything I needed. I closed my hand over it, with an instinct to hide it, to keep it safe.

Bob, too, must have felt like that. The care with which he'd hidden it revealed the strength of his instinct. And he hadn't known at the time how true that instinct had been.

Smiling at myself, I nevertheless followed his example.

There was in my suitcase a fresh unopened dressing for the cut on my chest, thoughtfully provided by Charles Stirling in case I needed it; but since the intermittent throbbing had faded to an intermittent itch, I'd left his original handiwork undisturbed.

Laying the key on the bedside table, I pulled off the old dressing to take a look: and dark, dry, and healthy, the slit was healing fast.

I fetched the new plaster and stuck it on, with Bob Sherman's precious key snug inside it against my skin.

Thirteen

ERIK CAME TO BREAKFAST with an expression almost as depressing as the freezing wet day outside. He brought two plates, heaped like the Matterhorn, over from the buffet, sat opposite me, and toyed with the foothills.

"Did you sleep well?" he asked.

"No."

"Nor did I. Kept hearing the bang of that bloody bomb." He looked at the smoked fish I had acquired before his arrival. "Aren't you eating?"

"Not madly hungry."

He raised a grin. "The condemned-man syndrome?"

"Thanks."

He sighed, adjusted his mind to the task, and began proving his stomach was as big as his eyes. When both plates were empty of all but a trace of oil and six dorsal fins, he patted his mouth with a napkin and resurfaced to the dangerous Sunday.

"Are you, seriously, going to the races?" he said.

"Don't know yet."

"I didn't bring Odin today. Left him with a neighbor." He drank his coffee. "I hired a bigger Volvo. A fast one. Here's the bill." He dug in his pocket and produced a receipt.

I took out my wallet and paid him. He didn't say leave it until later.

A party of English racing people came into the restaurant and sat in ones and twos together at a table near the window. I knew most of them: a top amateur jump rider, a pro from the flat, an assistant trainer, an owner and his wife. When they'd chosen their food and begun to eat, I drifted over to them and pulled up a chair.

"Hi," they said. "How's things?"

Things, meaning mostly their chances that afternoon, were relaxedly discussed, and after a while I asked the question I had joined them for.

"Remember the weekend Bob Sherman disappeared? Did any of you happen to come over with him on the same flight?"

The top amateur rider had. Glory be.

"Did you sit next to each other?"

He explained delicately that he had traveled first class, Bob tourist.

"But," he said, "I gave him a lift into Oslo in my taxi."

"Where did you drop him?"

"Oh . . . here. I was staying here, but he was going on to that trainer feller he rode for. He thanked me for the ride, and I think he said he would catch the Lijordet tram, if there was one. Anyway, I remember him standing on the pavement with his bag and saddle and stuff. But does it matter? After all, he rode next day, all right."

"Was the flight on time?"

"I don't remember that it wasn't."

I asked a few more questions, but the amateur remembered nothing else of much significance.

"Thanks, anyway," I said.

"Hope you get whoever did it," he said. He smiled. "I expect you will."

If he doesn't get me, I thought with a twinge, and went back to collect Erik.

"Where first?"

"All the railway stations."

"All the *what?*"

"The nearest railway station," I amended.

"Whatever for?"

"I want a timetable."

"They have them here at the hotel desk."

I grinned at him. "Which is the nearest station?"

He said doubtfully, "The Østbane, I suppose."

"Off we go, then."

He shook his head in exasperation, but off we went.

From the Østbane, I discovered, trains ran through Gol on the line to Bergen. Trains ran also to Lillehammer, Trondheim, and the arctic circle. Østbane was the main long-distance terminus in Oslo.

It had luggage lockers and it even had a C 14. But the locker was empty, the key was in the open door, and the tag was different.

I took timetables which included Gol, where Mikkel Sandvik's school was.

One never knew.

"What now?" Erik said.

"The other railway stations," I said, and we went there, but without finding any matching black tags.

"Where else would you find lockers like those?"

"Besides railway stations? At the airport. In factories, offices, schools. Lots of places."

"Available to a foreign traveler at eight-thirty on a Saturday evening."

"Ah . . . Fornebu. Where else?" Where else, indeed. "Shall we go there?"

"Later," I said. "After Sven Wangen."

Erik objected. "He lives in the opposite direction, farther out than the racecourse."

"All the same," I said, "Sven Wangen first."

"You're the boss."

He looked carefully several times in the driving mirror as we set off, but said he was sure we were not being followed. I believed him. Nothing could have stayed with Erik when he was really trying.

"Tell me about Sven Wangen," I said.

He pursed his mouth in much the same disapproving way that Arne had.

"His father was a collaborator," he said.

"And no one forgets it?"

He sniffed. "Officially, the past is past. But after the war, the collaborators didn't thrive. If some town wanted a bridge built, or a school, for instance, it would happen that an architect or a builder who had worked well with the Nazis would just not be the one to get the contract."

"But Sven Wangen's father was already rich . . . from shipping."

He looked at me sidewise while taking a sharp turn to the left and missed a lamppost by millimeters.

"Arne Kristiansen told me," I said.

"Inherited wealth is immoral," Erik said. "All estates should be distributed among the masses."

"Especially the estates of collaborators?"

He grinned. "I suppose so."

"Was the father like the son?" I asked.

Erik shook his head. "A hardheaded greedy businessman. He made a lot of money out of the Nazis."

"Surely that was patriotic of him?"

Erik wouldn't have it. "He did nothing for his fellow countrymen. He made money only for himself."

"The father destroyed the son," I said.

"Destroyed him?" He shook his head. "Sven Wangen is an overpowering boor who always gets his way. He's nowhere near destroyed."

"He's an empty person. Because of his father, I shouldn't think he ever had a chance to be normally liked, and people who are spurned for no fault of their own can become terribly aggressive."

He thought it over. "Guess you may be right. But I still don't like him."

Sven Wangen lived in the style to which he had been born, in a huge country house built mostly of wood, partly of stone. Even on a cold wet early-winter morning it looked neat, clean, and prosperous. Everything growing was sharply clipped into geometric precision, a regimentation totally uncongenial to Erik's casual, generous, and untidy mind. He stared around in distaste, his give-everything-to-the-masses expression much in evidence.

"All this for two people," he said. "It's wrong."

A middle-aged woman came to open the front door when I knocked, and showed me down the hall to a small sitting room with windows facing the drive. Through them I could see Erik pacing up and down in the rain, radiating Marxist disapproval and stamping the undeserving bourgeoisie into the gravel with each crunch of his heel.

Sven Wangen strolled into the room eating a sugary pastry and staring with cold eyes down from his great height.

"I'd forgotten you were coming," he said. "Have you solved everything yet?" A slight sneer. No friendliness.

"Not everything."

A small bad-tempered flash in the supercilious eyes.

"I've nothing to tell you. You are wasting your time."

They'd all told me that, and they were all mistaken.

Without a hat, Sven Wangen was revealed as going prematurely bald, the russet hair as thick as ever around the back and sides, but almost as thin as Erik's on top. He took a large sticky bite, chewed, swallowed: added another fraction to his overweight.

"The last day Bob Sherman rode for you, did he say anything unexpected?"

"No, he did not." He hadn't bothered to think about it.

"Did you take him for a drink to celebrate the winner he rode for you?"

"Certainly not." He started another mouthful.

"Did you talk to him at all—either before or after the race?"

He chewed. Swallowed. Looked closely at the pastry, prospecting the next area.

"In the parade ring, I gave him his orders. I told him I expected better than he'd just done for Rolf Torp. He said he understood."

Bite. Munch. Swallow.

"After the race, he unsaddled the horse and went to weigh in. I didn't see him again."

"While he was unsaddling, did he tell you how the mare had run?"

"No. I was telling Holth she needed a good thrashing to quiet her down. Holth disagreed. I didn't speak to Sherman."

"Didn't you congratulate him?" I asked curiously.

"No."

"Do you wish you had?"

"Why should I?"

You might need to eat less, I thought, but refrained from saying so. His psychological hang-ups weren't my affair.

"Did he mention delivering a package which he had brought from England?"

"No." He stuffed the rest of the gooey goody into his mouth and had difficulty closing his lips.

"Did you ask him to ride the mare next time he came?"

He stared, then spoke around the dough and currants. "He didn't come again."

"I mean, that last day, did you ask him to ride for you again?"

"Oh. No." He shrugged. "Holth always engages the jockeys. I just say who I want."

"You never telephoned to Sherman in England personally to discuss his rides for you?"

"Certainly not."

"Some owners do talk to their jockeys," I said.

"I pay Holth to do that sort of thing."

What a lot you miss, I thought. Poor fat, unloved, deprived, rich young man. I thanked him for his time and went back to

Erik. Sven Wangen watched us through the window, licking the sugar off his fingers.

"Well?" Erik said.

"He might have issued the orders, but he never killed anyone himself."

Erik grunted as he started the hired Volvo toward the gate. "Where now?"

"You're wet," I said. "Why did you stay out in the rain?"

He was almost embarrassed. "Oh . . . I thought I'd hear you better if you yelled."

We went in silence for five miles down the road and then he pulled up at a fork.

"You'll have to decide here," he said. "That way to Øvrevoll, and that way to the airport. The racecourse is much nearer."

"The airport."

"Right."

He blasted off down the road to Fornebu as if he were trying to fly there.

"Mind we aren't followed," I said.

"You're joking."

The thirty-mile journey, from one side of Oslo to the other, took just over half an hour.

No one followed.

C 14 was locked, and C 13 next to it had a key in its door with a black tag, just the same as the key to C 14. Both were large lockers in the bottom row of a three-high tier.

Erik, who had allotted himself full bodyguard status, stood at my elbow and peered at the ranks of metal doors.

"Are these the lot you're looking for?"

I nodded. "I think so."

"What do we do now, then?"

"We walk around for a bit to make sure there's no one here we know."

"A sensible idea."

We walked around and stood in corners to watch, but as far

as I could see every person in the airport was a complete
stranger. After drifting gently back to the lockers, Erik stood
stalwartly with his back to C 13 and looked ready to repel
boarders while I inconspicuously fished out the hidden key and
tried it in the lock next door.

The right key, no mistake. The locker door swung open re-
vealing a space big enough for two large suitcases: and on the
scratched metal floor, looking lost and inappropriate, lay a strip
of folded paper.

I bent down, picked it up, and tucked it into my inside jacket
pocket.

"See anyone?" I asked Erik, straightening again.

"Not a soul we know."

"Let's grab some coffee."

"What about the locker?"

I looked down at C 14 with its key in the lock and its door
open.

"We don't need it anymore."

Erik steered us to the airport buffet and bought coffee for
both of us and a couple of open sandwiches for himself. We sat
at a plastic-topped table amid travelers with untidy hand luggage and children running about doing what they were told not
to; and with an almost fluttery feeling of expectation I took out
the paper Bob Sherman had left.

I had supposed it would prove to be a base for blackmail:
incriminating letters or photographs no one dared show his
wife. But it proved to be neither of those things. It proved to
be something I didn't recognize at all.

For one thing, the paper was thinner than I had at first supposed, and only seemed to be thick because it was folded several times. Unfolded, it turned out to be a strip six inches across
but nearly three feet long, and it was divided into three columns which were intended to be read downward. One could
not, however, actually read them, as each inch-and-a-half-wide
column seemed to be composed of variously shaded blocks and
squares, not letters or figures. Down the long left-hand edge of

the paper were numbers at regular intervals, starting with 3 at the top and ending with 14 at the bottom. Across the top, in handwritten capitals, was a single heading: "DATA SUMMARY."

I refolded the strip and put it back in my pocket.

"What is it?" Erik asked.

I shook my head. "Don't know."

He stirred his coffee. "Knut will find out."

I considered that and didn't especially like it.

"No," I said. "This paper came from England. I think I'll take it back there to find out what it is."

"It's Knut's case," he said with a certain amount of quiet obstinancy.

"Mine as well." I hesitated. "Tell Knut I found the paper, if you must, but I'd rather you didn't mention it to anyone at all. I don't want it leaking out round Oslo, and if you tell Knut he will have to record it, and if he records it you never know who will see. I'd much rather tell him myself when I get back. Anyway, we can't make a useful plan of campaign until we know what we're dealing with, so nothing can really be gained by telling him now."

He looked unconvinced, but after a while all he said was "Where did you find the key to the locker?"

"In Bob Sherman's helmet."

His obstinancy slowly melted to resignation.

"All right," he said. "I won't tell Knut. He could have found the key first."

As logic it hardly stood up, but I was grateful. I looked at my watch and said, "I can catch the two-five to Heathrow."

"Right now?" He sounded surprised.

I nodded. "Don't tell anyone I've gone. I don't want any friend of yellow eyes waiting at the other end."

He grinned. "David Cleveland? Who's he?" He stood up and turned to go. "I'll give your regards to Odin."

I watched his untidy back depart forthwith through the scattered crowd toward the distant exit and felt unexpectedly vulnerable without him. But nothing dire happened. I caught the flight, landed safely at Heathrow, and, after thought, left my car where it was in the car park and took myself by train to Cambridge.

Sunday evening in midterm was as good a time as any to beard professors in their dens, but the first one I found was a loser. He lectured in Computer Science: but my Data Summary, he said, had nothing to do with computers. Why didn't I try Economics? I tried Economics, who said why didn't I try Geology?

Although it was by then getting on for ten o'clock, I tried Geology, who took one brief glance at the paper and said, "Christ, where did you get this—they guard these things like gold dust."

"What is it?" I asked.

"A core. A chart of a core. From a drilling. See those numbers down the left-hand side? I'd say they refer to the depth of each section. Might be in hundreds of feet. Might be in thousands."

"Can you tell where the drilling was done?"

He shook his head, a young earnest man with a mass of reddish hair merging into an undisciplined beard.

"Could be anywhere in the world. You'd need the key to the shadings even to guess what they were looking for."

I said, in depression, "Isn't there any way of finding out where it came from?"

"Oh, Lord, yes," he said cheerfully. "Depends how important it is."

"It's a long story," I said doubtfully, with a look at his clock.

"Sleep is a waste of time," he said like a true scholar, so I told him more or less exactly why I wanted to know.

"Have a beer?" he suggested when I'd finished.

"Thanks."

He found two cans under a heap of uncorrected essays and ripped off the rings.

"Cheers," he said, dispensing with glasses. "All right. You convinced me. I'll pass you on to the people who drew the chart."

I was astonished. "How do you know who drew it?"

He laughed. "It's like knowing a colleague's handwriting. Any research geologist could probably tell you where that chart came from. It's a research lab job. I'll give the managing director a ring in the morning and explain, and see if he'll help you. They're awfully touchy about these charts." He eyed it thoughtfully. "I shouldn't be surprised if there'll be an unholy row, because from what you've said I should think it was stolen."

The seeds of the unholy row were plain to see, next day, on the face of Dr. William Leeds, managing director of the Wessex-Wells Research Laboratory. An impressive man, small, calm, and decisive, he looked deeply disturbed at what I'd brought him.

"Sit down, Mr. Cleveland," he said.

We sat one each side of his managerial desk.

"Tell me where you got this."

I told him. He listened intently, without interrupting. At the end he said, "What do you want to know?"

"What this chart is about. Who could benefit from getting hold of it, and how."

He smiled. "Fairly comprehensive." He looked out of his big first-floor office window for a while at a row of leaf-dropping willows across a stretch of lawn. Deep in the heart of Dorset, the laboratory was set in ancient parkland, a Victorian country residence sitting easily beside new low flat-topped workaday workshops. Dr. Leeds's window overlooked the main artery of pathways linking the complex, a neat finger on the pulse if ever I saw one.

"Almost anyone could benefit from getting hold of it if they were unscrupulous," he said. "This chart cost perhaps half a million pounds."

My mouth fell open. He laughed.

"Well, you have to remember that drill rigs are enormously sophisticated and expensive. You don't get a core by digging a hole with a spade. This one"—he tapped the paper—"is only five inches in diameter but about fourteen thousand feet in depth. A fourteen-thousand-foot drilling costs a lot of money."

"I can see that it does," I said.

"Of course you couldn't sell it for that, but I should think this particular chart might be worth a hundred thousand, if you had a market."

I asked if he would explain in more detail.

"A chart like this is information. You can always sell information illegally if you know someone ready to buy. Well, suppose this core showed a deposit of nickel, which it doesn't, incidentally, and you knew exactly from which particular drilling it came, you would know whether it was worth investing money in the drilling company or not. For instance, during the Poseidon nickel boom in Australia, you'd have been able to make literally millions on the stock market through knowing infallibly in advance which of the dozens of prospecting companies had made the drilling that was richest in ore."

"Good grief," I said.

"It can work the other way, too," he said. "If you knew that a concession which has been expected to give a high yield is in fact not going to be good, you can sell out while the share price is still high."

"So it wouldn't only be people engaged in mining who would be ready to buy such a chart."

"Certainly not. The people who make most out of the earth probably don't know what a drill looks like."

I said, "Why sell the chart to someone else? Why not make millions on the stock market yourself?"

He smiled. "It's much safer to be paid a lump sum into a nice anonymous Swiss bank account than to start dealing in shares. Any geologist dealing much in significant shares would be detected at once."

"Do people approach geologists, asking them to sell information?"

"They do. We try to protect our geologists here by not letting them know exactly where the material they're working on has

come from. But obviously we have not been entirely successful." He looked bleak. "We know from past experience that a
working geologist is usually approached by a middleman, an
entrepreneur who buys information from the research source
and then sells it to a bigger fish who operates in the world
markets."

"Am I dealing with the middleman or the big fish?"

He smiled and shook his head. "Can't tell. But the middleman, I suspect, as you found the chart so close to source."

"What exactly do these columns mean?" I asked.

He picked up the chart and showed me. "The first column is
lithology, the composition of the rock layers. The second is the
original particle type, that means micro and macro fossils and
micrite. The third . . ." He compressed his lips, clearly most
upset by this one. "The third is a fairly new and highly secret
process, scanning electron microscopy. Our clients will be particularly furious that this finding has been leaked. They paid a
mint for it. We can stay in business here only as long as every
client remains convinced that the analysis he is paying for will
never be seen by anyone except himself."

I said, "This chart wouldn't be much use, though, without the
key to the various shadings."

"No." He thought. "If I had to guess, I'd say that this might
be used as a sort of appetizer, or a proof that the middleman had
the real goods to sell. We don't normally make up charts in this
form. This is an abbreviation. A condensed, composite edition.
Specially made."

"But would the rest of Bob Sherman's package be worth
anything without this chart?"

"Oh, sure. It depends what else was in it. A written analysis
would be just as good as a chart. If they had a written analysis,
it wouldn't matter all that much if they lost the chart."

I thanked him for his help. "Could you tell me where that
drilling was made—and what for?"

He glanced at it. "I can tell you in general just by looking at
it. But do you want to know precisely, to the half mile?"

"Please," I said.

"Then come with me."

He led me along a wide passage, through some swinging doors, and into a modern wing tacked onto the back of the original house. We were bound, it seemed, for the records department, but to get in there even the managing director had to announce himself to the inmates and get the door unlocked electronically from inside.

He smiled at my surprise.

"We usually pride ourselves on our security. We're going to have a great upheaval sorting out which of our people sold the information on this chart." A thought struck him. "I suppose you wouldn't like to come back and work on it yourself?"

I wouldn't have minded, but explained about the Jockey Club.

"Pity," he said.

He unerringly picked out one particular folder from the thousands in the filing cabinets which lined the walls. He knew exactly which company had commissioned the analysis, and he knew roughly from where the core had been taken.

He turned a few pages, comparing the chart with the notes.

"There," he said finally, pointing with his finger. "Those are the coordinates you want."

I looked over his arm. Read the coordinates.

Read the name of the company.

I'd never heard of it.

"Thank you very much," I said.

Fourteen

I CALLED TO SEE EMMA.

The cottage was warm and welcoming in the cold afternoon, alive with a glowing log fire and a huge vase of bronze chrysanthemums. None of the furniture had been replaced and the curtains were still at the cleaners, but Emma herself during the past week had made strides. There was at last a shade of color in her cheeks and the faintest of sparkles in her eyes. The pretty girl had indeed come back to life.

"David! How great to see you. Have a hot scone. They're just out of the oven."

We sat in front of the fire eating the scones with butter and jam and concentration.

"Golly, you must have been hungry," she said later, eying the almost empty dish. "I really made them to take over to Grandfather." She laughed. "Guess I'd better make some more."

"They were lovely." What with bombs and general chasing around, I had missed a lot of meals and picked at others. With Emma, for the first time in days, my stomach nerves felt safe enough to encourage intake.

"I don't know whether to ask," she said, "but have you found out anything about Bob?"

"Not enough." I looked at my watch. "May I use your tele-phone?"

"Of course."

I called a stockbroker I knew who owned racehorses and asked him about the share movements of the company which had commissioned the analysis of the core.

"That's easy," he said. "About two months ago, the share price started to soar. Someone had a hot tip, bought at the bottom, and made a real packet."

"Who?" I said.

"Impossible to tell, but probably a syndicate, considering the huge sums involved. All done through nominees, mostly on overseas markets."

I thanked him and rang off; and after that I called S.A.S., who made warm noises and said sure there was a free seat on the six-thirty. A lot of my mind persisted in telling me that there was another flight in the morning and widows were meant for consoling: well, maybe, but not this one, not yet.

I kissed her goodbye.

"Come again," she said, and I said, "I will."

At Heathrow I handed in the car I'd hired that morning in Cambridge, and squeezed into the six-thirty at the last call. I didn't seem able to help the tension that was screwing up again as we began the descent into Oslo, but a harmless taxi took me uneventfully to the hotel, where the reception desk resignedly let me choose my own room.

I telephoned to Erik.

"Where are you?" he demanded.

"At the Grand."

"For God's sake—didn't you go?"

"There and back."

"Did you find out?"

"Up to a point. I know what it is, but not who it belongs to. Look, could you give me Knut's home number?"

He told me. "Do you want any more driving done?"

"I'm afraid so, if you can face it."

"Count on me," he said.

I rang Knut, who yawned and said he'd just come off duty and wouldn't be back until two the following afternoon.

"Do you know a place called Lillehammer?" I asked.

"*Ja.* Of course."

"What's it like?"

"How do you mean? It is a big town. A tourist town in the summer, and a ski place in the winter. No visitors go there in October and November."

"If you wanted to meet someone secretly in Lillehammer, within fairly easy walking distance of the railway station, where would you suggest?"

"Not in a public place?"

"No. Somewhere quiet."

There was a pause. Then he said, "It might be better to walk away from the town itself. Down toward the lake. There is a road going down to the bridge over the lake. It is the main road to Gjøvik, but there is not much traffic, and there are some small side roads down to the houses round the lakeside. Is that what you want?"

"Sounds perfect."

"Who are you going to meet?"

I told him at considerable length. Somewhere along the way he shed his fatigue, because when he next spoke his voice was alert and even eager.

"*Ja.* I understand. I will arrange everything."

"I'll see you in the morning, then."

"*Ja.* Agreed. And—er—take good care, David."

"You bet," I said.

I rang Erik again, who said certainly he would come to breakfast, drive me to Knut's office, and get me to the station in time to catch the ten o'clock to Lillehammer.

"Is that all?"

"No . . . Would you meet me again when I get back? Four-thirty, I think."

"All right." He sounded almost disappointed.

"Bring knuckle-dusters," I said, which cheered him.

Next, Lars Baltzersen.

"Of course I've heard of that company," he said. "Their shares are booming. I bought some myself a few weeks ago, and already they show a good profit."

"Do you know anyone else who bought any while the price was still low?"

A pause; then he said, "Rolf Torp did. I believe it was Rolf who told me about them, but I can't be sure." He cleared his throat. "I have heard worrying rumors, though, that the really big buyers were in the Middle East. One cannot be sure. There is much secrecy. But it seems likely."

"Why would that be worrying?" I asked, and he told me.

Last of all, I telephoned Arne. Kari answered, her voice warm, amused, and full of memory from our last meeting.

"Haven't seen you since Friday," she said. "Why don't you come to dinner here tomorrow?"

"Love to," I said, "but I don't think I can."

"Oh. Well, how's the case going?"

"That's really what I wanted to talk about with Arne."

She said she would fetch him, and he came on the line. He sounded glad that I'd called.

"David . . . Haven't seen you for days," he said. "What have you been doing?"

"Ferreting," I said. "Look, Arne, I've had a piece of luck. Some man in a place called Lillehammer telephoned and said he could tell me something about Bob Sherman being killed. He said he almost saw it happen. He wouldn't say anymore on the phone, but I'm going to meet him tomorrow. The thing is . . . I wondered if you'd like to come with me. I'd be glad of your company, if you could spare the time. And he didn't speak very good English, so you could interpret for me, if you would."

"Tomorrow?"

"Yes. I'm catching the ten-o'clock train in the morning."

"Where in Lillehammer are you meeting this man?"

"On the road to Gjøvik, down near the bridge over the lake. He's going to be there at midday."

He said doubtfully, "I suppose I could."

"Please do come, Arne," I said.

He made up his mind. "*Ja.* I'll come. Are you still staying at the Grand?"

"Yes," I said. "But you are nearer the station. I'll meet you there."

"Right." He hesitated again. "I hope he isn't some lunatic, making up stories."

"So do I," I said.

I slept with my bed pushed right across the door, but nobody tried to get in.

Erik had brought Odin again to assist with the guard duty, although I now knew from longer acquaintance that the Dane's fierce appearance was only a front. A right great softy lived within the sandy hide.

Together nonetheless they conveyed me safely to the police station, where Knut met us, keenly awake a good five hours before he was due on duty. Up in his office I gave him the geological chart, which he inspected curiously.

"Don't lose it," I said.

He smiled. "Better to lose my life, I suspect."

"You'll get it photocopied?"

He nodded. "Right away."

"See you this evening, then."

We shook hands.

"Be careful," he said.

Erik and Odin stuck beside me while I bought my ticket and

walked to the barrier. It was the worst morning yet for jumpy
nerves, with me far outstripping Arne in the matter of looking
over my shoulder. By this evening, I thought grimly, I'd either
be safe or dead. It seemed an awfully long time to the evening.

Arne, already waiting on the platform, greeted me with a big
smile.

"What number is your ticket?" he asked.

I hadn't realized that each ticket bore a seat number on the
train, but it was so.

"I'll see if I can change mine to be next to you," he said, and
vanished on his errand at high speed. While he was gone I found
my allotted number, a window seat facing forward, halfway up
one of the large airy coaches. With only a few minutes to go to
departure time, about half the seats were filled with respecta-
ble-looking citizens, and I managed to look over my shoulder
only twice.

Arne returned with an air of satisfaction and the ticket for the
seat beside mine.

"That's better," he said, and gave all the worthy fellow travelers a severe inspection before sitting down. "I should have
waited for you at the ticket office. Didn't think of it in time."

Erik, with Odin still beside him, suddenly appeared on the
platform outside the window, rapping to attract my attention
and vigorously beckoning me to talk to him. I pointed to the
rear of the carriage, excused myself past Arne, and went to the
door to hear what Erik wanted to tell.

"I saw him," he said, almost stuttering with urgency. "Get off
the train and come with me."

"Who?"

"It'll go if you don't get off quickly. The man who planted the
bomb. Big, with a butterfly birthmark. I saw it. He was buying
a ticket—he dropped some change and bent to pick it up. I saw
his neck—and I saw his eyes. They really are a sort of yellow.
Very light and bright and odd. Do hurry, David. There was
another man with him. They got on this train, in the rear car-

riage. Three carriages back from here."

A whistle blew. He practically danced with frustration.

"Get off, get off."

I shook my head. "I'll find a way of avoiding them." The train began to move. "Thanks a lot. See you this afternoon. Mind you come."

"Of course I'll come."

The train gathered speed, diminishing my protectors second by second until I could no longer see the bewilderment on Erik's face or the patient lack of comprehension on Odin's.

"Who was that?" Arne asked as I returned to my place.

"Someone I hired to drive me around."

"Extraordinary-looking chauffeur, isn't he?"

I smiled. "His driving is pretty hair-raising as well."

"Tell me about this man we're going to see."

"I don't know much, really. He said his name was Johann Petersen."

Arne grunted. "There are dozens of Johann Petersens."

"He said he was at the races the day Bob Sherman disappeared. He said he would like to tell me something about that. He said he lived at Lillehammer and worked there in the timber yard. I asked him to come to Oslo, but he said he couldn't take the day off. He said he'd meet me during his lunch break today. It was very difficult to understand him clearly, as he spoke so little English. It'll be fine with you there."

Arne nodded, blinking away as usual. The train took things easy, sliding quietly through the outer suburbs in a typically unhurried Norwegian fashion.

"How will you know him?"

"He said he would know me. All I have to do is walk down toward the bridge carrying an English newspaper."

"Did you bring one?"

I nodded. "In my coat pocket."

The train was well heated. Coats were expected to be shed, and there was a rail at the rear equipped with hangers, where

Arne's coat and mine hung side by side.

The line ran north through farmland and woods and along-side an extensive lake. On any other day I would have enjoyed the journey, but it was extraordinary how a little fear could keep the mind focused close at hand. Old yellow eyes and his pal were a sight too near for comfort, and I'd developed an even worse over-the-shoulder compulsion because of passengers walking up the center aisle through the train. Every bang of the door from one carriage to the next had me looking to make sure.

A woman in a blue smock, pushing a trolley into the carriage, sold hot drinks, biscuits, and sweets. Arne bought me coffee. The trolley trundled away, and bang went the door behind her.

We stopped lengthily at a largish town, Hamar, a junction with masses of open windswept platforms and no air of shunting or bustle. Then on again, moving faster, on toward Lilleham-mer. Two and a half hours, altogether, on the train.

"I missed you at the races on Sunday," Arne said.

"Yes. I meant to go, but it was so cold."

He gave me a look of friendly contempt.

"I might be going home soon," I said.

"Are you?" He was surprised. "I thought . . . you'd never leave us without finding out."

"Well, after this trip today we should know a lot more. With a bit of luck. And then there's the key."

"What key?"

"I found a luggage-locker key stuck in Bob Sherman's riding helmet."

"You didn't!"

I nodded and told him about the trail to Paddy O'Flaherty's. "So you see, although I'll go home soon, we should have most of the answers."

Arne was enthusiastic. "That's great," he said. "All we have to do now is find what's in the locker the key fits." A thought struck him. "Perhaps it's that money. In the canvas bags—you know, the money that was stolen."

"It's a thought," I said. I didn't launch into explaining what actually had been in the locker; time enough for that later, as, from the way the other passengers were standing up and putting on their coats, it was clear we were close to arrival. The train ran beside Lake Mjøsa, and in the distance I could see the timber yard, with acres of pine-tree logs floating in the water.

Arne held my coat for me, and I his for him. He smiled a little sadly.

"Kari and I will miss you."

"I'll be back one day. I like Norway very much."

He nodded. The train passed the end of the bridge to Gjøvik, climbed a hill slowly, inched into Lillehammer station, and sighed to a stop. We stepped out into a stinging wind under a gray cloud-filled sky. So much, I thought, for all those happy holiday posters of sun and snow and people on skis showing their suntans and teeth. It was odd, too, how none of the far frozen North railway stations had sheltering roofs over the platforms. Perhaps no one ever stood waiting in the open air, so that roofs were redundant and there was some point in them all still looking like the last scene in *Anna Karenina*.

"Are you coming, David?" Arne said.

"Yeah." I stopped looking around vaguely and followed him through the main doors into the booking hall. At the far end of the platform, two men, bypassing the station buildings, had set off quickly in the general direction of the road to the bridge. One of the men was big, the other of the same build as my attacker in the flat. They were too far away for me to swear to it in court.

But I was sure, just the same.

The small booking hall was scattered with prospective travelers wearing limbo expressions, waiting for time to pass. There were seats around the walls, doors to washrooms, a window for buying tickets: all the amenities in one central area. Arne said he wanted to make a telephone call before we set off to the meeting with our informer down the road.

"Carry on," I said amiably.

I watched him through the glass wall of the booth feeding money into the slot and talking earnestly into the mouthpiece. He talked for a good long time, and came out smiling.

"All done. Let's go," he said.

"Arne," I said, and hesitated. "I know this is going to sound silly, but I don't want to go."

He looked dumbstruck. "But why not? This man might have seen who killed Bob Sherman."

"I know. But—I can't explain it. I have the weirdest feeling of premonition. I've had it before. . . . I can't—I can't ignore it. Something tells me not to go. So I'm not going."

"But, David," he said, "that's crazy."

"I can't help it. I'm not going."

"But what about the man?"

I said helplessly, "I don't know."

Arne grew impatient. He tried insults. He tried persuasion. I wouldn't budge.

In the end, he said, "Give me the newspaper. I'll go and meet him myself."

"But," I objected, "if my premonition means there is some danger down that road, it must be dangerous for you as well. I had a premonition about a street once before. . . . I wouldn't go down it, and a few seconds later several tons of scaffolding collapsed onto where I would have been. Ever since then, when I've a strong feeling against doing something, I don't do it."

He blinked at me. "If I see any scaffolding, I'll keep away from it. But we must see this Johann Petersen and hear his story. Give me the newspaper."

Reluctantly I handed him the previous day's *Express.*

"I'll wait for you here," I said.

He nodded, still not pleased, and set off on his own. I chose a place to sit at one end of one of the bench seats, with solid wall at my back and on one side. On my other side sat a plump teen-age girl in a shaggy sheepskin coat, eating herring sandwiches noisily.

A few people came. A train arrived and took most of them away, including my neighbor. Time passed very slowly.

An hour and a half between our arrival and the train back to Oslo. An hour and a half to kill. Correction, I thought wryly. To stay alive. I wished I smoked or bit my nails or went in for yoga. I wished my heart wouldn't jump every time people walked past the window in pairs. I wished I knew what views yellow eyes and brown eyes held on murdering in public, because if only I was sure they wouldn't risk it I could save myself a lot of fretting. As it was, I sat and waited and slowly sweated, hoping I'd judged their limit right.

When passengers for the Oslo train started arriving and buying tickets, I bought two myself, for Arne and me. I asked particularly for the most public pair of seats in the carriage, as observed on the way up, and although I had difficulty explaining what I wanted because the ticket seller spoke little English, I got them.

Back in my carefully chosen corner, I found myself flanked by an elderly man with an ear-flapped cap topping an elongated skull. He had heard me speak English at the ticket window and was eager to tell me that he'd been in England the year before on holiday with his son and daughter-in-law. I encouraged him a bit, and got in return a minute-by-minute conducted tour from Tower Hill via Westminster Abbey to the National Gallery. By the time Arne came back, a quarter of an hour before train time, we were chatting away like old friends.

Arne was looking anxious. I stood up to meet him, gesturing to the elderly man and saying, "We've been talking about London—"

Arne glanced at the man without really seeing him and abruptly interrupted. "He didn't come."

"Oh, no," I said.

Arne shook his head. "I waited. I walked down to the bridge twice. I showed the newspaper. No one spoke to me. No one even walked past looking as if they were looking for anyone."

I made frustrated noises. "What a bloody nuisance. I'm so sorry, Arne, to have wasted a whole day for you . . . but he sounded so definite. Perhaps he was delayed and couldn't help it. Perhaps we could telephone the timber yard."

"I did," he said. "They haven't any Johann Petersen working there."

We stared at each other.

I said depressedly, "I banked so much on him giving us some really vital information."

He looked at me uncertainly.

"My premonition was all wrong, then," I said.

"I told you."

"Yes, you did."

He began to fish out his wallet.

"I've got the tickets," I said, producing them. "Two seats together."

"Oh . . . good."

The train arrived, dark red and silver, and we climbed aboard. The seats were all I'd hoped, right down at one end, with their backs to the wardrobe end but facing the other seats in the coach. By a stroke of luck, my elderly friend of the London holiday took his place on the aisle three seats down. He had a clear view of Arne and me, and waved and smiled. I told Arne how friendly he had been. Like all Norwegians, I said.

Arne jerked a look over his shoulder. Only a row of hangers with coats; but he didn't look happy.

Two bright-eyed young girls came and sat in the seats directly facing us. I moved my feet out of the way of theirs, and smiled at them. They smiled back and said something in their own language.

"I'm English," I said, and they repeated "English" and nodded and smiled again. "And this is my friend Arne Kristiansen."

They put the introduction down to the eccentricity of foreign-
ers, saying hello to him with giggles. Arne said hello back, but
he was old enough to be their father and not interested in their
girlish chat.

The train started back toward Oslo. We talked for a while
about the nonappearance of Johann Petersen, and I said we
would just have to hope that he would telephone again.

"You'll let me know if he does?"

"Of course," I said.

The lady in the blue smock arrived, pushing her trolley down
the aisle. I said it was my turn to buy the coffee, and despite
Arne's protestations I did so. I also offered drinks to the two
girls, who thought it a great lark and went pink. They asked
Arne to see if it was all right for them to have orangeade, as they
didn't like coffee. The lady in blue patiently attended to all
Arne's translations and finally, with a smile, gave him my
change.

Arne began to wear the hunted look he often did in crowds.

"Let's go somewhere quieter," he said.

"You go," I said. "I rather like it here."

He shook his head, but he stayed.

To his relief and my regret, the two young girls got off at
Hamar, giggling goodbye with backward glances. No one em-
barked to take their empty places, but after the train had
started again my elderly friend got to his feet and came inquiringly toward us.

"May I sit here with you?" he said. "It is so interesting to talk
about England."

Too much for Arne. He rose abruptly to his feet and dived
through to the next carriage. The door banged behind him.

"Have I upset your friend?" asked the elderly man anxiously.
"I am sorry."

"He has problems," I said. "But not of your making."

Relieved, he launched into more reminiscences which bored
me to death but quite likely kept me alive. He was still there,

talking inexhaustibly, as we drew into Oslo. And on the platform, flanked by Odin, stood Erik anxiously looking out for me, just as promised.

There wasn't much time left. If they were going to make an attempt now, they were going to have to do it in the open.

I stepped off the train and turned toward Erik. And there between us, looking sickeningly businesslike, stood the two men I least wanted to see.

Fifteen

BATTLE NEVER COMMENCED.

Erik saw them at the same moment I did, and yelled "Police!" at the top of his lungs.

Every person within earshot stopped to look.

"Police!" he yelled again, pointing at yellow eyes and brown eyes. "These are thieves. Fetch the police!" And he repeated it in Norwegian, very loudly.

It broke their nerve. They looked around at the growing circle staring at them wide-eyed, and suddenly made a bolt for the exit. No one made much effort to stop them, and the chief expression on every beholder's face was astonishment.

Erik strode up to me and pumped my hand.

"Just putting your theory into practice," he said.

I looked blank.

He explained. "Knut told me you didn't think they'd kill you while people were looking. So I just got a few people to look."

"Thanks."

"Call it quits," he said with a grin, and patted Odin.

I discovered that the palms of my hands were wet and a lot of me was shaking.

"I need a telephone," I said.

"You need a good stiff drink."

"That, too."

I rang Knut. "I'm back at the terminus," I said.

"Thank God for that."

"Did it work?" I asked with some intensity, because I'd risked my skin for nearly seven shivery hours and no one could be entirely objective after that.

"Yes," he said, but there was an odd note of reservation in his voice. "At least . . . *ja.*"

"What's the matter?"

"You had better come here to the police station. It will be easier to explain."

"All right."

I stepped outside the box and almost fell over Odin, who was lying across the door like a medieval page. He gave me a reproachful look, stood up nonchalantly, and yawned.

I asked Erik, "Did you see Arne Kristiansen anywhere?"

"Who?"

I scanned the crowd without success. "Never mind. I expect he's gone home."

In gathering dusk, Erik drove sedately (only one near miss) to the police building, where I went upstairs and found Knut sitting alone and chewing a pencil. He gestured me to the visitor's chair and produced only the vestige of a smile.

"Well . . . we did everything you suggested," he said. "We planted the chart in a locker at Fornebu and put the key loose in the helmet in your room at the Grand. We sprinkled anthracene dust over every surface an intruder would touch and we waited at Fornebu to see if anyone would come."

He rattled the pencil along his teeth.

"Someone did come," he said.

"Who?"

He sighed. "You'd better come and see."

He led the way out of his meager office and down an uncarpeted corridor, and stopped outside a cream-painted door. Bright light from inside shone through a small glass panel in the door at viewing height.

"Look," Knut said.

I looked.

The room was small and bare, containing only a simple table and three chairs. One chair was occupied by a young uniformed policeman looking stolid. On another, smoking quietly and as calm as if he were back in his own boardroom, sat Per Bjørn Sandvik.

I pulled my head away from the glass and stared at Knut.

"Come back to my office," he said.

We went back and sat down as before.

"He came to Fornebu and opened the locker," Knut said. "That was at—" he consulted a note pad—"fourteen-thirty-five hours precisely. He removed the chart from the locker and put it in an inside pocket. I myself and two other officers went up to him as he was walking away from the lockers and asked him to accompany us to this police station. He seemed surprised but not—not deeply disturbed. I have arrested so many people. . . . Per Bjørn Sandvik did not behave like a guilty man."

He rubbed thumb and finger down his nose.

"I don't know what to make of him, David. He shrugged and said he would come with us if we liked, but he said almost nothing else until we got back here. He was completely calm. No sign of stress. None at all. He has been here now for about an hour and a half, and he has been calm and courteous the whole time."

"What explanation did he give?"

"We went into that interview room and sat on the chairs, with a constable to take notes. Mr. Sandvik offered me a cigarette. He said he had only been trying to help the investigation into Bob Sherman's death. He said Arne Kristiansen had telephoned to say that you had found a key which might lead to useful information, so he went to the Grand Hotel to fetch the key, which he recognized as having come from Fornebu, as he has often used those lockers in the past. So he went to the airport —to see what Bob Sherman had left there. He said he thought

it might have been the missing money, but it was only a paper.
He hadn't done more than glance at it when we stopped him."

"Did he give any reason for doing all this himself and not
waiting for Arne or me to get back or enlisting the help of the
police?"

"*Ja.*" He smiled a small tight smile to mock me. "He said Arne
asked him to do it. Arne wanted to prove to the racecourse
committee that he was worth his salary as an investigator, so he
telephoned to Sandvik as a member of the racecourse committee to tell him about the key. Arne apparently said that if he and
Mr. Sandvik helped with the case, the committee would not be
able to give all the praise to you."

"What do you think?"

He looked depressed. "Per Bjørn Sandvik is a leader of industry. He is much respected. He is being very reasonable, but if
we keep him here much longer he will be angry."

"And your superiors will lean on you?"

"Er . . . *ja.*"

I thought.

"Don't worry, Knut," I said. "We've got the right man."

"But he is so confident."

I nodded. "He's working on a false assumption."

"What's that?"

"He thinks I'm dead."

Per Bjørn Sandvik got a very nasty shock indeed when I
walked into the interview room.

Muscles around his eyes and mouth contracted sharply, and
his pale blue skin went perceptibly paler. But his resilience was
extraordinary. Within three seconds, he was smiling pleasantly
with the deceptive lack of agitation which was so confusing to
Knut.

"David!" he said as if in welcome, yet I could almost hear and
certainly sense the alarm bells going at panic strength.

"I'm afraid this isn't the happiest of meetings," I said.

He was making such an urgent reappraisal that the muscles

around his eyes were moving in tiny rhythmical spasms: which booted out of me any hint of complacency, because people who could think as quickly and intently as that in such adverse circumstances had brains to beware of.

Knut followed me into the room and told the young policeman to fetch another chair. While he went to get it, I watched Per Bjørn finish reorganizing his thoughts. Infinitesimally, he relaxed. Too soon, I reckoned: and I couldn't afford to be wrong.

The extra chair came, and we all sat down around the bare table as if to a simple business discussion.

I said, "It must have occurred to you by now that there was no Johann Petersen at Lillehammer."

"I don't understand," he said pleasantly, in his high distinct diction. "I thought we were talking about the locker key and Fornebu airport."

"We're talking about Arne Kristiansen," I said.

A pause. I waited. But he was too cautious now to take any step without prospecting for quicksand, and after some time, when he said nothing, I invited him a little farther along the path.

"You shouldn't rely on Arne," I said. "Arne is deep in, up to the neck."

No response.

"Come to think of it," I said. "Up to his neck and over his head, considering the amount of swimming he's done."

No reaction.

"All that messing around in the fjord," I said. "There was me thinking Arne had drowned, while all the time he had a scuba suit on under his red anorak. Nice snug black rubber with yellow seams, fitting right up over his head to keep him warm." I'd seen the black and yellow under his anorak. It had taken me days to realize it had been rubber. But then that chug down the fjord happened before I'd begun to be sure that Arne was on the other side.

"A strong swimmer, Arne," I said. "A tough all-round sportsman. So there he is standing up in the dinghy waving his arms

about as if to warn the speedboat not to run us down while all
the time signaling to it that yes, this was the dinghy it was
supposed to be sinking. This dinghy, not some other poor innocent slob out on a fishing trip. Arne swam ashore, reported an
accident, reported me drowned."

A pause.

"I don't know what you're talking about," Per Bjørn said, and
patiently sighed.

"I'm talking about Arne putting on his scuba suit and diving
into the pond at Øvrevoll to get Bob Sherman out of it."

Silence.

Arne had been sick when he saw the month-dead body. At
night, when he'd fished Bob out and wrapped him in the tarpaulin, it couldn't have seemed so bad: but in the light of a
drizzly day it had hit him a bull's-eye in the stomach.

"I'm talking about Arne being the one person who could be
sure no one saw him putting bodies into ponds, taking them out
again, and later putting them back again. Arne was the security
officer. He could come and go on that racecourse as he pleased.
No one would think it odd if he was on the racecourse first, last,
and during the night. But he could also make sure that the night
watchman saw nothing he shouldn't, because the night watchman would carry out any attention-distracting task Arne gave
him."

Nothing.

"This is speculation," he said.

Knut sat still and quiet, keeping his promise that he would
make no comment whatever I said. The young policeman's
pencil had made scarcely a mark on the page.

"Arne stole the money himself," I said. "To provide a reason
for Bob Sherman's disappearance."

"Nonsense."

"The impression of most people in the officials' room was that
the money had been put in the safe. And so it had. Arne himself
had put it there, as he usually does. He has the keys, in his official
capacity. He has keys to every gate, every building, every door

on the place. He didn't take the money during the five minutes that the room happened to be empty. He had all night to do it in."

"I don't believe it. Arne Kristiansen is a respected servant of the racecourse."

He sat there listening to me with long-suffering courtesy, as if I were a rather boring guest he was stuck with.

"Bob Sherman brought a packet of papers with him from England," I said.

"Yes, you've already asked about that. I told you I couldn't help you."

"Unfortunately for him, he was curious. He opened the package and saw what he had no business to see. He must have done this on the flight over, as he left some of the contents in a locker at Fornebu."

Per Bjørn slowly turned his good-looking head until he was facing Knut, not me, and he spoke to him in Norwegian. Knut made gestures of regret and helplessness, and said nothing at all.

"Bob Sherman was too fond of schemes for getting rich quickly," I said. "He was being paid for bringing the envelope, but it seemed to him that he could push the price up a bit. Very much his mistake, of course. He got bonked on the head for his pains. And no one discovered until long after he was dead and in the pond that when he'd opened the envelope he'd taken something out."

Per Bjørn sat impassively, waiting for the annoying gnat to stop buzzing around him.

I buzzed a bit more.

"Because what he took out was in a way a duplication of what he left in."

That one hit home. His eye muscles jumped. He knew that I'd noticed. He smiled.

I said, "Bob Sherman took the precaution of hiding the key to the Fornebu locker in his racing helmet. By the time he was brought out of the pond, it had been discovered that he had removed a paper from the envelope, but a search of his water-logged clothes and overnight bag failed to produce any sign of it. So did a search of his house in England. By the time I realized what must be going on, and came to wonder if Bob had some-how hidden the missing object in his racing saddle or helmet, others had had the same idea. His saddle, which had stayed on its peg in the changing room for a month after he disappeared, was suddenly nowhere to be found."

He sat. Quiet.

"However, the helmet with the saddle was no longer Bob's but Paddy O'Flaherty's. I told Arne about the exchange. I told him I'd found the key."

Per Bjørn crossed one leg over the other and took out his cigarettes. He offered them around, then, when no one ac-cepted, returned his case to his pocket and lit his own with a practiced flick on a butane lighter. The hand which held the lighter was rock steady.

"I didn't tell him that we had already opened the locker and seen what it contained," I said. "We wanted to find out who else besides Arne was looking for the missing paper, so we gave him an opportunity of finding it."

"Ingenious," he said. "What a pity you had made the funda-mental mistake of believing Arne Kristiansen to be connected with Bob Sherman's death. If he had been guilty of all you say, it would have been an excellent trap. As it is, of course . . ."

He delicately shrugged. Knut looked worried.

"There was the problem of the two men who searched Bob Sherman's house," I said. "If we didn't decoy them away, they would be available to fetch the key and open the locker. So we provided an urgent reason for them to leave Oslo. We invented, in fact, a possible eyewitness to the killing of Bob Sherman. I told only Arne Kristiansen that I was going to Lillehammer to meet this man, and I asked Arne to come with me. On the train, I told him about the key and said that as soon as I got back I was going to give it to the police. I told him that the police were expecting me to report to them at once on my return, to tell them what the man in Lillehammer had said. This meant to Arne that if I didn't return, the hunt would be on immediately and there might be no later opportunity to get into my room for the key. It had to be done quickly. A risk had to be taken."

I paused.

"You took it," I said.

"No."

"You believed no one knew of the existence of the key except Arne and myself. You were wrong. You believed there was a possible eyewitness to Bob's murder and you sent your two assassins to deal with him. You expected them also to kill me as well. They aren't very successful at that. You should sack them."

"This is ridiculous," he said.

I said, "I asked the reception desk at the Grand not to worry if anyone asked for my room number or my door key." And extremely odd they'd thought it, after all the hide-and-seek of the previous days. "We made it as easy as we could."

He said nothing.

Knut had sprinkled the room with anthracene dust, which clung invisibly to any clothes or flesh which touched it and showed up with fluorescence under a strong ultraviolet light. Anyone who had been in my room and denied it would have been proved to be lying. But Per Bjørn had outthought that one and hadn't denied it. He must have done a great deal of fast figuring during his nonspeaking ride from Fornebu to the police station. He couldn't have known about the anthracene, but he must have guessed that a trap so complicated in some respects wasn't likely to be naïve in others.

I said, "The paper you were looking for is a chart of a core taken from area twenty-five six of the North Sea."

He absorbed that shock as if he were made throughout of expanded polystyrene.

I gave him some more. "It was stolen from the Wessex-Wells Research Laboratory in Dorset, England, and the information it contains was the property of the Interpetro Oil Company. It is the chart showing exceptionally rich oil-bearing rock of high porosity and good permeability at a depth of fourteen thousand feet."

It seemed to me that he had almost stopped breathing. He sat totally without movement, smoke from the cigarette between his fingers rising in a column as straight as honesty.

I said, "The Interpetro Oil Company isn't part of the consortium to which your own company belongs, but it is or was mainly Norwegian-owned, and the well in question is in the Norwegian area of the North Sea. Immediately after Bob Sherman brought his package to Norway, the Interpetro shares started an upward movement on the world stock markets. Although a great deal of secrecy surrounds the buying, I'm told that the most active purchasers were in the Middle East. You would know far better than I do whether it is to Norway's advantage to have one of her most promising oil fields largely bought up by oil-producing rivals."

Not a flicker.

I said, "Norway has never really forgiven the citizens who collaborated with the Nazis. How would they regard one of their most respected businessmen who sold advance news of their best oil field to the Middle East for his own personal gain?"

He uncrossed his legs and recrossed them the other way. He tapped the ash off his cigarette onto the floor, and inhaled a deep lungful of smoke.

"I wish," he said, "to telephone to my lawyer. And to my wife."

Sixteen

KNUT AND I went back to his office and sat at his desk.

"Can you prove it?" he said.

"We can prove he went to the Grand, fetched the key, and opened the locker."

"Anything else?"

I said gloomily, "It's circumstantial. A good defense lawyer could turn everything inside out."

Knut chewed his pencil.

"The scandal will ruin him," he said.

I nodded. "I'll bet he's got a fortune tucked away somewhere safe, though."

"But," Knut said, "he must care more for his reputation than for just money; otherwise he would simply have left the country instead of having Bob Sherman killed."

"Yes."

We sat in silence.

"You are tired," he said.

"Yeah. So are you."

He grinned and looked suddenly very like Erik.

I said, "Your brother told me Per Bjørn Sandvik was in the Resistance during the war."

"*Ja.* He was."

"Nothing wrong with his nerve," I said. "Nothing then, nothing now."

"And we are not the Gestapo," Knut said. "He knows we will not torture him. We must seem feeble to him after what he risked when he was young. He is not going to give in and confess. Not ever."

I agreed.

"Those two men," I said. "Yellow eyes and brown eyes. They're too young to have been in the Resistance themselves. But . . . is there a chance their fathers were? Arne's father was. Could you run a check on the group Per Bjørn belonged to, and see if any of them fathered yellow eyes?"

"You ask such impossible things."

"And it's a very long shot indeed." I sighed.

"I'll start tomorrow," he said.

Some coffee arrived, very milky. I could have done with a triple Scotch and a batch of Emma's scones.

"You know," I said after another silence, "there's something else. Some other way . . . There has to be."

"What do you mean?"

"I mean, it was just luck finding that key. If Paddy hadn't swapped the helmets, we would never have found the paper at Fornebu." I drank the coffee. It wasn't strong enough to deal with anything but thirst. "But . . . they tried to kill me before they knew the chart wasn't in the pond with Bob Sherman. So there must be something else which they couldn't afford for me to find."

I put down the cup with a grimace.

"But what?" Knut asked.

"God knows."

"Something I missed," he said with gloom.

"Why would they think I would see it if you didn't?"

"Because you do," he said. "And Arne knows it."

Arne . . . My friend Arne.

"Why didn't he kill you himself, out on the fjord?" Knut

asked. "Why didn't he just bang you on the head and push you overboard?"

"It isn't that easy to bang someone on the head when you're sitting at opposite ends of a small dinghy. And besides, leading a beast to the abattoir and slitting its neck are two different things."

"I don't understand."

"Arne was keen for me to die but wouldn't do it himself."

"How do you know?"

"Because he didn't. Over the last few weeks, he's had more chances than anybody, but he didn't do it."

"You couldn't be sure he wouldn't."

"He's a complex person but his attitudes are all fixed. . . . If he didn't do it the first time, he wouldn't do it afterward."

A few more minutes dawdled by while I tried to concentrate on what I hadn't discovered.

Useless, I thought.

Yesterday I didn't know who had manipulated Interpetro Oil. Today I did. Did that make any difference?

"Oh, my Christ," I said, and nearly fell out of my chair.

"What is it?" Knut said.

"I'm bloody mad."

"What do you mean?"

"You remember that bomb?"

"Well, of course I do."

"It was such a sloppy way to kill someone," I said. "It might have gone off before we got back to the car. . . . It didn't kill us, so we thought of it as a failure. But it didn't fail. Not a bit. It was a roaring success. It did just what it was meant to."

"David—"

"Do you remember where I was going that afternoon? I didn't go, because the bomb stopped me. I'm so damned stupid. . . . It isn't *what* I haven't seen, it's *who.*"

He just stared.

"It's Mikkel Sandvik."

I telephoned to the College of Gol and spoke to the headmaster.

"Oh, but Mikkel isn't here," he said. "His father telephoned on Sunday morning to say that Mikkel must go and visit his aunt, who was dying and asking for him."

"Where does the aunt live?"

"I don't know. Mr. Sandvik talked to Mikkel himself."

There was some speaking in the background, and then he said, "My wife says Mikkel told her his Aunt Berit was dying. He went to catch the Bergen train. We don't know where he went after that. . . . Why don't you ask his father?"

"Good idea," I said.

"What now?" Knut said when I told him.

"I think I'll go and see Mrs. Sandvik, and see if she'll tell me where Mikkel is."

"All right. And I will do what I must about keeping Mr. Sandvik here all night." He sighed. "A man like that—it doesn't seem right to put him in a cell."

"Don't let him go," I said.

"Oh, no."

Erik had gone home long ago but Knut reckoned I was on police business and sent me to the Sandvik house in a police car. I walked through the arch into the courtyard, turned right, and rang the bell outside the well-lit imposing front door.

A heavy middle-aged woman opened it. She wore frumpy clothes and no makeup, and had a positive, slightly forbidding manner.

"*Ja?*" she said inquiringly.

I explained who I was and asked to see Mrs. Sandvik.

"I am Mrs. Sandvik. I spoke to you on the telephone a few days ago."

"That's right." I swallowed my surprise. I had thought she would already have known about her husband being at the police station, but apparently he hadn't yet made his two calls.

When we had left him, Knut had said he would arrange for a telephone to be taken to the interview room and plugged into the socket there, which I supposed took time. No one was positively rushing to provide facilities for a suspect, not even for Per Bjørn Sandvik.

It made it easier, however, for me to ask questions.

"Come inside," she said. "It is cold with the door open."

I stepped into the hall. She invited me no farther.

"Mikkel?" she said in surprise. "He is at school. I told you."

I explained about his Aunt Berit.

"He has no Aunt Berit."

Wow.

"Er . . ." I said. "Does he know anyone at all called Berit?"

She raised her eyebrows. "Is this important?"

"I cannot go home until I have seen Mikkel. I am sorry."

She shrugged. After a longish pause for thought, she said, "Berit is the name of an old nurse of my husband. I do not know if Mikkel knows any other person called Berit. I expect so."

"Where does your husband's old nurse live?"

"I don't know."

She couldn't remember the old nurse's surname, and she wasn't sure if she was still alive. She said her husband would be able to tell me when he came home. She opened the door with finality for me to leave, and with a distinct feeling of cowardice, I left. Per Bjørn had smashed up her secure world and he would have to tell her about it himself.

"He might be with his father's old nurse," I told Knut. "And he might not."

He reflected. "If he caught the Bergen train, perhaps the Gol ticket office would remember him."

"Worth a try. But he could be anywhere by now. Anywhere in the world."

"He's barely seventeen," Knut said.

"That's old, these days."

"How did Mrs. Sandvik take the news of her husband's arrest?"

"I didn't tell her. I thought Per Bjørn should do that himself."

"But he has!"

"She didn't know," I said blankly.

"But," Knut said, "I am sure he made his two calls almost half an hour ago."

"Bloody hell," I said.

He steamed out of the office at twenty knots and yelled at several unfortunate subordinates. When he returned, he was carrying a piece of paper and looking grim, worried, and apologetic all at once.

"They find it difficult not to obey a man with such prestige," he said. "He told them to wait outside the door while he spoke to his wife and his lawyer, as both calls were of a private nature. They did what he said." He looked at the paper in his hand. "At least they had the sense to dial the numbers for him, and to write them down. They are both Oslo numbers."

He handed the paper over for me to see. One of the numbers meant nothing. The other meant too much.

"He talked to Arne," I said.

I pressed the bell outside Arne's flat, and after a long interval Kari opened the door.

"David." She seemed neither surprised nor pleased to see me. She seemed drained.

"Come in," she said.

The flat appeared somehow colder, less colorful, much quieter than before.

"Where's Arne?" I said.

"He's gone."

"Where to?"

"I don't know."

"Tell me everything he did since he came home."

She gave me an empty stare, then turned away and walked

through to the sitting room. I followed her. She sat on the string-colored sofa and shivered. The stove no longer glowed with warmth and welcome and the stereo record player was switched off.

"He came home upset. Well . . . he's been upset ever since this Bob Sherman thing started. But today he was very worried and puzzled and disturbed. He played two long records and marched about. He couldn't keep still."

Her voice had the calmness of shock. The reality of whatever had happened had not yet tipped her into anger or fear or despair: but tomorrow, I thought, she might suffer all three.

"He rang Per Bjørn Sandvik's house twice, but they said he wasn't in. It seemed to worry him very much."

There was a tray on the coffee table in front of her laden with an untouched dish of open sandwiches. They made me feel frantically hungry, as I hadn't eaten since a pin-sized breakfast, but she gave them an indifferent glance and said, "He left them. He said he couldn't."

Try me, I thought: but hostessing was far out of her mind.

"Then Per Bjørn Sandvik rang here. Only a little while ago, but it seems hours and hours. . . . Arne was relieved at first, but then he went so quiet. . . . I knew something was wrong."

"What did he say to Per Bjørn? Can you remember?"

"He said *ja*, and no. He listened a long time. He said—I think he said—'Don't worry, I'll find him.'"

"That was all?"

She nodded. "Then he went into the bedroom, and he was so quiet I went to see what was the matter. He was sitting on the bed, looking at the floor. He looked up at me when I came. His eyes were—I don't know—dead."

"And then?"

"He got up and began packing a suitcase. I asked him. . . . He said, 'Don't worry me.' So I just stood there. He packed—he threw things into the case—and he was muttering away, mostly about you."

She looked at me intently but still with the numb lack of emotion.

"He said, 'I told him, I told him David would beat him. I told him at the beginning. . . . He still says David hasn't beaten him, but he has, he has.' I asked Arne what he was talking about, but I don't think he even heard me." She pressed her fingers against her forehead, rubbing the smooth skin. "Arne said, 'David . . . David knew all day. . . . He made the trap and put himself into it as bait. He knew all day.' Then he said something about you using some girls and an old man, and something about orangeade . . . and a premonition you invented. He said he knew you would be the end of everything; he said so before you came."

She looked at me with the sudden awakening of awareness and the beginnings of hostility.

"What did you do?" she asked.

"I'm sorry, Kari. I gave Arne and Per Bjørn Sandvik a chance to show they knew more than they ought about Bob Sherman's death, and they took it."

"More than they ought?" she repeated vaguely: and then overwhelmingly understood. "Oh, no. Oh, no. Not Arne." She stood up abruptly. "I don't believe it." But she already did.

"I still don't know who killed Bob Sherman," I said. "I think Arne does know. I want to talk to him."

"He's not coming back. He said he would write, and send for me. In a few weeks." She looked forlorn. "He took the car." She paused. "He kissed me."

"I wish . . ." I said uselessly, and she caught the meaning in my voice though the words weren't spoken.

"Yes," she said. "In spite of everything, he likes you, too."

It was still not yet eight o'clock and Per Bjørn was still in the interview room when I got back to the police station.

"His lawyer is with him," Knut said morosely. "We won't get a word out of him now."

"We haven't had so many already."

"No." He flicked the paper with the telephone numbers which was lying on his desk. "This other number—it isn't the lawyer's."

"Whose, then?"

"It's a big second-class hotel near the docks. Dozens of incoming calls; they couldn't remember one more than any other. I have sent a policeman down there with a description of the man with yellow eyes."

"Mm. Whoever he spoke to at the hotel, then, telephoned the lawyer."

"*Ja,*" he said. "It must be so. Unless Arne did."

"I don't think so, from what his wife said."

"He had gone?"

I nodded. "In his car."

He put his hand again on the telephone. "We will find the number and put out an alert: and also check with the airport and the frontier posts with Sweden."

"I know the number." I told it to him. He looked surprised, but I said, "I've been in his car, and I've a memory for numbers. Don't know why."

He put out his alerts and sat tapping his pencil against his teeth.

"And now we wait," he said.

We waited precisely five seconds before the first call came through. He scooped up the receiver with a speed which betrayed his inner pressure, and listened intently.

"*Ja,*" he said eventually. "*Ja . . . takk.* Thank you."

He put down the receiver and relayed the news: "That was the policeman I sent to the hotel. He says the man with yellow eyes has been staying there for a week, but this evening he paid his bill and left. He gave no address. He was known to the hotel as L. Horgen. My policeman says that unfortunately the room has already been cleaned because the hotel is busy, but he has directed them to leave it empty until we've searched it and tried for fingerprints. Excuse me while I send a team to do that."

He went out of the office and was gone a fair time, but when he came back he had more to tell.

"We've found Arne's car. It is parked not far from the quay of the Nansen shipping line, and one of their ships left for Copenhagen an hour ago. We are radioing to the ship and to Copenhagen to pick him up."

"Don't let them relax at Fornebu," I said.

He looked at me.

I grinned faintly. "Well, if I wanted to slip out by air I'd leave my car beside a shipping line and take a taxi to the airport. And Arne and I once discussed quite a lot of things like that."

"He'd know you'd guess, then."

"I'd pin more hope on the ship if he'd left his car at the airport."

He shook his head and sighed. "A good thing you're not a crook," he said.

A young policeman knocked, came in, and spoke to Knut.

He translated for me. "Mr. Sandvik's lawyer wants to see me, with his client. I'll go along to the interview room. . . . Do you want to come?"

"Please," I said.

With Per Bjørn, his lawyer, Knut, me, and a note-taking policeman all inside with the door shut, the small interview room looked overcrowded with dark suits and solemnity. The other four sat on the hard chairs around the plain table, and I stood leaning against the door, listening to a long conversation of which I understood not a word.

Per Bjørn pushed back his chair, crossed his legs, and set fire to a cigarette, much as before. His lawyer, a heavy self-possessed man of obvious worldly power, was speaking in an authoritative voice and making Knut perceptibly more nervous minute by minute. But Knut survived uncracked, and although when he answered he sounded friendly and apologetic, the message he got across was "No."

It angered the lawyer more than the client. He stood up, towering over Knut, and delivered a severe caution. Knut looked worried, stood up in his turn, and shook his head. After that the young policeman was sent on an errand, presently returning with a sergeant and an escort.

Knut said, "Mr. Sandvik," and waited.

Per Bjørn stood up slowly and stubbed out his filter tip. He looked impassively at the escort and walked calmly toward them. When he drew level with me at the doorway, he stopped, turned his head, and stared very deliberately at my face.

But whatever he was thinking, nothing at all showed in his eyes, and he spoke not a word.

Knut went home, but I spent the night in his office sleeping on the floor on blankets and pillows borrowed from the cells; and I daresay I was less comfortable than the official guest downstairs.

"What's wrong with the Grand?" Knut said when I asked him to let me stay.

"Yellow eyes is on the loose," I said. "And who knows what instructions Per Bjørn gave him?"

Knut looked at me thoughtfully. "You think there's more to come?"

"Per Bjørn is still fighting."

"*Ja.*" He sighed. "I think so, too."

He sent a policeman out to bring me a hot meal from a nearby restaurant, and in the morning at eight o'clock he came back with a razor. He himself, trim in his uniform, seemed to have shed yesterday like a skin and arrived bright-eyed and awake to the new day. I shivered blearily in my crumpled clothes and felt like a reject from a rooming house.

At eight-forty-five, the telephone rang. Knut picked up the receiver, listened, and seemed pleased with what he heard.

"*Ja. Ja. Takk,*" he said.

"What is it?"

He put the receiver back. "We've had a message from Gol. The man who was on duty in the ticket office on Sunday remembers that a boy from the college bought a ticket to Finse."

"Finse." I thought back to my timetables. "On the Bergen line?"

"*Ja*. Finse is the highest town on the line. Up in the mountains. I will find out if he is remembered at the station there. I will find out if anyone has seen him in the streets or knows if he is staying."

"How long will that take?"

"One can't tell."

"No." I thought it over. "Look, the train for Bergen leaves at ten, if I remember right. I'll catch it. Then if you hear that Mikkel is or isn't at Finse, perhaps you could get a message to me at one of the stops up the line."

"Have you forgotten yellow eyes?"

"Unfortunately not," I said.

He smiled. "All right. I will send you to the station in a police car. Do you want a policeman to go with you?"

I thought. "I might get further with Mikkel if I go alone."

On the train I sat next to a total stranger, a cheerful young man with little English, and spent an uneventful journey looking out at peaceful fields and bright little dollhouses scattered haphazardly on hillsides.

At Gol there was a written message: "Young man disembarkation to Finse the Sunday. One knows not until where he gone. The questions is continue."

"Thank you very much," I said.

The train climbed slowly above the timberline into a landscape of blue-gray rock and green-gray water. Snow scattered the ground, at first in patches, then in profusion, and finally as a thin white rug over every sloping surface, with sharp rock edges like hatchets showing through.

"Is small snow," said my companion. "In winter in Finse is two meters."

"Two meters deep?" I asked.

He nodded. "*Ja*. Is good for ski."

The railway ran for a time alongside a fiercely cold-looking wind-ruffled gray-green lake and slowed with a sigh of relief into Finse.

"Is hot summer," my friend said, looking around in surprise. "Is snow gone."

He might think so, but I didn't. Snow still covered everything worth mentioning, hot summer or not; and icicles dangled from every roof like stiff glittering fringes. Once I was out of the warmth of the train, the cold bit sharply, and in spite of my ear-covering cap and padded jacket I wrapped my arms around my chest in a futile attempt to hold on to my body heat.

I was met by the bulk of the Finse police force in the shape of a broadly smiling officer of turnstile-blocking size.

"Mr. Cleveland." He shook my hand. "We do not know where is this boy Mikkel Sandvik. We have not seen him in the village. There are not many strangers here now. In the summer, and in the winter, we have very many strangers. We have the big hotel, for the ski. But now, not many. We have look for an old woman who is called Berit. There are two. It is not one, because she is in bed in the house of her son and she is—er, she is—old."

"Senile?" I suggested.

He didn't know the word. "Very old," he repeated.

"And the other Berit?"

"She lives in a house beside the lake. One and a half kilometers out of Finse. She goes away in the winter. Soon, now. She is a strong old woman. In the summer, she takes people who come to fish, but they have all gone now. Usually on Wednesdays she comes for food, so we have not gone to see her. But she is late today. She comes in the mornings."

"I'll go there," I said, and listened to directions.

The way to the house of Berit-by-the-lake turned out to be merely a path which ran between the railway line and the shore, more a matter of small stones and pebbles through an area of boulders than any recognizable beaten track. With its roughnesses still half covered by crusty ice, it was easy to imagine that once the new snows fell it would be entirely obliterated.

Seventeen

I LOOKED BACK.

A bend had taken Finse out of sight.

I looked forward. Nothing but the sketchy path picking its uncertain way through the snow-strewn boulders. Only on my right could be seen any evidence of humanity, and that was the railway. And then that, too, ran straight ahead behind a hill while the shore curved to the left, so that in the end there was just me and the stark unforgiving landscape, just me trudging through an energetic wind on a cold, wild, and lonely afternoon.

The path snaked its way around two small bays and two small headlands, with the hillside on my right rising ever more steeply the farther I went, and then all of a sudden the house lay before me, standing alone on a flat stony area spread out like an apron into the lake.

The house was red. A strong crimson. Roof, walls, door—the lot. The color stood out sharply against the gray and white of the shore and the darker gray-green of the water; and rising beyond it at the head of the lake stood dark towering cliffs, thrown up like a sudden mountain against the Northern sky.

Maybe it was a grand, extraordinary, awe-inspiring sight. Maybe it should have swelled my spirit, uplifted my soul. Actu-

ally it inspired in me nothing more noble than a strong desire
to retreat.

I stopped.

Surely Sandvik wouldn't have sent his son to this threatening
place, even if he did urgently want to hide him. Surely Mikkel
was half the world away by now, with Arne cantering posthaste
in his wake to look after him.

Damned bloody silly place to build a house, I thought.
Enough to give anyone the creeps, living with a mountain on
the doorstep.

I went on. The house had a landing stage with a motorboat
tied to a post like a hitched horse in a Western. It also had
looped-up lace curtains and geraniums on the windowsills. Red
geraniums. Naturally.

I looked in vain for smoke from the chimney, and saw no one
staring out at me as I approached.

I banged the knocker. The door was opened right away by a
ramrod-backed old woman, five feet tall, sharp-eyed, entirely
self-possessed. Far, very far, from dying.

"*Ja?*" she said.

"I'd like to talk to Mikkel," I said.

She took a very brief pause to change languages, and then, in
a pure near-Scots accent, said, "Who are you?"

"I am looking for Mikkel."

"Everyone is looking for Mikkel." She inspected me from
head to foot. "Come in. It is cold."

She showed me into the living room, where everything was
in process of being packed away in crates. She gestured around
with her fine-boned hand. "I am leaving now for the winter. It
is beautiful here in the summer, but not in winter."

"I have a message from his father," I said.

"Another one?"

"What do you mean?"

"Already one man came this morning. Then another. Both of
them said they had a message from his father. And now you."
She looked at me straightly. "That is very many messages."

"Yes. I have to find him."

She put her head on one side. "I told the others. I cannot judge which of you I should not tell. So I will tell you. He is on the mountain."

I looked through the window to the wall of rock and the end of the lake.

"Up there?"

"*Ja.* There is a cabin up there. I rent it to visitors in the summer, but in the winter the snow covers it. Mikkel went up there this morning to bring down the things I do not want to leave there. He is a kind boy."

"Who were the other men who came?"

"I don't know. The first one said his name was Kristiansen. They both said they would go up and help Mikkel bring down the things, although I said it was not necessary; there are not many things and he took the sleigh."

"The sleigh?"

"*Ja.* Very light. You can pull it."

"Perhaps I had better go up there as well."

"You have bad shoes."

I looked down. City casuals, not built for snowy mountains, and already darkly wet around the edges.

"Can't be helped," I said.

She shrugged. "I will show you the path. It is better than the one round the lake." She smiled faintly. "I do not walk to Finse. I go in the boat."

"The second man," I said. "Did he have extraordinary yellow eyes?"

"No." She shook her head decisively. "He was ordinary. Very polite. Like you." She smiled and pointed through the window. "The path starts over there behind that big rock. It is not steep. It winds away from the lake and then comes back. You will see it easily."

I thanked her and set off, and found almost at once that she was right about the shoes. One might be able to see the path easily, but that was because it was a well-worn track through the snow, patterned widely on either side by the marks of skis, like a sort of mini-highway.

I slithered along in the brisk wind, working around the hillside in a wide, upward-sloping U; but it proved to be not as far as I'd feared, because long before I expected it I came to the top of a small rise and found below me, suddenly only a few yards away, a sturdy little log hut, built, in the traditional Norwegian pattern, like a roofed box standing on a slightly smaller plinth.

It was already too late to make a careful, inconspicuous approach. I stood there in full view of a small window: so I simply walked straight up and looked through it.

The cabin was dark inside and at first I thought it was empty. Then I saw him, huddled in a corner, with his head bent over his knees, slowly rocking as if in pain.

There was only one small room. Only one door. I put my hand on its latch and opened it.

The movement galvanized the figure inside into action, and it was something only half seen, half instinctive, that had me leaping sideways away from the entrance with adrenaline scorching down to my toes. Blast from a shotgun roared through the doorway, and I pressed myself against the heavy log wall alongside and hoped to God it was impervious to pellets.

A voice shouted something hysterically from inside.

Not Arne's voice. Young. Stretched to breaking.

"Mikkel," I said. "I will not harm you. I am David Cleveland."

Silence.

"Mikkel . . ."

"If you come in, I will shoot you." His voice was naturally high-pitched like his father's, and the tension in it had strung it up another octave.

"I only want to talk to you."

"No. No. No."

"Mikkel . . . You can't stay here forever."

"If you come in, I'll shoot."

"All right. I'll talk from here." I shivered with cold and wholeheartedly cursed him.

"I will not talk to you. Go away. Go away."

I didn't answer. Five minutes passed with no sound except the blustering wind. Then his voice from inside, tight and frightened. "Are you still there?"

"Yes," I said.

"Go away."

"We have to talk sometime. Might as well be now."

"No."

"Where is Arne Kristiansen?" I asked.

His reply was a high keening wail that raised goose bumps up my spine. What followed it was a thoroughly normal sob.

I crouched down low and risked a quick look through the door. The gun lay in one hand on the floor and with the other he was trying to wipe away tears. He looked up and saw me, and again immediately began to aim.

I retreated smartly and stood up outside against the wall, as before.

"Why don't you tell me?" I said.

A long pause of several minutes.

"You can come in."

I took another quick look. He was sitting straight-legged on the floor with the gun pointing at the door.

"Come in," he said. "I won't shoot."

"Put the gun on the floor and slide it away."

"No."

More time passed.

"The only way I'll talk," he said, "is if you come in. But I'll keep the gun."

I swallowed. "All right."

I stepped into the doorway. Looked down the double barrels. He sat with his back against the wall, holding the gun steady. A box of cartridges lay open beside him, with one or two scattered around.

"Shut the door," he said. "Sit down opposite me, against the wall. On the floor."

I did as he said.

He was slight and not full-grown. Brown hair, dark frightened eyes. Cheeks still round from childhood; the jawline of an adult. Half boy, half man, with tearstains on his face and his finger on the trigger.

Everything movable in the bare little cabin had been stacked in a neat pile to one side. A heavy table and two solid chairs were the total to be left. No curtains at the single small window. No rugs on the bare wood floor. Two collapsible camp beds, folded and strapped together for transport, leaned against a wall. A pair of skis stood beside them.

No logs by the cold stove, and no visible food.

"It'll be dark soon," I said. "Within an hour."

"I don't care." He stared at me with burning eyes and unnerving intensity.

"We should go down to Berit's house while we can still see the way."

"No."

"We'll freeze up here."

"I don't care."

I believed him. Anyone as distracted as he was tended to blot even extreme discomforts out of his mind: and although he had allowed me into the hut, he was far from coming down off the high wire. Little tremors of tension ran in his body and twitched his feet. Occasionally the gun shook in his hands. I tried not to think gloomy thoughts.

"We must go," I said.

"Sit still," he said fiercely, and the right forefinger curled convulsively. I looked at it. And I sat still.

Daylight slowly faded and the cold crept in inexorably. The wind outside whined like a spoiled child, never giving up. I thought I might as well face it: the prospect of the night ahead made the fjord water seem in retrospect as cozy as a heated pool. I put my padded mitts inside my padded pockets and tried to kid myself that my fingers were warm. And it was a minor disaster that the jacket wasn't really long enough for sitting on.

"Mikkel," I said. "Just tell me. You'll explode if you don't talk to someone. And I'm here. So just tell me. Whatever you like."

He stared fixedly through the gathering dusk. I waited a long time.

"I killed him," he said.

Oh, God.

A long pause. Then, on a rising note, he said it again, "I killed him."

"Who?" I said.

Silence.

"How?" I said.

The question surprised him. He took his gaze for one moment off my face and glanced down at the gun.

"I—shot—"

With an effort, I said, "Did you shoot Arne?"

"Arne." The hysteria rose again. "No. No. No. Not Arne. I didn't kill Arne. I didn't. I didn't."

"All right," I said. "All right, Mikkel. Let's wait a bit until you can tell me. Until you feel it is the right time to tell me." I paused. "Is that O.K.?"

After a while, he said, "*Ja*. O.K."

We waited.

It got darker until it seemed that the only light left was the reflection from the window in his eyes. I could see them long after the rest of him dissolved into one amorphous shadow, two live agonized signals of a mind desperately afraid of the help it desperately needed.

It must have occurred to him as to me that after total darkness I would be able to jump his gun, because he stirred restlessly on the floor and muttered something in Norwegian, and finally, in a much more normal voice, said, "There is a lamp in a box. On top of the things."

"Shall I find it and light it?"

"*Ja.*"

I stood up stiffly, glad of the chance to move, but sensing him lift the gun to keep me where it mattered.

"I won't try to take the gun away," I said.

No answer.

The heap of gear was to my right, near the window. I moved carefully, but with many small noises so that he should know where I was and not be alarmed, and felt around for the box on top. Nothing wrong with his memory: the box was there, and the lamp in it, and also a box of matches.

"I've found the lamp," I said. "Shall I strike a match?"

A pause.

"*Ja.*"

It proved to be a small gas lamp. I lit it and put it on the table, from where it cast a weak white light into every corner. He blinked twice as his pupils adjusted, but his concentration never wavered.

"Is there any food?" I asked.

"I'm not hungry."

"I am."

"Sit down," he said. "Where you were."

I sat. The gun barrels followed. In the new light, I could see down them a lot too well.

Time passed. I lit the lamp at four-thirty in the afternoon and it was eight before he began to talk.

By then, if I was anything to go by, he had lost all feeling from the waist down. He wore no gloves and his hands had turned blue-white, but he still held the gun ready, with his finger inside the trigger guard. His eyes still watched. His face, his whole body were still stiff with nearly unbearable tension.

He said suddenly, "Arne Kristiansen told me that my father was arrested. He told me he was arrested because of you."

His voice came out high and his breath condensed into a frosty plume.

Once he had started, he found it easier.

"He said my father wanted us to go to Bergen . . . and on a boat to Stavanger . . . and fly—" He stopped.

"And you didn't go," I said. "Why didn't you go?"

The gun shook.

"They came," he said.

I waited.

He said, "I was talking to him. Outside. About going away."
A pause. "They came over the hill. On skis, with goggles."
Another pause. "One of them told Arne to step away from me."
After a longer pause, and with an even sharper burst of remembered terror, he said, "He had a knife."

"Oh, Mikkel," I said.

He talked faster, tumbling it out.

"Arne said, 'You can't. You can't. He wouldn't send you to kill his own son. Not Mikkel.' He pushed me behind him. He said, 'You're crazy. I talked to his father myself. He told me to come here to take Mikkel away.' "

He stared across at me with stretched eyes, reliving it.

"They said my father had changed his mind about Arne going. They said they were to take me themselves on a ship to Denmark and wait until my father sent money and instructions. Arne said it was not true. They said it was true. . . . And they said Arne was going no farther than right here. . . . He didn't believe it. He said not even my father would do that. He watched only the one with the knife, and the other one swung a ski stick and hit him on the head. He fell down in the snow. I tried to stop them—they just pushed me off—and they put him on the sleigh—they strapped him on and pulled him up the path."

The panic he had felt then came crowding back into his face. He said painfully, "I remembered the gun in the cabin. I went inside and loaded it . . . and put on my skis and went after them to stop them. . . . But when I found them they were coming back without the sleigh, and I thought—I thought—they were going to—they were going to—"

He took a deep shuddering breath. "I fired the gun. The one with the knife—he fell down. . . .

"I fired again," he said. "But the other one was still on his skis. . . . So I came back to the cabin because I thought he would come after me. I came back to reload the gun. But he didn't come. . . . He didn't come. . . .

"You came," he said. "I thought it was him."

He stopped.

"Did you know the two men?" I asked. "Had you ever seen them before?"

"No."

"How long was it before I came?" I said.

"I don't know. A long time."

"Hours?"

"I think so."

I hadn't seen any of them on my way up.

"Killing is wrong," he said jerkily.

"It depends."

"No."

"To defend your life, or someone else's life, it would be all right," I said.

"I—I believe—I *know* it is wrong. And yet I—when I was so afraid—" His high voice cracked. "I have done it. I despise killing and I've done it. And I would have killed you, too. I know I would. If you hadn't jumped."

"Never mind," I said: but the horrors were still there in his eyes. Making it deliberately an emotion-reducing question, I asked, "Have you known Arne Kristiansen long?"

"What?" His own voice came down a bit. "About three years, I suppose."

"And how well do you know him?"

"Not very well. On the racecourse. That's all."

"Has your father known him long?"

"I don't think so. . . . The same as me. At the races."

"Are they close friends?"

He said with sudden extreme bitterness, "My father has no close friends."

"Will you put the gun down now?" I said.

He looked at it.

"All right."

He put it beside him on the floor. A relief not to be looking down those two round holes.

The lamp chose that moment to give notice it was running out of gas. Mikkel switched his gaze from me to the table, but the message of fading light didn't seem to pierce through the inner turmoil.

"The lamp is going out," I said. "Is there a spare gas cylinder?"

He slowly shook his head.

"Mikkel," I said. "It is freezing and it will soon be dark. If we are to survive the night, we must keep warm."

No response.

"Are you listening?"

"What?"

"You are going to have to face life as it is."

"I . . . can't . . ."

"Are there any blankets?"

"There is one."

I began to try to stand up, and he reached immediately for the gun.

"Don't be silly," I said. "I won't hurt you. And you won't shoot me. So let's just both relax, huh?"

He said uncertainly, "You had my father arrested."

"Do you know why?"

"Not . . . not really."

I told him about the oil transaction, playing down the disloyalty—to put it no higher—that Per Bjørn had shown to his country, but there was, it seemed, nothing basically wrong with Mikkel's brains. He was silent for some time after I'd finished, and the muscles slowly relaxed, limb by limb.

"Once he had been found out," he said, "he would lose his job. He would lose the respect of everyone. He wouldn't be able to live like that—not my father."

His voice at last was sane and controlled; and almost too late. The lamp was going out.

"The blanket is in the beds," he said.

He tried to stand up and found his legs were as numb and useless as mine, if not more so. It kicked him straight back to practical sense.

"I'm cold!"

"So am I."

He looked across, seeing our predicament squarely for the first time.

"Stand up," he said. "Walk about."

Easier said, but it had to be done.

"Can we light the stove?" I said. "There are four more matches, the cardboard boxes, and the table and chairs, if we can break them up."

We had both by then tottered to our feet. The lamp shone with one candlepower, sadly.

"There is no ax," Mikkel said.

The lamp went out.

"I'm sorry," he said.

"Never mind."

We jumped up and down in total darkness. Funny if it hadn't been urgent. Blood started circulating again, though, to the places where it was needed, and after half an hour or so we were both warm enough to give it a rest.

"I can find the blanket," Mikkel said, and did so. "Shall we share it?"

"We certainly shall."

We both wore warm jackets and he, when he remembered where he'd put them, had a cap and mitts like my own. We laid the folded canvas beds on an insulating foundation of cardboard boxes, and wrapped ourselves from the waist down in one cocoon in the single blanket, sitting close together to share every scrap of warmth. It was too dark to see what he was thinking, but there were faint tremors still, occasionally, through his body.

"I took the rest of the bedding down to Berit's house yesterday," he said. "On the sleigh."

"Pity."

The word switched his thoughts. He said abruptly, "Do you think Arne is dead?"

"I don't know," I said. But I did think so.

"What will happen to me for killing that man?"

"Nothing. Just tell it as you told me. No one will blame you."

"Are you sure?"

"Yes."

"I am as bad as anyone else who kills," he said, but this time there was adult acceptance and despair in his voice, not hysteria. I wondered if it were possible for a boy to age ten years in one night, because it would be better for him if he could.

"Tell me about Bob Sherman," I said, and felt the jolt that went through him at the name.

"I . . . can't . . ."

"Mikkel, I know that Bob brought the stolen surveys from England to give to your father—"

"No," he interrupted.

"What, then?"

"He had to deliver them to Arne. I didn't know they were for my father when I—" He stopped dead.

"When you what?"

"I mustn't tell you. I can't."

In the darkness I said calmly, almost sleepily, "Did Bob tell you he had brought a package?"

He said unwillingly, "Yes."

I yawned. "When?"

"When I met him in Oslo. The night he came."

I wondered if he felt in his turn the thud with which that news hit me.

"Where in Oslo?" I said casually.

"He was outside the Grand with his saddle and his overnight bag. I was walking home from a friend's house, and I stopped. He said he might go and catch the tram. I asked him if he would like some coffee first, so we walked along to our house. I carried his saddle." He paused. "I liked Bob. We were friends."

"I know," I said.

"My father was out. He usually is. Mother was watching television. Bob and I went into the kitchen, and I made the coffee. We ate some cake my mother had made."

"What did you talk about?"

"At first about the horses he was riding the next day.... Then he said he had brought a package from England, and he'd opened it, and it didn't contain what he'd been told. He said he had to give it to Arne Kristiansen at the races, but he was going to ask a bit more money before he handed it over."

His body trembled against mine within the blanket.

"He was laughing about it, really. He said they'd told him it was pornography, but it wasn't, and he didn't know what it was even though he'd seen it. Then he took the package out of his case and told me to look."

He stopped.

"And," I said, "when you saw what was in the package, you knew what it was?"

"I'd seen papers like that before. I mean ... I knew it was an oil survey. Yes."

"Did you tell Bob what it was?"

"Yes. I did. We talked about it a bit."

"And then?"

"It was late. Too late for the tram. Bob took a taxi out to Gunnar Holth's stable, and I went to bed."

"What happened the next day?"

"I promised—I promised I wouldn't tell anybody. I didn't tell the police. I mustn't tell you. Especially not you. I know that."

"All right," I said.

Time passed. It was almost too cold to think.

"I told my father about Bob Sherman's package on the way to the races," he said. "He took me in the car. I only told him for something to say. Because I thought he might be interested. But he didn't say much. He never does. I never know what he's thinking."

"Nor do I," I said.

"I have heard people say he looks kindest when he is being

most cruel. When I was small, I heard it first."

"Is he cruel to you?"

"No. Just . . . cold. But he is my father."

"Yes."

"I think I want to tell you. . . . But I can't."

"All right."

A long time passed. His breath and body movements betrayed his wakefulness and the churning thoughts in his mind.

"Mr. Cleveland? Are you awake?"

"David," I said.

"David. Do you think he meant those men to kill me?"

"No, I don't."

"He told them where to come. He told me to come to Finse. He told Arne Kristiansen to come to Finse. And those men."

"He did," I said. "But I think perhaps they spoke the truth. I should think he meant them to take you out of the country after they had dealt with Arne. They were very clumsy to let you see them actually attack Arne, but then they have more strength than brains, those two. Arne is the only one who could go into court and give conclusive evidence against your father; and I do think that your father is ruthless enough to have him killed to prevent that."

"Why do you think so?"

"Because he sent those two men after me, too."

I told him about the boat in the fjord, the knife in Chelsea, the bomb in Erik's car.

"They're terrible men," he said. "They frightened me the instant I saw them."

He relapsed into silence. I could almost feel him thinking, suffering, working it all out.

"David?"

"Yes?"

"It was my fault Bob died."

"Certainly not."

"But if I hadn't told my father that Bob knew he'd brought an oil survey—"

"Arne would have told him," I said flatly. "You can go on saying 'if' forever. If Bob hadn't opened the package. If your father hadn't been ruthless enough to get rid of him. But all these things happened. They all happened because your father is both greedy and proud, which is always a pretty deadly combination. But also he learned how to live a secret life when he was young. Against the Nazis, it was good. Everyone admired him. I think perhaps he's never lost the feeling that anything anti-authority is daring and therefore all right. I imagine he put the police into the place of the Nazis, as the enemy to be outwitted. He thinks like lightning, he gives away nothing under questioning, he takes tremendous risks coolly, he arranges without mercy for people to die. He's still acting the way he did when he was twenty. He always will."

Time passed.

"David."

"Yes?"

"I'll have to tell you," he said.

I took a deep breath. It felt icy in my lungs.

"Go on," I said.

He paused again. Then he said, "I was talking to Bob at the races. He laughed and told me it was all fixed, Arne was going to drive him to the airport afterward and pay him extra for the package."

He stopped.

I waited.

His voice went on, hesitant but at last committed.

"By the end of the races it was dark. I went out to the car to wait for my father. He is often late because of being on the committee. I sat in the car and waited for him. I hadn't talked to him at all at the races. I usually don't see him much there. He's always busy."

He stopped again. His breathing grew heavier, more disturbed.

"Most of the cars went. Then two people came by and in some passing headlights I saw they were Bob and Arne. I was going to call out to them—I wish I had—but I couldn't get the window down fast enough. . . . And then they were over by Arne's car. They were talking face to face. I could only see them now and then, you see, when car lights pointed that way as people went home. But I saw another man walk up behind Bob and raise his arm. He held something shiny. . . . Then he brought it down."

He stopped. Gulped a bit. Went on. "The next time I could see, there were only two people there. I thought—I couldn't *believe*— And then one of them turned and came toward our car. I was scared."

He shuddered violently.

"But he just opened the boot and threw something into it that clinked, and then he got into the driver's seat, and he was smiling."

A long pause.

"Then he saw me sitting there, and he looked absolutely astonished. And he said—he said, 'Mikkel! I'd forgotten you were at the races.' "

His voice was full of pain.

"He'd forgotten me. Forgotten me."

He was trying not to cry.

"My father," he said. "My father killed Bob Sherman."

Eighteen

WE WENT DOWN TO FINSE at first light, he sliding easily on his skis, I scrunching and slipping in my city shoes. If I looked anything like he did, I had blue-gray circles around my eyes, hollows at the corners of my mouth, and a certain over-all air of extreme weariness.

He had said little more during the night. He had rolled his head onto my shoulder at one point and fallen exhaustedly asleep, and in the early morning, when he stirred, he had been calm and apparently untroubled, as if the final unburdening of the horror he'd lived with through eight long weeks had quietly set him free.

I left him with the warm comforting people of Finse, and went up the mountain again with several local men. This time I went on skis, shuffling along inexpertly up the slope. They waited for me, making jokes. They had cheerful faces, carefree smiles. And the sun came wanly through the clouds, the first time I'd seen it in Norway.

We reached the hut and went on past it, up beyond where the path petered out into a flat field of snow. Two of the men were pulling a sleigh, a lightweight affair sliding easily on ski-like runners—just like the one old Berit has, they said.

Brown eyes was lying face down in the snow.

Dead.

But he hadn't died from gunshot wounds: or not primarily. He'd died from exposure and cold.

The men from Finse looked in silence at the trail leading away beyond his body. He'd been pulling himself along, crawling. The snow where he'd been was streaked black with his blood.

They wrapped him in canvas, put him on the sleigh, and turned to go to Finse.

"I'll go that way," I said, pointing to where brown eyes had come from.

They nodded, consulted, and sent a man with me, as they didn't trust my rudimentary ability on skis.

We followed the bloodstained trail up a shallow slope and onto a sort of plateau whose far edge was a smooth horizon against the pale gray sky. The trail ended in a jumble of tracks that the man from Finse, whom I had filled in on details, rapidly interpreted.

"This is where he was shot. See the blood. There was another man with him." He pointed to a set of ski marks setting off at a tangent across virgin snow. "That man is an expert cross-country skier. He went fast. He left the other man lying here wounded in the snow. He did not come back with help. If he had, he could have followed the trail of blood."

Yellow eyes had just upped and left. But Knut would find him in the end.

"The two men came across to here, skiing fast and easily," my guide said, and pointed to tracks stretching away across the plateau.

"There are other tracks over there," he said, turning to his right and stretching out his well-gloved hand.

"Let's look," I said.

We went over.

"Two men," he said, "pulling a loaded sleigh."

Although I expected it, it hit in my gut.

"They came that way," I said, pointing back toward the hut.

He nodded. We went back along the trail until we found the marks of Mikkel's skis beside it.

"The boy came to here. Stopped. Then he turned and went back. You can see from his tracks that he was disturbed when he came. And panic-stricken when he left. Look at the depth and the sharpness and the small steps."

"We might find the cartridges," I said.

He nodded. We looked for a while and found both of them, bright orange cylinders on the snow.

"And now . . ." I gestured ahead along the trail which Mikkel had been following: two men and a loaded sleigh.

The marks ran regularly across the plateau toward the horizon. We followed.

The horizon proved to be not the end of the world, but the brow of a hill. Down the other side, the slope was steep, short, and sharp-edged, and far beyond it, mile upon mile, lay a vista of snow-scattered peaks. We were standing at the top of the mountain cliffs above the lake where Berit lived.

The marks of the two men on skis stopped at the brow of the hill and turned back.

The marks of the sleigh ran on straight and true to the edge.

"I want to go down there," I said, and unclipped my skis.

My guide didn't like it, but produced a rope from around his waist. He tied me to it, and paid it out foot by foot, standing foursquare and solid at the top of the slope.

I went down slowly in my borrowed boots, finding the snow surprisingly glassy and having to be careful not to slide. Having to concentrate, too, on not feeling giddy, and finding it as difficult as ever. When I stood at length on the edge, I could see all the lake stretching away, with Berit's house a crimson blob far down to the left.

Beside my feet, the marks of the runners looked shallow and crisp, speaking of speed. And they ran on without pity, pointing straight out into space.

The drop in front was six hundred feet. The ruffled green water lay secretively below. Nothing else. Nothing to see.

Arne, I thought. Flying through the air on a sleigh, down to his death.

Arne . . . who didn't look over his shoulder the one time the enemy was really there.

Arne, my treacherous friend.

You would have sworn that around the snowy cliffs you could hear crashing chords of Beethoven echoing in the wind.